"Don't worry, it's not as bad as you're thinking."

"Some of the old blokes only want some kind words and a cuddle and you get paid just the same. And it can't be worse than lying splattered at the bottom of the cliffs, which is where you'd be now if you hadn't met Madeleine."

Sarah shivered. She recalled jokes she had heard about a "fate worse than death" whispered at parties and never fully understood. Outside her window a bird landed on the nearest branch and broke into a noisy laughter. Was any fate worse than death? she wondered. At least there were possibilities in being alive.

She turned to Renee. "I know nothing at all about any of this," she said. "You'd better let me know what I'm in for."

MADAM SARAH

Janet Quin-Harkin

FAWCETT GOLD MEDAL • NEW YORK

A Fawcett Gold Medal Book
Published by Ballantine Books

Library of Congress Catalog Card Nubmer; 89-91901

ISBN 0-449-14636-7

Manufactured in the United States of America

First Edition: February 1990

Finally one for John,
Also grateful thanks to my Australian kin for all their hard work in background research when I wasn't there and hospitality when I was.

Prologue

FOR ONCE THERE HAD BEEN MUSIC. OLD ARMY friends of Major Hartley had returned on leave from India and were staying for a few days. The major pronounced them a confounded nuisance; nevertheless, he went out of his way to give the impression of the English country squire. A shoot was arranged in the stubble of the wheat fields and the kitchen was afterward full of feathers and pheasant. There were many courses at dinner, and wines were brought up dusty from the cellar. A butler was borrowed from the Bowyers, whose estates bordered Wickcombe. And after dinner there had been music.

For the little girl, used to the silence and the bleakness of life in the big empty house, the sights and sounds and smells had been almost overpowering, even from her position at her open nursery window, two floors above. Janet, who was usually nursemaid as well as housekeeper, was downstairs supervising the extra help in the kitchen, or she would not have allowed Sarah to lean out, dressed only in her nightdress. It was mild for October and the French doors to the terrace were open. Laughter floated up. An elegant lady walked out onto the terrace, accompanied by a tall, distinguished gray-haired man. A lively waltz was struck up on the piano inside, and Sarah watched as the gray-haired man slipped his arm around the lady's waist and began to twirl her, right there on the terrace.

Sarah could stand it no longer. She tiptoed to the door of her nursery, crept cautiously along the passage and down the servant's staircase. From the kitchen she could hear Janet's clipped Scottish voice barking instructions to the village girls. Everyone in the kitchen was too occupied to notice a tiny four-year-old in a nightdress slip past the open doorway and out into the night. She ran around the side of the house and stood on the other side of the yew hedge peeping through into the brightly lit drawing room. Inside was a whirl of color as couples spun to the music. Although it was colder outside than it had seemed and the thick dew on the grass numbed her bare feet, Sarah hardly noticed, so entranced was she by the silk gowns, the glittering jewelry, and the music. To be held in someone's arms like that and to twirl around the room must be the most wonderful feeling in the world, she decided. In a life devoid of touch, except for Janet's rough hands as they tucked in prickly blankets or pulled on scratchy cotton pinafores, Sarah tried hard to imagine what it must feel like to have arms holding you while you twirled. Out there in the cold dewy grass, Sarah began to twirl, too, wrapping her arms about her as she moved to the music, faster and faster . . .

It was all of five minutes before Janet found her and dragged her in disgrace back to bed. "I don't know what the ladies and gentlemen would have thought if they'd seen you out in your nightygown," she had said, her voice cracking with horror. "They'd have thought they'd come to a house of heathens. I don't know what got into you, I'm sure. You're usually such a good wee thing . . ."

Later she had wrestled with her conscience before reporting the matter to Sarah's father. "I think we're going to have trouble with that wee lass, sir," she had said, "if we're not extra careful. Her mother was wild as a lassie, I remember."

Major Hartley had frowned. "We've caught it young enough, thank God," he said. "Children are like dogs. As long as you train 'em young enough . . . I'll advertise for a governess."

"But the wee lassie's only four, sir," Janet had said. "Is that not a wee bit young for the reading and writing?"

"Nonsense," Major Hartley snapped. "Discipline and order, that's what she needs. Keep her busy enough and we'll soon stamp out any wild ideas she might have . . . not that another ridiculous event as tonight's is likely to be repeated in a hurry. The Scott-Browns are off to India for another seven years, thank God."

Sarah, curled into a little ball in her bed, her freezing toes tucked inside her nightgown in the hope of warming them up, knew nothing of this. She was already making plans for the future. One day she was going to be a fine lady and wear silks and jewels, just like the lady who had danced on the terrace. And one day a handsome, gray-haired man was going to put his arm around her waist and she would twirl and twirl . . .

One

"WAKE UP, MISS, OR YOU WON'T SEE THE HEADS!"

Sarah Hartley struggled to regain consciousness, rising to the surface like a diver from very deep water. The message was repeated, this time more urgently. "Come on, miss, we're just about to pass the Heads. You don't want to miss them, do you?"

The message made no more sense than the first time, when she had still been down in the green depths. For a moment she lay there in half-darkness, taking in a ceiling only a few inches above her head and a face that floated, like a disembodied head close to her own face. Even this did not make sense. She had been dreaming that she was back at Wickcombe and had expected to see the white fluttering curtains of her own room with Janet's pinched little face appearing above a tea tray. This face was round and moonlike, staring at her, expressionless, rimmed with black hair. Then the head beside her spoke for a third time. A hand appeared to shake her arm.

"What's the matter with you? You're dead to the world this morning. Come on, wake up. I know you want to see the ship go through the Heads and the captain says we'll be there in a few minutes."

Sarah finally kicked her consciousness to the surface, parting green depths and identifying the face that peered at her with concern.

"Oh Jessie," she said. "It's you."

"Who did you think it was, Mata Hari?" Jessie's round moon face broke into a big grin. "You was certainly sleeping deep this morning. What did they put in that trifle last night?"

Sarah sat up, ducking to avoid the ceiling above her head. "I was dreaming I was back at Wickcombe," she said, pushing her long ash brown hair out of her eyes. "I thought you were Janet waking me with breakfast."

Jessie laughed easily. "No such luck. You're not up with the first-class snobs remember? If you want breakfast, you'd better look lively and get up to the dining room. And if you want to see the Heads, you'd better look livelier still and get up on deck."

"Oh, the Heads!" Sarah said, smiling at her own dimwittedness as she remembered that this was the name for the outcroppings of sandstone marking the entrance to Sydney Harbor. "We're really about to go into Sydney Harbor?"

Jessie nodded. "Isn't it exciting?" she asked. "I can't believe we're really here. I was beginning to think I was going to spend the rest of my life in this poky hole—no offense meant, miss. But now we're really here. We're going to be off this old ship in a few hours and my Tom will be waiting there, and your Jim . . ."

Sarah slid herself down from the top bunk and reached out for her robe hanging on the door. "I can't believe it either," she said, her face lighting up. "Sometimes I actually wondered if I'd imagined it all—if Jimmy didn't really exist and I wasn't really going to Sydney to marry him. Almost every morning I've expected to wake up back at Wickcombe with Janet standing over me and my father pacing downstairs, yelling that I'm sleeping half the day away."

She walked to the mirror and began to pull a brush through her long, heavy hair. "I hope Jim still recognizes me," she said. "I hope I still recognize him. Two years is a long time." Her gaze shifted to the small photo in a silver frame, perched on the narrow shelf beside her brushes and soap dish. It was a picture of a tall, fair young man, stiff and erect in his army uniform. Sarah shook her head and turned back to Jessie. "I look at this photo every night, but it doesn't really look like him. It's so stiff and formal—like one of those "We Want You in the Army" posters! It doesn't show the way his eyes crinkle at the sides when he smiles—or the way they twinkle."

Jessie smiled as if she understood. "They'll be twinkling all right when he sees you coming down that gangplank," she said. "And I hope my Tom's will, too. They'd better, if he knows what's good for him!"

Sarah laughed and took an outfit from the closet. "Do you think this will be right to meet him again?" she asked, holding it up against her and peering critically into the mirror. "It's really old-fashioned, I know. Look how long it is and it still has a waist all pinched in—but it was impossible to get anything new made with my father hovering around . . ." Her voice trailed off . . .

Jessie sniffed. "Sounds like a regular old one-of-them!" she commented. "You're well rid of him and that's the truth. I don't go much for fathers myself. Me own wasn't much better. Had the belt off his trousers before you could say Jack Robinson if you ever answered him back. I swear my backside has still got lines all over it from that belt. I'm not going to treat my kids like that, that's for sure . . ."

"Jimmy won't be like that," Sarah said pensively. "I don't believe Jimmy could hurt anybody—he's so gentle and kind. He cried as much as I did when he had to go home—he said he couldn't bear to see me cry!" She smiled—a secret smile at the memory of it. Then she tossed back her hair and reached for her towel. "I know—I'd better hurry up and get on deck," she said, interpreting Jessie's face. "I'll just pop down the hall and take a quick bath; then I'll be right with you."

"You and your baths," Jessie said. "It ain't natural to want to wash every day. My mum used to say it soaked away the top layers of skin if you sat in it too long. The way you go on, I reckon you've only got a couple more layers to go before your skin's all gone and your innards fall out."

Sarah laughed, thinking how much she would miss Jessie and her dry cockney humor. "I'm making the most of baths now because I know I won't get too many on the farm," she said. "Jimmy said that when water's short, it all has to go to the sheep. I just hope we don't get a drought until I'm used to living there." She paused, looking at her face in the mirror—her pale English complexion, the grave gray eyes fringed with long dark lashes, the slightly hollow cheeks, and the long straight aristocratic nose of her purebred ancestry. How would that face look after a year on a sheep farm, she wondered.

Jessie came and stood behind her. "There's a lot we'll have to get used to, if you ask me," she said. "And a lot we'll have to do without. I know Paramatta's much nearer to Sydney, but it's still primitive. The lav's still down at the bottom of the garden, if you can imagine that! Tom says that they don't think it's hygienic here to have that sort of thing near the house. I can't imagine myself running through the fields in the middle of the night to meet the call of nature, can you? I might bump into a kangaroo and die of heart failure!" And she laughed merrily. Sarah thought privately that there wouldn't be much that would phase Jessie.

"If only we weren't going to be so far away from each other," she said hesitantly. "It would make everything so much easier if I knew somebody nearby."

"I'd like it, too, miss," Jessie said, "but cheer up—you'll soon make friends, and of your own type, too, I shouldn't wonder. Lots of posh people come out to the colonies after the war, they say. Too many folks got too restless to settle down in boring old England after the excitement—and I say good luck to them! You can't deny that the big old families were born to rule, and that's the truth. You take the Havershams I used to work for: there'd always been a Haversham for Justice of the Peace in Maidstone. Right back to olden times. They was born to it, see? I mean, you can't expect folks like me and my Tom to be magistrates and the like, can you?"

"But they are, Jessie," Sarah said. "You'll have to learn that we're all equal here. And I do wish you'd learn to stop calling me miss. I'm just plain Sarah now. You're just as good as me here, or rather I'm just as good as you."

Jessie grinned awkwardly. "I know, but it doesn't seem right, does it? I was brought up to service. Chambermaid when I was just fourteen to the Havershams and in service to them ever since. Probably would have been all my life if my Tom hadn't been sent to France and come back with big ideas. And it wasn't such a bad old life . . ." her face grew wistful at the memory.

"Still," Jessie said, "I suppose I'll learn to make a good old life here, even though it will be strange to start with—what with them kangaroos hopping about all over the place and the heat and all. As long as my Tom is with me, I reckon I'll get along just splendid. And you'll have your Jimmy. That's all that counts, isn't that right?"

Sarah nodded. "I'm sure it is, Jessie. As long as we have Tom and Jimmy to take care of us, nothing much can go wrong, can it?"

"Then, for pete's sake, stop waffling around and get up on deck with me. I want my first glimpse of my new home. Come on—I'll give you a hand. It'll likely be the last time you have a maid to dress you in quite a while."

With that she skillfully removed Sarah's robe and handed her

her garments in the correct order, lacing stays and doing up buttons with great speed and agility.

I am going to miss her so much, Sarah thought. *I never thought she'd come to mean anything to me . . .* She remembered the first day on board the ship, almost six weeks ago. She remembered her revulsion at the size and smell of the tiny cabin down on G deck, the vibration of the engine making everything quiver, and the stale air still reeking from the cigars of a former occupant. It was her first taste of her new life, bringing home forcefully for the first time how very much she had given up to marry a quiet Australian boy she had not seen for two years and hardly knew. When Jessie had appeared as her roommate, chirping away nonstop like a cheerful cockney sparrow as she unpacked her cheap cotton dresses and hung them next to Sarah's silks, Sarah had almost gone to the purser and demanded better accommodation. The one thing she had inherited from her domineering father had been his pride, and having to share a room with a servant girl, knowing that she had no money to pay for anything better, was almost more than she could endure. She had fought the strongest urge to walk straight off the ship and catch the next train home again, except that she no longer had a home, or a father. He had made that very clear to her. She had made her bed, he told her, and now she had to lie in it. She was no longer his child. She was only Mrs. James Alison to be . . .

She shivered with a sudden chill.

"What's the matter, miss, cold?" Jessie asked, fastening a final button at her neck. "You won't have much chance to be cold, once we land, I'm thinking. They say the heat's something terrible in the summertime."

"I'm not cold, Jessie," Sarah said, taking her hair and twisting it into a tight knot at the base of her neck. "I was just thinking about things and how final everything is. We're twelve thousand miles away from our homes, half a world away from everything we've known, and there's no going back . . ."

"Not having second thoughts about Lieutenant Jimmy, are you, miss?" Jessie asked softly.

"Not about Jimmy," Sarah said firmly. "If there's one thing I do know, it's that I want to marry Jimmy and that he'll do everything he can to make me happy."

"There, then, what are you griping about?" Jessie asked. "Not many girls can say they've found someone as perfect as your Jimmy, from what you tell me—a gentleman but not a sissy. That's a rare combination. You certainly don't see it too much among them young men you used to mix with, I'll be bound. Lot of pansies I bet they were, if you ask me!''

Sarah laughed out loud. ''You're right, Jessie. They certainly were a lot of pansies. I should have had died of boredom if I'd had to marry one of them. Come on, race you up on deck!''

Giggling and struggling, they fought their way down the narrow corridor, not looking at all like two young women about to be married.

Two

IT TOOK FOUR FRUSTRATING HOURS TO MOVE DOWN Sydney Harbor, not because of the length of the journey, but because their way was impeded by wave after wave of uniformed officials of the Australian Government. First came the medical inspection in Watson's Bay—a laughable parade of hands past a man in white shorts and a peaked cap.

''I haven't had to show me 'ands since I was a nipper in school,'' Jessie whispered to Sarah. ''Do they only let in people with clean fingernails?''

Sarah smiled. ''It's supposed to stop people with certain diseases like smallpox from coming in.''

Jessie nudged her. ''Do they think someone wouldn't have noticed if a person with smallpox sat down next to them at a table for all this time? I know I wouldn't have ate me food next to a man with scabs all over him! Don't have much brain down here, do they?''

After the health inspection came the next line for immigration and customs. Finally they were allowed to move on down the harbor, past the elegant homes on sandstone bluffs. Before them were the tightly huddled houses of working-class neighborhoods and the cranes from the line of docks, looking like French can-

can dancers with legs raised high. The great white ship let out a blast from its rear funnel as tugboats inched it toward the dock. Jessie grabbed at Sarah in alarm.

"Why don't they ever warn you when they're going to do those things?" she demanded. "Nearly gave me heart failure and my Tom wouldn't half create if he found me dead of heart failure after he'd paid for my ticket."

Sarah laughed and turned to gaze fondly at Jessie. At first she had found the macabre cockney humor incomprehensible and felt as if she were sharing a cabin with a creature from the moon, but as the long, dreary voyage had dragged on, with empty hour upon hour to fill as they drifted through the Indian Ocean, she had come to appreciate her companion's ability to laugh at anything. She had also come to realize for the first time that people like Jessie had learned at an early age to laugh rather than cry, because in their lives there was a lot to cry about. Jessie's stories of baby brothers dying because they couldn't afford a doctor, of fathers who drank and gave mothers black eyes every Friday night, had opened her eyes to the world outside Wickcombe. Until she had met Jessie on the boat, she had not realized that other people struggled to survive while she was deciding what to wear and whether to go out hunting. Even the laborers on her father's farm always had enough good food to eat and seemed to enjoy life. It was hard for Sarah to digest that people like Jessie grew up expecting life to deal them bad cards. And now she was also headed for a life that would have hardships and disappointments. Jimmy wrote about sheep dying and bushfires destroying houses. She knew she'd be far from medical help, far from civilization and she didn't know whether she would be able to cope. She hoped she would. Her father had always boasted about the good stock she came from, how a Hartley had never turned away in the face of danger or despair. She could recount all the incidents from famous battles when Hartleys distinguished themselves, risking lives for their men. There had been portraits of them above the great staircase at Wickcombe—tall, somber men with steel-hard eyes, gripping sword hilts; but hadn't they also been afraid before Waterloo or Balaklava?

If they can fight battles, then I can cope with a strange new life, she determined as she peered down at the sea of ant-sized people below on the dock. *I want Jimmy to be proud of me, and above all, I don't want to give my father the satisfaction of seeing me fail.*

The tugboats tooted impatiently to each other. Great lines were thrown ashore. The crowd of ants surged toward the quayside, hundreds of little hands waving so that the crowd looked like a giant insect, fluttering feelers. Jimmy was in that crowd. His hand was one of the feelers. Soon she was going to feel his strong hands around her waist again, crushing her to him so fiercely that she could hardly breathe.

She gave a happy sigh, leaning down over the railing, trying to distinguish his upturned face from the thousands around him. *Whatever happens,* she decided, *it will be better than marrying some oaf like Tony Watson-Smythe and only having tea parties to look forward to!*

She grinned at Jessie, who was likewise peering over the railing.

"It's no use," she said. "We'll never recognize them from this distance. Let's fight our way to near the gangplank and maybe we'll see them coming up!"

"Good idea," Jessie said. "I just hope my poor Tom don't get trampled in the rush. Him being undersized and all. He always was a skinny little runt, poor little sod," and she laughed fondly. Sarah could see her brain working, thinking how she was going to take care of him and fatten him up nicely.

A cheer went up as the gangplanks were slid into position. The first rank of people surged up them like invading forces. Jessie and Sarah were crushed against the railing as passengers recognized loved ones and pushed to get through. The noise level rose alarmingly. "Fred! It's me, over here! Lizzie! Lizzie! Aunty Sue! Cousin Alf! Mum!!" The sea of faces turned itself into individuals who laughed and hugged and cried all around them. Jessie clutched at Sarah's arm. "There he is," she shrieked. "Tom! Tom! Over here!"

The perky little man, who reminded Sarah instantly of a cockney sparrow, looked up and laughed in delight. "Well, blow me. It's my Jessie! How are you then, love?"

To Sarah's amusement Jessie did not fling herself into his arms, but instead stepped back a pace, looking at him critically. "As well as can be expected after the long trip, thank you Tom," she said very primly.

Tom looked at her uncertainly, as if he had picked up a pet

kitten who might be a tiger in disguise. "Well go on then, give us a kiss," he said.

"Not here, Tom, with all these people watching," Jessie said. "What will they think?"

"They'll think that I've waited nearly three years to see my best girl again and I deserve a kiss," he said, wounded.

"They'll be plenty of time for that when we're married," Jessie said. "First let's think about getting my stuff off this ship. Is the ceremony all planned like I told you?"

Tom beamed again, proud of having done something right. "Just like you said, Jessie. Nice little Methodist Church over in Paddington—Bethel Chapel on Oxford Street—and it even has a hall for celebrating afterward. At four o'clock this afternoon so that gives us plenty of time to get your stuff loaded into the lorry. My mates drove me over from Paramatta with the lorry so we'll have someone to celebrate with, then they'll drive us home tonight."

"Tonight?" Jessie asked. "You mean we're not going to have a honeymoon at a hotel or nothing?"

"Have a heart, Jessie love," Tom's face clouded over. "Them hotels cost something shocking, you know. I wanted to have some money saved for you to choose furniture. We've got a nice little cottage of our own now, you know. The boss let me have it for a real cheap rent. No more sleeping in with the other grooms. I know you'll make it real homelike soon. I just got the essentials for us . . . like a bed . . ."

"One track mind you've always had, Thomas Bates," Jessie said, making contact with him for the first time as she dug him in the ribs.

"Who was thinking about hotel rooms then?" Tom demanded.

"Well, that's only right and proper and what a girl can expect," Jessie said haughtily.

"We'll have a good old blowout at the hall," Tom said. "Me mates been out and bought the food and booze. Whole keg of beer and oysters—you should see the shrimp and oysters you can buy here, Jessie! Talk about eat well! You'll be as fat as a pig if you're not careful."

Jessie took his arm. "Well, let's get cracking then," she said. "All this talk of food has made me peckish and Sarah and me had an early start today . . ." The mention of Sarah made her turn to her friend at the railing.

"Oh Sarah, I almost forgot you were there. Have you spotted your Jimmy yet?"

"Not yet," Sarah said, trying to keep her voice even.

Jessie came over and peered down. "Crowd's thinning out," she said. "I hope he remembered the right day."

"Maybe he couldn't get away," Sarah said wistfully. "He did say in his last letter—the one I got in Ceylon—that he might not be able to leave because this was the busiest time of year with the sheep. But he promised he'd try and get someone to keep an eye on the place. I'm sure he'll try to make it . . ." Her voice trailed away and she gave Jessie a bright smile. "You go along and get your things. You don't have to wait around with me."

"Oh no, miss, we'll stick around a few more minutes, won't we Tom?" she asked. "After all these months apart, a few more minutes don't seem too important." She took Tom's arm and jerked him toward Sarah. "Tom, I'd like you to meet my good friend, Sarah Hartley," she said proudly. "She took good care of me on the trip and made sure I didn't get shipped off as a white slave in one of them bazaars in Cairo!" She looked across at Sarah and giggled at the memory. Tom held out his hand stiffly toward Sarah, "Pleased to meet you, miss," he said.

"I'm pleased to meet you, too, Tom," Sarah said. "I've heard so much about you I feel that I know you already. Jessie and I did nothing but talk for six weeks."

"Nothing bad I hope," Tom said uneasily.

Sarah smiled. "I probably know all your guilty secrets," she confided. As she spoke, she never once took her eyes off the traffic up and down the gangplank. It had now turned into a two way procession with trunks and cases disappearing down to the dock on the shoulders of porters. There were very few people standing down below now who did not have their luggage with them. She turned back to Jessie.

"Please don't wait any longer for me," she said. "It really doesn't look as if he's coming. I expect an emergency came up and he left a message for me. I'll go and see the purser and find out where messages would be sent."

"Well, if you're sure, miss—I mean Sarah," Jessie said uneasily. "I would like to get my cases off so that I can get changed for the wedding . . ." She reached out impulsively and took

Sarah's hands. "Look, if you're still in Sydney by this afternoon, why don't you come to my wedding?"

"That's very nice of you, Jessie," Sarah said, smiling but embarrassed, "but I'm sure . . ."

"No, honestly, miss," Jessie insisted. "I'd really like you to be there. You see, I won't have anybody of my own there. No bridesmaids or nothing. It would mean a lot to me . . . ."

Sarah smiled at her fondly. "I'll try, Jessie. If I'm still around, I'll be there."

"That's wonderful, miss," she said. "And if you can't wait around for it and I don't see you again, keep in touch, won't you? I hope you and your Jimmy are as happy as Tom and I plan to be."

"I'll write, Jessie," Sarah said. "And I wish you both all the best."

Jessie wiped a tear away as she took Tom's arm and led him down the deck. As soon as they were almost out of earshot, Sarah overheard him saying, "What did you have to go and invite her for? We don't need no toffs at our wedding. Put a real damper on things that will!"

And Jessie's voice, loudly reprimanding him. "I want her and that's that. She's a real good friend to me, however posh she speaks!"

Then they were swallowed up into the crowd. With a sigh, Sarah turned away and fought past porters to the purser's office.

"If there was a message for you, it would be down at the company's office on the docks, miss," the purser said. "You can't miss it. Little blue shack just to the right as you come off the ship. They'll put you right."

Sarah stood in the hallway, hesitating about what to do next. If she unloaded her luggage and then Jimmy came to her cabin, he'd find her gone and not know what to do next. But, on the other hand, if he wasn't coming and wanted her to meet him somewhere else, she'd need her luggage with her and there might not be any porters around by then . . . A strapping giant of a man passed her and she made an instant decision.

"Porter? I have some bags that need removing," she said. The porter touched his cap immediately. "Over in first class are they, madam?"

Sarah smiled. "Down on G deck," she said. "I've come out to marry a poor farmer!"

The man's big ugly face broke into an answering smile. "Don't worry about it, miss," he said and began lumbering down the stairs.

A few minutes later she was standing outside the *Orient Line* office on the dock with her two trunks beside her. The office was crammed with people. She squeezed in and fought her way to the counter. The clerk checked through a message board.

"Doesn't appear to be anything for Hartley," he said.

"Are you sure?" Sarah asked hopefully.

"You can look for yourself," the young man said, pointing across at a board filled with messages. "Sometimes the names get copied down wrong."

Sarah looked. There was, indeed, nothing. The small shed was stifling and thick with tobacco smoke. She steadied herself against the counter, trying to make her brain think in an orderly manner against the hubbub of voices around her.

"This is the only place a person would leave a message for passengers?" she asked once more.

The young man had already moved on to the next customer and looked back at her unwillingly. He shrugged his shoulders. "As far as I know," he said.

She almost opened her mouth and blurted out, "Then what do I do now?" but she was not going to let a supercilious young clerk with center-parted, slicked down hair have the satisfaction of seeing her distress. Instead she said in what she hoped was a calm voice, "Then perhaps you will be good enough to direct me to a place from which I may telephone or send a telegram?"

"Head post office on Martin's Place," he said, turning back to his present customers.

"Can I walk there?" she asked, but this time he ignored her.

She stepped out into the bright sunlight again, noticing the clarity of the blue sky, the brightness of the red roofs on the other side of the harbor, the sparkle of the water for the first time. It was an incredibly pretty place and one that would have been fun to explore if it were not for the tight knot of fear that threatened to choke her any moment. Why hadn't Jimmy left a message? There must be some mistake—perfectly logical explanation . . . It was misfiled by another slicked-down clerk or Jimmy, out on the borders of his large property, had got his days wrong and was just this moment standing at the local post office sending off a message to tell her where he'd meet her . . .

She rummaged through her handbag and brought out the neat bundle of his letters. She hadn't even given much thought to where she was going, expecting Jimmy to be there at the docks, ready to whisk her away to a new life.

"Don't worry about the wedding details, I've got everything planned nicely," he had written in his last letter. "It won't be a fancy ceremony, I'm afraid. We haven't even got a church in Ivanhoe yet . . .

Ivanhoe, Sarah thought. *At least I know the name of the nearest town.*

On impulse she pushed back into the crowded office. "Can you please tell me how I get to Ivanhoe?" she asked.

Several faces looked at her in silence.

"Never heard of it," one man muttered.

"Some place out back-o'-Bourke, most likely," another man agreed.

"Will they know down at the post office?" she demanded, her temper beginning to rise at the constant wall of unhelpfulness.

"If it's in New South Wales, they can look it up in a book," the first man said.

Sarah left the office again and ran into her porter, staggering past with a new load. "Is there anywhere here I can leave these trunks for a while?" she asked. "The party I expected to meet me is not here yet and I have to go and telephone."

The big man nodded. "Not supposed to officially, but I'll pop them into that roped-off area over there. The stuff there's for further shipment and nobody will touch it today. Come and find me when you want it picked up again."

Sarah opened her purse for a tip, but he shook his head. "My pleasure, miss. We Aussies don't go in for that. All as good as each other down here, see. Hope it all works out all right for you. Pretty young girl ought to have someone to meet her."

Then he walked on again, leaving Sarah in somewhat better spirits. At least one person on this continent had been pleasant and kind. She asked directions and began to walk in the direction of Martin's Place. The warm sun on her back felt good and the sidewalks were clean. Shoppers came out of department stores with packages, and businessmen walked briskly discussing money and golf. It was good to be back in a civilized city again—a city where people spoke English and looked English.

She began to feel more confident. This was all just a temporary misunderstanding. In a few days they'd be laughing over this . . . it would even be the sort of thing she'd tell their grandchildren: "And what about the time your grandfather forgot to come and pick me up at the docks because he had the wrong month on his calendar?"

The head post office was solid and Victorian-looking. Feet echoed across marble floors so that most people crossed on tiptoe. The man at the counter in the telephone section looked forbidding, dressed very formally in a dark suit and high, starched collar, but he turned out to be polite and helpful. He looked up Ivanhoe in a big book, then shook his head. "We have no service there yet," he said, "although it is planned, I believe, when they start putting the railway through past Trida. But there's not the money for that sort of expansion just now."

Sarah digested this information. "So there is no telephone service to Ivanhoe?" she repeated. "Where would be the closest place I could phone?"

"They have the telegraph office in Trida because of the railway," the man said, doubtfully. "But that's a good forty miles away, I think."

"Would they send a telegram out from there?" Sarah asked.

The man stared past Sarah, mulling over this. "I think it would likely as not go out with the postie," he said.

"The postie?" Sarah asked at the unfamiliar term.

"When he makes his mail rounds," the man said seriously. "You'd do just as well to send a letter. They would go with the postie, too, around once a week I imagine. It would get there just as quickly."

Sarah sighed. "I can be there, in person before that," she said. "You say the railway goes to where?"

"Trida," the man said.

"Then that's what I'd better do," Sarah decided. "No doubt it will be easier to get information once I'm out there. I'm sure there must be a system for sending messages . . ."

"Maybe," the man said.

"So can you tell me the way to the train station?" Sarah asked.

"Just keep on down George Street," the man said. "You can't miss it."

An hour later she was sitting on one of her trunks in the

middle of Central Station. All around her people hurried, trains belched steam, whistles sounded, and porters trundled barrows piled high with luggage. It seemed that everything and everybody in the world had a place to go except her. From the booking clerk she had found that the train for Trida left at six-thirty in the evening and got into Trida at noon the next day. Not wanting to leave her luggage again or waste money by having it put in the left luggage, she had sat on it beside the platform. The time passed very slowly and her worries began to creep one by one to the surface of her consciousness. She fought back the desire to cry, determined that an English girl of good breeding should not be seen sniffling in public at the first sign of reverse in her life. *After all,* she gave herself a rapid pep talk, *things have all worked out until now, haven't they? Father forbade you to see Jimmy again and yet you still kept in touch. He managed to save up enough to send your ticket, and you got up enough nerve to walk out of Wickcombe? It will sort itself out, I'm sure.*

The clock on the ornate tower above the station chimed four, waking Sarah from her reverie and reminding her that Jessie's wedding would be taking place at his very moment.

When she had found that the train did not leave for four more hours, she had been very tempted to go to that wedding. She admitted to herself that it was not so much to keep Jessie company, as to cling to the two people in the whole of Sydney whom she knew. She realized all too well that the train would be taking her hundreds of miles away from them, with just the hope that Jimmy would be waiting at the other end to keep her going. She had another reason for staying put on her trunk beside the platform. If, by any chance, Jimmy had been delayed at the ship and arrived to find her gone, this would be the one logical place to come to. She let herself indulge in that daydream—she would look up toward the entrance arch and Jimmy would be there. He would spot her across the crowded platform . . . run toward her . . . "Can you ever forgive me?" he'd beg. "The stupid train was delayed two hours! Cow wandered onto the line and got itself wrapped around the engine. I was nearly frantic with worry and I bet you were, too . . ."

"It's all right, Jimmy. Nothing matters now. You're here and I'm here. Let's go home and get married . . ."

A train nearby let out a piercing whistle that brought her back to the present. A porter with a high load almost ran into her and swore under his breath as he steered around her. She heard Tom's comment echoing through her head: "What did you go and invite her for? We don't need no toffs at our wedding!" It seemed that there was no place for her on the entire continent of Australia! She swallowed hard again. "I'm not going to give in now," she muttered. "I must just be brave until tomorrow, then everything will be all right."

Three

THE TRAIN PUFFED PONDEROUSLY OUT OF THE STAtion into the setting sun. The world outside was bathed in glowing evening colors so that the red-tiled roofs of the neat suburban houses looked even redder than before. Sarah settled back against her corner, staring out with half-seeing eyes. Streets passed slowly, rows of tenements decorated with ironwork balconies, factories with chimneys belching out smoke, and then patches of green—a cricket ground with white figures standing on it, back gardens full of bright flowers, and then fields and small farms, horses poking heads over fences, rows of neat green crops. It was hard to imagine that it was October and that in England the fields would be bleak, the trees mere bare bones with icy winds rattling the few remaining leaves.

As the train drew into Paramatta station, she got to her feet and watched carefully, trying to spot the racing stables where Jessie would be living; but all she saw was a collection of brick buildings with tin roofs glinting in the sunlight. More fields followed. Small farms, cultivated fields, white houses shaded with tall trees, in fact, nothing resembling the descriptions Jimmy had given her of Orwell, as he had named his farm out beyond Ivanhoe. Again she took out the bundle of his letters. "It's not the best property in the world," he had written a year before, "but it's all that I could afford, and I think that with hard work I can make a go of it. You English wouldn't call it a farm at all—you'd think it was a desert with no use for anything, terrible soil, hardly any grass, no water, no trees, but out here people raise sheep successfully on land like this because they buy enough land to graze one sheep to the acre. I'm not even doing that to start with. The farm is around a thousand acres and I've just enough money to buy two hundred sheep to get me started—or rather, I've put the down payment on two hundred sheep and hope to pay off the balance with the first spring lambs and the first shearing. They seem like good solid animals, but I'm not the best judge of sheep—they are fat and woolly and all look pretty much the same to me. No doubt I'll soon learn better."

Sarah paused and smiled to herself. She could almost hear Jimmy speaking those words out loud. He had that endearing way of laughing at himself and of being prepared to tackle anything. He had smiled in the same way when he had left on fighter missions over Europe. "I'll be a little busy Tuesday night," he'd say. "I've got a dinner date with the Kaiser, or rather with the Red Baron and his friends." He grinned as he said it, never once giving the slightest hint of being scared or of knowing the odds of his returning safely were not very favorable. Sarah sat up every one of those nights and gave a small prayer of thanks every morning when she counted the number of returning aircraft at the nearby Royal Flying Corps aerodrome. Jimmy must have been a pretty good fighter pilot because he came back from every mission with both wings on his plane. If anyone could make a go of farming a desert with no water and no trees, Jimmy could . . .

Sarah closed her eyes and smiled to herself. Even living in a desert didn't seem too terrible with the thought of Jimmy beside her. She had dreamed of being with him again every night of the two years they had been parted. She had written to him almost every day and he wrote back faithfully, not every day, but whenever he had time—letters full of details about the farm and the sheep and all the stupid mistakes he had made to begin with. Then finally came the letter in which he announced proudly that the new season's lambs would provide the cash to buy her ticket. And that letter happily coincided with her twenty-first birthday. She was able to go into her father's study and announce, "I won't be needing a twenty-first party father, since I won't be here. Jimmy, who you said would never amount to anything, has managed to save enough to pay my fare out to marry him. I'll be leaving on the next boat!" And for once in his life he could not find the words to answer her. It was only several weeks later, as Janet accompanied her to the taxi, that he appeared at the door and told her quietly that if she crossed that threshold, she would no longer be his daughter. She had crossed.

"You never even gave Jimmy a chance, Daddy," Sarah muttered to herself in the empty compartment. "You were determined from the very first that he was no good."

Her mind went back to that day in 1918 when she had first met him, walking along a country lane near her home. It was spring and the banks were full of primroses. Sarah had stopped to pick some when she noticed him watching her. He was wearing an officer's uniform that she recognized as a flyer from the nearby base, but he didn't look like the young officers father had occasionally invited in for drinks. He was tall and strong-looking, with a tanned face and bright blue eyes. He seemed to be bursting with life and vitality, in contrast to the pasty-faced English boys who draped themselves languidly on sofas. When he opened his mouth to speak, she could tell instantly why he had looked so different.

"G'day, miss," he said, touching his cap. "I hope you'll pardon the liberty, but I wondered if you could tell me where there's a good café round here where a bloke can get a decent cup of tea in the afternoon. All they serve down at that base is dishwater."

He smiled and Sarah smiled in return. "There's a little café in the village," she said. "The Cosy Corner. I'm not sure how good their tea is, but I'm sure it's better than dishwater."

"Thank you, miss," he said. "Much obliged." He half turned to go, then he looked back at her. "I don't suppose you'd consider joining me for a pot of tea and a cake, would you? It gets very lonely stuck in the middle of the wilds like this."

Sarah's strict English upbringing took over. "I'm afraid that wouldn't be right at all," she said in her best English manner. "You see, we haven't been introduced."

His face fell and she could see him blushing beneath that tan. "That's all right, miss. I quite understand. I didn't mean any harm," he said. "I was only asking you for a cup of tea, not to run away with me to Brighton . . ." and a sudden wicked smile flashed across his face, making him irresistible.

Sarah had given in to that smile. "You're absolutely right," she said. "What can be wrong with having a cup of tea with somebody? I'd love to come."

They walked together to the café that afternoon, talking non-stop as they walked, drank tea, and then walked home again. After eighteen stuffy years imprisoned in a nursery with a succession of stuffy governesses and a very severe father, he was like a breath of fresh air. In her rare meetings with boys at hunt balls and Christmas parties, she had either been tongue-tied or bored. With Lieutenant James Alison she was neither. He treated her like a person, not a girl, and she responded the same way. He was obviously very homesick and told her all about his Aunty Mabel, who had raised him in a small town in New South Wales and whose death had caused him to enlist, about kangaroos and kookaburras, about good Aussie beer and thick steaks. When it was her turn, she could find nothing amusing or exciting to tell him. Her mother had died when she was born and her father was determined to keep her tied to the house forever, a perpetual housekeeper and companion for him. She had been denied the privilege of going away to school, denied the privilege of her class of being a debutante and being presented to the king, and since Wickcombe was so isolated, even denied many companions of her own age.

By the end of the first meeting they knew that they were kindred souls. They made each other laugh. They shared in each other's sorrows. They met at the little café about once a week. He sometimes left letters for her with the gatekeeper at Wickcombe. She always left replies. Then her father found out and behaved as if she was holding secret meetings with the Kaiser. She brought Jimmy to meet him, in the hope that Jimmy's charm and gentleness would influence the older man to like him. The meeting was a disaster. Her father called him a social climber trying to ape his betters and forbid him to see his daughter again. Neither of them obeyed him. The meetings, now being totally in secret, were somehow all the sweeter and more exciting. It had been the war's end that drove them apart. When it was over, Jimmy was shipped back to his native land. They met for one last time and he asked her to marry him. She agreed. He bought her a ring with a small diamond in it, kissed her passionately for the first time, and left. She had met him not more than twenty times and on that short acquaintanceship had promised to give up her comfortable life, her family, and her country.

She glanced down at the ring, now worn openly and proudly on her finger. It was nothing like the flashy emeralds and diamonds of their acquaintances in Suffolk, but it seemed much nicer to her: a sincere ring, a true plighting of troth.

"Tomorrow," she murmured.

The train had begun to climb. Sarah stood to look out of the window, but there was no obvious sign of hills ahead. Nevertheless, they were going steadily upward. The air, when she opened the window away from the smoke, smelled fresher and the colors of the eucalyptus trees glowed in the clear air. They stopped in small towns—Penrith and then Springwood. Finally at Katoomba men walked down the platform with an announcement that they would be making a fifteen minute tea stop. Sarah thought that eight o'clock in the evening was a funny time for tea, but got out with most of the other passengers. She noted there were hardly any women on the train. They were mostly men and mostly dressed for farm work with broad-brimmed hats and big boots. They looked, to Sarah, like her idea of American cowboys.

"Excuse me," she asked a friendly-looking older woman, "but is the train going to stop again for dinner?"

"Is what?" the old woman asked, looking strangely at Sarah. "Didn't you hear the man? This is the tea stop. You pick up your tea in the buffet over there."

"Oh," Sarah said. Maybe dinner was not a meal in Australia. Maybe they just had tea, the way children did in English nurseries. She followed the woman into the poky little station buffet, expecting to find bread and butter and jam tarts. Instead men were standing around, wolfing down meat pies and great mugs of tea. It turned out that the choice of food, by the time Sarah got to the counter, was meat pie or sausage roll. She chose the meat pie, but it was so unappetizing that she could only take a couple bites of it.

She realized, with concern, how very little money she had on her and wondered how many other things she would have to pay for before it ran out. She had never had any money of her own. Her father made her ask for anything she needed and only handed over the money if he thought the cause was worthy. Unworthy causes had been Janet's birthday and new dresses. It had, in fact, been Janet who had lent her her own meager savings to come on the trip. "Never know when a little cash might come in handy," she had said. Then, when Sarah had refused to take it, "What if you found yourself stranded in one of those heathen ports and the ship sailed without you? I'd feel a lot better knowing you had at least enough money to get yourself posthaste to the British consul!"

Sarah smiled to herself wistfully. If only Janet were here now. She would take charge as always, more of a sergeant major than housekeeper—the only one not to be afraid of her father, eyeing him with her severe Scottish face and telling him he'd likely burst a blood vessel if he didn't stop his blustering!

The meat pie left a bad taste in her mouth. The other passengers showed no signs of reboarding the train, so she decided to stretch her legs. The platform was unfenced and led straight across to a sandy area between a few houses. It was almost dark but the sky still glowed behind eucalyptus trees. To her left the trees seemed to come to an end. She walked toward them and found her arm grabbed by a stranger. As she gasped, he tipped his hat to her.

"Better watch your step, miss, or you'll fall off the mountain," he said in the slow Aussie twang.

"Mountain?" Sarah thought she was probably being made a fool of.

"Down there, miss," he said. She stepped forward and gasped. Beneath her feet the ground fell away hundreds, if not thousands, of feet, plunging sheer to an almost unseen valley below. She looked back at her rescuer.

"Thank you, I had no idea . . ."

He grinned, that same boyish Aussie grin that had been so endearing with Jimmy. "Queer country this," he said. "Even our bloody mountains go down and not up!"

She laughed with him.

"Where you heading then, miss?" he asked, nodding when she told him.

"My word, that's out back-o'-Bourke!" he commented.

"Where is this Bourke that everyone talks about? It doesn't seem to be on the route."

He laughed again. "Fresh out from the old country, are you miss? Back-of-Bourke just means way in the outback, miles from everywhere. There is a town called Bourke, but it's not near here. And what, if I may be so bold to ask, will you be doing out beyond Trida?''

Sarah smiled. ''I'm meeting my fiancé. He's bought a farm out beyond Ivanhoe and we're going to be married.''

The man tipped his hat again. ''Good on yer, miss,'' he said. ''We need more pretty girls like you out there. Pretty bloody boring for a bloke if he don't see a nice bit of skirt once in a while, even if she is someone else's sheila!''

The train whistle summoned them back to their seats. The stranger escorted Sarah back to hers then left her with a nod and a wink. The encounter revived Sarah's spirits. The fact that there would be men like that, polite and respectful in their uneducated way, made the prospect of life ''back-o'-Bourke'' seem more bearable.

The train started again, crawling now as it negotiated mountain bends, sending out shrill notes of warning into the fading light. The food lay in a solid lump in Sarah's stomach, being shaken around by the violet swaying of the train as it rounded each curve. She got up and began to pace up and down, wondering what the food would have been like at Jessie's wedding. What would they be doing now? she wondered. Would the feasting on oysters and shrimps still be going on or would they already be heading back toward the little cottage in Paramatta and the honeymoon night?

That thought brought her to a halt, leaning against the closed door of the compartment. She, too, might be facing a honeymoon night tomorrow. Not that she was worried about it—Jimmy would be kind and understanding, she knew, but it represented such a giant unknown. From the overheard conversations in English powder rooms, she understood that it was simply ghastly and that even the most civilized man became like an animal. That did not seem possible with Jimmy and yet Sir David Cameron seemed the meekest, mildest little man and it was his wife who had been describing his animal behavior when Sarah had come unexpectedly into the room. The conversation had ceased immediately, of course. She ranked as a *Pas devant les jeunes filles,* a muttered French phrase of warning with which cultured English people broke off interesting conversations whenever servants or innocents intruded.

The problem was that most conversations had been broken

off before she could get more than a hint of anything. Her father had not encouraged friends her own age. The girls she was thrown together with at hunts were horribly dull and only wanted to talk about their horses. No knowledge could be extracted from Janet, who had a very Puritan idea about what was proper for young girls to know. In fact, Sarah doubted that Janet knew any more than she did, having been put into service at age twelve and remained an old maid in what must have been the least lively household in England.

Was Jessie feeling scared right now? Sarah wondered. She doubted it. At least Jessie had some idea of what to expect. Sex had become one of the topics they discussed most as the boat passed through the Red Sea and they had lain in deck chairs, too lethargic to do anything but talk for days at a time. Jessie laughed herself silly about Sarah's notion that people must do it from behind like animals. "I've watched pigs and dogs," she said indignantly when Jessie started laughing until tears ran down her cheeks. "Why should people be any different?"

"Because we don't run around on four legs, silly," Jessie stammered. "Believe me, I know what I'm talking about. When I was first in service, the kitchen maid, Rita, her name was, was being courted by the underfootman. Well, he was the "over-footman" where Rita was concerned. Used to come up to our room every night almost and I was unlucky enough to share a bed with her. I always used to pretend I was asleep, of course, but how could a person sleep with all that bouncing up and down? Sometimes I thought I'd roll right out—or get seasick!" And she convulsed with laughter again.

Sarah considered these details again. The tea-party ladies she had overheard spoke of the pain, but Jessie had maintained she never heard Rita complaining. The only moaning she did was for more, Jessie maintained. That must indicate that she actually enjoyed it, or she wouldn't risk smuggling the underfootman up to her bed every night. Sarah thought back to that one kiss, when she promised to marry Jimmy and he said good-bye. They had kissed before, of course, but the previous kissing had been limited to a delicate brushing of her lips, as if she were made of fragile porcelain and might break. The final kiss started like that, too, then Jimmy gave a strangled sob and crushed her into his arms. She could still remember the unfamiliar, exciting feel of his body against hers, of his mouth against hers. In a life where physical contact had been almost nonexistent, limited, in fact, to Janet's daily brushing of her hair, Jimmy's embrace seemed at the time almost overwhelming. She had to fight against wanting to push him away. But after he had gone, she yearned to repeat the moment, feeling his hard body, his demanding lips in her dreams.

"Oh Jimmy," she whispered, sitting down again in her corner and leaning her face against the cool leather of the seat back. "Just let everything be all right tomorrow."

Four

NEXT MORNING THE SUN CAME UP TO A VERY DIFferent landscape. This was the Australia Jimmy had described: wide vistas of yellow earth, dotted with isolated gum trees. Sheep stood in pools of shade munching at the sparse yellow grass. Riverbeds over which they passed were dry or mere lines of puddles. The horizon seemed to stretch away into infinity. When Sarah opened the window, dust blew in.

All of that long night she had dozed fitfully, her fears magnifying themselves as the night progressed. At one moment she had almost convinced herself that Jimmy had found another girl and not found the courage to stop Sarah's arrival. With the morning she had to admit that this fear, at least, could not be true. Jimmy would never deliberately hurt anyone. If he had fallen out of love with her, he would have told her. Anyway, she argued, whatever the reason, she was going to find it out in a few hours from now.

Sometime during the night they had stopped at a deserted station. Sarah opened her window and looked out. The sign on the waiting room said ORANGE. The station seemed larger than most and lit street lamps beyond seemed to hint that they were at a large town, but nothing moved on the platform and the only sound was the night wind, rustling the eucalyptus trees that grew along the station fence. Sarah shivered. The night was surprisingly cold, or her fear had made it seem so.

As the waiting time continued, a few passengers got down from the train and began to pace the platform. Sarah did not dare to leave, in case the train took off again without her. At last the sound of a shunting engine could be heard. Maybe there was only one line of track, and trains had to wait their turn, Sarah wondered. If so, it was very poorly timed that two trains should approach it at the same moment, seeing that they had only passed one other train in the past several hours. She peered further out of the window, but could not see the other train until a dreadful jolt nearly threw her out onto the platform below. A railway official came out of nowhere and hurried past.

"Excuse me," Sarah called to him, trying to keep the alarm from her voice, "but what is happening please?"

She half expected him to say that there had been a crash and he was going to rescue the survivors, but instead he looked up at her in annoyance at having been delayed. "Special coach been added. The premier's getting on the train here."

"Who?"

"Col Murphy's getting on. He's going to Broken Hill." Then he ran on before Sarah could ask any more questions. With his strange accent and rapid speech, she hadn't understood a word that he had said, but she gathered that an important person must be joining the train, or they would not have added a special coach for him.

At least it can't be royalty, she thought with a smile. *I thought everybody was supposed to be equal in Australia!*

Curiosity made her keep watching, although the open window was chilling her compartment. At last a group of men was hustled across the platform, all talking loudly, and doors banged on the special coach. It all happened so quickly that Sarah had no time to observe any of them, but she did notice that they wore city suits and hats, not cowboy boots and wide brims like the other passengers. A few men still stood on the platform, apparently the send-off committee. As Sarah continued to watch, a large head leaned out of the special coach window—a head crowned with a shock of gray curly hair and now without a hat on it.

"What happened to me grog, Harry?" the man demanded

loudly in a strong Australian twang. "I'm not going to survive this journey without my case of grog."

"It's with your baggage, Col."

"You'd better not have taken it, you bastard," the gray-haired man shouted and gave a huge laugh. "I'm going right over to find it now. And then I'm going to count it, too! I don't trust you country types . . . only don't let my constituents know that." He broke into a deep, rich laugh that was drowned by a piercing shriek from the train's whistle.

"Look's like we're moving, then," the big man shouted, waving to those remaining behind. "Thanks for your hospitality, Harry. Thanks, mates—hope it goes well—and if I'm not back within a week, send a search party!" Then he laughed as the train began to jerk forward with horrible screeching and groaning. Sarah was about to pull her head in when the big, gray-haired man looked down the train and caught her eye. Instead of hastily looking away again, as any English gentleman would have done, he gave her a broad wink. Blushing furiously, Sarah pulled her head inside. What must he have thought of her? He probably considered she was a brazen hussy for daring to peer out of a train window in the middle of the night! She closed the window and settled herself back in her corner, determined to sleep.

Instead she found sleep impossible. The noise from the special coach kept up unabated all night—loud laughter and even singing, as from a barroom. The noise continued until just before dawn, when Sarah dozed off into fitful sleep. She was woken by a ticket collector, tapping on the door of her compartment and she sat up hastily, straightening her dress and blinking her eyes in the strong daylight.

"Just coming into Condobolin, miss," he said, sliding the door open and touching his cap to her. He took her ticket and clipped it. "Breakfast stop—I expect you could do with a nice cup of tea. It's a long night sitting up, isn't it?"

Sarah nodded. "Especially when there was too much noise to sleep," she said.

He grinned. "My oath—there was noise all right. Still, we could hardly ask them to keep it quiet, could we?"

"Who exactly are they?" she asked. "I watched them get on in Orange."

"It's Col Murphy, miss," the man said.

"Who is he?" she asked. Then, because his face looked as if she'd just asked who King George was, "I'm sorry, I've only just arrived here. I don't know much about Australia yet."

"He's the premier, miss," the man said. "You'll soon be hearing more about him, I don't doubt. Makes headlines wherever he goes, miss. A real wowser."

"A what?"

"Sort of stirs up trouble," the man said. "You either love Col Murphy or you hate him. He's not your middle of the road politician, that's for sure."

"He's the prime minister, then?" Sarah asked, still confused and finding it hard to imagine a prime minister who shouted out so crudely and winked at strange girls.

"No, miss. The premier of New South Wales. The prime minister's of the whole country. The states have premiers—just like little countries within a big country, you could say. Only Col Murphy probably has more power than the federal prime minister. He has to please everybody, see? Col just has to please his bloody self!"

"Oh, I see. Thank you," Sarah said stiffly. "So he's visiting his constituents?"

The man grinned. "He's up for reelection. He's going courting, that's what he's doing. Promising them everything. He's heading out for Broken Hill and what's the betting he'll promise them their railway? It stops at Trida right now, you see. They were going to build it through, but the war sort of put a damper on things."

The train had begun to slow and isolated houses could be seen along a dirt road, each shaded by its dusty eucalpytus.

The man looked up. "Here we are," he said. "This is Condobolin. Nice little town. Used to be the terminus until a couple of years ago. It's pretty down by the river, but I don't think you'll have time to see it. Anyway, I expect you want your brekkie more. Nice cup of tea and you'll feel right as rain."

Condobolin did not look like a former terminus, but a dusty town with one main street. Her fellow passengers, sauntering ahead of her to the little refreshment room, their hats tipped forward against the fierce morning sun, helped to enhance the feeling of a wild Western town. The buildings all had wide overhangs to shelter the sidewalks from the sun. The sidewalks and the street were both made of dirt and clouds of it rose when a lone car lurched its way past, bouncing through the potholes.

Col Murphy stared out of the open window as the train sped through empty countryside. His city jacket, well-tailored and silk-lined, was now up in the rack and Col had rolled up his shirtsleeves and taken off his tie. A big bear of a man, with the coarse bones and ruddy complexion of his Irish peasant ancestors, he looked now even more like a farmer or even a dock-worker than a premier of the richest state in Australia. After a while he turned back from the empty scrubland and grinned at the young man, lounging in the opposite corner, fanning himself with a magazine.

"Bloody godforsaken place, isn't it, Jack?" he asked the young man.

Jack Hemmingway, his new secretary and aide, presented a stark contrast to his boss. He alone in the coach had not removed his tie. His shoes were still highly polished, inspite of the dusty streets, and he wore a gold signet ring on his little finger. Freshly back from a degree in politics at Oxford, he represented the other side of Australia—the descendant of younger sons of English aristocracy who had come out with no hope of inheriting at home and had made good lives for themselves while still maintaining the standards and ties of their homeland. Many thought him an unlikely choice for adviser to a people's premier, running on a labor ticket, but Col Murphy was no fool. It might be the workers who elected him, but the finance to run a state had to come from somewhere, and the workers did not have the money. Col liked a finger in both pies. In addition, he appreciated Jack's quick wit and sharp sense of humor.

Jack stopped fanning himself and laughed easily. "One of these days your big mouth is going to get you in trouble, Col," he said.

Col grinned. "Who's going to tell on me?" he asked. "None of these blokes, if they want a job for another three years. When you've known me longer," he added, "you'll realize that I know pretty well when to keep quiet and when to talk. I've been in politics so bloody long that there's not much I don't know . . . but just between you and me, this is a bloody godforsaken place."

Jack continued to smile. "I thought you were supposed to

like the country—your residence has to be in Sydney, but your heart's out in the great open spaces. Isn't that what you said to them back in Orange?"

"Of course I did, you drongo. If I'd given the same speech in Sydney, I'd have said the opposite, wouldn't I?" and he laughed again—his big booming laugh that made several of those still dozing in the compartment stir and open their eyes. He leaned back on the windowsill again, letting the wind play havoc with his unruly hair. "And, as a matter of fact," he said slowly, "I do like the country—but not this sort of country. Marjorie's sort of country is what I like—green paddocks, a few thoroughbreds trotting around in them, iced drinks served by the butler and fresh oranges picked for breakfast—that's my sort of country. I wouldn't mind retiring to one of Marjorie's properties one day . . ." He stared out, feeling the immensity of Australia, contrasting it in his mind with the white picket fences and shaded colonial mansions where his wife's family lived. For a second he pictured himself in riding breeches, whip at his side, going out for a morning canter. Then he laughed at the incongruity of the street kid from a Sydney slum playing at master of hounds and turned back to Jack again.

"Not that Marjorie will ever let me escape from being premier," he said. "She enjoys being queen of Sydney too much. She only keeps me for the prestige!" and he threw back his head and laughed again.

"How you can be so bloody cheerful at crack of dawn I don't know," Frank Harris, his longtime friend and well-known labor leader, growled, peering out from under the brim of his hat.

Col kept on laughing. "You know me—I got stamina," he said.

"Bloody well must have," Frank grunted to Jack. "He drank most of that whiskey himself. I only saw a couple of little glasses—how about you?"

"I needed it most," Col said belligerently. "I've got that bone shaking ride to Broken Hill ahead of me, and then I've got to sound like I know what I'm talking about when I get there. I need my wits about me, too . . . I don't want to go promising them anything I can't deliver just because I'm dying for my bed."

Jack smiled lazily. "I thought you planned to promise them their railway anyway?"

"I might," Col said mysteriously. "It will depend on a lot of things."

"Such as?" Frank demanded.

"Such as who in Broken Hill is willing to put up some good-faith money . . . I'm not financing the bloody thing out of my pocket!"

"Kickback, you mean?" Jack asked serenely.

"Good-faith money," Col growled. "And also I'm meeting a bloke at Broken Hill . . ."

"What sort of bloke?"

"A geologist sort of bloke. He's been out doing a little investigation for me. Everyone's talking about this uranium stuff that is supposed to be able to blow up the world. He thinks he might come up with some out beyond Broken Hill. If he still thinks that, it will be worth opening up the area . . ."

"But it's worth it now, Col," Frank said. "Do you realize all that ore is going by rail down to Adelaide because South Australia was smart enough to put in a track to a town in our state? Doesn't make sense to me."

"It's all a question of money, Franko," Col said. "Is it cost effective to put in three hundred miles of track—and the stations—and maintain it—to ship out silver and zinc? Besides, motorcars are getting better by the minute. What's to say they won't come up with new fast trucks that can transport more cheaply? If they find this uranium, then by all means I say go ahead, since I get the feeling that all the world's going to want to keep enough around to blow each other up . . . but apart from that . . . the economy's shaky. Everyone's talking prosperity, but I don't like the sound of what I'm hearing from Europe at all. It might just not be the time to expand . . ."

He turned back to the window again.

"You watch him, son," Frank Harris said with a sideways grin to Jack. "You've heard him now, but quite likely at the meeting this evening he'll be telling them with a dead straight face that the railway's as good as completed. Trouble is that he always manages to get away with it. He must have an honest face or something!"

The two men laughed. Col did not turn back to them. He was staring out at the vast, empty landscape. *This is my state,* he thought, feeling the amazement that came to him from time to time when he realized what he had achieved. *All this bloody empty land and I'm in charge of it all. If my mother could only see me now. God, she'd never have believed it. She always said I'd come to a bad end with my big ideas . . .* and he laughed, this time silently, to himself.

Five

JUST BEFORE NOON THE TRAIN FINALLY ROLLED into Trida. Sarah leaned out of the window, looking for a porter. The only porter was busy down the train, helping down the premier and his party. Local officials waited, sweating uncomfortably in suits and hats, then put on delighted expressions to shake hands with the emerging party and whisk them away to waiting cars, while the porter pushed their mountains of baggage behind them. Obviously that task must have exhausted him for the rest of the day, since he did not come back to the platform again. When the porter showed no sign of returning, Sarah attempted to drag her two large trunks down from the train by herself. After several men had walked past without appearing to notice her struggle, a tall cowboy did say, "Here, let me give you a hand with those, miss," and lifted them down as if they weighed nothing at all. He stood them on the platform and Sarah thanked him.

"Where you going on to, miss?" he asked. "Old Barney there will take them to the hotel for you, if that's where you're staying."

"I'm not staying," Sarah said firmly. "I've got to get to Ivanhoe and then to a farm beyond there."

The man nodded politely. "Ask old Barney," he said. "He knows everything. I've got my mates waiting." Then with another nod of his head, he walked off the platform and climbed up into a horse-drawn buggy. The premier's cars started off, too, with the necessary shouting and waving. This time Sarah would have welcomed being noticed and maybe then offered a ride, but the group was removed from the station so efficiently that they had no time to notice her. The remaining passengers cleared quickly and soon Sarah was standing alone in the shade of the awning. Even the engineer climbed down from his perch and sauntered off into town. Sarah dragged her two trunks to the side of the platform beside a bench and then walked through the small office to the bright sunlight beyond.

Trida was a replica of the place where they had stopped for breakfast and whose name Sarah had already forgotten. One dusty main street, some sad-looking roses in front yards, bright bottlebrushes making splashes of color beside tin roofs. Two horses were tied outside a store. No sign of cars here, nor of people, for that matter. The only living creatures besides Sarah seemed to be the flies, which descended on her in black clouds, settling on her body, her face, even her eyelids if she didn't continually brush them off. A light wind was blowing and dust swirled and stung. Sarah fought back the fear and depression that threatened to engulf her. This journey was rapidly turning into a nightmare version of the game she played with her older cousins when she was a small girl. These cousins had formed a secret club that Sarah kept asking to join. They would always promise she could join their club if she passed the initiation rites. But no matter how many terrible things she did—collecting a bag full of spiders, walking into the cellar in the dark, she never managed to satisfy them, and the next round of challenges were always more horrible and impossible than the round before. At that time Sarah was not wise enough to realize that her cousins had no intention of admitting her to the club and that the impossible quests were only a way of keeping her out. Later she had understood their motives and wondered why she had ever wanted to be in a club with two such horrible people. In fact, she had forgotten all about the club until this moment.

"Maybe this is another Labors of Hercules," she thought to herself with a grim smile. "If I come through all the tests, I'll win the fair knight!" and she laughed because the whole thing was so absurd and her nerves were stretched tauter than a violin string.

The laugh produced a reaction. A partition slid open and a face peeped through it.

"Can I help you, miss?" the old man asked. Old Barney, surely.

"I hope so," Sarah said politely. "I have to get to Ivanhoe from here. Can you tell me if there is a bus service or something?"

The old face creased into a thousand wrinkles as the man chuckled. "This ain't Marble Arch, lady," he said. "There is a coach through once a week. Cobb and Co., you know. But they just been through yesterday." He turned to look into the distance where a cloud of dust could be seen. "You should have asked old Col for a ride. He'd not have said no to a pretty face," and he gave a wheeze that might have been a laugh.

"I was still trying to get my trunks off the train when they left," Sarah said reproachfully. "Is there anyone else heading in that direction I could ride along with?" she asked.

Barney shrugged his shoulders. "Postie goes out that way once a week," he said. "But he's not heading there till Friday. The hotel could put you up . . ."

Sarah moved restlessly. She did not want to stay three more days in this godforsaken place if she could help it. "And there's no telephone or telegraph out of here?" she asked.

Barney didn't even bother to answer that one. Sarah brushed away flies that threatened to buzz into her mouth each time she spoke. "So I'm stuck here until Friday?" she asked.

Barney stared out into the distance, as if he was about to have a vision. "Unless there's someone else going on in that direction," he said. "I seem to remember Bert Williams talking about going that way. You can check with him."

"Bert Williams?" The next round of initiation.

"He's a bullocky."

Sarah nodded, unwilling to display more ignorance. Barney inclined his head sideways. "He'll be over at Lockhart's store, likely enough."

"Lockhart's store?"

"If he ain't at the pub."

Sarah looked the length of the deserted main street. "Can you watch my two trunks?" she asked.

The ghost of a smile crept across his face. "Who'd want to steal them, lady?" he asked. Then his face brightened up. "You're in luck. There he is now—see the old bandy bloke coming out of the hotel? That's him. That's Bert Williams." He yelled across the street. "Hey, Bert. Get over here. Got a young lady that wants to meet you."

The old man shuffled across the street, kicking up a cloud of dust. He looked at Sarah as if she was an inanimate object.

"Young lady needs to get to Ivanhoe, Bert. Didn't I hear you saying you was headed that way?"

"Out Kenilworth," he muttered.

"You got to go through Ivanhoe to get to Kenilworth you daft drongo," Barney said with a wheezing laugh. "So you can give the young lady a ride as far as there, can't you?"

Bert continued to size her up. "No worry," he said at last. He still stared at her, unblinking.

"Are you leaving soon, Mr. Williams?" she asked, trying to charm him with a friendly smile.

"After me tucker," he growled, then pushed his hat back on his head, as if the long speech had confused him.

"After what?" Me tucker might be anything from a nap to the spring rains.

Barney wheezed his laugh again. "Young lady's fresh out from Pommie Land. She don't talk Strine yet."

"Better learn, hadn't she?" Bert Williams mumbled.

"So you'll be leaving about two o'clock then Bert?" Barney asked for Sarah's clarification.

Sarah's face lit up. "Two o'clock this afternoon? That's wonderful, Mr. Williams. And you really don't mind if I ride along?"

He snorted this time, which sounded like a no.

"Her bags are right here, Bert," Barney said. "You can swing around and pick them up on your way can't you?"

Bert nodded then began to slouch off again. Halfway across the street he remembered and turned back. "Cost you," he said.

Sarah tried not to let anxiety show on her face. Her money was being eaten away very quickly. Was this old man going to use her desperation to make money for himself?

"Of course I intend to pay you, Mr. Williams," she said firmly. "How much do you think would be fair?"

Bert Williams glanced for a second at Barney and luckily Barney spoke up. "I reckon five bob ought to do it, don't you Bert? Buy you a few beers at the Australasia, won't it?"

Bert nodded. "Right oh," he said and shuffled on. Sarah sighed with relief. At least she could afford five shillings. She used the waiting time to walk down to the general store and buy herself a lump of cheese and some biscuits rather than face the lunch in the hotel. Then, at two o'clock, Bert Williams appeared with a team of four bullocks and a wagon piled high with sacks. Sarah climbed up beside him and they set off at a snails pace.

The journey to Ivanhoe took four uncomfortable hours. The wagon shook and bounced over the dried, rutted track until Sarah felt like a sack of potatoes herself. The bullocks kept up an even pace, not quite fast enough to drive off the flies who tormented them and the two humans equally. Sarah's head swam with the heat and her clothes stuck to her unpleasantly. It seemed as if the whole universe had been transformed into orange earth and blue sky, never ending in all directions. Several times Sarah found herself dozing off and waking again with a jerk as the wagon hit a bump. She held on tightly, wondering if Bert Williams would bother to stop for her if she ever rolled off in her sleep. The ride became a blur of half sleeping, half waking until she was not sure which was dream and which reality. She began to doubt that Ivanhoe ever existed . . . or Jimmy ever existed.

Then, around six o'clock, she saw uneven shapes on the horizon—square, man-made shapes that turned themselves into houses and sheds. They drove down the one street of Ivanhoe and Bert jerked the bullocks to a halt. Without another word to her he lifted down her trunks and then disappeared into the bar of the hotel, leaving Sarah, once again, alone in the street. This town was even more deserted than the ones before. In the fierce evening light the tin roofs glowed unnaturally red. Sarah looked up and down the street. There were tin-roofed bungalows straggling along the main street, each fenced with it's own little garden. One had a rickety sign outside announcing, POLICE STATION. Another sign in the window said, CLOSED. Next door the general store was also closed. The only sound of human activity was coming from the bar of the grandly named Australasia Hotel—a large wooden structure with a balcony running the full length of its front, creating a shady porch underneath. The hotel was painted white, but could have done with a coat of paint. Taking a deep breath, Sarah followed Bert Williams into the pub.

As her eyes became used to the darkness, she could see she was in a big room with a mahogany bar running its full length. Several male figures were propped up against this bar and a large female was standing behind it, chatting with one of the men. Nobody looked up as Sarah came in, so she cleared her throat and then said, "Excuse me," loudly.

This had an instant effect. There was complete silence as every head in the room turned toward her. The large woman behind the bar straightened up and glared at her. "This is a bar. Gentlemen only," she said firmly. Her face was so weather-beaten that she looked as if her skin was made of leather.

Sarah felt her cheeks coloring. "I'm sorry, I just wanted to ask . . ."

"No ladies allowed." The woman said, very firmly this time. "Do I make myself clear, miss?"

Sarah felt her temper rising. She was hot, tired, thirsty, and very confused. She stepped back to the door and, making sure she did not lean in around it, she yelled, "Then do you mind telling me where I go for information if you're the only people in this town and I'm not allowed in here?"

The woman's expression didn't change one bit. She jerked her head. "Ladies' Lounge. Entrance 'round the corner."

Sarah stomped out and around to the side of the hotel, entered at a frosted-glass door marked Ladies Lounge and found herself on the other side of the same big room, divided by the same bar. The situation was so absurd that she almost wanted to laugh. The woman at the bar turned toward her, "Now miss?" she asked pleasantly, "what can I do for you?"

"I've come out here to see Jim Alison," Sarah said.

"Jim Alison? Never heard of him," she said bluntly.

"He has a farm out here . . . Orwell, it's called."

The woman's expression did not change.

"He wrote that the nearest town was Ivanhoe," Sarah pleaded.

The woman chuckled. "We're the nearest town to a couple of hundred square miles, miss," she said. "I don't recognize the name. Maybe I'd recognize the face. I'm better with faces than names. Can't be much of a drinker or I'd know him."

"I'm sure he isn't," Sarah said.

"Orwell, you say the property's called?" the woman asked. "Hold on a minute and I'll ask the boys." She turned back to the other side of the room.

"Any of yous know a bloke name of Jim Alison?" she called. "Got a place called Orwell?"

"Orwell?" one man asked, looking at Sarah with interest. "Think I heard of that one. Likely he's out on the station, miss."

"The station?" Sarah was now very confused and frustrated

enough to burst into tears. "But I thought the railway ended back in Trida. That was what they told me."

General laughter. "The sheep station, miss," the man explained. "That's what we call our properties out here."

A young man who had been almost asleep down at the end of the bar pushed his hat back on his head and looked up at Sarah. "Jim Alison?" he asked. "Wasn't that the bloke fell off his horse couple of weeks back?"

A wave of relief shot through Sarah. Jim had fallen off his horse. He was probably lying up with a broken leg, unable to come to meet her.

"Tall fair bloke?" the man asked. His speech was badly slurred.

Sarah nodded. "Is he all right?"

"Broke his neck, I heard."

"Where is he now?" Sarah stammered.

"Where is he?" the man looked confused. "They'd have probably buried him out on the station. We don't have a graveyard in town here."

The room began to spin around violently. Sarah clutched at the cool mahogany of the bar to stop herself from sliding to the floor. "Are you sure it was him?" she asked.

Nobody was.

"You can check with old Paddy, the policeman," one man suggested. "He'd likely know. Had to fill out the death certificate and all that."

"But Paddy's not here right now," another volunteered. "He's off over Beilpajah way. Case of poddy dodging."

"Jake Cotrell would know," someone suggested. "Wasn't he the one who found him?"

"Jake Cotrell?" Sarah repeated like a parrot.

"Out on Woomera," the landlady explained.

"Woomera?" Sarah asked.

"Big station about thirty miles from town. You boys reckon Jake would know?"

"Too right," the first man said. "His station was next door to the Alison bloke, wasn't it? Old Jake would know. He's a mucking good bastard. He's right."

Sarah had stood, her hands gripping at the curved mahogany edge to the bar, watching one speaker then the next, as if she was watching an unreal scene from a play—remote from real life and unconnected with her. She forced herself to think, to come to grips with reality again.

"How do I get out to this Woomera?" she asked sharply. "I've got to find out what happened."

"This Jim Alison was a relative of yours?" the woman asked, looking at her skeptically.

"I'm . . . I came out here to marry him," Sarah said.

The woman looked her up and down. Her face expressed very clearly what she thought of posh young English girls who showed up in Ivanhoe. "Can you ride a horse?" the woman asked.

"As it happens I ride very well," Sarah said, her pride overcoming all other emotions for a second. "Can I rent a horse from you?"

"You'd never find your way," the woman said, "but Tommy here might take you. What do you say, Tommy?"

The big man who had been talking to the landlady leaned across the counter to be part of the conversation. "You can take this young lady out to see Jake Cotrell in the morning, can't you?" she asked. "Seeing it was her financy who got killed?"

The big man nodded. "It's a fair ride, miss," he said, "but I don't mind taking you."

"Then you'll need a room here for the night," the landlady said. "I'll have your bags sent up." She reached beneath the bar and took out a key. "Number three is free," she said, "and nice and quiet out the back."

Numbly Sarah took the key and stumbled up the uneven stairs to a long, gloomy landing up above. The key turned in the lock and she let herself into a small, narrow room. It was furnished with an iron-framed bed, a chair with a broken leg, and a marble-topped table in the corner containing a Victorian jug and basin. The walls were white plaster, peeling in places and adorned with two hideous prints of dogs and pheasants. Sarah walked mechanically across to the bed and lay down on top of the cover. She could feel the lumps in the mattress through the layers. She closed her eyes. An evening breeze had sprung up sending a cooling breath through the open window and causing the white lace curtains to billow out. Sarah half-opened her eyes to watch them the way she always watched the curtains in her room at home. *I'm not here at all,* she thought as exhaustion fought with emotion, *I'm in my own room at home and all this was a horrible dream. Soon Janet's going to bring me my tea . . .*

As if on cue there was a tapping at her door. But it wasn't Janet who came in. It was the leathery lady innkeeper, carrying a tray. "I thought you wouldn't feel like eating down with the men tonight, so I brought you something up to your room," she said, putting it down none too gently on the marble table. "What you need now is a good meal. You get that inside you and you won't do too badly. Brought you up a glass of brandy, too. My treat. Do you a power of good."

Then, without waiting for Sarah to say anything, she turned and left. Sarah raised herself enough to look at the tray. Two dishes were steaming on it—on one, four lamb cutlets lay between mounds of mashed potato and watery cabbage, and on the other, lumpy custard half concealed a huge slab of spotted dick. With a sigh Sarah lay back down again. She was not at Wickcombe after all. She was very, very far away.

Six

THE NEXT MORNING SHE LEFT WITH TOMMY PRESTON at first light. She had, surprisingly, been able to sleep, maybe with help from the large glass of brandy, which had been the only part of her supper she had touched, and in the morning she woke refreshed. The landlady had woken her with a large cup of tea and a slab of bread and butter. Sarah drank the tea and ate the bread mechanically, then she washed and put on all clean clothes, moving as if she were a mechanical toy and not a person at all and as if constant motion might stop her from thinking.

When she appeared downstairs in her neat English riding habit, she saw Tommy Preston's mouth twitch in a smirk, but he didn't say anything. The horse was very large and she was glad for all her experience with her father's hunters. The saddle and harness were unfamiliar to her with the long stirrups and the horn at the front, but she soon adjusted to them, learning to relax rather than sit stiffly upright as she had been taught in

England. Tommy Preston looked at her with approval. "You know about horses, I can see that all right. Lived on a farm back in the old country, did you?"

Sarah nodded. "I've been riding since I was three years old. My father bought me a little piebald pony. His name was Squibbs. We kept him until I was almost grown up and much too big to ride him . . ." Her voice trailed off at the thought of Squibbs and home and happy memories.

"Do folks still use horses to get around in the old country?" he asked.

"Not very much," Sarah said. "We have proper roads. Most people have cars now, and there are good bus services and railways . . ."

"Just like here, right?" he asked seriously and it was only the twinkle in his eye that betrayed his dry sense of humor.

"Right," she said.

"No sense in buying a car out here," Tommy went on. "A few stupid bastards tried it and broke their axles in the first week. Mr. Johnson over at Kenilworth has one, but then he's rich enough to buy another when the first one breaks." He turned to her and grinned, then went on thoughtfully, "No—I don't see horses getting shoved out for a while, which suits me fine. I like horses. Good steady fellows, don't let you down like a car. Don't run out of petrol on you or break down . . ."

Sarah opened her mouth to say that they threw people off their backs and killed them, but she saw that he'd also thought of that too late. "It's not usually the horses fault if there's an accident," he said quickly. "Get their foot in a pothole maybe or trip over some barbwire some mucking bastards left lying around. That happened to me once. Got twenty stitches across my head."

As if they were both aware that they had started in on a subject they didn't want to continue, they rode on in silence. The flies settled on them every time they slowed to cross a dry creek bed or a stony patch. The sun was already very hot and there was no shade. A pair of big crows flew up from the track as they approached. Once there was a blur of movement through the grass ahead as something moved very fast and shot across the track, bounding incredibly high as if on springs.

"Kangaroo," Tommy muttered. Sarah tried to focus on it, but it had already gone.

Later they passed a solitary tree—a huge, twisted ghost gum that created a welcome pool of shade. Its bark, unnaturally white, hung from its thick trunk and branches in untidy strips and its branches were covered with large white blossoms. As they approached, the blossoms rose into the air, squawking and wheeled away.

"Cockatoos," Tommy said.

Sarah was feeling stronger with every moment that she had stepped into Alice's Wonderland, where flowers flew and animals bounded on springs. Every new sight seemed to blend with the unreality. Nothing had made sense since she stepped off that ship back in Sydney. Now she would no longer be surprised if the horse turned to speak to her or those weird rocks on the horizon got up and danced.

They paused to water the horses as they passed a river that still had several puddles along its bottom.

"When do we reach Jake Cotrell's farm?" she asked, pushing back a sweat-soaked strand of hair that had plastered itself to her forehead.

Tommy looked around, then jerked his horse's head up again. "We've been on his land for a good hour," he said. "Another hour to the house, though."

They set off again. The constant bumping and rubbing of the saddle was beginning to make Sarah uncomfortable. She was glad in a way of physical discomfort. Anything that could take her mind off the terrible fear that threatened to engulf her was welcome. She counted fence posts, noted blisters on her palms from the reins, and even licked at beads of sweat as they dripped down onto her lip. Then suddenly they came upon a side track, leading away from the main one. A primitive board was tacked to the fence. ORWELL J. ALISON, PROPRIETOR, was printed on it in faded letters.

"Oh," Sarah gasped. She turned her horse. There was a gate across the path and beyond that a tree sheltering a shack. "Oh," she said again. She slid from her horse and began to walk toward the gate. It was all just as Jimmy had described in his letters: "There's a patch I've started to dig for you for a kitchen garden," he had written. "I know you won't want the moldy vegetables we can buy in Ivanhoe and I imagine you'll want some flowers. Women always want flowers, don't they? Anyway, I've started some geranium cuttings so they should be going by the time you get here and I've put in a bottlebrush. They bloom anywhere!"

She pushed open the gate. She could see the patch of red by the door where Jimmy had started his geraniums for her. As she began to walk up that sandy path, a dog ran barking from the shack. The dog was followed by a figure that came out of the house and stood looking at her—a tall man standing in the deep shadow of the porch.

"Jimmy!" she yelled and began to run. They had got it all wrong. He wasn't dead after all. He was here, waiting for her. "Jimmy! They told me you were dead!"

Then the man pushed back his hat slightly and she saw that it wasn't Jimmy at all. It was nothing like him. It was a tall dark man, very lean and wiry with thick brows and dark, deep-set eyes. He stared at her coldly. "Can I help you, miss?" he asked.

"This is Jimmy Alison's farm," she said firmly.

"Was," he said. "He was killed a couple of weeks back. Poor bloke. Never was much of a horseman—nor a farmer, although he tried hard, I'll give him that."

"Do you work for him?" she asked.

His eyes narrowed. "Me?" he asked. "Jimmy couldn't afford to hire a bloody Abo even." He stepped toward her. "My name's Jake Cotrell. I own the property next to this. In fact, if you arrived here from town, you've been riding through my land."

"Then you were the one who found him," Sarah exclaimed.

"Found Jimmy! Too right," he said. "Poor little bastard. Of course he'd been lying there for a couple of days by the time I got to him, so he wasn't a pretty sight. We only knew because my man Billy came across his horse running loose. Don't know what happened. Horse was all right. As I said, he never was much of a horseman. Takes years to turn a city boy into a farmer . . ." He paused and looked at her speculatively. "You're not a relative of his? We understand he was an orphan with no kin."

"I was going to be," Sarah said, fighting to keep her voice even. "I'm Sarah Hartley. I came out here to marry him. Surely he told you that?"

"Can't say that I remember it," Jake said slowly, not taking his eyes off her for a second," but we didn't go in for talking much, me and Jimmy. Didn't get along too well for some reason. He didn't take kindly to advice. Came out from England, did you?"

"That's right," Sarah answered warily. He had almost smiled at her and she found the smile more dangerous than the scowl that had preceded it.

"What a shame," he said. "All that way for nothing. What will you do now, do you think—go home again?"

"I don't know," Sarah said bleakly. She had not allowed herself to think about the future until she was sure that Jimmy really was dead. "Can I see his grave?"

Jake Cotrell shrugged his shoulders. "Nothing to see, really. My man Billy and I dug a spot near where we found him. Over stony creek way on the boundary between my land and his. Put a couple of big stones on it to mark the place in case the parson wants to say some prayers or something when he comes around next. Was he C. of E. or Catholic do you know?"

"He wasn't anything," Sarah said. "After all the killing he saw in the war, he said religion didn't seem to make sense anymore."

Jake nodded as if he agreed with the sentiments.

Sarah looked around at the jingle of Tommy Preston's harness. In the newly dug earth of the vegetable patch, some brave little beans had been growing under netting. They were now almost all withered. "What's happening to the farm now?" she asked. She was finding it very hard to make her tongue and lips move. "Are you taking care of it for him until it's sold?"

"That's all done," he said, matter-of-factly. "Seeing that he didn't leave a will or any next of kin, I agreed to take over the land in payment of the debt he owed me . . ."

"Debt?"

"I sold him the sheep. He's only paid me for half of them. He was going to pay me the rest with the spring lambs this year but as I said, he wasn't much of a farmer. Lost about a hundred to fluke and the floods. The constable said it was only right that debts get paid off first and there wasn't anything else to pay off with except the land. It's not worth much . . . bloody useless piece of land really, all bloody rocks and saltbush . . . and seeing as how there was no other claim on it . . ."

"But he had no right," Sarah interrupted, choking back the anger that was mounting in her throat. "He couldn't just give you Jimmy's land! And there is a next of kin! I'm the next of kin and I want Jimmy's land."

Jake Cotrell continued to stare at her. Again there was that hint of a smile. "How do you figure that one, miss?" he asked. "You weren't actually married to him, were you?"

"Of course not, but he intended to marry me," she said.

"A lot of gentlemen say a lot of things they don't really mean to young ladies, I would imagine," Jake Cotrell said.

"How dare you!" Sarah exploded.

"Not that I'm suggesting this was the case here," Jake said. "I'm sure Jimmy Alison was a good, straight bloke."

"Jimmy was planning to marry me yesterday. He sent me my fare from England and the ceremony was all arranged."

"If you say so, miss," Jake said.

"I'm sure intent to marry will stand up in a court of law," Sarah said icily.

"If you can prove it, maybe, although I'm not sure about that," he said evenly. "Of course, I'm no lawyer . . ."

"Let's go into the house. There must have been a marriage certificate. He wrote that he'd got one—and the ring. They'd stand up in a court of law!"

"I've been through the house. There was no certificate or anything else," he said.

"You had no right!" she shouted, "No right at all. That was trespassing. I shall report it to the policeman when he returns."

"Well, you see, the policeman was with me," Jake said. She felt that he was enjoying this. "We had to go through his things to see if there was a will or next of kin . . . We didn't find anything like that. You can come inside and look for yourself if you like!"

Seven

HE TURNED AND LED THE WAY BACK INTO THE cabin. Sarah followed him, standing in the doorway until her eyes became used to the darkness. Inside it smelled musty, rather like the cellars back home, as if nobody had used it for a long time, but it was very neat. Sarah had always imagined Jimmy would be a neat person. He always looked as if he had taken great care over his uniform and his appearance. The cabin was sparsely furnished, but Sarah knew this was because he wanted her to be able to choose her own furniture. In fact, the table looked as if he had made it himself from boards. Pots and pans were concealed on a shelf behind a tacked-up curtain. Another tacked-up curtain in the bedroom hid his clothes. Sarah almost choked when she pulled it back and saw his good suit hanging there, his shoes standing neatly below it, as if just waiting for their owner to return. She turned abruptly and walked out, back into the living room.

"You want any of this stuff, I'm sure you're welcome to it," Jake said. "The clothes are too small for me."

A picture sprang to Sarah's mind of Jake Cotrell, calmly trying on all Jimmy's things, walking off with those he liked, and reluctantly leaving the clothes because they were too small. She looked away in disgust and opened a box on the shelf. "My letters," she exclaimed. "Surely you saw my letters. Didn't they give you a hint that I was due to arrive?"

"I don't read private letters," he mumbled gruffly, "and it wouldn't matter whether we knew you were arriving or not. He hadn't paid me for my sheep. Nearly two hundred quid still owing. It was only right and proper that I got that back and I know he didn't have that many sheep left. If you want that land, you can just pay me the two hundred pounds and it's yours. You pay me that and I'll willingly give you back the land. It's no use to me, really. Most of its not even good enough for sheep. I told Jimmy that. Too much mineral in the water, for one thing. Told him he was wasting his time."

"But this was the only land he could afford," Sarah said softly. "He knew it wasn't much good, but it was better than nothing. It was all he could buy with the money from the soldier scheme."

He came around the table and stood behind her then. "Look miss," he said in a kinder voice. "I'm sure this has been a big shock to you. Why don't you go on back to the city where you belong? There's nothing for you here. Even if you got this land, what would you do with it? It costs money to pay men to run a sheep station and you wouldn't want to live out here alone, would you?"

"I don't know," she said honestly. "I honestly don't know. Jimmy might want me to make a go of his farm . . ."

"Jimmy would want you to be safe and happy some place," he said. "Out here's no place for a woman. You take my advice and go home, back to good old England."

"I can't do that," she said simply. "I have no home there anymore."

He raised his eyebrow.

"My father threw me out when I left to marry Jimmy," she said. "He's not the sort of man who changes his mind."

"I see," he said. "You could always try Sydney? I hear there are more jobs for women these days."

"Yes, I suppose I'd better do that," she said. At the back of her brain a thought kept nagging that she wanted Jimmy's land. She knew she'd been cheated out of it and Jake Cotrell most probably knew that, too, but it would take a lawyer to get it back now and lawyers were very expensive. "I need to get a good job," she said out loud.

"Short of money, are you?" he asked bluntly. In England, in the society in which she moved, such a question would have been unthinkable—the ultimate insult. Out here it almost seemed natural.

"Yes," she said honestly. "Very short."

"I could offer you a job," he said.

"You?"

"Yeah—don't look at me like that. I'm talking about a fair dinkum job. I need a cook. My Abo, Billy—his wife died couple of months back. I've been without a cook since. You know anything about cooking?''

She thought of herself back at Wickcombe. She had been in charge of selecting daily menus since she turned thirteen. Her father had insisted that she learn this task as mistress of the household. She was very good at planning dinner parties and knowing that poached sole went before baron of beef. She had watched the cook enough times and the cook had let her make fairy cakes and toffee when she was small . . . ''A little,'' she said.

''It's only very simple stuff,'' he said. ''But Billy and me, we're shagged out by the time we get back at nights and neither of us knows a thing about cooking . . . so, what do you say?''

She looked at Jake Cotrell, knowing that she did not like him, knowing that he now owned Jimmy's land. She also knew that in her purse she probably had just enough money to get her back to Sydney. What if she was stuck for a week in Ivanhoe—she wouldn't even have the money to pay her hotel bill. And when she arrived back in Sydney, what would she do then? Even the cheapest hostel would cost something and it might be a while before she found a job . . . Jake Cotrell waited motionless by the door. She looked at his profile, etched against the harsh light: an angular face, a very determined chin, hard eyes . . . this was a man who expected to get his own way all the time . . . *but I don't have to like him,* she reasoned. *He'd be gone all day and this would be a way to make enough money to get myself safely back to Sydney. I'll only stick it out for a month or two, just until I've enough money. He's using me, so I'll use him . . . and I would be close to Jimmy for a while longer—have a chance to go through his things, give him a proper grave stone . . .*

She looked up at Jake. ''All right,'' she said. ''I'll take your job.''

''Good on yer,'' he said with that same hint of smile. ''We'll ride over to Woomera right away. I can show you around and give you a bite of tucker. Where are your things?''

''They're back at the hotel in Ivanhoe.''

''I'll send Billy in for them with the wagon, if you like,'' he said. ''Don't make sense you riding back all that way. If he starts now, he can be back by nightfall.''

A thought flitted across her mind. ''I will have my own room and everything?''

She saw the quick grin. "Think you'd have to share with the Abo like Queenie used to?" he asked. "Don't worry. You'll have your room. Come on, let's get out of this place. It gives me the creeps."

He walked out of the door. Tommy Preston was standing patiently with the two horses in the shade. "Find out everything you wanted to know, miss?" he asked.

"Everything," she said.

"So it's back to town, right?"

"No, we're going over to Woomera with Jake Cotrell," she said. "He's giving us lunch and he's offered me a job."

"A job?" Tommy sounded horrified. "What sort of job?"

"He needs a cook, apparently. His last cook died."

"Oh, too right," he said. "Poor old Queenie. I heard that a snake got her."

This was a terrible country, Sarah thought. People fell off horses and died of snake bites. What she wanted to do more than anything was run straight back to Sydney. Surely she could find a nice safe job in a big city—in a dress shop maybe, or as companion or governess. There must be plenty for a well-bred young English girl to do. Maybe somebody here, even Jake Cotrell, would lend her some money to get her back safely. After all, he owed her . . . She put the thought from her mind. She would not ask Jake Cotrell for anything. She would work for him for a month or two, then she would take his money and leave. Somehow she would make enough money to pay a lawyer and then she'd get Jimmy's land back. She had survived the news of Jimmy's death without fainting or any of the hysterics that might have been expected of her in England. Surely she could survive anything for two months . . .

"You're not going to take this job, are you?" Tommy was asking.

"You don't think I should?"

"You're too . . . fancy," he said uneasily. "You're not used to the life out here."

"I would have had to get used to it if I'd married Jimmy," she said. "I'm strong, and I do need a place to stay right now."

"Well, if you're sure," he said, very hesitantly.

"You don't trust Jake Cotrell?" she asked.

He looked toward Jake, emerging from behind the shack,

leading a sleek horse. "Jake's all right," he said. "He's a good bloke. Knows his stock, but . . ."

"But?"

"No, I reckon he's a good bloke," Tommy stammered as Jake drew level with them. They mounted again and rode back up the track. Half an hour later they arrived at Woomera homestead. It was bigger than Jimmy's little place, but scarcely more elegant. There was a long, one-storied building with a porch running the full length and three sheds behind it. Beside the sheds were two big water tanks, painted rusty red, and a windmill turned out in the field beyond. There was also a fenced-in corral with shelter at one end and two horses standing in the shade. There were no geraniums around this porch, no attempt in fact, to make the place any more than a collection of huts. There was nothing growing, not even a tree to shade the house, just red dust that rose up under the horses hooves and settled in your nostrils. Tommy dismounted and helped Sarah from her horse. Her legs were beginning to feel shaky. She couldn't tell whether this was from unaccustomed riding or tension. She had to steady herself on the fence rail as she walked toward the house.

"I don't feel anything," she kept repeating to herself. "I am made of stone. I am white marble. I don't feel."

But her legs would not stop shaking as she climbed the three steps onto the porch. A primitive bed was rigged up behind a screen at one end of the porch. There were basins and jugs on a bench, indicating that the main life of the household happened out here.

"Come on through, I'll show where you're going to be," Jake said, walking ahead of her up the steps and into the house. Again there was one central living room, but the kitchen was separate at one end, containing a large black, wood-burning stove, and at the other end there was a bedroom.

"You can have this," he said. It was tiny and contained a cot and a few hooks on the wall. The basin and jug stood on the floor. A hat and man's pants hung from the hooks. Sarah stepped back uneasily. "But this is your room," she said.

"I'll get my clobber out right for you," he said. "I sleep out on the porch anyway. Always have. It's too stuffy for me in here. You can do what you like with the room. Doll it up if you want to."

He turned and walked out again while Sarah stared bleakly at the flypaper, black with captured flies, the cracked, plastered walls; the uneven wooden floor. The smell of stale clothing and horses sweat was almost overpowering. Unlike Jimmy's cabin, nobody had cleaned this place for weeks. There was nothing in the room that was pleasing to the eye, no possible way that she could ever "doll it up." She walked back through the living room, noting the empty beer glass with its rim of flies, the dirty plates stacked on the kitchen table, the red dust thick on everything.

Jake had brought out some cold lamb, bread, and pickled onions. Tommy was already tucking in and helping himself to the jug of beer beside it. Sarah ate sparingly, finding it hard to swallow every mouthful. She kept trying to form the words to say, "I'm sorry, but I can't stay here. I'll ride back with Mr. Preston," but every time she tried to say them, she knew that she couldn't leave yet. She couldn't leave Jim's things to be pawed over by strangers, then sold off by Jake Cotrell. If she could just stay around for a while, maybe there would be a sympathetic magistrate and he'd award her compensation and she wouldn't have to worry about paying her way back to Sydney . . .

Then Tommy finished his beer, wiped away the foam with the back of his hand and got up. "I'd best be on my way then," he said. "You're sure you don't want to come back with me?"

No, she wanted to shout, *I'm not at all sure. Don't go.* But instead she nodded and stood there like a statue, watching him ride away. Jake Cotrell appeared behind her. "Here," he said. "Clean sheets for the bed." And he flung the off-white pile into her arms. "I'll go and find Billy, and he can fetch your things. Then I'll show you what's for tea."

She heard him ride away soon afterward. It was only when she was finally alone in that poky little room that she allowed the tears to come.

Eight

JAKE COTRELL APPEARED AGAIN SOON AFTER SHE had attempted to clean up the room. She had only cried for a few moments before she regained control of herself, just a few silent tears that escaped from her eyes and trickled down her cheeks however hard she blinked and fought to keep them back. She had washed her face with cold water immediately, determined that Jake Cotrell would not see her weakness. Then she had taken his offensive smelling clothes out onto the porch, made a bundle of his old bedclothes, and even dragged the mattress outside to beat it with a broom. She could feel her shirt sticking to her back, but she could not stop herself from working. If she could only keep busy enough—busy until she was too exhausted to stay awake, everything would be all right.

She hadn't heard Jake ride up and the first thing she knew of his presence was a yell from the kitchen. "Meat for our tea's on the floor," he called. "You'd best get started on it if we want to eat tonight."

She walked through to answer the summons, then leaped back, stifling a scream, as she almost walked into a dead sheep, lying on a sack, its dead eyes staring at her from the bloody, skinned face.

"Is this your idea of a joke?" she called after him, anger replacing her fear.

He paused at the doorway, the bead curtain already parted in his fingers and looked back, puzzled. "Joke? No, it's dinner. What we always have. One sheep lasts us about a week. I did skin it for you first. I figured you might not know how to do that—Queenie always skinned her own."

"You want me to cook a whole sheep?"

He laughed. "Stone the flaming crows, woman—where do

you think you'd cook a whole sheep? Cut it up first, of course—what do they do in England?"

"In England the meat comes ready to be cooked," Sarah said, "from the butcher."

"Oh, of course, in England!" he said. "I forgot. You won't be much use as a cook if you can't even cut up the bloody meat."

"I didn't say I wouldn't," Sarah said haughtily. "It's just that I don't know how to begin. You show me this time and I'll do it in the future."

"Fair enough," he said. "Let's get it up on the table and get me the chopper from the hook over there."

An hour later the sheep was lying in unrecognizable pieces. Sarah had been unable to find an apron and the sack he gave her to drape around her waist had not prevented her clothing or her hair from being spattered with blood. She brushed back her hair from her face with a bloodstained hand, too exhausted to even think of washing it.

"What do we do now?" she asked, trying to sound brisk and efficient and not give him the satisfaction of noting that the chopping and cutting had been too much for her. He had been condescending enough as it was, getting a few digs in about spoiled little English girls until she was ready to turn the chopper in his direction.

"We'll have the leg tonight," Jake said. "You can put away the rest of it."

"How do we stop it from going bad in this heat—do you have an icebox?" Sarah asked.

Jake laughed again. "Icebox?" he asked. "Where do you think I'd find ice in the middle of the outback? Use your head. I've got a meat safe on the back porch where it's fairly cool. Put it in there."

"But won't it go bad before we can eat it all?"

"Too right," Jake said. "We just throw away what we can't eat. Only use the legs and the chops first. They're the best bits. When it starts to go off, Queenie used to make a big stew . . ."

"That seems very wasteful," Sarah said. Her eyes met his, both staring coldly at the other.

"So what do you want me to do—go hack a few chops off one of the sheep that's running around?" he demanded. "For pete's sake, woman—if you want meat out here, you kill a sheep. There's no other way."

"I see," she said. She started to put the various cuts onto plates and carry them out to the meat safe. It was an inadequate-looking wooden box, screened at the front and buzzing with flies. The temperature out here was hardly cooler than at the front of the house and Sarah thought privately that no meat would last in here more than a day or so. A jug was standing on a table. She poured some water over her hands and face then went back into the kitchen to start dinner. It took her a good half hour to get the wood stove going, and when she finally produced a roaring fire, she almost wished she hadn't, since the temperature in the kitchen soared to unbearable levels. A search around the kitchen and the shed behind it produced one sack of potatoes, already sprouting and two onions, also already sprouting. No vegetables, no seasonings of any kind and Jake was nowhere to be seen. She expected he'd be sarcastic again when he came home and found only potatoes roasting beside the leg of lamb and a few onion slices dotting it, but she was too tired to care.

By the time he turned up, when the sun had turned into a red ball, sinking behind distant blue hills, the delicious smell of cooking lamb was wafting from the oven.

"Smells good," he said, throwing down his hat on the table. "I thought you'd be a bit of a no-hoper from the look of you."

"A no-hoper?"

He grinned. "Bloody flaming useless," he said.

"You were wrong, weren't you?" she asked calmly. "I come from good stock. Hartleys have never been known to give in."

He grinned again. "Then get the flaming meal on the table, woman. I'm starving," he said.

"Do you always have to swear?" she asked, turning toward the kitchen.

"Swear? I don't swear."

"Not much. It's flaming this and bloody that."

"That's not swearing. Not real swearing anyway. I know words would make your hair curl."

"My hair already curls sufficiently, thank you," she said primly, "and where I come from no gentleman would ever dream of swearing in front of a lady. And I am a lady, even if I have to be somebody's cook at the moment."

He opened his mouth to say something to her, then closed it

again. For the first time since they met, it appeared that she had the upper hand.

"Well, you'd better get off your high horse and flaming well get used to it," he said after an uneasy pause, "because that's the only talk you'll hear around here."

He sat at the table, spreading his long legs and leaning back in his chair.

"Do you always leave your hat on the table while you have a meal?" she asked, removing it and hanging it on a hook.

"I know where to find it then," he said. "It never bothered me."

"It bothers me."

He looked at her critically. "I hope you're not going to turn into a nag," he said.

"You've mentioned several times that I'm a prim English girl," she said. "You're right. I am. And as such I have certain standards I will not sink beneath. For example, I notice that you have not even bothered to wash before dinner . . ."

"Wash?"

"Yes, wash. I'm not sitting down to a meal with a man who's caked with grime. It's disgusting."

"Then eat in the kitchen," he said.

"Very well, I will." She took the roast leg of lamb from the oven, cut several large hunks, which she put on his plate, and put it down not too gently in front of him.

"Your dinner, sir!" she said.

He got up and sighed. "Oh, very well," he muttered. "I'll go wash, only for pete's sake sit down and eat. You give me the willies, hovering around like that."

She smiled as she walked back to the kitchen, feeling her face muscles relax. This must be the first time she had smiled since . . . since when? she asked herself. *Since I said good-bye to Jessie maybe.* How very long ago that seemed—another lifetime away. She turned back toward the table in the dining room at which the tall, lean man had just sat down again. "I washed my hands—satisfied?" he asked her.

After dinner he poured himself a second beer and walked out to sit on the porch. Sarah put a pan of water on the stove. She realized suddenly that she needed to obey the call of nature. *One thing I will not do is ask him about toilet facilities,* she thought grimly. *There has to be one somewhere. I'll find it my-self.*

She searched carefully through the house, then opened the doors of both sheds before she finally noticed a little outhouse at the edge of the paddock. Then she remembered Jessie's comments about not being hygienic having them near the house. As she strolled toward it, she heard Jake call after her. "Watch out for the spider! He gets mad if you shake him around."

"Very funny," she muttered to herself, embarrassed that he should have spotted her mission. She opened the door and was overpowered by the stench. The toilet was just a wooden seat built over a box sunk into the ground. By the smell of it, it had not been emptied in years. Her urgent need fought with the nausea that rose in her throat. The need won. She took a big gulp of fresh air from outside and then closed the door. As she did so, something scurried up the inside of the door and sat perched along the top of it. Sarah's heart almost leaped into her throat. She could see the thick, hairy legs hanging over the top of the door. He was sitting there, waiting for her to come out again. Did spiders drop on you? she wondered. Did they leap off at you? Were they poisonous?

This is an awful place, she thought, her heart pounding. *Everything about it is horrible. And I'll never come in here again. I'll just wait until Jake is far away and then I'll sneak out into a field—anywhere but here!*

The smell finally became worse than the spider. Very cautiously she opened the door, stopping, and stepping back each time those legs moved. They seemed to be waving at her in warning. Then, as the spider began to come down the side of the door toward her hand, she flung the door open, leaping past it and rushing out as fast as she could. She fled back to the house and, coming around a corner bumped into a person. She looked up into a fierce black face and screamed.

"Hey, hold on there, missy. Billy won't hurt you none," said a deep, rumbling voice and two black hands grabbed her arms to steady her.

"Oh," she said, panting with shock. "You're Billy. I didn't think . . . I wasn't expecting somebody black."

Billy's coal black face creased into a wide smile. "Didn't boss tell you I be Abo-fella?" he asked.

"I suppose he did," she admitted.

The smile increased. "You ever see a white Abo-fella?" and he chuckled at the joke he had made. "I bring your things, missy. I put in house. I take fine care they don't get shooked up."

"Thank you, Billy," she said.

Billy hung around nervously. "Boss tell me Misser Alison, him your fella. I sorry, missy. That too bad."

"I'm sorry, too, Billy," she said quietly, thinking that this was the first person she had met who had shown her any sympathy. Then she remembered. "I'm sorry about your wife, too," she said.

He nodded slowly. "That bad, too, missy. Her poor leg—it swell up something shocking and her shouting and hollering all night . . . she asking me to put her out of her misery."

Sarah shuddered. "And there wasn't anything you could do, I suppose?"

"Not after brown snake bite you," he said. "Boss try slicing her leg with the knife, but it don't do no good. The poison acts too quick, you see." He sighed as if poisonous snakes were just something one had to expect from life. "She good lubra, my Queenie," he said. "Too much yabber, but a good woman. It too quiet now."

"At least you'll be able to eat again now," she said, trying to sound bright. "There's plenty of lamb and potatoes left in the kitchen.

"Thank you, missy. Just put my plate on the window ledge and I fetch. I don't come in house."

"Why on earth not?"

His eyes opened wide. "Boss don't want no dirty Abos in house, missy."

She eyed him carefully, thinking privately that he didn't look any more dirty than Jake Cotrell had done, but she didn't feel up to getting into a fight at this moment. She smiled at Billy. "I'll bring you a plate," she said.

That night she lay on the lumpy bed, covered only with a sheet, too tired to sleep. She heard Cotrell stomping about on the porch outside. The stale smell of his clothing still permeated the room, making her feel that she couldn't breathe. She heard the horses moving in the corral and the bleating of far off sheep. She was still consumed by the feeling of complete unreality, longing for someone to pinch her, for Janet to shake her and tell her her tea was on the bedside table.

How long can I keep going here? she wondered. Images of the past day flitted through her head—dead sheep staring up at her, hairy legs of the spider on the outhouse door, Billy's black face, the red dust on her white shirt, the horizon that went on forever, and through them all Jake Cotrell's face, looking down at her as if she was the best joke to come around in a long while. "I hate him," she muttered, "but he won't get the better of me."

NINE

ALTHOUGH SHE DID NOT REALIZE IT AT THE TIME, her anger was like adrenaline pumping through her system. It kept her going at a time she might easily have given up. To know she was trapped alone, without friends, in a place as alien as a distant planet, that she had no family, no husband to take care of her, and that she had to survive, might have made a sheltered girl of her background give up and crumble under the strain. Sarah's anger kept her going. In fact, she nurtured her anger with each passing day, adding to the previous day's insults a list of more inexcusable behavior to be held against Jake Cotrell for future revenge. It was not that he was horrible to her: he spoke to Billy as if Billy deserved no more than his sheepdogs, but to her he was always fairly polite. She noticed that he even attempted to temper his language and had cut back to one bloody per sentence. But she could not forgive the look of triumph that lurked behind his smile. When his eyes held hers, his smile was saying, all too clearly, "I own the land that should have been yours and now I own you, too." She was an additional prize he hadn't expected, and he was making the most of the unique situation. He knew she had no money. He knew she could not run away until he paid her and he was enjoying it. She was sure it was the sort of thing he'd boast about one day: "Did I ever tell you about the time I had this posh English girl working for me as cook? My word did she think a lot of herself, but I soon licked her into shape . . ."

"Just you wait," Sarah muttered to herself every time she walked away from him, but the days drifted on and sometimes, when she stepped outside the front porch and stared into the limitless horizon, she realized how trapped she was. It was the sort of place where people could lose count of days and weeks. She wondered if it was the sort of place where people could go insane. So she threw herself into her work, scrubbing the filth from the blackened kitchen range, scrubbing the table and floors, anything to keep herself completely occupied so that she fell asleep each night from exhaustion. After one week she was sick of the sight of mutton. They ate it for every meal—chops with bread for breakfast, cold between bread for lunch, and hot with potatoes for dinner. Jake did not seem to think it strange that they had no vegetables, no milk, except condensed in a can, no butter, or anything else to make meals more appealing.

"What do stations with little children do for milk?" she demanded.

"Keep a cow," he answered.

"Then why don't you keep one?"

"Never saw the need," he said with that same amused look. "I gave up drinking milk when I was a nipper. I only need it for my tea and the tinned's fine for that."

"I think it tastes disgusting," she said, "and what about vegetables? You could easily start a vegetable garden the way Jimmy did. Then you'd have fresh vegetables every day instead of moldy old potatoes."

"You're very welcome to try if you want," he said. "Spade's in the back shed. I can pick up seeds and stuff when I'm in town, no doubt."

She knew he'd got her there. Starting a vegetable garden implied permanence, a long-term commitment that she was not willing to make. She would survive on cold mutton and baking soda bread for the next few weeks.

"But what about puddings?" she insisted. "Don't you ever want a pudding after your dinner?"

"I don't mind a good suet pud," he confessed.

"We've nothing to make one with!"

"We've got some cocky's choice, I think," he said in answer to her complaint.

"Some what?"

"Cocky's choice—golden syrup," he said, his half-hidden smile telling her that he had scored another point. "And there's flour and sugar. You can make yourself something with that, can't you?"

"I can't even make pastry without fat," she had complained.

"What about the lard from the lamb?" he had asked scathingly. "What's that then?"

"But the pastry will taste all meaty . . ."

"You'll get used to it. Queenie always used that. Made bloody good pies, I remember. Billy and me used to take one in our lunch when we were out on the boundaries."

She began to count days by the amount of time the sheep lasted. Neither Jake nor Billy took any days off at the weekend and she only knew she'd been there a week when another dead sheep appeared on the kitchen floor. This time Billy was there to skin it for her and help cut it up. She began to say something about the way Jake treated him, but he did not seem to think there was anything unusual in his treatment.

"Him good boss-fella, Mr. Cotrell," he said. "Him good to Queenie when she died."

"But that doesn't give him any right to . . ." she began. "He doesn't own you, Billy."

She saw from his eyes that he didn't understand her.

They had a good meal that evening—she attempted to make jam tarts and they were fairly successful so that all of them felt full and content. Jake, as usual, took a beer out to the porch and sat watching the sun go down. She was about to start the washing up when he called to her.

"Why don't you bring yourself a glass and sit with me?" he asked. "You're always scurrying around like a little mother hen. Give yourself a break, woman, for pete's sakes . . ."

"I like to work," she said, defensively. "It stops me from thinking."

He poured a glass of beer and handed it to her. "Get that inside you. You need to know how to relax."

She took it, taking a wary sip at the foam. It was warm and bitter, but not unpleasant. He motioned to the chair beside him and she sat.

"Came from a farm in England, did you?" he asked. "Anything like this?"

Sarah smiled. "Nothing like this. Neat green fields, fat cows, lots of trees, flowers, fruit . . . nothing like this."

He eyed her critically. "First time I've seen you smile. I began to think your lips were locked like that. Nice to know you are human . . ."

"I've tried not to be human," she said quietly. "It hurts less when you don't think."

"Think? Oh, you mean about young Jimmy?"

"You don't think that's a natural thing to do?" she demanded. "The boy I loved was killed. My whole world fell apart. I have nothing now—of course I miss him. I don't know if I'll ever stop missing him."

"You think you're the only one who's hard done by," he said at last, "but you're wrong. Most families in Australia can tell you about a son or a father who didn't come back from the war. And it was a stupid war—somebody else's war, fought far away on somebody else's land. It was nothing to do with us. We should have kept our bloody noses out of it!"

"I suppose that's why you didn't go and fight," she said stiffly.

"Who says I didn't go?" he asked. "I did my bit like all the rest. I was even quite keen on it to start with. You should have seen me marching off in my new uniform. Thought I looked a real wowser! It didn't take me long to change my mind, though . . ." He took a gulp of beer then stared out past her. "You heard of a place called Gallipoli?" he asked.

She nodded. "I know there was a big battle fought there. The Turks pinned down the allied soldiers, didn't they?"

"They weren't very allied," he said bitterly. "They were all ANZACS. Aussie boys and Kiwis, all straight from the Bush, never seen a war before. I was one of the first—some joker told us to go ashore and capture the Turkish positions. Bloody laugh that was. They were up on the cliffs with bloody great guns and we were sitting on the beach with nowhere to hide. As soon as we stepped up on the beach—boom, boom, the Turks would cut us down. Then they'd take those of us who were still alive back to the ships, patch us up, and send us back again. I was shot four times and sent back four times. It was only when they couldn't find any more of me to patch that they finally admitted

I was wounded and shipped me back here. I suppose you'd call that lucky. Plenty of my mates never made it past the first time. We buried them on the sand with little tin crosses we made from hammered-out bully beef cans. Whenever I think of Gallipoli, I think of those bloody crosses winking at you in the sun. You could see them from out on the ships."

"I'm sorry," she said quietly, noting that he always walked stiffly, as if walking were not an easy thing for him.

"Don't worry about me," he said with a laugh. "I come from tough country stock—got a hide like a goanna. Takes a lot to make me fall apart, in fact, I thought of offering them my skin for their combat uniforms. Better than the bloody useless cotton stuff they gave us! That didn't even keep out the fleas!" He laughed again, then looked down at the glass in his hand. "I don't know what made me talk about it. I never do. None of the blokes here know a thing about me or my past. I just wanted you to know that you weren't the only one who'd been dealt a raw deal."

"You're not from around here then?" she asked.

He looked at her strangely, sideways. "I'm from Queensland," he said. "My family had a big spread up there. Queensland's not like here. Plenty of rain, you see. Grass this high and big fat cattle and sugarcane. Oh, it's a bonza place up there."

"So why didn't you stay up there?" she asked.

He laughed. "You see, while I was away, fighting for king and country, my brother stayed home, on account of his weak eyes. So when I get back, I find that he's helped himself to my girl as well as taking over the running of the farm from Dad whose just had a heart attack. I wasn't going to stick around and watch them living happily ever after, so I took my share of the money and I got out."

"I'm sorry," she said again.

His eyes narrowed. "I don't want your pity," he said. "I just wanted you to know that you weren't the only one."

The next morning, he was as cold and impersonal as ever, and Sarah felt that he regretted the beer that had made him open up to her because he did not invite her to join him on the porch again.

After two weeks she finally brought up the subject of money. "I just wanted to know when I get paid," she suggested, her cheeks pink with embarrassment.

"What do you think I am, a flaming bank?" he snapped. "I don't print my own money, you know. You'll have to wait until I get into town and I've not been able to get away. I've got the shearers coming soon and I had to get the sheep rounded up."

"I understand," she said, "but I am an employee. I've a right to know when I can expect my wages."

"You'll get your bloody wages," he said. "I'll go into town for you. We need lamp oil anyway."

"And while you're there," she added, not wanting to waste an opportunity, "we need more flour and if you bring some yeast, we should have proper bread and vegetables. Can't you buy some fresh vegetables?"

"Like greens you mean?"

"Yes, greens."

"I hate greens. My mum always made me eat my greens when I was a little nipper. Never touched them since."

"You're supposed to eat greens to keep you healthy."

He stared down at her insolently. "There's not many men could take me on in a fight," he said. "You want to watch me lifting the sheep when the shearers come. I'm as fit as any of them, right enough."

"Very well, no greens then, but we could do with a little variety. Surely you can buy seasonings or dried fruit in town, or a tin of lard?"

"Like I said, a bloody nag," he muttered as he left the room, but she noted he did not sound angry.

He did not come back from town until it was almost dark. Sarah had already lit the lamps in the living room and taken the stew off the hottest part of the fire to keep it from burning, wondering if he had decided to spend the night there and not risk a late journey back. She walked to the window uneasily when she heard the dogs start barking, in time to watch them streak across the yard, tails wagging furiously as Jake rode up. When he came in, he seemed to be in a good mood. It was clear that he had been drinking in the hotel. Sarah could smell it on his breath and his speech was slightly slurred.

"Here's your bloody money," he said, "I thought two pounds a week, since you get your food and everything . . . oh, and I've got all those things you nagged me about." He dumped a sack on the table and Sarah drew out delightedly a jar of Vegemite, a can of lard, flour, onions, and even some carrots. He smiled benevolently at her enthusiasm.

"Oh, and you've got a letter," he said, throwing that down beside the groceries.

"A letter?" For a wild moment of hope she thought that the letter might have come from England—her father was begging for her to come back, he had sent her fare home . . . She glanced down at the envelope and almost cried out loud when she saw the words Mrs. James Alison. It was like being haunted by a ghost. She recognized Jessie's childish, rounded script. Jessie! She had almost forgotten about Jessie during the last days. It had been too painful to think of somebody else being happily married and living the life she had expected to lead. But now she clutched the letter to her possessively. Somehow it was very important that she still had a contact with the outside world. Somebody in Australia knew her—she was not trapped alone and totally friendless at the edge of the world. There was hope of escape.

"I didn't know you had anybody out here," Jake said suspiciously.

"The girl I came out with on the ship," she said. "She got married. She's living at a racing stables in Paramatta."

"I see." His tone indicated that he had already lost interest. "Good job that I went into town today," he said, pulling his boots of and kicking them across the floor. "I heard the bloody shearers are already over on Kenilworth. They might have missed me all together and then I really would have been up the bloody creek."

As happened often, Sarah only understood half of what he said. She was beginning to tune into Australian slang, but he used so many unfamiliar expressions that she always played it safe and guessed their meaning from further conversation. She didn't want to give him the satisfaction of telling her she didn't know anything.

"So you met the shearers?" she asked politely.

"Didn't meet them. I told you they were over at Kenilworth, but I managed to send a message out with a bloke to tell them to stop by on their way south. If you don't remind them, they forget about little stations like me."

"This is a little station?" she was genuinely surprised, remembering how many hours it had taken to ride across his land.

"My word yes," he said. "The big stations, they're bonza places to work. The shearers like going there. They've got electricity, some of them and big, cool shearing sheds with fans and everything. Some of them are even getting airplanes now, I hear. Of course, it takes them a couple of days to cross their land so it would be worth it."

She began to dish up his dinner, carrying in the plate of stew. He ate noisily, telling her between slurps about all the town gossip. She realized as he talked that they had slipped into a relationship, whether she liked it or not. It did not matter that she disliked him. He was her one human contact, apart from Billy, who hardly ever dared talk to her, and she needed to hear his human voice.

He finished his stew and pushed his plate away from him, stretching out his long legs, the way he always did, and tipping the chair back.

"Funny thing they were saying in town," he said casually. His eyes caught hers. "Lot of talk about you and me, there was . . . about how you chose to stay on out here with me . . ." His eyes did not leave hers for a second. "Some folks were suggesting, apparently, that there might be something in it . . ."

His lips curled in a smile, as if he could sense her discomfort.

"I hope you dispelled their insinuations instantly," she said.

"I did what?" he asked suspiciously. "I'm only an ignorant Aussie, remember?"

"I meant that I hoped you told them the truth about us. That you didn't let them keep any wrong impressions."

His smile broadened. "What do you think?" he asked, teasing her. "Oh, don't look like that. I told them they'd got it wrong."

She got up from the table and began to carry out his plate.

"Although, now I come to think of it," he said as she made for the door, "it does seem like a bit of a waste, doesn't it?"

She turned back, her cheeks flaming with embarrassment.

"I mean to say—you're a woman and I'm a man and we're neither of us bad-looking and we're both young and there is only one bedroom in the house . . ."

His eyes were still lingering on her, mocking. Sarah fought to keep her composure. He looked at her expression and threw back his head, laughing. "Just joking, for pete's sakes. Can't you take a joke? My word, it's like living with Queen-bloody-Victoria!''

"I didn't find it very funny,'' Sarah said. "Now, if you'd excuse me, I'd like to go and read my letter.''

She shut the door of her room firmly behind her and stood against it, feeling the cool firmness of the wood. Then she sat on the edge of her bed and opened Jessie's letter. It was painful to read, assuming, of course, that Sarah was now Mrs. James Alison and living just as happily as she was.

"I was so sorry you didn't manage to get to our wedding after all, but I suppose your Jimmy was impatient to get back, just like my Tom was!'' she began. "We had a real good blowout too—I'll say that for my Tom—he ain't stingy! We had a great bowl of oysters and shrimps and you should have seen the beer! We was all having such a good time that we didn't want to leave and go back to Paramatta. Bumpy road they got out here, haven't they? That truck ride back to Paramatta seemed to go on forever. Thought I was going to throw up more than once!

"Still—I can't say that Paramatta's a bad place. Lots of nice big trees and the lawns around the big house are something lovely, but I hope your place is a bit more spacious than ours. We haven't got enough room to swing a cat here, although it's a nice enough little house and sheltered by nice big trees.'' She went on to describe her trip into town to buy furniture and how busy she was making curtains and cushion covers. It all sounded so homey and civilized and so very far away.

"Remember all our little chats on the boat?'' Jessie's letter went on. "I hope you've had all your questions answered by now and you can tell all them old ladies back in England that they was wrong. I don't find nothing wrong with it, personally, except that men don't seem to be able to get enough of it. But I expect your Jimmy is still quite the gentleman, like you always said he was, and I expect he's treating you real nice and gentleman like. Tom's not bad, when it comes to that. He tries so hard to please me, bless him. He bought me the most horrible scarf when he went into town last time. I didn't have the heart to tell him that the colors did not go together and I'd never wear it!''

Sarah looked up as she heard Jake moving around on the porch. Nervously she closed up the letter, too tense and too heartsick to go on reading. For the first time she was aware that just a fly screen was between herself and his bed on the porch outside, and they were the only two white people within fifty miles . . . he had claimed that the whole thing was a joke. He had laughed loudly at her embarrassment. But it didn't really matter whether he had intended his suggestion seriously or not. He had introduced a dimension to their relationship that had not been there before, and now that it had been introduced, it would not go away. Sarah hugged her arms around herself, thinking of his mocking smile and realizing just how helpless she was.

TEN

THE SHEARERS ARRIVED ON A HOT AFTERNOON about a week later. Sarah had finally persuaded Jake to let her ride to see Jimmy's grave and then go over to Orwell and go through his things. She had to wait for a day he could spare Billy because he was obviously not going to let her go riding off alone. Finally the sheep were all rounded up, waiting for the shearers and Billy was sitting on the step of his little hut, fixing a harness and humming to himself in his low, growling voice. Sarah decided this would be a good moment to approach Jake. She had hovered between playing the helpless female and appealing to his mercy to lend her a horse and an escort, or acting as if it was her right and duty to be allowed to go through her fiancé's things. She chose the latter, determined that Jake Cotrell was never going to see any sign of weakness in her if she could help it.

"Since we don't seem to take any weekends off on this station," she began and noticed the wary look come into his eyes immediately, "I'd like to know when it will be convenient to pick up the items that belong to me over at Jimmy's place. There are my letters and presents I've sent him and we could certainly use some of the new pots and pans he bought. Your old frying pan is a disgrace . . ."

He continued to eye her warily, looking as he always did when she attacked, as if she was a dangerous, unknown species of animal. "So you want to go over to Orwell?" he asked.

"Would today be convenient?" she asked. "Billy seems to be sitting around without much to do and none of us will get any time off when the shearers arrive."

Jake shrugged. "I suppose today's as good as any," he said. "You can ride a horse, that one's for you . . . only stay close to Billy and do what he says. I don't want another broken neck or snakebite on my hands."

"Don't worry," she said smoothly. "I don't intend to be buried on your property. I want a proper gravestone."

They set off at a good pace, moving through land emptied of sheep, already mustered for the shearing. Hardly anything moved in the shimmering heat. Fat lizards scuttled across their path and again there were kangaroos on the horizon, but it was a harsh, unfriendly landscape. They came, at last, to Jimmy's grave, marked only by two gray stones in a sandy hollow. A few gray bushes guarded it from the force of the wind and a ghost gum, its bark gleaming eerily white, loomed on a rise beyond. The thought crossed Sarah's mind that the gum was actually Jimmy's spirit, unable to rest until it had received a proper Christian burial. It was on the tip of her tongue to ask Billy if the tree had been there before, but she felt foolish once she opened her mouth. Instead she squatted in that hollow, feeling the warm sand through her skirt, her hand pressed to the sand, trying to imagine that just below that surface, Jimmy was buried. Was he wrapped in anything or just lying there, smothered in sand? If you scraped away and dug down, would it still look like him or would he already be a shriveled mummy? It was all too improbable to be real. She had thought that by going to his grave, she would feel his presence and come back comforted. Instead she could not feel that he was here at all. She got to her feet. Wherever Jimmy was, it was far far away. It was almost as if he had never been.

They rode on in silence as if Billy respected her privacy. She did not stay long at Orwell. It no longer felt as if Jimmy had ever lived there. Some small animal had gnawed its way through the remains of his flour sack and there were neat, white footprints across the floor. There was a large spider's web across the window and something scurrying about in the rafters above. It was like sleeping beauty's palace—something that had been asleep for a long while. She found that she no longer wanted anything that could not be useful to her. She took his shirts, since she could wear them herself and roll up the sleeves. She took the good cooking pots and let Billy help himself to the remainder of the clothing. Billy's eyes grew wide as he picked up the riding boots.

"Go ahead, Billy, they'll only go to waste here," she said.

He looked around warily. "Them no belonga boss?"

"They don't belong to your boss," she said firmly. "They belonged to Mr. Alison and even if your boss managed to get the land in repayment of a debt, he certainly has no claim over Mr. Alison's private things. Please help yourself and don't worry about it."

Then she left the room, feeling that Billy would be uneasy about pawing over things while she was still there. She did take all the papers she could find, convinced that the marriage license would turn up in an unlikely place among them, and she found his war medals in a drawer, which she also took. Then she walked out. Billy followed her, walking uneasily in his new boots. The pots and pans clinked and clanged musically on the saddlebags as they jogged home. Long before they approached the homestead, Billy's sharp eyes had picked out something wrong.

"Some fella done come!" he stated. "Stone flaming crows, shearers must have got here. Boss he be one mad fella, him skin me alive for not being here."

"Relax, Billy. He said you could come with me," she said, smiling at his agitation. "And besides, it's almost dark. The shearers wouldn't be able to start work until morning."

As they drew closer, they saw that several horses were roaming loose in the corral and smoke from a camp fire was rising behind the house. The dogs barked at their return and Jake came round the house immediately.

"Shearers just got here," he said.

"Am I supposed to be cooking their tea?" she asked, wondering how many men there were and how she would cook for that many.

"I've given them a sheep and they've got it roasting out on the fire right now," he said. "That will keep them going for tonight, but they'll expect their breakfast and keep the kettle on all day for tea and you might make one of your stews for tomorrow night. They're not bad."

"The men or my stews?" she asked in amusement.

"Yer stews," he said. "I don't know so much about the men."

She suspected that was the closest to a compliment she'd ever get from him. She slid from her horse. "Good thing I brought the big pot over from Jimmy's house," she said. "I'd never make enough stew for a crowd in your little saucepan."

He followed her toward the house. "Get what you wanted over there?" he asked.

"I didn't bring back much," she said. "No good brooding on the past."

"Too right," he agreed.

Several shouts came from behind the house, followed by noisy laughter. Jake grabbed her arm, spinning her around. "Look—keep away from those blokes," he said. "Unless you have to take them a pot of tea or something . . ." She looked up at him, inquiringly. "I don't want them distracted from their work," he said. "I'm paying them and I don't want my ewes all cut up with their mucking shears." He released her arm and went back toward the front door. "A joker can spoil a fleece with one bad cut," he said. "I don't know half these blokes. New ones show up on the team every year. I hope they know what they're doing . . ."

And he went leaving Sarah confused as to whether he was worried for her safety or for the safety of the fleeces he was paying for.

She met the men at breakfast next day. She had heard them moving around at their outside camp at the first light of dawn and quickly put a big kettle of water on the stove for their tea. There were five of them, big brawny men, all with leather skin and eyes habitually screwed up against the fierce light. They wore tattered undershirts that revealed big knotted muscles and they all smelled as if they hadn't bathed in years. It was hard to tell how old they were. They greeted Sarah politely enough and thanked her for the tea and bread. As she walked back to the house, she heard one of the saying, "I didn't know Cotrell had got himself a wife."

"He didn't," came the reply. "She's the cook."

"I wouldn't mind a cook like that, wouldn't you, Blue?"

came the sharp reply and there were words in the laughter that Sarah didn't quite catch.

The men started work immediately after breakfast. The long shed behind the house was cleared for shearing and the men stood in a line, bent over, a sheep imprisoned between their knees while they removed its fleece with swift clicking of the shears. The whole process took around a minute and Jake and the dogs selected the next victim. They worked without stopping, pausing to spit on the wood floor, to swear when the shears nicked a sheep's skin, or to take a hurried drink as the heat in the shed grew. Fat, heavy sheep waddled in and skinny sheep ran out, fleeing to the safety of the herd like spinsters, who in their worst nightmares find themselves unclothed in public. As the day drew on, the group of fat sheep dwindled and the number of nimble skinny ones grew. Many of the skinny ones had telltale cuts to the speed of the shears. Some had black splotches on them where the tar-bucket had been used to stop serious bleeding. But most of them did not look the worse for their ordeal. In fact they seemed to be relieved to be spared the weight of their coats.

Sarah continued to bring pots of tea across and Jake always took the pot from her. She was glad of this because the smell in the shed was becoming more overpowering as the day's heat grew. At last the shearing was completed and the men greeted the sight of the stew pot with enthusiasm. Jake sank down wearily over his own meal, not wanting to talk, and afterward took his beer out to the porch as usual. She noted that he did not invite the men to join him. He was definitely a man who did not welcome company.

Darkness fell and Sarah moved about the house, lighting the oil lamps, heating the big pans of water for washing up and her evening bath. The shearers were in high spirits. They had lit a camp fire again and the sweet smell of wood smoke drifted invitingly into the kitchen. She could hear voices raised and laughter coming from behind the shed. It contrasted with the usual silence and awoke a longing for human company, for tea parties, hunts, and Christmas dances . . . all the things she would never know again. When an accordion began to play, the sound was almost too much for her. Rousing Irish jigs and haunting popular melodies from the war hung in the warm night air. When she finally went out to collect the dirty plates, she stood at the edge of the firelight, watching the silhouetted figures as they swayed to the music or lifted mugs of beer to their lips.

The pile of dishes wavered in her hand and the sound of the shifting china caused one of them to turn around. Sarah shrank back into the shadows, but she had been seen.

"Come on, darlin', don't be shy!" the man called out. The others looked up. "It's the little cookie girl, standing out there all alone and lonely," the man said. "Come on over and join us . . ."

"I've got washing up to do," Sarah said, glad that the darkness was hiding her confusion.

"Don't you let that old bastard Cotrell work you too hard," the big man by the fire growled. "Come on over and join us. You need yer fun, too."

"I really ought . . ." Sarah began but the man rose up and grabbed her by the wrist. He took the plates from her, put them on the wagon bed and led her forward. "Come on, my little beaut, let's have a dance then. Dance music, Charlie! I haven't danced since God knows when!"

The mouth organ struck up a lively Irish reel. The large man was remarkably nimble on his feet. Sarah felt herself twirled around, her feet flying as her arms caught his. She didn't know the steps and she suspected that the man did not know them either, but there was a feeling of excitement as she flew over the rough ground and her skirts sent up sparks from the fire.

Another man had got to his feet. "Come on, Bluey, don't hog her all to yourself," he laughed. He threaded his arm through Sarah's free one and spun her clear of the first man. The sensation of unreality, of flying, of being one of the sparks from the fire, grew as she was twirled from partner to partner. At last only the man with the accordian was still seated, the others all clomping around in their big boots as rough arms grabbed her and released her again. Some of them were none too steady on their feet, Sarah noted, and their breath smelled of something other than beer. She began to feel dizzy from the constant twirling.

"I've got to stop!" she called out and tried to break free.

"Oh, no you don't. Come back here!" the first big man, the one they called Blue, commanded, laughing as he grabbed at her. He missed her arm as she wrenched free and his hand latched onto her blouse instead. There was a frightening ripping sound. Sarah gasped. The accordion faded to silence. She looked down at the front of her blouse, hanging open, revealing half a white breast. For a second she sensed the men were horrified at what they had done. If only she could have moved quickly enough, she could have fled back to the house and the whole incident would have been over. But the horror made her back away clumsily, her hand clutched to the remnants of her blouse. As if it was an idea just dawning in his mind, the big man called Blue walked slowly toward her. He took her wrist and pulled her hands away from her.

"What do you think, boys?" he asked quietly. "Think Cotrell would mind?"

Sarah looked from one face to the next. The faces had changed. The good-natured gaiety had disappeared. They were looking at her hungrily, like wolves. Only now did she realize what they were thinking and the thought flashed through her mind that Jake and Billy would come and save her. She opened her mouth to scream, but a big hand came over it at the same time as she was pulled backward to the ground by her hair.

"Hold her still for me, Charlie," the big man growled, his voice choking, "and don't let her make any noise." Another hand replaced the first over her mouth. It was a soft, podgy hand and it tasted of the lamb stew she had just cooked. It crushed against her teeth. She tried to bite it but she couldn't move her jaws. She was conscious of two men kneeling on her arms, holding her shoulders and head. Above her everything seemed to be happening in slow motion—the grinning faces, eyes, and teeth lit by the fire, all looking down at her hungrily, excitedly. The big man was fiddling with the buttons that held his trousers. She watched, fascinated like a rabbit before a snake, as he reached into the opening and brought out a long whitish thing. It seemed to move with a life of its own as it came closer and closer to her, waving in front of her face. She could see his jeering, triumphant face looking directly down on her. Then, suddenly impatient, he threw up her skirts and cursed impatiently as he tried to pull down her panties. She wriggled in terror as she felt him kneeling on her thigh, forcing her legs apart with his huge knee. Her captors at either side responded by holding her more firmly. She could feel the stones digging into her, the man's weight crushing her, the hand almost covering both nose and mouth so that she could hardly breathe.

Maybe that would be the best thing, she thought. *Just let them suffocate me. Then at least I wouldn't have to know about it . . .*

"Come on, Blue, get on with it," another voice growled.

"You'll get your turn soon enough," Blue leered as he lowered himself onto her. His enormous weight was crushing her. She tried to wriggle. It was impossible, there was no hope, no chance of rescue . . .

And then suddenly there was a shout. "What the hell do you think you're doing?" Jake Cotrell's voice, knife-edged and commanding. He strode forward and noticed Sarah's feet, sticking out from the melee of men.

"Get off her right now, you bastard," he ordered.

"Oh, come on, Cotrell, you'll get your turn soon enough," one of the men jeered. They all laughed.

"I said get off her!" Then almost instantly, there was a crack. It sounded like a shot and Sarah wondered whether there would be a shooting match and she would end up getting shot by mistake.

"You jokers know what I'm like with a stock whip," Jake said and again there was a crack. "So you get out of here now unless you want backsides you can't sit down on for a month of Sundays."

The whip cracked again. Sarah felt the holds on her gradually released. Blue staggered to his feet. "Why don't you mind your own bloody business, Cotrell," he growled. "You might be fucking sorry you interfered."

"She is my business, you bastard," Jake said evenly, "and I'd even go rescue a bloody Abo girl from you lot. Lot of bloody animals. Don't even see my dogs behaving the way you did. Now pack your things and get out of here."

"You think you can make us, Cotrell?" the big man asked.

Jake looked down at him and a smile curled at his lips. "I used to do a stunt once, when I was in the army. Used to make the blokes laugh. I used to take a bloke's cigarette out of his mouth with my stock whip—and your cock's a little bit bigger than a cigarette! Only just, mind you!"

At that there was laughter from the other men and the tension was broken. One by one they slunk away. One of them looked back at Sarah and she saw regret in his face. He almost said something, then he slunk after the others.

Slowly she sat up and began trying to right her skirts and underclothes, then with her hand over her exposed breast, she got unsteadily to her feet. She could feel nausea at the back of her throat, as if her dinner might come up the moment she opened her mouth. As she staggered, Jake came over and grabbed her arm fiercely. "Are you all right?" he demanded.

"I'll be all right," she murmured. Somehow she could not stop her teeth from chattering.

"That wasn't what I meant," he snapped. "I meant did I get there in time? Did he already rape you?"

"No, I don't think so," she stammered.

She saw him smile then. "You'd have known it if he had," he said dryly. "I take it you're a bloody virgin. Oh, you'd have known it all right."

He led her back toward the house. She looked over her shoulder fearfully. "Those men—do you think they might come back?"

He shook his head. "Nah. They won't be back. One thing those blokes don't want is trouble with the law. They won't be back."

He sat her down in a chair and reached for a bottle of whiskey he kept on a high shelf. "Go on, drink this," he commanded. "It's good for shock."

She forced some of the burning liquid between her chattering teeth and felt its warmth spreading through her limbs.

"Better now?" he asked.

She nodded.

"Bloody stupid thing to do—to go out there when they've been drinking all evening," he said. "You can't blame the poor buggers. They don't see a woman in months and then you come tripping out, all sweet and virginal with your titties half hanging out. It's more than most men could stand . . ."

She got to her feet. "I think I'll go to my room now, if you don't mind. I'll finish the washing up in the morning."

He nodded again. "Yeah, you go get yourself a good night's sleep. You'll feel better in the morning."

She turned back and looked at him. "Jake—I want to thank you for saving me," she said. "That was a very brave thing you did. There were five of them . . . you were very brave and I'll always be grateful. . . ."

A smile spread across his face. "They always said I was a selfish bastard," he said. "I don't like to share my things. When anyone has you, it's bloody well going to be me."

Eleven

NEXT MORNING IT WAS HARD TO THINK OF THE INcident as anything more than a very real nightmare. She woke to the sound of Jake whistling as he dressed on the porch outside. He didn't say anything more to her than a nodded G'Day as she went to get water from the tank. There was no sign of the shearers except for a blackened patch of ground where their camp fire had been. Fleeces were spread out to dry in the sun. Billy was already working on the first of them, rolling them into tight bundles and flinging them onto the back of a wagon. He did not look up when she walked past him and Sarah wondered if he knew about last night and was tactfully avoiding her eyes.

"Got to get those fleeces into town," Jake said casually, passing her to inspect Billy's work. "The broker from Sydney will be up . . ."

Wild hope flashed through Sarah's mind. She could persuade Jake to take her into town with him, then stow away with the fleeces, even ask the wool broker to help her get back to Sydney, back to civilization, away from this red earth and shimmering horizon—anything to get away. After last night she would never feel safe again. She hugged her arms to her, longing for drawing rooms with lace table cloths, chatter about the latest fashions, a roaring fire in a big brick fireplace while the wind howled outside, tea at four o'clock precisely—all the facets of genteel English life she had found so restricting and boring now represented sanity and security.

She caught him as he walked in to breakfast.

"I want to go into town with you," she said calmly, even though her knees were shaking under her skirts. "If you can pay my wages up to date, I'll get the next transportation back to Sydney."

He looked at her steadily. "You might at least give me time to find a new cook," he said. "I'm placing an advert in the *Sydney Morning Herald*—see what that brings. Can't you hold on for a week or two?"

She looked down at her feet, horrified that she might start crying at any moment and not wanting him to see her finally break down.

"What happened last night," he said slowly, "it could happen anywhere, you know. The streets of Sydney aren't exactly safe. You'll need a place to stay . . ."

"I don't care," she mumbled. "I've just got to get out."

"Tell you what," he said. "I'll try and bring a newspaper back with me. You can answer adverts in that. Maybe get yourself a nice job looking after kiddies or something, but you don't want to go rushing off with no plans. You could wind up worse than you are here."

She opened her mouth to say that she didn't see how that could be possible, but he put his hand on her shoulder. It was the first time she ever remembered him touching her and she started like a frightened animal. "Hang on," he said, "it's only me. You don't have to worry about me. If I'd wanted to come through that screen one night, I could have, you know."

"I know," she said, and her voice trembled. "But I still have to get out of here. I don't belong out here—it scares me—everything's so hostile. I'll never get used to it."

"Would you have quit on old Jimmy, too?" he asked.

She turned on him angrily. "That was different. That would have been different, I mean. Jimmy and I loved one another. That would have made all the difference in the world."

"Would it?" he asked, eyeing her seriously. "The same bad things would have happened. Your babies might have died because there was no doctor and your home might have burned down in the next bushfire. These are badlands here. Bad things do happen. You've got to learn to be the sort of person who doesn't give a damn to survive here. It's my betting that you and your Jimmy would never have made it."

"I'd have made it if I had to," she said, holding her head up to stare at him defiantly. "I wouldn't have let Jimmy down."

"How about letting me down?" he asked. "You were full of gratitude to me last night, weren't you? And now you're all set to walk out on me before I find myself another cook."

She opened her mouth then shut it again. It was true. Until last night she was secure in the knowledge that she owed him nothing, but now she was in his debt. He had saved her, however much he joked about his motive afterward. Hartleys did not abandon someone to whom they were indebted.

"Maybe I can hold on for a little while longer," she said. "Just until you find another cook."

"Good on yer," he said, patting her playfully between the shoulders as he walked past. Then he turned back with a grin. "Wasn't any room for you on the wagon anyway."

That final quip was like a shot in the arm. It reawoke her anger and the fighting spirit of the Hartleys was active again.

"You better bloody well put in that advert!" she yelled after him, "because I'm only staying two more weeks, not a day more!"

He looked back, still grinning, his eyes screwed tight against the fierce sunlight outside. "I thought swearing offended you," he said smoothly, as he disappeared round the side of the house.

I hate him, she muttered to herself, banging pots and pans noisily down on the counter. *I hate his smugness. Doesn't anything or anyone matter to him? He doesn't care a damn about last night or about my feelings—he only wants to get his precious wool into town!*

He did not come home until very late that evening and he was very drunk.

"Here's your bloody paper," he slurred, tossing it to her. "Go on—find yourself a swanky job in the city where the master can grab you in the linen closet or the butler can feel you up in the pantry . . . don't think you'll be any safer than here because it's not true. You should know by now that men only want one thing and they go bloody 'round the bend when they can't get enough of it . . ."

The way he looked at her, calculating in his drunkenness through half-open lids, made her shrink back into the kitchen.

"Here's your dinner," she said, putting it down on the table with a loud bang and turning to go again.

He grabbed her wrist as she moved past and she let out a little gasp of fear. He eyed her smoothly.

"You don't have to be scared of me, you know. I'm not one of them blokes . . . even if you are a good-looking sheila, I'll wait until you want to. You'll come around in the end, no doubt about it."

She snatched her wrist free, holding it as if it had been burned. "Let me make one thing clear to you, Mr. Cotrell," she said, trying to stop her voice from trembling. "When I give myself to a man, it will be to a man I love and respect, not because I'm desperate."

His eyes had taken on that amused look again. "And if you never find this man you're looking for?"

"Then I'll be quite happy to die an old maid," she said and flounced from the room to his laughter.

Once again the next morning he was sober and treated her with indifference, apparently no more aware of her presence than that of his station dogs. While he was away, she studied the newspaper and wrote letters to three families who wanted governesses or companions, plus a bookstore in Sydney. She looked at the finished letters lying on the table beside her bed and wondered impatiently how long it would be before somebody went into town again. Would Jake let Billy ride in and mail them for her? If he didn't send them soon, the positions would all be filled long before the letters even reached their destinations. She slapped her hand down on the table in frustration, sending her brushes and combs dancing. It was unbearable to be totally dependent on another human being. All her life she had been at the mercy of someone else's whims and decisions. Every penny of money begged from her father, every item of clothing approved by him, every trip to London considered and rejected. And now it seemed that she had traded one Wickcombe Hall for another. She had written letters to set herself free, but their ever reaching the first stage of their journey to the city was still at the mercy of Jake Cotrell. If he didn't want them to get into town, they never would.

As it happened, he was surprisingly agreeable about taking the letters into town for her. "Going in next week," he said. "The wool broker should have sold my stuff by then and there might be a check waiting for me. You can come in yourself if you'd like—see if there's anything we need in the store." He paused and grinned again. "Have to show those jokers I'm not mistreating you. There's rumors going around I've got you chained to a bedpost!"

It was always the same with Jake, she thought. If he did anything nice, he always had to spoil it.

Twelve

BEFORE THEY COULD GO INTO TOWN, THE WEATHER changed. Until then it had been monotonously hot, dry, and changeless. Every day Sarah had woken to vivid blue skies and every evening the sun had gone behind the western hills in a glowing red ball. But one morning Sarah woke to a wind rattling the beads on the door curtain. She went outside to fetch water, the wind snatching at her robe. There were clouds on the horizon—puffy white clouds like small children put in their paintings. Billy came out of the shed, carrying a saddle he had just polished.

"There are clouds," Sarah said delightedly. "Does that mean we'll finally get some rain?"

Billy stood, sniffing the wind, his nostrils flared like an animal. "Maybe soon," he said, "but not this time. This wind not coming good for raining. Watchem clouds—you see them cloud goin' right past us. No rain left in them clouds. If this wind start blowin' other way 'round, we get rain—maybe."

"You mean that maybe we won't get rain soon?" she asked. "Won't there be a drought if it doesn't rain soon? Won't the sheep die?"

Billy's mouth spread into a big smile, displaying his very white teeth. "This no drought yet. Still got water in stock ponds. If we get no rain longa time . . . then maybe drought. Then sheep go die. Missy be long gone walkabout."

Sarah nodded, realizing that this was true. She would be long gone before any drought. Why was she worrying about sheep dying? In a month's time it wouldn't even matter.

The wind whipped up, stinging her bare legs with sand and making her clutch her skirts.

"Is there often a wind like this?" she asked, alarmed.

"Wind from hills always big wind," Billy said. "Sometime bad wind, too. Take care in wind. Sheep know. When sheep come down to shelter, they know bad wind."

Sarah glanced around. There was no sign of sheep around the station. She went back into the house. Jake was stomping around with no shirt on and his boots unlaced.

"Bloody southerly," he muttered. "Now everything will taste of grit for the next week and I've got to go out and mend bloody fences."

"Do you have to go today?" Sarah asked, putting breakfast dishes on the table. "It's blowing really hard out there."

"Too bloody right I do," he said. "Billy saw kangaroos up at the north end again. Big reds this time. Bloody things go clean through fences like they're not there. So bloody stupid, too, because they could jump the things easily enough, but they never do, the buggers. Always go right through them and half a mile of fence to replace."

"So you'll want me to pack you a lunch?" she asked.

"Right oh." He began lacing his boots. "Oh, and get me my flannel shirt, will you? That keeps the wind out better than the other one."

She handed him the shirt, thinking suddenly that they had slipped into a parody of husband and wife all too easily. *But it's only going to remain a parody!* she thought firmly.

"You'd better close the shutters 'round the back," he instructed as he buttoned his shirt. "Or the house will be full of bloody sand by the end of the day."

"How long do winds like this last?" she asked.

He shrugged his shoulders. "Sometimes a southerly passes through and blows itself out in a couple of hours. Sometimes they hang around a couple of days or more. That's why I can't wait to get the fences fixed. I'll have half my sheep over on Kenilworth if I don't look sharp."

He ate a hurried breakfast then left. Sarah closed the shutters as instructed, wrestling with the force of the wind. When she thought about getting food ready for the evening meal, she discovered that she should not have left the meat out in its wire-fronted safe. It was encrusted with an orange red covering that reminded her sharply of the Christmas hams back home at Wickcombe, fresh from the butcher and covered in crispy bread crumbs. She had to scrape and wash the leg of lamb several times before it was free of dirt, and by that time, it was the only item in the house that was. Her own white apron was streaked with red dust, a fine layer covered the kitchen table and all the plates. When she went out to the tank, the bucket came up with a thick layer floating on it. Jake was right, everything did taste of grit.

The wind kept blowing all day. It seemed to build up a pressure inside her head so that she felt as if she would explode if she didn't get out. She stood on the front porch, sheltered from the main blast, watching balls of dead weed go tumbling past to be caught on fence wires. The horses stood together in their shelter, nose to tail, flicking dust not flies. This thought made Sarah smile. *At least there are no flies today,* she thought. *I must be learning to be thankful for small mercies!* It occurred to her that the Reverend Milton, at St. Mary's Church, Wickcombe, might be surprised and impressed by her spiritual development. He frequently told her father that she was a most unspiritual young person and not the least grateful for the blessings God had so bountifully bestowed upon her.

I suppose he was right, she thought as she left the shelter of the porch and started to walk across the yard, driven by the wind in her back.

As she came to the top of the gentle rise, she was started to be greeted by a sea of faces. Sheep were standing in neat lines, packed close together, looking ridiculously like crowds outside a London clearance sale, waiting for the doors to open. They gazed up at her steadily, but they did not attempt to move away. Their unblinking stares unnerved her and she hurried back toward the house.

In the yard she met Billy with the dogs at his heels, a plate of scraps in his hand.

"I feed them early tonight, missy," he said. "In case it gets bad later."

"What sort of bad?" she asked hesitantly.

He nodded toward the horizon. "It look bad back there. It pass by God willing."

Out on the southern horizon, where there was normally a sharp line between earth and sky, there was now no horizon. There was a band of darkness that had no defined edge, like a supernatural thing that was swallowing the land.

"What is it?' she asked. "Is it a storm?"

"That willy-willy, missy," Billy said.

Usually Sarah found his Pidgin English fascinating, but at this moment she wanted to slap him. "A what?" she asked sharply.

"A willy-willy—more than storm. Full of spirits—Billy seen the spirit lights!"

"You mean a thunder storm?" she asked impatiently. "You're talking about lightening?"

He shook his head as if he was sorry for her stupidity. "Not lightening, missy. Spirits that make light. They hang there, and if you follow them—they take you off and you lose your way. Real bad. Pray God it doesn't come this way."

"And Mr. Cotrell's still out," she commented, peering out to the north, as if she expected to see the figure of a horseman approaching.

"Boss him smart fella," Billy said. "Him know how to get home safe. You go back in house and shut it up good."

"I've put the shutters on," Sarah said.

"You make sure they on proper," Billy said. "You take rags and papers and stuff them around the doors and windows and you bring in all things from the porch."

She did not question the fact that he was giving her orders. She did what she was told, conscious that the brown wall was gradually moving up from the southern horizon, expanding to blot out earth and sky.

About five o'clock it reached them. One minute there was blue sky and sun. The next it was like London in a November fog. She could hear the wind wrestling with the shutters, the dirt particles pattering like rain on the tin roof and the wooden walls. The air was so thick that she could no longer make out the fence and the two horses in the paddock were ghostly shapes. She wondered if she should do something about them and couldn't decide what. She hoped Billy had been sensible enough to retire to his own hut and shut the door.

The storm went on. She glanced more than once at the clock on the shelf, glad for some definition of time because it was impossible to tell if night was falling or not. What would Jake do out in a storm like this? Surely even he could not find his way home in this swirling chaos?

Suddenly she heard the dogs barking. She leaped up and wrenched open the door, expecting to see Jake striding up the steps the way he always did. But instead of Jake's towering figure, Billy's little black face peered at her, a kerchief held around his mouth, no longer black but red, matching his red shirt and his red pants. There were muddy tears on his cheeks.

"Missy, I think something bad happen to boss!" he panted, coughing the dust from his throat.

Dust swirled into the house, stinging at her eyes and getting into her nostrils. "Has he come back?" she answered.

"Look there, missy," Billy said, pointing out into the gloom toward the gate.

Sarah stepped out onto the porch and stared hard. The air was swirling as if it was alive. Through the dust swirls Sarah could make out a dark shape. Something was beyond the gate—a form, not moving.

"I can't see," she complained. "Is it the boss?"

"No missy," Billy said quietly. "Not boss, just horse belonga boss."

"He's not with it?" she shouted. "Why's the horse just standing there? Maybe he's just fallen off and the horse won't leave him. Come on, Billy, let's go see."

"You best stay here, missy," Billy said, but the waver in his voice told her that he was afraid of the spirits in the willy-willy and not at all happy at going out into it alone.

Swiftly she grabbed the old sacking apron and flung it over her head. The dust blinded her almost instantly and her mouth was coated with dryness. The wind tossed her like a rag doll and she would have fallen if Billy hadn't steadied her arm. They reached the gate and the trembling horse on the other side of it. Billy examined it.

"No wound," he said. "Horse good. Where boss?"

"Maybe he was mending fences and the horse bolted when this storm arrived?" Sarah suggested, shouting to be heard above the wind, keeping the sack over her mouth.

Billy dismissed this. "Boss not stupid fella. Him tie up horse good. I think him have accident—see saddle tight for riding. Him make loose when he tie up horse. Only make tight again when he ready to ride. And see—here bag belonga him. Look—water bottle and gun and all. Boss never leave his gun."

"Then he must have had an accident," Sarah agreed. "I wonder when and where. Do you think it was far from here, Billy? Do you think we should go look for him?"

Billy stared off into the swirling darkness. "This horse been runnin' longa way," he said. "Him running fast, too. I think maybe him get scared and run home. We never find boss tonight. Best wait."

Sarah had no desire to go out into the impenetrable darkness. "Yes, I think we'll have to wait," she agreed. "It will be night soon anyway. There's nothing we can do tonight. In the morning we'll both go look for him."

"In the morning this bad storm gone away, God willing," Billy said. He took the horse's bridle. "This horse scared bad, him one big shiver," he commented as he led the horse into the paddock. Sarah made to follow, then looked back. Through the bushes along the crest a light was bobbing.

"Look Billy, there he is, he made it back after all," she called, turning toward the light. "He even brought his lantern with him . . ."

"No missy!" Billy yelled after her. "Come back here. That spirit light like I told you!"

Sarah was already running, stumbling over the uneven ground. She heard Billy's frantic shouts and dismissed them. Of course it wasn't spirits. It was a very visible little light—the sort of light a lantern would make, and Jake was trying to find his way back.

"Jake—you've made it. Down here!" she called as the light appeared to go parallel to the house and not toward it. Suddenly two ghostly black figures reared up in front of her, taller than her and silent. As she watched, rooted with fear to the spot, they walked past her with strange bobbing walks, merging into the darkness. She screamed, taking in a mouthful of grit that had her coughing and retching. Billy ran to grab her arm.

"Come back inside, missy," he pleaded. "That bad spirit light."

"Those figures—did you see them?" she asked, trying to stop her heart from hammering furiously.

"Them emu, missy. Them big bird—not hurt you. Come away into the house, missy," he pleaded. Sarah continued to stare, watching the light bob into the distance. It reached the fence, hovered above it, and went out. Her heart was still pounding as she allowed Billy to lead her and the trembling horse back to the house.

Thirteen

THE DUST STORM BLUSTERED ON INTO THE NIGHT, with rattling shutters and dirt pattering like hail on the iron roof. Sarah slept fitfully, waking to the panic of feeling that she was being suffocated as dust clogged her nostrils, coughing and weeping muddy tears onto her pillow. In the morning her eyelids were swollen so that the face that looked back at her from the mirror had an odd Oriental touch to it.

She had woken with the very first light, conscious of the silence, realizing that the storm had finally blown itself out. She did not even have to look outside the house for evidence of its passing through. In spite of the cloths she had tucked around windows and doors, sand was piled on windowsills, had coated all the furniture with a fine, red layer, and was scattered over the floor so thickly that it crunched as she walked across the room. In the living room, where the door to the outside had been opened several times, it lay in miniature drifts against the walls and furniture legs.

Sarah walked across the living room floor and cautiously opened the front door. The porch was barely recognizable under a thick layer of sand with a gentle slope marking where the steps down had been. The two horses stood together under the shelter at the end of the corral. Apart from their tails, nothing moved outside. The sky was clear and cloudless, the sun shone. Only the fact that the fence around the homestead had disappeared in one area under a sloping sand dune gave a clue to the might of the storm.

As Sarah scanned the horizon looking for any sign of life or any hint that Jake might have tried to make it toward the house, there was a bright flash of color and a flock of rosella parakeets—dazzling in iridescent reds, peacock blues, and emerald greens—fluttering in to land on the newly formed sand dune, chattering excitedly like children on a first outing to the beach. Sarah forced her entranced eyes away from them and headed back into the house to get dressed. She had to make some quick decisions on what to do about Jake. She had lived out here long enough to know that a wrong decision could cost him his life. Should she send Billy into town to get help or should she go with Billy right now to look for him?

Why am I so concerned? she asked herself. *Would he be so anxious to come out and look for me if I was lost in a storm?*

The reply came back instantly. It didn't matter one bit what Jake would or would not have done. She was a Hartley and Hartleys did not let people down. Wickcombe Hall was full of medals that her ancestors had won charging into the midst of the enemy to rescue their men. *Wouldn't father be surprised to find out that she was Hartley after all, just when he had told her that she wasn't?*

She dressed in riding breeches and one of Jimmy's white shirts and met Billy coming across the yard, the dogs at his heels. "Are you ready to come with me and find Mr. Cotrell?" she asked.

He gave her his big, flashing smile, "I ready," he said.

"Do you think we ought to get help from town first?"

He shook his head. "No time, missy. If he no have water bottle alonga him, he go die pretty damn quick."

"Then let's get going," Sarah said. "You saddle up the horses and I'll get together some food and drink to bring with us."

Ten minutes later they set off with Taffy, the blue cattle dog, running ahead of them excitedly, the horses hooves making no more than a muffled thud as they came in contact with the soft sand beneath. The sheep were no longer huddled together in the hollow, but had wandered off again, looking for grass beneath the new coating of dust. There were no signs of last night's horse tracks. In fact, the whole surface was smooth and glistening. Billy set their course without hesitation, leading her across a featureless landscape. They passed no signs of wildlife. Sarah kept her eyes open for the emus she had seen last night, but saw nothing to indicate they had been here. She wondered if they had been spirits of the storm after all, belonging to that strange light that had hovered above the fence and gone out.

The sun rose in the sky, beating down on them and casting short black shadows behind each horse. Sarah's irritated eyes smarted with the glare. She pulled her hat down farther over her eyes and scowled. Now she understood why most of the outback folk had a permanent bad-tempered look. It was not from temper after all, but from their constant frowning at the sun.

"How much longer, Billy?" she called to him.

"Maybe not long now, missy," he said and again she did not know whether he was telling the truth or just trying to please her by saying what she wanted to hear.

They came to a half-buried wire fence that Sarah assumed must be the property boundary. Was this the fence Jake came out to fix? Suddenly Billy started pointing excitedly. "Look, missy! New wire!"

Sure enough, the wire strands glittered in the fierce sunlight. Jake had been working here the day before. They rode along the new section, finding nothing.

"What's on the other side of that fence, Billy? Someone else's property?"

"That Kenilworth," Billy said with reverence in his voice. "That Mr. Johnson's place."

"Would he have been likely to have gone to Kenilworth station?" she asked. "Or could the people from Kenilworth have found him and taken him back?"

A broad grin spread across Billy's face. "Mr. Johnson, he don't like boss too much. I think he let him lie. Anyway, Kenilworth station two days ride from here."

"Then where can he be?" She heard the desperation in her voice.

Billy shrugged his shoulders. "Find place to hide, maybe?"

Sarah stared across the featureless landscape. Several stunted bushes were the only shelter she could see. Not even a gum tree in sight.

"Him maybe buried in sand," Billy suggested. As usual there was no trace of emotion in his voice. Sarah thought that if he found Jake alive or dead, he would give no reaction.

Sarah gazed out across the silent landscape. There was not even the faintest wind-sigh today. The dry bushes did not stir. Far over in Kenilworth some big black birds rose in the air squawking. *Crows, probably,* she thought. *Some poor sheep got trapped in the storm.*

"Do you think the crows have found a dead sheep, Billy?" she asked.

"I wondering same thing, missy," he said.

"You don't think that could be Mr. Cotrell lying over there? He could have wandered there by mistake . . . There's still a gap in the wire."

For a second he looked amused. "Not by mistake," he said, shielding his eyes as he peered at the wheeling forms of the crows.

"What do you mean?" she asked sharply.

Billy looked away.

"Why would Mr. Cotrell go over there on purpose?" she asked. "There's no shelter there . . ."

"Him not looking for shelter," Billy said evenly. "I think maybe Mr. Cotrell think Kenilworth not miss a few sheep in the storm."

"You think he was stealing their sheep?" she asked, horrified. "Surely he wouldn't do a thing like that?"

"Maybe not," Billy said. He wouldn't say any more.

"I think we should go and look anyway," she said, urging her horse forward. Billy hung back. "That Mr. Johnson's land. He shoot people who come there—think they comin' to take his sheep."

"Then you wait here," she said. "I doubt he'd shoot a woman. We can't risk leaving your boss lying there."

"All right, missy. You go. I wait," he said. Sarah commanded her horse into a canter. Sand flew up as the hooves thudded down. At the sound of the horse the birds rose again, laughing harsh laughs as they flapped away. Sarah slid from her horse as she made out something lying beside a saltbush. Holding the horse's reins, she walked slowly forward, half-afraid of what she would find. Even a sheep with its eyes pecked out would not be a pretty sight—but a human—a human she had known and spoken to . . . she had never seen a dead body in her life.

She fought back the desire to hurry back to Billy's side. Had Jimmy's eyes been pecked out when Jake found him? He'd already been there a couple of days, Jake had said. She tied her horse to the bush and walked cautiously around it. A foot was protruding from the sand. His leg was half buried. He was lying on his front, he hat shielding his face and his arm thrown over his hat for further protection. He was not moving. She stood looking down at him.

As she stood there, she found herself wondering: had Jake once stood like that over Jimmy's body? She could see the scene very clearly—Jimmy lying in the sand, Jake towering over him, casting a long cool shadow across him. Unsettling thoughts began to creep into her mind. Had Jimmy really been dead? How easy it would have been to turn away again, to ignore a plea for water, knowing that you would get your hands on another spread of land if its owner unfortunately died.

She continued to stare down at Jake and felt her power. How easy it would be for her to ride back to Billy and tell him she had found nothing. Then she could take back Jimmy's homestead and Billy could work for her and nobody would ever know . . . *Stop it immediately!* she commanded herself. It must be the heat that warped people's thinking. It didn't matter how little she liked Jake, she wasn't going to leave him lying half-covered in sand for the crows.

"Over here, Billy!" she yelled.

At the sound of her voice the body on the sand stirred and groaned. She was down on her knees immediately.

"Jake?" She tried to turn him.

Instantly he was very much awake. "Get your flaming hands off my mucking leg!" he shouted.

She leaped back as if she had been burned. "Well!" she said, mustering all that was left of her English dignity. "If that's all the thanks I'm going to get . . ."

His eyes opened slowly then, focusing on her. "Oh, it's you," he said, his voice croaking. "I must have been dreaming. I thought you were one of Johnson's men and you were trying to drag me along . . ."

He pushed back his hat and squinted at her. "I can't see a bloody thing," he muttered. "My eyes got all caked up."

"Billy's with me," she said. "We'll soon have you out of here."

"I can't move my bloody leg," he muttered. "I think it's broken."

She couldn't resist the question: "Fall off your horse, did you?"

He rubbed his eyes hard so that he could get a good look at her. "Of course I didn't fall off my bloody horse, woman. The thing went crazy, without any warning, and went down in the sand . . ."

"I see," she said. She had an absurd desire to smile.

"Bloody horse was real spooked," he repeated. "Couldn't do a thing with him. I saw the storm coming up and started to head for home. Barely got on the horse when the wind starts blowing like billy-oh and I couldn't see a flaming thing so I thought I'd follow the boundary line until it got better." He tried to prop himself up on his elbow and grunted in pain again. "Bloody leg," he muttered. "Bloody horse—I'll shoot the bastard."

"So what happened?"

"This bloody light appears, right in front of us," he said, rubbing his eyes incredulously, as if he could still see it. "Bloody light, I tell you. I've never seen anything like it. Nobody around but this bloody light's dancing up and down."

"I know," she said. "We saw one last night. It moved along and then just went out. Billy says it's spirit lights."

"He would," Jake grunted. "Primitive little bastard."

"So what do you think it was?" she asked.

He shrugged his shoulders, then winced with the pain of slight movement. "How should I know—must have a perfectly good explanation, I suppose." He looked around. "Where's Billy?"

"He's here," she answered.

"Then let's get me back home before I croak," he said. "Mucking leg. What a bloody stupid thing to happen to a bloke. Now I'll be crook for weeks. Who'll take care of my mucking sheep?"

"We'll manage," Sarah said calmly, not allowing her own thoughts to enter. "The first thing is to get you back to the house. Do you think we can get you onto a horse?"

"Have to if I don't want to walk," he said.

"I could always send Billy down to Kenilworth station and have you brought there in a buggy," she said, "You know you're on Kenilworth land."

"I am?" he asked turning innocent eyes on her. "I must have strayed through the gap in the fence. Never did get it finished."

"So shall I send Billy to get Mr. Johnson?"

That produced a reaction. "No, don't do that."

"Why not? You said yourself they'd got everything there. You'd get better treatment."

"They might not understand that I'd just . . . wandered . . . onto their land," he said. "You know what a suspicious bastard that Johnson is! Just get me onto a horse and I'll be fine."

It took all of their combined strength, plus several swear words that Sarah had never heard before and whose meaning she could only guess at, to drag Jake onto the saddle of Billy's horse. Jake's face was deathly white and the sweat was running down it like tears as they tried to walk the horse home at an even pace.

Fourteen

WHEN JAKE WAS SAFELY INSTALLED IN HIS BED ON the porch, Sarah dispatched Billy into town to find a doctor. By nightfall Jake was sleeping peacefully, his leg in a clean white cast and an injection of morphine having removed the pain for the moment.

"He'll need some looking after for a while," the doctor had said to Sarah as he left. "He was very dehydrated and there's a good chance of infection. Call me again if his temperature shoots up." He looked at her, as if really noticing her for the first time. "You're a relative?" he asked.

"Heavens no. I'm just helping out temporarily. I was planning to go to Sydney as soon as possible."

He nodded again. "You're not the sort of person I expected to meet on a station like this, although I've been out here long enough to be surprised by nothing."

"I came out here to get married," she said, "only my fiancé died."

He nodded with understanding. "Oh, you're the one. I've heard about you. Young Jimmy Alison, wasn't it? I'm very sorry. It must have been a terrible shock for you."

"I'm getting over it," she said. "I decided to stay on and

help Mr. Cotrell until he found another cook. I was hoping to leave very soon . . ." Her voice died away as she looked back at the sleeping figure. She sensed the doctor looking at her with sympathy.

"I'm afraid he won't be back on his feet for a week or so," he said. "He's a strong person. He may make a miraculous recovery. A lot of these sheep men do. You see someone with a smashed pelvis or a crushed skull and then two weeks later you pass them on a horse. You have to be tough to survive out here." He laughed, the sort of friendly laugh people like doctors always gave back home in England. Her own doctor had laughed like that when he visited her with chicken pox, or the time she fell out of an apple tree. "Now young lady—what have you been doing to yourself this time?" The laugh became the one familiar thing in weeks of nightmare unfamiliarity. As he walked to his buggy, she had to stop herself from running after him, from grabbing at his sleeve and begging, "Take me with you. Just get me away from here!"

But she stood without moving on the front step and waved politely as he drove away.

As the doctor had predicted, Jake did, indeed, get worse. He woke during the night, tossing with fever and clawing at his cast. She had to stop him from trying to get up, mopping at his forehead with cool towels and getting more pain-killing pills down his throat. The fever raged on and he slipped into delirium, seeing processions of undertakers dressed all in black walking up the front steps, and black-winged horses hovering over the roof.

With morning his fever subsided a little, then rose with the midday sun. Sarah hardly left him, her own nerves stretched to breaking point, feeling giddy from lack of sleep. With night, the hallucinations returned and he cried out as more undertakers came up the steps. As Sarah sat up with him in the middle of the night, sponging his face, trying to calm his terrors, she fought back her own fear as his unreality became hers. She could almost see those undertakers moving silently up the front steps and almost hear the beat of horse's wings on the roof.

About three in the morning, she must have nodded off to sleep for a few moments, for when she opened her eyes, he was looking at her. His eyes were clear and focused on her face.

"Sarah?" he asked and his voice sounded cracked, like an old, old man.

It was the first time she ever remembered him speaking her name. It had always seemed to her that he avoided it purposely before. She bent toward him.

"Do you want something?"

"What time is it?"

"You mean what day is it, don't you?"

He looked alarmed. "Have I been lying here for more than a day?"

"Two days."

"Christ!" He tried to sit up. "Whose taking care of my bloody sheep?"

"Relax," she said calmly. "Billy's doing a great job. He's much more intelligent than you give him credit for. All you have to do is rest and let that leg heal itself." She got up. "I've made some broth—do you think you could try some? I've only been able to get a little water down you."

He nodded. "I'll try," he said. "I do feel a bit hungry."

She brought in the broth and fed him, like a child from a spoon. He accepted meekly, even letting her wipe his chin as some liquid ran down it. After a few sips, he lay back, exhausted.

"Can't manage any more right now," he said. He closed his eyes. "Think I'll take a little sleep," he murmured. Then he opened them again, focusing on her face. "Sarah?"

"Yes?"

"I thought I was a gonner."

"You're tough. You'll make it."

"Those bloody undertakers," he muttered. "Are they still here?"

"They were only a dream—a fever dream, Jake."

He shook his head. "I saw them. I heard them coming up the front steps . . ." Anxiety clouded his face again and he began to sweat. "You won't let them take me, will you?"

Sarah put a restraining hand on him. "No, I won't let them take you. Don't worry."

He lay back and gave a sigh of content, like a small child. Then he turned to look at her, examining her face carefully.

"You're all right, you know that?" He paused, as if thinking. "I wouldn't have had a chance without you."

She laughed off her embarrassment. ''You? If I know you, you'd have crawled home twenty miles and still survived.''

''No, I mean it,'' he said. ''I wish you'd stick around a bit longer. Who knows—maybe you'd even learn to like me.'' He gave a tired little smile and closed his eyes again.

She didn't answer, embarrassed by his sudden gentleness, frightened that she might trap herself into something she dreaded.

''Sarah?'' he asked again. ''If I don't come through this . . . if I kick the bucket . . . you tell my brother about Orwell. Tell him you get the money from it . . . tell him . . .'' His voice drifted into silence. For a long moment Sarah held her breath, waiting for him to breathe, convinced that he had just died. Then he gave a long, gentle sigh and she saw that he was asleep again.

The next morning he was awake and impatient, with no hint of last night's tenderness.

''How do you think I'm feeling?'' he asked when she brought him a cup of tea. ''My bloody leg aches like billy-oh and my head feels like it's about to split open, and I've got no way of taking care of my stock for bloody, flaming weeks. Otherwise I'm just fine and dandy.''

''I can see you're fast on the road to recovery,'' Sarah said, smiling as relief flowed through her. He'd be up and around soon and she would be free to go . . .

After that he was a terrible patient, refusing to take medicines that he no longer thought he needed and claiming that a shot of whiskey did him more good. It was obvious that his leg gave him a lot of pain whenever he tired to move it, but he refused to give up, determined to defy the doctor and start walking again.

''Same damn leg they tried to put out of action at Gallipoli,'' he told her once. ''They said I'd never walk properly again after that, but I showed them they were wrong.''

Sarah recalled the hint of a limp he always had in his stride and wondered if it would be worse once the cast came off. Would he really be able to manage his station alone, to put in long hours in the saddle and run after sheep? Were those same worries at the back of his mind and was that why he was so incredibly bad tempered? Having never been noted for his sweet nature and good manners, Jake's temper was now twenty times worse. He swore at her for the least little inconvenience: the soup was too hot or his boots were not in the right place. In a way Sarah was glad of this treatment because it made her yearning to leave grow stronger with every moment and would allow her to leave with no twinge of guilt. "In two weeks his cast comes off," she would mutter to herself in the kitchen. "Two weeks. I'll be in Sydney for Christmas!"

She had gone up to London to see the Christmas lights once when she was a small girl, when a kindly neighbor had persuaded her father to allow her the treat. She had been entranced by the store windows, full of fairy-tale models and snow scenes, of fairy lights strung across the streets and magic snowflakes and candles winking back from every rooftop. In her mind, in the sterility of the outback, this was how she imagined Sydney. Music would be coming from every doorway. Crowds of happy people would be jostling in the streets. She'd find a job, maybe as governess to a nice family, or in a shop of some sort—a bookstore or a dress shop, and by the end of the month, she'd be part of those Christmas festivities, one of those happy, jostling people.

So she bore Jake's complaints and rages with a stoic smile, counting the hours until she would escape. She noted with growing uneasiness, however, that his treatment of Billy also became worse with each passing day. He had always treated Billy abominably, she felt. He talked to the aborigine as if he were no better than a dog. Now that he had to rely on Billy for so much of the station work, he was always finding fault, always yelling. Billy accepted everything with his normal lack of emotion. Sarah tried to talk to Jake about it, but she got nowhere.

"He's an Abo. He's used to it," he said, grinning at her across the breakfast table.

"But have you ever thought that he'll just up and leave one day if you go on yelling like that?"

He continued to grin. "Nah," he said. "He won't leave. He knows which side his bread's buttered. Besides, where would he go? Not many stations take on Abos down here in New South Wales. I brought him down from Queensland with me. His tribe would never take him back, now he's been contaminated by the white men and he likes his white tucker too much, too!" He laughed easily. "He's stuck here whether he likes it or not."

"Is that what you think about me, too?" Sarah asked uneasily. "Do you think that I'll never leave because I'm trapped here?"

He looked at her steadily. "You can go tomorrow if you want to," he said. He tried to get up and sank back into the chair, cursing. "Bloody leg," he muttered. "Hand me down that whiskey bottle will you?"

"You've been drinking too much, Jake," Sarah said firmly. "You can't start in the mornings now or you'll not be able to do your work properly."

"I sure as hell can't do my work without it," he growled. "I need something to deaden the flaming pain, for Christ's sakes. Are you going to give me the flaming bottle or have I got to get it myself?"

With a stony stare she handed him the bottle. He put it to his lips and drank noisily. He was about to put it back on the table, then changed his mind. "Maybe I'll keep it with me," he said. "I'm going to be on my feet a lot today."

Before the accident Sarah had hardly seen Jake touch spirits. He liked his beer after dinner, but he seemed to be able to handle that well. It made him relaxed and mellow. The whiskey might have deadened his pain, but it made his temper even worse. Sarah wished she dared to take the whiskey bottle and hide it until he came back to full sanity, but she had seen enough of Jake when he lost his temper to be just frightened of him. She decided to speak to the doctor about it when he next came out. Maybe the doctor could scare sense into him, although she doubted it.

When he came home that evening, he looked terrible. His face was haggard and his eyes were bloodshot.

"You ought not to have stayed out all day," she soothed, putting a meal before him. "The doctor warned you to take things easily."

"Bloody doctor!" he spat. "What does he know about anything. Bloody leg aches all the time. Can't put my weight on it right. Reckon he's set the mucking thing all screwed up."

Sarah eyed him warily, noting the slight slur to his speech. "Have you been drinking that whiskey all day?" she demanded.

"Too bloody right," he commented, looking up belligerently. "How else do you think I managed to get on a horse."

"You got on a horse? You must be out of your mind."

His eyes narrowed. "You mind your business, woman," he

said. "Your job is to bloody cook and keep my house clean. That's all your bloody job is—and you don't do that too bloody well. This stew's half burned again!"

"That's because you've eaten dinner at five for the past week and now it's seven," she said coldly. "And you won't have to put up with my bad cooking much longer, since I'll be out of here as soon as your cast comes off."

"No bloody use anyway," he mumbled. "Cold little bitch. Any normal girl wouldn't want to sleep alone. S'not natural. Don't know what you're missing."

"Will that be all now, sir?" she asked, in her most clipped English voice, "because if so, I'll retire to my own quarters."

He burst out laughing. "Retire to my own quarters? That's a good one. Someone's going to have to take you off your high horse one day—Miss Bloody Pom—show you what life's really like!" He put the whiskey bottle down on the table with a bang and leered across at her defiantly. Sarah threw back her head, turned, and walked from the room. She undressed and prepared for bed, trying to write more of her half-finished letter to Jessie, but unable to put her racing thoughts in order. *Oh, Jessie,* she thought. *If only you knew how much I envied you! To be settled with someone you love—to know where life is going—to have something to work for . . .* she glanced down at the paper. *How can I tell her any of this?* she asked herself. *How can I say anything that doesn't sound as if I'm wallowing in self-pity?* And yet she was loathe to break off the correspondence with the only friend she had on the continent. She was just describing the dust storm when she was startled by a scream. The scream was followed by another, of a tormented animal in agony. She leaped up and rushed outside. The screams were coming from behind the house. They were interspersed with cracking and whistling sounds and even growls. Sarah wondered what terrible Australian animal could be attacking the dogs? As she came around the corner, she froze, horrified by what she saw. By the square of light from the kitchen window, Billy was cowering on the dust, his hands over his head, while Jake stood behind him, his stock whip raised, an unnatural snarl on his face.

"You bloody little black bastard," he growled. "You black bastard." The whip came cracking down again. Billy screamed but didn't try to defend himself.

"I'll teach you," Jake snarled. The whip was raised again,

but this time, before it could strike, Sarah leaped forward and grabbed at Jake's arm. "Stop this! Stop it right now!" she commanded.

"You stay out of this!" Jake roared. "Do you know what this little black bastard has done?"

"I don't care what he's done," Sarah said, still using all her strength to hold onto his whip-hand. "It doesn't give you the right to whip him like an animal."

"I do what I like on my own station!" Jake growled. "Billy's my Abo and I'll whip him if I want to! When I find five newborn lambs dead because this stupid little bastard . . . " He fought to raise the whip again.

"I sorry, boss," Billy whimpered. "I sorry. I not know."

"You're sorry!" Jake shouted, "Let go of my flaming arm, woman, or you'll be sorry."

"No, you'll be sorry," Sarah shouted back. "Go on, Billy. Go in your house and lock the door. He'll calm down when he's got the alcohol out of his system."

Billy scuttled away like a frightened beetle. Sarah released Jake's hand and stood looking at him defiantly. "There," she said trying to sound calm and hoping he could not see her heart pounding wildly. "Now let's cool down shall we, and we'll talk about it rationally in the morning." Then, before he could do or say anything, she turned and walked ahead of him back into the house.

Sarah shut her bedroom door behind her and let out her breath. Although her knees were still shaking, she felt elated. She had fought a battle and won, the way Hartleys were supposed to fight battles, with dignity and presence. *If only father were here now,* she thought, a smile curling around her lips. *He'd never believe I was turning into a Hartley after all* . . . a memory swam into her consciousness: her father striding into the drawing room during afternoon tea. It must have been winter because there was a roaring fire in the grate and her father's cheeks, normally florid, were almost glowing. He had crossed the room without speaking, helping himself to a scone that he crammed into his mouth before he spoke. "Finally taught that blighter Higgins a lesson he won't forget," he said, rubbing his hands before the fire. "Caught him beating his wife again and gave him a damned good thrashing. Now you know how it feels, I told him, and he scurried away like a cur!" It was strange that she should have imitated her father so closely without knowing it. Her father would have had to admit that he was proud of her—something he had never done in his life . . .

She left the coolness of the bedroom door and walked across the room, pausing to splash water on her face from the china jug. She was just drying her face and had the towel over her eyes when the door was thrown violently open. She dropped the towel in horror as Jake stood there, his hands on his hips, eyeing her with contempt. She fought to muster her dignity. "What do you think you are doing?" Her voice came out harsh and brittle. "This is my bedroom!"

"Wrong," he said crossing the floor toward her. "This is my bedroom. This is my house and this is my property." He grabbed her by the arm, holding her so tightly that she cried out. "And that's my Abo out there," he went on. "You made me look like a fool in front of my Abo."

"You already looked like a fool," she said, her voice not betraying her fear. "Any man who lashes out like that ought to be taught a lesson!"

His hand dug into the flesh on her arm, wrenching her arm upward. "You and your bloody high and mighty English ideas!" he sneered. "You seem to forget a few things! You seem to forget that you're my servant here and you're in my house and that I'm a man and you're a woman—you've got to learn, understand me—you've got to learn to keep your place, woman!" His voice slurred as he yelled at her. She tried to twist free of him.

"Let go of me at once. You're hurting me!"

A grin spread across his face as if he was enjoying inflicting pain. "I do what I like on my own property," he said, still smiling. "I'm master here!" He grabbed her shoulder and pulled her toward him, his mouth half-open, intending to kiss her. She wrenched her head sideways, so that his lips made contact with her hair. "Let go of me," she said again. "You'll be sorry if you don't, Jake. You'll really be sorry in the morning."

"Wrong again," he said, shaking with a belly laugh, "I'll be sorry if I do. Now, will you stop fighting like a little wild cat?"

"I'll fight until you let go of me," she said trying to bite at his hand, which still held her arm.

"Won't do you any good," he said, holding her very close

to him. "You may get yourself hurt because I'm much stronger than you!" He threw her back onto the bed, lost his own balance because of the cast on his leg, and landed with his whole weight on top of her. Her head banged against the iron bedstead and she lay there, stunned and winded. She could feel him struggling with her nightdress, attempting to unbuckle his own pants. She fought to get her breath and struggle, but his weight was crushing her, his heavy plaster cast digging into her thigh, his belt buckle and all his buttons scratching through the thin fabric of her nightdress. She wriggled and tried to scream, but his mouth clamped down hard on hers, almost smothering her as he drove his tongue hard into her mouth. She fought to get her hands free, to get any part of her free of him. Finally she wrenched a hand free and grabbed at his hair, pulling his head backward with all her might. He released her from the kiss, gulping in air, and before she could make any use of her momentary advantage, he slapped her hard across the face. She could feel tears trickling down her cheek, though, whether they were from the force of the blow or from fear, she didn't know. Her whole head was singing and stinging from the violence of that blow. She didn't dare resist any further as she felt him driving her legs apart. His mouth crushed onto hers again as she cried out with the pain. He was pushing into her body with incredible force. He grunted with impatience as her body did not yield to him immediately and bore down on her harder, thrusting desperately against her until she felt her flesh being torn apart as he entered her. White hot pain surged through her. She screwed up her eyes tightly against the unbearable, burning, tearing, thrusting. Surely he must know how he was hurting her! If only he knew he wouldn't go on—he was a human being, after all—a man she had talked to and eaten with. He wouldn't want to inflict such terrible pain! She opened her eyes so that her terrified gaze might bring him back to sanity.

As soon as she looked at him, she could tell it was hopeless. He was lost in the world of his passion, and she had ceased to exist for him as a person at all. He was staring out at nothing, eyes clouded with passion, thrusting into her with all his strength and weight, while his tongue anchored her mouth to him as he jerked her up and down. It seemed as if he would go on forever, but suddenly he became wilder and more desperate, clutching her to him and throwing her down as if she were a rag doll, until he finally collapsed on top of her with a shuddering sigh.

Fifteen

FOR A LONG WHILE SARAH LAY THERE, TOO BRUISED and frightened to move, with Jake's heavy body on top of her. She waited, praying for him to move, to go away and leave her alone, but he didn't stir, and his rhythmic breathing finally told her that he had fallen asleep. Not daring to breathe, she wriggled herself from under him. He responded by grunting in his sleep and flinging out a long arm around her, pinning her to the bed. Again she waited patiently, her eyes fastened on him all the time, until his breathing had become deep and regular again, before she carefully lifted his arm and inched the bolster pillow into her place. It was only when she was standing safely on the cool wood of the floor that she let herself breathe again. The thought that he might wake and want her again, or abuse her for daring to get out of bed set her heart racing—pounding so loudly in her chest that she was sure he would hear it.

As she stood, she felt the warm liquid trickling down her legs, bringing about a wave of revulsion so violent that she almost vomited. A great shudder went through her body as she recalled his possession of her, and she rushed through to the kitchen, splashing water over her body desperately as she tried to wash away all traces of him. The cold water also helped to calm her racing mind so that, by the time she was drying herself on the kitchen towel, feeling the gentle night breeze through the mesh of the kitchen fly screen, she was able to think more clearly.

"I've got to get away from here now," she thought. "I can't stay another minute." She gazed out into the darkness of the night. A half-moon gave enough light to define the line of the paddock fence and the sheds. Would there also be enough light to travel by? "Keep calm," she instructed herself. "This needs thinking through.'' It was obviously no good running out into the night when the nearest building was more than thirty miles away and missing the town could mean dying of thirst in the featureless outback. *But it's not good waiting until morning and then telling him I'm leaving,* she thought, trying to calm the whirling panic in her brain. *He probably wouldn't let me go now. He thinks he owns me . . .* Again she fought back the revulsion. If she had ceased to exist as a human being for Jake, then the reverse was also true. She could no longer equate the snoring figure on the bed with a man who had talked to her pleasantly sometimes and who had even begged her to stay on because he needed her. He was a dangerous monster and the sooner she got away from him, the better. The doctor was due out again before the end of the week, and he would surely give her a ride into town, but she couldn't afford to wait around that long. She had to be far away by the time Jake awoke.

"I'll take one of his horses,'' she thought. "That's the only way I could be out of here by morning. And I'll take Billy, too. He won't want to stay here after tonight. We'll both get into Ivanhoe and then we've got a chance . . .''

She crept back into the bedroom to find some clothes. Most of her garments were in the drawers and she didn't dare open one for fear of waking Jake, so she limited herself to what was hanging on the wall pegs. *When I'm safely settled somewhere else, maybe I'll write for my things,* she decided. *He won't dare not send them, not if I threaten him with the law . . .* this new aspect of the situation made her pause and think. Surely, all she had to do was ride into Ivanhoe, go to the constable, and report Jake Cotrell for rape. There were laws about raping innocent women everywhere, weren't there? Maybe he'd even be thrown in jail and she'd get her farm back . . . Hastily she crammed what she could into a bag, regretfully leaving her best clothes and most of her changes of underwear in their drawers and slipped out the back door.

She had to tap several times on Billy's door before there was an answer.

"What you want?'' Billy asked cautiously.

"Billy, it's me—Sarah,'' she whispered back. "Open the door quietly.''

The door opened and Billy's black face peeped out, his eyes looking extra large and bright as the moonlight caught them.

"What you want, missy?" he asked, "It middle nighttime."
"I know, Billy. How are you feeling—are you all right?"
"I good," he said, looking at her cautiously as if he was afraid she might want to come into his hut and dress his wounds for him.
"Billy, I'm so sorry about what happened."
He shrugged his shoulders. "It Okay. Boss not bad fella. Tonight he take one drink too much."
"But it's not all right, Billy," she said. "No man has a right to treat another human being like that."
She saw the wary look come into his eyes, as it always did when she spoke to him of such things.
"Billy," she said. "I'm leaving this place. I want you to come with me."
"You leaving—on account a me?"
"Not on account of you only, Billy. On account of me, too," she added. "Mr. Cotrell thinks he owns people as well as land. We've both got to get out of here."
Billy was already shaking his head. "This my place," he said. "I no got other place."
"You'll find another place. You're a good stockman."
"This my place," he said. "I belong here. You belong here, too, maybe?"
"No Billy," she said firmly. "I've never belonged here. I belong back in civilization with polite people and nice clothes and good food. That's where I belong and that's where I'm going right now." His eyes became wistful. "No leave us, missy. I miss you. Boss miss you, too."
Sarah gave a grunt of scorn. "I'm sorry to leave you alone with him, Billy. I wish you'd come. Maybe I could even help you find work . . ."
But she could tell from his face that he couldn't even contemplate the possibility. "You good woman, missy," he said. "You make Billy happy."
"Then if you won't come with me, perhaps you'd help me," she said. "I need to get into Ivanhoe without Mr. Cotrell knowing. Can you take me?"
"You go into town?" he asked. "Tonight?"
"Why not?" she asked. "There's some moon, isn't there? Could you find the way?"

"Walking? I no get back before morning and boss be real mad, maybe kill me next time."

"I wasn't planning to walk," Sarah said. "I was going to take Jake's horse."

Billy's eyes became frightened. "They shoot folks who steal horses."

Sarah laughed at the absurdity of it. "I wasn't planning to keep it," she said. "I just wanted to borrow it to get into town. If you'd come along with me, you could take the other horse and ride back with both of them. You'd be back before Mr. Cotrell woke up." As Billy still looked scared, she continued, "If you don't come with me, I'll have to go on my own, and I don't know the way."

Alarm showed instantly in Billy's eyes. "Don't do that, missy. No good thing to do. You get lost and you die. Stay here. Stay here with Billy."

"I can't," Sarah pleaded. "I can't stay with your boss one more minute. He . . ." She broke off, unable to express anything of what had happened to Billy. But it seemed as if Billy sensed or understood her fear. He nodded slowly. "All right. I take you. We go without saddles, though. Boss he hear and wake up if we put on saddles."

"Fine with me," Sarah said, "I'm not taking much stuff anyway."

Billy glanced down at the small bag beside her and nodded again. "Okay. We go then," he said. Sarah followed him across the yard and to the corral.

By the first pearl gray light of dawn she stood alone at the outskirts of Ivanhoe, wondering what to do next. Billy had long departed, hurrying to get back to the station before he was discovered and now that she had time to think, she was scared and confused. She knew that coaches only came through a couple of times a week. What if she had to wait around for several days and Jake came looking for her? Would the people of Ivanhoe allow him to drag her back unwillingly? Would they listen to her side of the story if she told it? Should her first task be to go to the constable? She looked across at the neat, iron-roofed bungalow that housed the policeman. If he believed her and arrested Jake—what would happen then? Would she have to stay around for a trial, would Jake go to prison and lose his land because nobody was left to take care of it? She moved uneasily from one foot to the other, wrestling with the problem. She wanted to punish Jake, she wanted it badly—not just for his last, unspeakable act to her, but for the many, lesser acts before—the stealing of her land, the degrading of Jimmy, and the many small humiliations he had put her through. He deserved to be punished, and yet she was not sure that she could revel in the total destruction of a man. Even now she could not wish him the loss of everything. *After all,* she decided, *what I want most of all is to be free of this place and now I am really going. By tonight I could be in Sydney!*

This thought made her pick up her bag again and head toward the hotel. Mrs. Gallagher, the landlady, would know how to get her out of town if anyone did. There was already a wisp of smoke coming from the brick chimney above the tin roof. Otherwise nothing stirred in the town, except for a dog who trotted along the main street, minding his own business. As Sarah approached the hotel, Mrs. Gallagher came out, a mat in one hand and a carpet beater in the other. She paused when she saw Sarah, screwing up her eyes to look at her.

"My word," she said without much surprise. "What happened to you?"

"I . . . I'm going back to Sydney," Sarah said, finding that her voice trembled when she least wanted it to.

The older woman continued to stare. "Lover's tiff?" she asked, "He beat you up?"

"Not exactly," Sarah said. "and we were not . . . I mean, I was only the cook there, nothing more, in spite of anything you've heard." She was going to say that they were not lovers and then realized that this was not longer strictly true.

"Whatever you say, dearie," the woman said, her smile hinting that she didn't believe Sarah. "You'd best come inside before the rest of the town sees you like this and get washed up. How did you get out from the station—walk?"

"I borrowed a horse," Sarah said. "Billy took it back."

"And how is Jake?" the older woman asked chattily as she led Sarah through the back door and into a large kitchen. "We've been hearing all about his accident. I gather he can get around a bit now. Not quite incapacitated?"

"No," Sarah said shortly, "he's not."

"That's good," the older woman said. "Seeing as he'll have to fend for himself again now."

Her tone hinted that Sarah was the one in the wrong for running out on him, and Sarah was glad that she hadn't gone to the policeman and told him the whole story. It was becoming more clear by the minute that anyone in this town would be on Jake's side, not hers. Mrs. Gallagher drew a pan of water, adding warm water from a large kettle and put it down on a side table with a clean white towel. "Here, you can wash here and get yourself tidied up a bit, too. Then you can come through for some breakfast."

She left Sarah alone in the kitchen. There was a small round, fly-bitten mirror on the wall and Sarah glanced into to, recoiling with a shock at the sight of her own face. Her upper lip was bruised and swollen, there was a bruise on her cheek, and her hair looked as if somebody had dragged her through a bramble hedge. She dipped the towel into some cold water from the jug and held it to her lip and cheek, but it didn't seem to have much effect on the bruises. Then she ran her brush savagely through her hair and twisted it back into a tight knot. By the time she had rearranged her hastily buttoned blouse, she looked almost respectable again, although she was now very conscious of the swollen lip and hesitated to go through into the dining room to find the hostess.

Luckily the lady appeared with a large tray in her hand and started putting steaks onto plates.

"You can help yourself and eat back here if you like," she said. "There will be a big crowd through in the room. Thought you might want it private-like."

Sarah nodded gratefully and found that she was very hungry. She ate the steak and eggs that would have horrified her on her arrival in Australia, enjoying the taste of butter and marmalade afterward. She drank several cups of strong tea and felt almost human again by the time the landlady came through with a stack of dirty plates.

"Thank you very much," Sarah said, rising awkwardly to her feet. "Now, perhaps you can tell me how much I owe you and how I can get to the station in Trida and on to Sydney."

"Got a bit of luck for you there, too," the landlady said, looking pleased with herself. "If you're really set on going, that is . . ." She looked at Sarah inquiringly.

"I'm really set," Sarah echoed. The landlady shrugged her shoulders. "In that case," she said, "Mr. Johnson's in having breakfast and he's driving to the train to pick up his wife. Said you could ride along—you know, Mr. Johnson from Kenilworth!''

So half an hour later Sarah found herself seated in the leather-upholstered seat of an elegant open-topped car, beside Mr. Johnson, whom Sarah found cultured and amiable.

He asked her about England and confided that his son was currently at Cambridge. They hoped to pay him a visit next winter if the wool prices fulfilled expectations. He had also been at Cambridge and he knew the part of the country that had been Sarah's home. ''All those wide, lazy rivers with the sail barges on them,'' he said. ''So much lovely water everywhere. I expect you miss it.''

Sarah swallowed hard and her reply came out as a choked, ''Yes, I do.'' He must have sensed that he was treading on dangerous ground because he went on quickly, ''My wife's been on a shopping spree to Sydney.'' He gave a little sigh. ''Maybe I should have brought the bullock cart instead. She claims she doesn't get to Sydney often enough, so she makes up for it by going berserk! We've been invited to a house party this weekend and she claims she doesn't have a thing to wear . . .'' He turned and smiled at Sarah.

She found it so unreal, sitting beside a civilized man, making small talk about new clothes, that she almost wanted to slap herself and see if she was hallucinating. *Maybe I finally went mad,* she thought. She smiled back at him, but tried to keep her face straight ahead so that he would not see the worst of her bruises. But Johnson behaved like a perfect gentleman. If he noticed her strange appearance, he refrained from mentioning it, and the nearest he came to prying was to mention that she hardly seemed a likely candidate for the outback life. ''Cotrell's place is not exactly a palace, is it?'' he said with a grin, ''although he should be making enough money with the number of extra sheep he acquires!''

Sarah thought it wiser to say nothing. She looked out at the scenery, which now seemed interesting and teaming with wildlife. Pink galah cockatoos were feeding beside the road. A streambed was bright with green budgerigars and once an emu ambled across the road like a lanky elderly spinster, giving them a haughty stare when Mr. Johnson hooted the horn at her. The wind streamed through Sarah's hair, giving her a pleasant feeling of freedom. Last night and the weeks preceding it were all taking on the quality of bad dreams—no longer real or important. A bubble of hope was growing inside her head. She was riding in a beautiful car with a pleasant, normal, cultured man and soon she would be on the train back to Sydney, which would be populated by such people as he.

This is the turning point, she said to herself. *From now on everything's going to get better and better!*

Sixteen

"I'VE INVITED THE JOHNSONS FOR THE WEEKEND," Marjorie Murphy commented to her husband as she propped herself up to apply another coating of suntan oil to her body. Her body, clad in a white, boned one-piece sunsuit, seemed to be made of polished bronze, with not an ounce of spare flesh on it—the result of dedicated hours of exercising and sunlamps.

Col Murphy, resting in a deck chair with the daily paper over his head, removed the paper and scowled at her.

"What did you want to go and do a damn fool thing like that for?" he demanded.

"Like what?" she asked, surprised.

"Inviting the bloody Johnsons!" Col growled.

"But I thought you liked the Johnsons!" Marjorie said, looking peeved.

"In small doses," Col said. "But not right now. I thought we came out here to get away for a few days so that I could take a rest before the nitty-gritty of the election started."

"Of course we did, darling," Marjorie said soothingly, "but just because we're in the country does not mean we have to shut ourselves away like hermits. Some stimulating company will do you good. All those dreadful laborites hovering around you are too depressing for words. If I don't talk to somebody civilized soon, I shall scream. In fact, if anyone mentions the words *unions*, *workers*, or *fundamental principles* once this weekend, I shall personally shoot them."

Col grinned. "But it's the unions who are going to get me in again," he said, "and you do like being Mrs. Premier, don't you my dearest?"

"You know I do," she said, "which is why I agreed to come away from town in the middle of the racing season. I want to make sure my entry is in top form to win the election and if sitting in the dreary countryside will do it, then I suppose I'll suffer."

"How about suffering a little more and canceling the Johnsons?" he asked hopefully.

"Darling, I can't," Marjorie said, her voice showing well-bred horror. "You can't cancel somebody when you've just asked them to drive two hundred miles."

"Hell," Col muttered.

"And Colin," Marjorie said reproachfully, "please try to watch your language when Elvira Johnson is here. You know she was convent educated."

Col chuckled. "If the worst thing she's come up against in life is someone saying *hell* in her presence, then she hasn't done too badly," he said. "I'm forty-three years old, Marjorie. I can't change the way I am now . . . and what's more I don't want to. I never was a one for show or pretense. You knew that when you married me."

"I know," she said with a sigh. She finished rubbing on the oil and picked up a nail file. "Journeys do horrible things to my nails," she said. "I always manage to chip at least one. Next time I shall bring my manicurist along."

"Fine with me as long as she's that slim little piece with the big brown eyes," Col said.

Marjorie lowered her sunglasses and peered at him coldly. "That's my hairdresser," she said. "My manicurist is Ivan—the young man from Russia with the lovely long fingers."

Col chuckled again. "I'm not that desperate," he said. "I haven't got around to fancying a poke with a bloke yet. There's still a few virgins left in Sydney."

"Don't be disgusting, Colin," Marjorie said. "I know you only do it on purpose to annoy me, but don't do it anyway."

"You always were a bloody prude," he said. "Anyway, I need to get it out of my system now so that I can mind my Ps and Qs when Elvira Johnson is here. Now there's a woman who gives me the willies—if ever there was a bloody virgin queen it was her. How she managed to produce three sons, I'll never know.''

Marjorie raised her glasses again to frown at him. ''I won't take any more of this teasing, Colin,'' she said. ''You are to behave yourself when the Johnsons are here! No crude remarks or innuendos at dinner.''

''Innuendos?'' He asked, a big grin spreading. ''Is that what one dago asks another—you wanta me go inuendo?''

''Colin!'' she frowned. ''I mean it. The Johnsons are generous contributors to your campaign fund as well as Elvira being my close friend. You are to behave yourself, understand me?''

''Yes, ma'am,'' he replied meekly and put the paper back over his head.

When the Johnsons finally arrived after lunch, Col played genial host, with no hint in his manner that they were not completely welcome. He thumped Ralph on the back, complimented Elvira on her new clothes, and personally mixed cocktails for them on the terrace.

''It's so lovely and civilized here,'' Elvira said with a sigh, laying her head against the cushion behind her. ''I should never have agreed to come right after shopping in Sydney. Now I'll be discontent for months when I get home.''

Ralph smiled at her affectionately. ''She's been nagging me for the past twelve hours to buy her a plane. Apparently that's the latest thing—you buy your own plane and then you can pop and visit friends all over the place.''

''It makes perfect sense, doesn't it, Marjorie,'' Elvira said, stretching out her hand languidly to her friend. ''Just think—you and I could have lunch together while these two old bores are busy working. We'll both get planes and then we can phone each other and meet halfway. Wouldn't that be fun?''

''I don't know where she could keep a plane in the middle of Sydney,'' Col said, taking a long gulp from his drink.

''A seaplane, darling,'' Elvira explained. ''They make seaplanes. You could keep it on the harbor and just roar off whenever you wanted to.''

''Doesn't sound like a bad idea at all,'' Marjorie commented. ''Just think, Col, I could keep tabs on you, too. You'd go off on one of your political tours and you'd never know when I'd pop in on you.''

For a second she held his gaze, challenging and cold. Then he laughed, his big, booming laugh. ''You weren't thinking of piloting this plane yourself, were you?'' he asked. ''If so, God help the harbor ferries. The only time you tried to drive your own car, you took out a lamppost and a garden wall.''

''Only because some idiot had left it in reverse,'' she snapped, ''and besides, streets are far too narrow. I have the whole sky to make mistakes in if we get a plane. I think I'll buy one as soon as we get back to Sydney—what about you, Elvira?''

''She has to wait to see what wool does,'' Ralph said quickly.

''Isn't everyone saying this is a bumper year?'' Marjorie asked.

''You can have too much of a good thing,'' Ralph said. ''All these soldier settlers raising sheep—we could find the market's flooded. And what happens if we get another dry year? We'll have all these smallholders with sheep on their hands and no way to feed them. It's only the big stations like ours that have enough water to keep going for a couple of dry seasons.''

''Then you'll buy up all their poor starving sheep for nothing, as a gesture of kindness, and make yourself a fortune again,'' Col said bluntly. ''I know how your mind operates.''

''The rate I lose them, I need to be constantly buying them,'' Ralph said smoothly. ''My neighbors all think I've got so many that I won't miss a few. My boys told me the fence was down again all along my western boundery. Blighter named Cotrell . . . funny thing, I gave a lift to a young English girl—a good class girl, too—when I picked up Elvira from the train yesterday. My word, she looked as if she'd taken a beating. She was Cotrell's cook. I think he knocked her about a bit and she was leaving. I didn't like to ask, and she didn't volunteer so we'll never know.''

''Just like a man,'' Elvira said. ''I'd have wormed every juicy detail out of her, wouldn't you, darling?'' She turned to Marjorie.

Marjorie gave a languid smile. ''It sounds very fishy to me that a young English girl should want to be a cook on an outback station. Are you sure she was the cook and not something a little more cozy?''

Col got up. ''You women,'' he said. ''Like vultures, waiting to tear each other to shreds. It's a good thing women don't rule the world, Ralph, or we'd have little wars every day."

"Which might have prevented the sort of terrible, final wars that men always seem to wage," Marjorie said. She, too, rose to her feet. "Are you coming in to change, Elvira? I'll have Stevens run you a lovely long bath."

Elvira sighed contentedly. "You hear that, Ralph. A lovely long bath. You don't know what those words do to me, Marjorie. Ralph has provided me with most luxuries a person requires to live, but he can't provide me with lovely long baths. If we use the bore water, of which there's always enough, it's so full of minerals that the sponge gives up the ghost and turns into a hard little brown ball, poor little thing . . ." She gave a tittering laugh. "I'll see you gentlemen many many hours later." She followed her hostess toward the house.

Ralph Johnson got to his feet and, by silent agreement, the two men began to walk down the steps and onto the lawns.

"My God, you've got a lovely place here," Ralph commented. "Elvira would be in seventh heaven if she could grow flowers like this."

The two men stood on the wide steps and gazed out across the pleasant view. Wide lawns gave way to green pastures with sleek horses and fat cattle in them. There was a little lake at the bottom of the hill and English shade trees dotting the pastures. Beyond, fold after fold, blue wooded hills melted into the distance. Col sighed with pleasure.

"Trouble is we don't see enough of it," Col said. "I'd happily spend half the year out here, but Marjorie doesn't like the country. For her there's no point in being alive if you're not constantly admired and adored . . . and I can hardly come out here alone, seeing that it's her property."

"I thought the husband owned all in a marriage?" Ralph asked.

Col snorted. "Didn't you ever hear about our marriage settlement? I thought that was common knowledge. Her folks would only agree to let her marry me if we drew up this long legal list of dos and don'ts. They wanted to make sure the properties went to her when they kicked the bucket. They thought I'd just squander her birthright . . . I was just a young backbencher in those days, with big ideas but not much else. Marjorie thought I could make something of myself if she pushed hard enough, but her folks didn't share her optimism. So all I own is the clothes on my back."

Ralph laughed. "Oh, come on, Col. I know you . . . you're as sharp as they come. You've got little bits stashed away here and there."

"Maybe little bits," Col confessed, "but I can't get my hands on this place, or the Sydney house. We have a good marriage, Ralph. I can't kick her out because I like playing country squire. She can't kick me out because she likes playing Mrs. First Lady!" He laughed again, but the laugh was harder this time.

"So how's the election coming along?" Johnson asked. "I haven't been in Sydney for so long, I'm way behind the times. Is McKinnon giving you a good run for your money this time?"

Col smiled. "It'll be close. He's promising a lot he can't give, of course. Prosperity if the unions give us freedom to expand and produce. Prosperity if we keep our faith in England . . . a farm for every returning soldier . . ."

"Those aren't good things?" Johnson asked, more by way of challenge than from conviction.

Col looked straight at him. "I don't like all this talk of prosperity, Ralph. You say you haven't been in Sydney for a while. If you had, you wouldn't like what you saw. There are men with one leg standing on street corners. Twenty blokes fighting for one job. They're only taking farms because there's nothing else for them."

"Then we should make something else," Ralph said. "Surely McKinnon and his ideas for expansion and production are a good thing?"

Col sighed. "It all comes back to Europe, doesn't it? It's no good growing all the wheat and all the wool in the world if there's no market for it. England's still staggering from the effects of the war and England has all the wool market. You must know what will happen if we keep on producing wool at this rate—there will be a glut and the price will plummet. The same goes for everything else. We can't outproduce Europe—we have to wait for Europe to recover before we see real prosperity here. In the meantime, we have to make sure there's enough work for everyone. Unions keep the employers from getting too greedy."

"And the unions also vote you into office," Ralph said.

"Too bloody right," Col agreed. "Between you and me, I'm not at all sure about the bloody unions. All the soldiers came back from Europe with too many bloody big ideas. We have to make sure the unions don't get too big for their boots and start telling their bosses how to run things. That's why I have to be so careful. I need their help, but I can see what they could do to a country if they put their minds to it . . . and there are more damned Bolsheviks around than people think . . ."

"You think we might have a little Russia on our hands?" Ralph asked with amusement. "You think the Australian people would follow like sheep the way the Russians did?"

"I just think they're very good at stirring up trouble," Col said firmly. Two dogs came running up from the river, springer spaniels with dripping wet coats. They bounded up to Col, sending a shower of spray over both men. Col bent to pat them. "Been after my ducks again, have you, you blighters?" he asked fondly. He looked up and caught Ralph Johnson's eye. "In spite of my reputation, I don't like trouble," he said. "I had enough fighting when I was a kiddie in the slums. I'm getting old, Ralph. Now I prefer a quiet life."

Seventeen

AS SARAH SAT ON A BENCH OVERLOOKING THE HARbor at the Domaine Park, some three days later, she was no longer so sure that the turning point had come. The harbor water glistened in the midday sun and the air echoed with the loud toots of busy ferryboats constantly coming and going. All around Sarah was the bustle and elegance she had longed for: the city was a strange mixture of Northern architecture set in a Southern landscape. Her recollection of Sydney when she first arrived had been hazy—bright water and a Victorian post office only standing out clearly in her mind. Now, after tramping the streets for three days, she had time to observe it. What she saw was a city of contrasts—tall office buildings, ponderous Victorian monstrosities, trams clanking their way on rails that dazzled in bright sunlight. On some streets she could easily imagine herself back in London. But then she would turn a corner and find a park shaded with date palms, dotted with bright barrows of the Italian street vendors selling freshly squeezed orange and lemon drinks and she would remember that London was very far away. It was also a city that somehow lacked London's elegance. It had clearly grown up as a sprawl, with no master plan, its docks lined with humble wooden sheds, its harbor views shielded by great warehouses, and its parks bordered by rows of poor terraced houses.

She had liked it very much at first, for it possessed a vibrancy and life that were almost overpowering after the silence of the outback. All the people seemed to be young and tanned, the fruit stalls piled high with the freshest fruit and the big department stores full of the latest fashions. It was clearly a city with plenty of money to spend. She had not noticed the beggars that first day, and she had not ventured to the slums behind the railway station to see the men leaning on fence posts staring out with blank expressions at the squalor.

Now, after three days of wandering, she had seen both sides and was trying to reconcile them in her mind, as well as find out where exactly she fit in. Here on the grass a crisp wind from the ocean was blowing. Children in neat white uniforms ran squealing across the grass on one side while a tolerant teacher watched them. Two women dressed in the latest short skirts and the latest bobbed hairstyles walked past her, their arms full of parcels.

"Which one do you think will be right for the party?" one asked the other in clipped English tones.

Sarah stared after them longingly and bit into a sausage roll—all the lunch she dared to buy now that her money seemed to be going at an alarming rate. She had already paid for the first week at the Emily Huxstep Memorial Hostel for Women—a bleak establishment close to the railway terminus. The travelers' aid people at the railway station had directed her there when she asked for a cheap, clean, temporary accommodation. It was cheap and clean all right, but that was all that could be said for it. The long dingy dormitories were lined with iron cots, and the only decorations on the army green-painted brick walls were lists of rules and the penalties that would follow their being broken: No food or drink to be brought into the hostel. Expulsion on second occurrence. No music or singing. No cigarettes.

No gentlemen callers. Hostel closed between 9 A.M. and 5 P.M. No exceptions. Hostel doors locked at 10 P.M. and nobody admitted after that hour, no exceptions. Mandatory chapel service every Sunday morning. No drying underwear on the windowsills, etc., etc., etc. There was a different rule on almost every wall. In fact, the hostel sounded suspiciously like the boarding schools some of her friends had been sent to. School away from home had sounded exciting and adventurous to Sarah, however strict the rules were—far preferable, at any rate, to the dreary governesses who came and went and to a father who shouted at her every time he tried to explain anything. After a couple of nights in the Emily Huxstep Memorial, Sarah thought rather more kindly of her father for sparing her the ordeal. She was not the kind of person who liked to be fettered by rules and would probably have spent her boarding school career in permanent trouble.

She had hoped, when she put down her small bag on the lumpy bed covered with its gray army blanket, that at least she would be among friendly people again—girls of her own age to talk to and share experiences with. However, the other girls in the Charity dorm (the rooms were each named after a virtue that presumably Emily Huxstep, whoever she was, possessed in great abundance) had only exchanged a few words with Sarah before they all decided that she was not one of them and therefore potentially dangerous. They were all working-class girls, most of them fresh from the country looking for work in the big city. There were a couple of English working-class girls with strong Northern accents among them, but they, too, regarded Sarah as a creature of another species. Unlike Jessie, they were not willing to give her a chance to be friendly. Her questions to them about home and the trip out were rebuffed and she heard them giggling about "Miss La-de-da!" In fact, the suggestion quickly passed around the room that she was a spy, planted by the management to find out which rules were being broken.

It's only for a little while longer, Sarah thought to herself, finishing her sausage roll and even licking the crumbs from its paper wrapping. *I should have found a job soon and then I can move in somewhere better . . .* the thought trailed off even as it passed through her brain. In the past days she had discovered that finding a job was not going to be a simple process. She had first tried the sort of jobs she would like to do: saleswoman in a bookstore or dress shop. On each occasion, as soon as they heard her accent, they had sent her away: "There aren't even enough jobs for our own young men back from the war," one bookstore owner told her coldly. "Men that lost limbs fighting for your bloody country."

After that she switched from walking the streets looking for store jobs to scanning the newspapers for jobs as companion or governess. There didn't seem to be any, but there was an advertisement for an employment agency specializing in domestic vacancies. She made an appointment to see them and wondered whether knowing how to cut up a whole sheep and make damper bread would qualify her for the position of a city cook.

The interviewer was an elegant older woman, dressed in an old-fashioned tight-waisted dress, trimmed with feathers and lace. Her hair was piled high and secured with pins in the prewar fashion. Her accent was pseudo-English, as if she had spent many years practicing to erase the Australian twang but hadn't quite succeeded. "You desire a position as a cook?" she asked, looking Sarah up and down. "You have had experience?"

"Yes," Sarah said. "I've just been working as a cook on a sheep station."

"Ah!" The face broke into a smile that cracked the white casing of makeup. "You have your references with you then?"

"Well, no," Sarah stammered. "I don't actually have a reference with me . . ."

"You were dismissed?" The voice was sharp again now.

"No!"

"Then your reason for leaving was?"

Sarah felt the blush spreading across her cheeks. She wondered what the woman's reaction would be if she told her the real reason and couldn't help smiling. "I . . . er, felt too shut away out there, and it was only supposed to be temporary. My fiancé died, you see. I went out there to get married, but I had to support myself instead." She hoped that maybe the poignant story would touch the woman's heart, but the woman's face froze back into a mask again. "I'm sorry," she said. "My agency would never place anybody without a reference. We have our reputation to think of. I suggest you write to the people on the station and ask them for a reference as soon as possible. Otherwise, I can't see you finding employment . . ."

Sarah bit her lip as she thought of that interview. She was

hardly going to write to Jake and ask him for a reference. Did that really mean that domestic jobs were barred to her in Sydney? Was there nobody in the city desperate enough for a cook or even a kitchen maid to hire her without a reference? If only she knew where to start. It would help if she knew her way around the city and which areas were considered good and which bad. The hostel area certainly qualified as the latter! She got up and began walking back down into the town. A van drove past, loudspeakers blaring from its roof. "If you vote for me I'll make sure that . . ." she heard before it turned a corner. Sydney was in the middle of election fever. Although elections were the furthest thing from Sarah's mind right now, she seemed to be one of the only people who did not care. Most people she passed wore buttons or ribbons in red or blue, with their candidates name on them. Banners with VOTE LABOR OF ELECT THE COUNTRY PARTY FOR PROSPERITY hung from balconies. Newspaper headlines proclaimed, "Keep ties with Britain," says McKinnon, or "Col says No to Imperial Preference!" They meant nothing to Sarah and she skirted loud political arguments that broke out here and there along the street with the amused caution of the outsider.

George Street was thick with shoppers buying Christmas presents. The store windows glittered with fake snow and Christmas trees, looking ridiculously out of place against the blazing blue summer sky and the shoppers in light cottons. Would she still be in the Emily Huxstep Hostel by Christmas, she wondered? That would hardly be the jolliest celebration in the world. The management would probably be putting up a notice in the next few days saying: No festivities allowed, she thought grimly, but at least it would be better than spending Christmas with nowhere to go at all. She just prayed that her money would last that long.

She bought an evening paper and sat on the steps of a building, dutifully circling all the ads to which she could reply. She even circled some ads for cooks out in the country, thinking that they might be more desperate and therefore less likely to want references. It also passed through her mind that her handwriting was neat and educated and that she might be finally reduced to forging letters from titled people she had known back in England. "This is to introduce Miss Hartley, a hard working girl of charming disposition," she wrote on the side of the newspaper and laughed at herself. An evening breeze swept down the street, ruffling the pages of the newspaper and making her shiver. Once the sun set, the evenings were still chilly here beside the ocean. She headed for the little cafeteria she had found where they served meat pie and mashed potatoes for ten pence. She washed it down with a cup of very strong tea, lingering as long as she dared before the waitress started sweeping very deliberately around her feet, giving her cold stares.

It was almost dark as she headed past the station toward the Emily Huxstep Memorial. The rush hour crowds had thinned—all normal people being now safely back with their own families or else sitting in their theater or cinèma seats. The streets behind the station were in contrast to the bright shopping streets she had passed through before. Some aborigines sat in the gutter, drinking. They did not even look up as she passed them. Jazz music was coming from inside a club. A man wandered out, wearing a big red rosette proclaiming VOTE LABOR on his lapel. He looked her up and down, then passed her without speaking. Sarah picked up her pace and hurried on. On the next street corner two girls were standing. They were dressed most inappropriately in short satin dresses with black fishnet stockings beneath them. Their faces were heavily made up with large blackened eyes and red gashes for mouths. Sarah glanced at them curiously, wondering if they were actresses dressed for a play, then gave one of them a second, longer look. Surely that was Joan, who had the bed next to hers in the hostel—little Joan from the outback who wrote letters home all the time and hardly spoke to a soul? She was about to speak to the girl when two sailors came past. There was the briefest exchange of words and the two girls disappeared with them, leaving Sarah confused.

When she got back to the hostel, she noticed that Joan's belongings had been removed from the shelf beside her bed.

"New girl coming in tonight," the big, beefy girl called Ruby said as she noticed Sarah staring at the empty bed. "Joan left."

"I saw her," Sarah said. "At least I'm pretty sure it was her. She was all dressed up strangely."

"See, Ruby, what did I tell you!" one of the other girls yelled. "I told you she was going to be a tart."

"A tart?" Sarah's knowledge of tarts was limited to jam, treacle, or almond.

"You know," the other girl said with a giggle, "a tart—one of them."

"She don't know," Ruby answered scathingly. "She ain't like us, Ida. She's grown up pure as the driven snow. She don't know what ordinary people have to do sometimes, whether they like it or not!"

She turned and glared at Sarah, who was still confused and wondering what she had said wrong.

"I wouldn't have thought little Joanie would do that, though. Would you?" a third girl joined in, coming to sit on the empty bed.

"There's no knowing what you'll do if you get desperate enough," Ruby said, folding her tree-trunk arms across her large stomach. "And poor old Joanie was getting pretty desperate. That old cow downstairs told her she'd have to be out of here by the end of the week if she didn't pay up and she was no nearer to finding a job . . ."

"I didn't mean that," the other girl said, interrupting Ruby. "What I meant was that Joanie didn't seem the type. No experience, I meant. I wouldn't have thought she'd even know what to do."

"She'll learn quick enough," Ruby said, still frowning. "Anyway, it's not hard. All she had to do is lie there and let the men do the work!"

This produced giggles from the other girls.

"Quiet, Rub, you're offending Miss Prissy over here," Ida said with a dig at the large girl's ribs.

"Oh, well, pardon me, your ladyship," Ruby said with a mock bow to Sarah. "I don't suppose they talk of such things at Buckingham Palace or wherever it is you're from."

The girls went into more peals of laughter and were soon back in another conversation that excluded Sarah. She pretended to be reading as she lay back against the hard frame of her bed, but in reality she was worrying about Joan. She still didn't completely understand what Joan was doing, but she worried about her. Of all the girls in the hostel, Joan had been the only one who had touched her most. The others were hard, beefy girls who swore like men and didn't seem to bat an eyelid when one of the matrons of the hostel shouted at them for breaking rules. Joan had seemed vulnerable. She was always to be seen, sitting cross-legged on her bed, writing page after page of letters in childish printing. Sarah had caught a glimpse of one page. It had said, "So don't you and Dad worry about me. I'm doing just fine and I'm going to make you all proud of me."

One by one the girls began to get ready for bed. Sarah went along to the bathroom and washed as much of herself as she could in the cold water in the basin. Baths were only allowed once a week and cost three pence each. Luckily the other girls did not seem to be too enthusiastic about washing and most evenings she could guarantee the bathroom sinks to herself. As she came back into the room, the other girls were huddled together, whispering. They looked up, guiltily when Sarah came in, making her wonder if they planned to do away with her during the night. She pretended, as usual, to take no notice of them and climbed into bed. She shut her eyes but could hear the whispers still going on.

"So what can we do about it?"

"It's her own bleedin' fault. I kept warning her about him."

"Well, now she's really gone and done it. She'll be out on her ear and then what will she do?"

"Maybe he'll marry her?"

"Not him. I shouldn't be surprised if he ain't got a wife and kids out back-o'-Bourke. He's too gussied up by half."

"Well we can't just leave her out there, poor little sod."

"You want to be the one who walks by old poker face and opens the door for her?"

"If only there was a fire escape or something."

"Ha! What do they need fire escapes for—they wouldn't care if we all burned in our beds."

Sarah lay there, trying to make sense of this conversation, then she finally sat up, her curiosity roused. The girls were clustered around the window, peering anxiously out.

"What's happening?" she asked. Immediately their faces were closed, suspicious. "Nothing," one of them mumbled.

"Just looking at the moon. Go back to sleep," Ruby said. But as she was talking, there came a whistle from down below. Sarah got out of bed to look for herself.

"There's somebody down there," she commented, seeing the figure in the shadows waving madly.

"It's Gertie, miss," one of the girls confided. "She was out with the Albert again and she's missed lock-up time. Now she'll be out on her ear and serve her right. None of us liked him . . ."

"But Gertie's all right, isn't she?" Sarah asked, trying to picture Gertie's innocuous face.

"Oh yes, there's nothing wrong with Gertie," the girl said.

"So can't we find a way to get her back in?"

"There's only the front door," Ruby said. "And you're very welcome to walk past old hatchet face if you want to and let her in yourself."

Sarah was peering out of the window. Gertie began to wave again. "If she got to that bit of roof up the fire escape, we could lower a sheet and she could climb into here," she suggested, she and a young friend having once done the same thing for a dare.

"Oh, I don't know," someone muttered. "Bit dangerous, that looks."

But Ruby was already leaning out of the window. "Gertie—climb up the fire escape to the roof and we'll get you across," she called down in a hoarse whisper. Soon Gertie's head appeared on the flat area to their left. Sarah took the sheets from her bed and knotted them together, then she lowered them, flinging them across to the surprised Gertie. "Hang on tight and we'll pull you in," she commanded. "You can steady yourself on the drainpipe."

A few moments later they were all red in the face with exertion and Gertie was lying panting across Sarah's bed. "I thought that was me last moment on earth," she said, half giggling. "Oh look—I tore me one pair of stockings."

"Lucky that was all you lost," Ruby said. "We nearly all wrecked our innards heaving you up. You must weigh a ton."

"We're just grateful it wasn't you, Rub," Ida said, giggling. "They don't make sheets to hold your weight."

The girls laughed, releasing tension at the end of an adventure. Then their laughter froze as the door was flung open and Miss Simkins, the hatchet face from downstairs, stood glaring at them.

"What is all this unseemly noise?" she asked. "Lights out is supposed to be at ten-fifteen. It is now ten-twenty." Her gaze went to the open window. "And what is this all about?"

"It was I, Miss Simpkins," Sarah said, stepping forward between Gertie and the knotted sheet on the bed. "I'm afraid I caused a slight problem by opening the window. I'm used to sleeping with my windows wide open at home and apparently these girls are not. I opened them and we had a slight argument about closing them again. I'm sorry if I caused a disturbance, but I find it very hard to sleep with no air in the room."

The woman eyed her suspiciously, torn between wanting to put her in her place and being impressed by her obvious upper-class bearing. After a long stare, during which she tried to out-stare Sarah and lost, she drew herself up to her full height. "This is not the Ritz, Miss Hartley," she said. "We do not bend our rules to the wants of the individual. You will just have to learn to sleep with your windows closed until you find more suitable accommodations. Now, back to bed, all of you." Then she swept out. The girls crowded around Sarah, grinning at her in delight.

"That was bloody marvelous," they laughed.

"You're all right miss. You're not the snob we thought you was."

Gertie gazed at her adoringly. "I'm real grateful to you, miss," she said.

Ruby came and sat on her bed. "What's your name then?" she asked. Sarah told her. "And what's a Pommie toff like you doing in a dump like this?" Sarah gave her a censored version of the story while the girls listened in silence.

"Blimey, Sarah," Ida said, "we had no idea you'd been through all that. We thought you was one of them spoiled little toffs straight off the first-class boat. We couldn't understand what would make you come here, unless you was studying poor people for a newspaper or something."

"So now you see," Sarah said. "I'm in exactly the same boat as most of you. Worse than some of you because you still have families back on farms. I have nobody and no job . . ."

"You said you were a cook out on the station?" Ruby asked. "A real cook—meat and potatoes stuff?"

Sarah nodded. "Starting with the dead sheep."

"Streuth," Ruby commented. "You don't look as if you could skin a rat." She got up and began to pace the room. "I can't promise nothing, mind you, but I might know of a job for you."

"You might?" Sarah asked, her face lighting up.

Ruby's face returned to its habitual sneer. "Of course, it wouldn't be no piece of cake. Dirty job actually—long hours, and terrible pay, but it's a start. I work in the hospital kitchen and one of our girls just left. Needed to get married in a hurry, if you get my meaning. So right now we're one girl short. If you want to come along with me tomorrow, I'll introduce you to the supervisor."

"That's wonderful, Ruby," Sarah said. "I really appreciate it."

The next morning she was hired to work in the kitchen of the Royal Women's Hospital. The work would have horrified her two months ago—peeling mounds of potatoes, washing out porridge-caked saucepans, and serving huge pans of evil smelling stewed meat, but now she was as excited as if she had been hired by the prime minister as his private secretary. She had a job. She would be paid a weekly wage and things could only start getting better.

On Christmas day Sarah chose to work overtime—as much for the company as for the extra wages. It turned out to be a wonderful day, with a true spirit of goodwill between patients, doctors, and domestic staff. She was kissed several times under a piece of mistletoe by young doctors. They all sang carols together around a giant tree and she got a little harmonica in a cracker at teatime. In the evening the kitchen staff gathered for a big dinner. It seemed to Sarah that they had saved all the best pieces of turkey for themselves and she gorged as much as anybody on turkey and stuffing, Christmas pudding, and brandy sauce, washing it all down with sweet, cheap wine until she almost floated home, feeling contented for the first time in months.

Eighteen

THE NEXT MORNING SARAH VOMITED MOST OF HER Christmas dinner into the nearest basin in the bathroom.

"You look like death warmed up," Ruby commented as she staggered back to bed.

"It must have been that cheap wine," Sarah said, lying back down and closing her eyes. "Thank heavens I don't have to work until midday."

"I bet that was your first hangover, too," Ruby said, laughing at her. "You certainly knocked back the booze last night. Still, it was worth it, wasn't it? All that lovely food and drink? They really did us proud."

Sarah groaned and closed her eyes, trying to erase the thought of mounds of turkey, lying in rich, brown gravy and steaming Christmas pudding from her swimming head.

By midday she felt much better and was able to go to work without more than a twinge of nausea at the sight of vats of turkey stew and rehashed pudding, but next morning she vomited again and had to spend half her shift at work rushing out to the outhouse.

"What's up?" Ruby whispered as Sarah came back from one of her quick departures.

"I feel terrible," Sarah groaned. "I think I must have got a bad bit of turkey and I've come down with food poisoning."

Ruby jerked her head. "Go on, take the rest of the day off. Not much happening. Most of the patients have gone home for Christmas. I'll cover for you."

Sarah gratefully accepted her offer, but once she was in the fresh air and paused to sit in the park, she felt suddenly ravenously hungry. She bought a sticky bun and a cup of coffee and instantly felt quite well again. She enjoyed the rest of the afternoon in the sunshine, feeling twinges of guilt when she thought of Ruby working for her, but not many twinges of stomach.

"I needed that afternoon off," she thought. "I haven't had much rest in a long while. I'll be right as rain tomorrow."

But she wasn't. Worried now, she popped in on her way to work to the morning surgery of Doctor O'Brien. He turned out to be another jolly man, another stereotype of genial doctors everywhere.

"Now, my dear, and what seems to be the trouble?" he asked, making Sarah wonder whether there was actually a course in medical school in how to look genial. She pictured it to herself. "First smile. Then rub hands together so . . ." She forced the smile from her face, which was not hard as another wave of nausea came over her.

"I think I must have food poisoning," she said. "I've been

vomiting for three days in a row, ever since I had a big turkey dinner."

"Dear me," the doctor said. "Vomiting all day, without stopping?"

"No, not all day. I'm usually feeling fine again by noon."

She detected a change in the man's smile. "Any other symptoms? Any diarrhea?"

"No," Sarah shook her head. "Just vomiting and terrible nausea. It makes me feel quite faint sometimes."

The doctor nodded wisely. "And your menstrual cycle?"

"I beg your pardon?"

"Your monthly periods—they are quite normal?"

Sarah blushed at the question, considering it completely out of place. "Yes, of course. That is . . . I've never been really regular."

"And this month? When was your last period?"

"Not this month yet. Not since sometime in . . . maybe November?" Her pride began to overcome her embarrassment. "Look, doctor, what has this to do with food poisoning?"

"My dear girl," the doctor said. He was rubbing his hands again. "Is there any possibility that you might be pregnant?"

"Pregnant?" the word stumbled out in horror. "Of course n . . ." she stopped, terrified at her thoughts. Surely that one act of violence could not have resulted in . . .

"So there might be," the doctor said, still rubbing his hands. He leaned forward in his seat. "You see, my dear. You have just been describing very clearly to me the symptoms of early pregnancy. If you let me examine you, I can probably confirm my diagnosis."

Sarah still sat like a statue. The doctor's face seemed to her to have turned into a mocking, grinning mask.

"I take it," he said, "that this is not welcome news to you? That there is some reason why you and the young man cannot be married right away?"

Sarah continued to stare at him as if he was talking a foreign language. She imagined sending Jake a letter telling him that he had to marry her. She imagined being married to Jake and shuddered. The doctor detected the shudder.

"Sometimes it is the simplest thing," he said. "Even if you aren't completely in love with the boy. There are so many complications otherwise . . . your family—do you think they will be understanding?''

''I have no family,'' Sarah said coldly. Suddenly she wanted this interview to be over, to escape from this kind, grinning face, and lose herself in the crowds of the city.

''And you don't think there is any possibility of marriage?''

''No.''

''Ah,'' the doctor leaned back thoughtfully. ''There are institutions for young girls in distress,'' he said. ''The church runs a very excellent one, I believe. The girls earn their keep doing sewing and such and the institution places the babies for adoption. They might have a vacancy, although . . . there is much immorality in the world these days.'' He paused and looked at her, as if deciding whether she, too, had been responsible for immorality. ''I could put you in touch with them,'' he said. Sarah nodded and he began to write an address.

''In the meantime,'' he went on, back to his genial, doctor-self, ''this is the address of the public antenatal clinic. Go to them and they'll give you advise on what to eat and all that.''

Sarah stumbled out of the office into blinding, summer sunlight. It seemed like a perfect day—gentle breezes, birds singing, everyone else in great spirits—the whole world mocking her. *You thought you were free at last,* the laughing world seemed to be saying, *you thought things were finally going well, but that was only to trick you. You'll never be free. You are trapped for the rest of your life . . .*

She began to wander through the crowds, milling around the main station. They were all dressed up for midsummer outings, carrying picnic baskets and parasols, children dancing excitedly, and fathers mopping sweat from their foreheads as they sought to keep control of their broods. Everywhere Sarah looked, the world seemed to be composed of families. A young family passed with a small baby in a pram. Sarah eyed it with fascination. Could it really be possible that in a few months time she would own something like that wriggling, squirming, smiling bundle? Even as a small girl she had never enjoyed playing with dolls. Janet had always called her a tomboy and wrung her hands in despair when she came home with torn dresses and mud on her best shoes. ''You wait until you have a family of your own,'' Janet had warned, ''if you can ever find a man to marry you, that is!''

Now she was to have a family of her own, it seemed, minus the necessary father. The whole idea was so incredible that she almost wanted to laugh. It couldn't be possible. The doctor had got it all wrong. She had allowed herself to be swept along with the crowd, up into the main hall of the station. Realizing where she was at last she took refuge in the station bookstore and browsed through family health books until she found the information she needed. "The first symptoms of pregnancy are usually a missed menstrual period, followed by morning sickness and a tendency to feel faint. The breasts are sometimes tender . . ." Sarah put a hand up cautiously and touched her breast. It felt bruised. She took it away as if her breast burned her, returned the book to its shelf, and hurried from the shop.

The big clock above the booking office struck eleven, making her realize that she was now late for work. Even that did not seem to matter anymore, since she probably wouldn't be keeping the job as soon as anyone found out . . . when did people find out? she wondered. Her education, as Jessie had discovered long ago on the ship, had been sadly lacking in matters of reproduction. All she knew about having babies was that your stomach got big and that you screamed a lot when you had them. Sometimes women even died, she knew also, since her own mother had suffered that fate. Maybe that would be the best thing, she concluded, trying to view the whole situation impersonally, because I don't see much future for a baby or me if I can't work and have no home . . .

"Vote McKinnon! Elect the country party for prosperity!" a young woman screeched, thrusting a pamphlet into Sarah's face. It was so incongruous that Sarah wanted to laugh. Just how could Mr. McKinnon, whoever he was, assure her prosperity at the moment?

On the loudspeaker a voice blared out, "Blue Mountains excursion leaving on platform three. Nonstop to Paramatta."

Sarah looked up. Jessie! She had forgotten all about Jessie! Maybe there was some hope after all. If Jessie could take her in, just for a while . . . she could work for her keep . . . all she needed was a place to sleep . . . She found herself running to the ticket office and then sprinted to catch the train.

Not bad for a mother-to-be, she thought with a grin as she swung herself on board as it began to move out.

An hour later she was standing outside an imposing gateway,

decorated on either side with stone lions, their feet on massive balls. On the crest of a rise stood a beautiful brick residence, adorned with wide balconies and white shutters. A raked gravel drive swept up to the main house. A spotlessly white picket fence surrounded the property, and in the greenest of green fields beautiful horses were standing quietly in the shade, many with pretty foals beside them. Sarah's knowledgeable eye took in the quality of the horses. She had lived close enough to Newmarket Racecourse in England to have friends who bred racehorses and she knew that these were of the highest quality.

In her past existence she would not have hesitated to go in through that white gate and walk to the front door of that house, demanding to see the owner. But now she was no longer Miss Sarah Hartley of Wickcombe, who could hold her head high with the best of English gentry. She was a girl from a hostel and a kitchen and she hung back, scared.

"Don't be ridiculous," she told herself. "You've a perfectly good reason for being here. It's not as if you've come to burgle the place!"

She forced herself to push open the gate and went in. She was halfway up the drive when she heard the crunch of boots and a groom came toward her, a racing saddle over one arm.

"Can I help you, miss?" he asked, eyeing her as if trying to sum her up.

"Yes please," Sarah said, "I'm looking for Mr. and Mrs. Thomas Bates. Perhaps you could tell me where to find them."

The man looked confused. "I'm afraid you must have the wrong address, miss," he said. "The master here is Mr. Steele."

"Oh, I'm not looking for the master," Sarah said, smiling at the misunderstanding. "Mr. Bates is one of the stable boys. I've come to see his wife, Jessie."

The groom's face looked even more confused. "Young Tommy?" he asked. "I'm sorry, miss. I felt sure by the way you spoke that you'd be visiting the boss." He jerked his thumb. "Cottages are over that way, down behind them trees."

Sarah followed the path, convinced that he would have escorted her personally if she had been visiting the master. The path went on and a wave of nausea swept over her as she began to feel weak from hunger. She hurried down the hill and came at last to a row of tiny huts behind large eucalyptus trees. A figure was hanging out washing. She looked up and let out a shriek of delight. "Sarah! Lord love us, it's Sarah!" and rushed toward her, arms outstretched.

The hug from Jessie was the nicest thing that had happened to her in so long that she had to fight back tears.

"I never thought I'd see you again, Sarah love," she said. "What are you doing here?"

Sarah mumbled her carefully prepared speech about having a day off and deciding to pay a call.

"I'm so glad you did," Jessie said. "I hoped you'd come to Sydney when I got your letter telling me you were looking for a new job. So sorry to hear about Jimmy, by the way. What a shock that must have been. Still, life must go on, mustn't it? Just one minute while I put these sheets up and then we'll go inside and I'll make us a nice cup of tea."

Babbling all the way, Jessie gathered up her washing basket and led Sarah toward the end cottage in the row. "Tom won't be back for a while," she said. "They've got a big race meeting coming up for New Year next week, so the boys have been working nonstop. Not that they pay them any extra, but you know how it is. Seems that we're lucky to have a job at all these days . . ."

She held open the door and motioned Sarah to go inside first. "Don't break your neck," she said. "Like I told you—ain't enough room to swing a cat, but we're getting on all right."

Sarah stepped into a small, dark room. It was about the size of the maid's bedrooms back at Wickcombe, but this was not a room but a house. Close to the front door was a large easy chair. A bed was pushed against the front wall, covered with a bright rug to make a sofa during the day. A chest of drawers was squeezed in beside the bed and a curtain hid clothes hanging on hooks on the wall. An oilcloth-covered table took up most of the middle of the room and another matching curtain hid a small sink, draining board, and shelves against the back wall. It was obvious that Jessie had already put a lot of effort into the house because the furniture all shone with polish and there were bright pillows and pictures everywhere. It shouted to Sarah that this was a home where happy people lived.

"Park your bottom," Jessie said, indicating the armchair. "That's Tom's chair but he won't mind, I daresay."

Sarah sat gratefully because her legs were beginning to feel weak again.

"So tell me about everything," Jessie said, bustling with the kettle. "Tell me how you got back to Sydney and what you're doing now and where you're living . . ."

"Oh, no," Sarah said, trying to bluff with a laugh. "Hostess has to tell first. I can see that you're happy here. You've done marvels with the place."

Jessie beamed. "I've put a lot of work into it, that's for sure. You should have seen what a dump it was when I first got here. Of course, there are limits to what you can do with the size. Tom calls it a bread box—but it is rent free and we're going to save for a place of our own. That's our dream for one day—an acre or two and some chickens—they call them chooks here by the way, ain't that a laugh? They do talk funny, don't they? I don't know how many times I've had to say to the other girls, 'Why don't you talk the king's English?' " She laughed at the thought of it.

"You get along well with the other families here?" Sarah asked.

"On the whole," Jessie said. "Some of the other wives are real nice, but there's a bit of bad feeling that we're English and we're keeping an Australian boy out of a job. There aren't enough jobs for all the returned soldiers, so they say. But I figure that my Tom did his bit, fighting in the same war as them. I don't stand no lip from nobody!" She laughed again, then her eyes lit up. "Oh, and guess what? Me and Tom are going to have a little nipper. I'm already a couple of months along. Didn't waste any time, did we? I don't think Tom's too thrilled. He says we'll have to sling a cradle from the roof because he can't see how we can squeeze another body into this room, but I told him that he'd have to get used to it because the rate we're going, we'll have four or five of them running around shortly!"

She poured boiling water into a big, brown teapot and began to put cookies from a tin onto a flowery plate. Sarah tried to eat daintily, even though her stomach was crying out for immediate food.

"Sorry about the store-bought biscuits," Jessie said. "I usually do my own baking, but I've been feeling so sick with the baby that I haven't wanted to look at the sight of dough. You can't imagine how bad you feel at times. Like that time we were both seasick in the Bay of Biscay, only worse.'' She put the tea things on the table and began to pour. ''Now,'' she said, smiling happily. ''Now you know all about me. Let's hear about you.''

Sarah sipped her tea politely and told Jessie about the hostel and the hospital kitchen.

''Don't sound right up your alley,'' Jessie said with sympathy. ''Educated young lady ought to be working somewhere posh. Still, I bet you'll find the right sort of job soon enough and when you're companion to Lady Whatsit or secretary to the prime minister, then I'll come up to Sydney with my string of little ones and I'll visit you. I'll say to the kids, 'See that grand lady! That's what your ma could have turned out to be if only she wasn't saddled with brats like you!' '' And she went into peals of laughter again.

When the tea was finished, Sarah made the excuse of having to return on her excursion fare and headed back to the station. *Last door closed,* she said to herself. She felt surprisingly calm. She looked out of the window all the way back to Sydney, noting how the countryside glowed with flowers and birds, how rich the colors were and how deep the sky. Back in Sydney she caught a bus out to Watson's Bay and followed the road up to the Heads—remembering how she had thought of Wickecombe and Janet when Jessie had woken her. She smiled fondly when she thought of Jessie. *At least things worked out well for her,* she thought. *I'm glad. She deserved some happiness. I'm glad one of us got it.*

The paved road ended and she walked along a narrow path to the cliff tops. On either side, sandstone slabs fell sheer away to pounding, swirling water. She walked over the springy turf smelling the rich sea-smell and feeling the spray on her lips. On one side the harbor was bright with sails and ferryboats, on the other the ocean stretched out a thousand miles before it met New Zealand. *This is the end of the Earth,* she thought. *The very end of a whole continent.*

She walked slowly and without pausing until she came to ''The Gap,'' where the path passed over a narrow bridge. Here the sandstone had been washed away and the last part of the Heads was virtually an island, standing with its ankles in pounding surf. A railing surrounded the area—a railing about three feet high. Sarah leaned on the railing and looked down. She watched great waves rush between the sandstone cliffs, then recede again, leaving seaweed-covered rocks. Seagulls drifted below her. The boom and roar of the water echoed back from the steep sides. The railing wasn't that high. She was glad for a tomboy childhood. It would be easy for her to hitch up her skirts and vault over. If anyone saw, it really didn't matter anymore if she showed her legs! Again she smiled as if she perceived the enormity of the joke. Not that there was anyone to see. She had passed nobody on her way up here. She was all alone at the end of the world. In a way that was comforting, too.

She was in the process of hitching her skirt when a voice spoke right beside her.

"It's not as easy as you think, you know."

Sarah turned to see an exquisitely dressed woman. She was wearing gray silk—dress, stockings, and shoes in matching gray. Although it was summer, her dress was trimmed with mink. Her hair had been black and was streaked prettily with gray across the front, blending in with a neat little gray hat. Her face was perfectly made-up and the hand that rested on the railing beside Sarah was tipped with long, red nails and decorated with one large solitaire ruby. She did not look at Sarah but stared out past her, as if she was observing something Sarah could not see. For a moment Sarah wondered if the woman had, indeed, spoken to her.

"I beg your pardon?" she asked in her most formal British manner.

"It's not as easy as you think," the woman repeated. Her voice, deep and smooth, at first had sounded like a cultured English woman, but now Sarah heard a hint of an accent, French maybe, beneath the perfect vowels.

"I'm sorry, I don't know what you are talking about," Sarah said, still frostily British.

"I know you do," the woman said, still staring past Sarah. "You were thinking of throwing yourself off The Gap. A favorite spot for people to end it all. I just wanted you to know that it's not as easy as you think."

"You think I wouldn't go through with it?" Sarah asked, amazed at the bluntness of the woman.

"Oh, I'm sure you would. I could tell instantly you were a very determined young woman. I just wanted you to know that it's not always successful."

"I beg your pardon?"

"Not everyone dies. If a wave happens to break the fall, the body may merely be smashed against rocks. People have lived on with broken backs or damaged heads . . ." for the first time she turned to look at Sarah and Sarah was amazed at the force of her gaze. Her eyes were almost tiger golden and Sarah could feel them looking right through her. "I would at least think it over if I were you," she continued.

"There's nothing to think over." Sarah looked away, reality beginning to overwhelm her again.

"That's only your opinion now. You probably think there is no other way out."

"There is no other way out."

"And I tell you, *ma petite*, there is always another way out."

"How would you know," Sarah said, turning on her fiercely. "You probably don't know what it's like to have nowhere in the world to go, nowhere to turn. I suppose you're one of these do-gooding women who use up empty hours saving poor souls. Well, thank you for your kindness, but this soul does not want to be saved."

The woman actually smiled. Sarah saw those tiger eyes dancing. "Ah yes," she said with satisfaction, "I think you'll do perfectly." She paused, as if calculating. "So he wouldn't marry you, my dear, or couldn't."

"I wouldn't marry him," Sarah stammered, thrown off guard by the question and wondering if this woman could read minds. "Not if he was the last man on earth!" she added, her anger returning.

The woman nodded wisely. "I have a suggestion," she said at last. "Why don't you come and have tea with me. I think I might be able to help. I have a wide circle of acquaintances, you know. There may be a perfectly simple way out of this, after all. Will you at least come? If you decide afterward that all is, indeed hopeless, then I shall have my chauffeur drive you back up here and at least you will have had the pleasure of my cook's eclairs before you go."

Sarah looked at her and laughed. "I don't know what to say," she said.

"Don't say anything. Just follow me. My car is parked at the end of the road. I was on my way home when I watched you begin to climb and guessed where you were going." She turned and began to walk back along the path with neat little steps.

Sarah stumbled after her. "I don't even know your name," she mumbled, "and I probably won't be able to repay your kindness . . ."

The woman paused as a tall chauffeur in gray livery opened the door of a gray, shiny Rolls Royce. "My name is Madeleine Breuner," she said with a little smile, "and I'm sure we'll find a way."

Nineteen

MADELEINE BREUNER WALKED UP TO THE LARGE figure who was standing, elbows on the terrace wall, looking out into the velvet night. The big house was built on the cliff tops, overlooking the ocean, and the dull thump and roar of Pacific breakers could be heard down below. Lights spilled from the open windows of the house, and music and laughter floated down the lawns.

"So here you are, my darling," she said in her soft, well-bred voice. She put a hand on his shoulder. "Why are you hiding? The guest of honor should not run away from his own party! I believe congratulations are in order."

Col Murphy, looking somehow too large for his black evening suit, turned toward her and idly kissed the hand that rested on his shoulder.

"Hello, sweetie," he said. "I didn't think you'd be coming tonight! Marjorie would hardly have sent you an invitation, would she?"

Madeleine laughed. "Hardly," she said. "But I'm not a gate crasher. I'm here because Sir Hubert did not wish to come alone. You know how every woman in Sydney is trying to marry her daughter off to him, just for the title. They don't realize that he's one of the boys, of course. At least he's safe with me!"

Col laughed and covered her tiny hand with his. "I'm glad you came," he said. "Lot of old farts except you. This is not my idea of a victory party . . . all the bloody country set, talking about how many Melbourne Cups their bloody horses have won. Of course, we have to have them because they put up the money for the campaign.''

Madeleine laughed and slid her arm through his, leading up away from the wall as though she were a tiny tugboat and he a giant ocean liner. ''But you are now head of the state for another three years. You can clap your hands and send them all away.''

Col allowed himself to be led up the path. ''I wish,'' he said. ''Did you see the majority? What I've got for myself is three years of headache. One vote we can be defeated on, and we're out. It will probably be the free milk for kiddies bill or something equally harmless that brings me down, you see.''

''I don't think so,'' Madeleine said. ''The common people still love you. They were dancing in the streets as we drove here.''

Col grinned. ''You know us Aussies,'' he said. ''Any excuse for a beer! But they weren't any too sure about voting for me this time. They've fought a war and they want their share of prosperity. When they believe McKinnon and his country boys can give it to them and I can't, I'm out. I know that.''

Madeleine gave his arm a sharp slap. ''I will not permit such talk! You must be gay on a night like this. Come on—I've brought you a case of Dom Pérignon as a present.''

''You're very good to me,'' he said, giving her a friendly wink.

''And you,'' she said smoothly, ''are very good to me, too.'' They began to approach the laughing group standing at the entrance to the marquee Marjorie Murphy had had erected on the back lawn. Madeleine withdrew her hand from his arm. ''Your wife is frowning,'' she said with a tiny laugh. ''That is not good for her face, I think. She will have to summon her masseuse immediately to get rid of the line on the forehead. I had better join Sir Hubert . . .'' and she slipped away, walking smoothly on tiny high heels across the grass. Col watched her go with a grin. He'd hear about this from Marjorie tomorrow . . . *But I'm entitled to have a few of my friends,* he thought. *It's my bash, after all . . . although I'd rather be down in the bar with Franko and the boys . . . or dancing in the streets down in Surrey Hills . . .*

He put on his hearty smile as he moved among the crowd.

"Hello Melvin, good to see you, glad you came Ginny, darling, nice of you to celebrate with me, Patti . . ." He moved among them with ease, slapping backs, shaking hands, brushing kisses on cheeks. Marjorie, as usual was at the center—a Paris-dressed sun around which lesser planets radiated.

"Oh, there you are, darling," she said to Col. "Colonel Neville is here. Isn't that nice of him?" She took his arm, possessively. When he was close enough she muttered, "Where the hell were you? I thought at least you'd have sense enough to stay around on an occasion like this!" She turned to the portly red-faced man, sweating in immaculate tails. "Here he is, Colonel. Can I get you another drink?"

The two men stared at each other, measuring strength like two boxers entering the same ring.

"Have some champers, Colonel," Col said, grabbing a glass from a passing tray.

"Don't mind if I do," Neville said, accepting it without taking his eyes from Col's face. "I suppose congratulations are in order."

"That's big of you," Col said, still staring without blinking, determined not to be the first to look away.

Neville smiled, a smile that didn't reach his small, piggy eyes. "Big of me, my arse," he said. "You've given me better sport than any premier before you. I've always got a bone to pick with you. You're always good for a rip roaring editorial. Between you and me, if McKinnon had really got in, I'd have had nothing to print for three years. We agree on everything."

Col did not smile. "I didn't think there could be two men that thick in one state," he said.

The annoyance did not register on the colonel's face. "Just make sure you keep your bloody unions under control, that's all I can say," he said.

Col actually threw back his head and laughed at this remark. "That's all you've been saying ever since I was elected back in 'sixteen," he said. "You've already called me unpatriotic, anti-productive, and anti-royalist," he went on. "There's nothing left to call me, is there?"

"But your majority's not what it was this time, is it?" the colonel asked easily. "You have to make sure you don't step on toes anymore, Murphy. In fact, one step wrong this time and I'll crucify you."

"Is that a warning or a threat?" Col asked, not sounding too alarmed. "I thought you'd know by now that I don't take anything your rag prints too seriously."

"It was a promise," the colonel said. "And if you don't take me seriously, you're a fool. All those people who voted for you take me very seriously, that's why so many of them voted for McKinnon this time instead of you."

Col smiled. "They voted for him because they want a change. It's human nature. One party in office for two terms and they always want a change, however well the bloke at the top is doing."

The colonel snorted. "With a majority of twelve, isn't it, I'd learn to take me seriously if I were you. I'm telling you right now, Murphy, I don't want to hear any more about slowing expansion, or halting the soldier settlement scheme, or any of these stupid anti-Imperial Preference statements . . ."

"In that case, Colonel," Col said. "You'd better close your ears. I'm trying to prevent a boom and bust in this state and you should be, too, if you had any sense." He drained his glass and held it out to be refilled. "They all want too much too soon," he said, "and even you should be able to see the danger of having England as our only trading partner. Another war like the last one, and she'll be wiped out."

Colonel Neville did register to this. His normally florid face became bright purple. "Another war?" he asked. "There will never be another war. Our young men did not die in vain, Murphy. They died so that another monster like the Kaiser can never arise."

Col took a meditative sip of his champagne. "I hope you're right, Colonel," he said. "Christ, I hope you're right."

"Your trouble, Murphy, is that you're so damned unpatriotic," Neville blustered. "Comes from being Irish, I suppose."

Col smiled. "Yes, I don't suppose my ancestors had too much love for the British . . ." He looked around, hoping for escape, and found it. "I think our mutual friend has someone you'd like to meet," he said, indicating across the marquee where Madeleine could be seen, entering with Sir Hubert. "He's just back from England. He can give you the latest from Parliament. Also the latest gossip, which is what your rag thrives on, isn't it?"

He did not wait for an answer but crossed to meet Madeleine.

"My dear," he said easily. "I think you know Colonel Neville," The two bowed to each other. "And Sir Hubert Townsley recently arrived from the old country. Sir Hubert, I'd like you to meet Colonel Neville, one of our more flamboyant newspaper owners."

"Ah, the famous Colonel Neville," Sir Hubert said. "They were talking about you at my club. England's staunchest ally, they called you. More British than the British, eh?"

"I don't ever forget our mother country, or our king," Colonel Neville said. "We owe everything to England."

"Yeah, including being shipped out here against our will, some of us," Col interrupted.

Madeleine laughed. "Our premier is very proud of his convict ancestry. It has become quite the *in* thing to own a convict ancestor. People are actually inventing criminals in their family tree."

"Not me," Col said. "Mine are quite genuine, but not criminals. Irish freedom fighters—that's not the same thing at all."

"Do you have any relatives left in Ireland?" Sir Hubert asked. "Because the Irish are still making the most confounded nuisances of themselves."

"I've got enough to worry about with Australian politics," Col said tactfully. "Don't have time to follow other people's squabbles."

Madeleine sensed the tension growing and stepped between the men. "Do tell us the latest gossip from London, Hubert," she pleaded.

Sir Hubert's face broke into a smile. "I've got one tidbit you'll want to hear," he said. "I understand that H.R.H. the Prince of Wales, is coming out here in June."

"How exciting," Madeleine said. "You'll have to entertain him, Col. I hope you don't forget me on your guest list."

"I think you'd be wasting your time, darling," Col quipped. "From what I hear, he's a bit of a pansy."

Colonel Neville snorted again. "He's a young man who's led a sheltered life," he said.

"So had I when I was his age," Col said. "But I still knew what to do."

"You can't miss an opportunity to run down royalty, can you?" Neville blustered. "At least my paper will give him a royal welcome."

"If he can read it among the typos and scandals on the front page," Col said. He looked up and stiffened. "Excuse me a moment, please. I've got to see a man about a dog."

He slipped through the crowd and took the arm of a thin, swarthy man with brilliantined hair who stood in the shadows of the entrance.

Madeleine took Sir Hubert's arm quickly. "And I'd love a stroll on the lawn, Hubie," she said. "It's too stuffy in here on a hot night like this. Please excuse us, Colonel."

The colonel bowed. "Madam," he said, and turned away.

"What was that all about?" Sir Hubert asked Madeleine as they came out of the tent and Col was nowhere to be seen.

"I imagine Col's gone to have a little discussion."

"Who was that man?"

"His name's Garglioni or Garbarini or something," Madeleine said. "He's in the import/export business."

"How fascinating," Sir Hubert said. "What does he import?"

Madeleine laughed. "My dear, you are so naive," she said. "By import/export one means drugs, of course."

Sir Hubert looked horrified. "What could Col want to discuss with him?" he asked.

Madeleine glanced over her shoulder. "Probably how much money his boss needs to pay for Col to let the stuff bypass customs, I imagine," she said.

Sir Hubert frowned. "He likes to live dangerously."

Madeleine considered. "I'm not sure its likes to or has to," she said. "He's been walking a tightrope for many years now."

Sir Hubert glanced toward the house where Col's bulky figure could be seen emerging from the French windows, coming back toward them. "Let's hope he doesn't fall off," he said.

Twenty

SARAH OPENED HER EYES AND FOCUSED ON STRIPS of sunlight on a white wall. The room was plain but not austere. The simple white chest beside her bed held a spray of fresh flowers and the pillowcases were trimmed with lace. A fan turned lazily from the high ceiling, making the room deliciously cool. Through the half-open window sweet scents wafted in and strange birds were calling, birds that Sarah had never heard before, some musical as flutes and others chatting to each other in secret languages. Sarah let her gaze roam around the room, trying to shake off the feeling of complete unreality.

For the past two days, since she woke in this room, she had been floating in and out of consciousness, dreams mingling with waking until she was not sure if the pretty red-haired nurse who offered her cool drinks and took her temperature belonged to the real world or to that of her fantasies. Her mouth could still taste the sickly sweetness of chloroform.

Any moment I'm going to wake up and find I'm back in the hostel, she told herself, sitting up a little stiffly to look out of the window. She took in flowering shrubs, green lawns sloping down to the glittering waters of the harbor, a yacht anchored at a neat wooden dock, and as backdrop, the tall buildings of the city across the water. She shook her head again. Nothing made sense anymore. Nothing had made sense since Madeleine Breuner had appeared and spirited her off in the gray Rolls to a tea with tiny cucumber sandwiches and thumb-size eclairs served from silver and Spode. After tea there had been phone calls and then she was riding in the Rolls again, this time with just a chauffeur and no Madeleine, crossing the harbor on the car ferry to the North Shore and pulling up outside an imposing three-story brick house.

She still did not fully understand what was happening to her, but let herself be ushered into a leather-furnished consulting room, as she had allowed herself to be escorted to the Rolls instead of jumping off a cliff. She should not have been alive at all at this moment, so there did not seem like much to lose. Madeleine had seemed so cultured and efficient that Sarah could only suppose she was a rich benefactor, in the way that fairy godmothers appeared in books. As a child she had not enjoyed fairy tales too much, never believing that pumpkins could turn into coaches or handsome princes could show up on white horses. Her own life had been one of such monotonous practicality, even to the same meal served on the same day of the week, for all of her twenty-one years. If a visitor arrived on Monday, he would get meat pie, since meat pie was always made from Sunday's roast. There were no excesses in her house—her father taking one glass of port after dinner every night and wine being offered with Sunday lunch. There were no extravagances either. New clothes were allowed when old clothes fell to pieces. In such a world ball dresses at the wave of a wand seemed hardly likely. Janet, of course, coming from the wilds of Scotland, had always believed in the wee folk and even told stories from her own experience of their existence: "And my own great-uncle it was, riding home, saw them dancing in the fairy ring, as clear as I see you standing there before me!" Even though Sarah had been very young when she first heard this story, her own common sense had dictated that Uncle Hamish could have been mistaken, riding home late at night, on his way back from the pub.

She smiled now at the memory of it. What would Janet say if she could see Sarah now, she wondered? Of course, Janet would be shocked, she remembered. Janet—so completely innocent about the ways of the world, would probably not even realize that such clinics as this existed. Sarah did not even understand fully herself what had happened to her. Madeleine had simply told her that she had made arrangements with a doctor friend and that, "everything would be taken care of and there was nothing to worry about." Sarah had accepted that, as she had accepted the ride home in the Rolls. She had accepted the murmured mention of future discretion in her interview with the doctor—who was tall and distinguished and did not rub his hands once. She had accepted the wad of chloroform placed over her nose with only a moment's panic, and had awoken to this pleasant room, where dainty meals were brought to her every time she woke again.

Since waking, she had only seen the red-haired nurse and had hardly exchanged more than a murmured thank you with her. As the effects of the anesthetic finally faded, she began to wonder about the future. When would she be allowed to leave this place? Where would she go then? Would she ever see Madeleine again? And last, but by no means least—was she definitely no longer pregnant? She had kept the latter thought pushed firmly to the back of her mind because she sensed, from the doctor's murmured warnings, that what had just happened to her might not be strictly legal. She didn't understand much about having babies, such things never having been mentioned in public at home, but she reasoned that somehow the baby had been removed. She tried to feel sorry for it, but instead only felt an overwhelming sense of relief. After all, it would not have lived anyway if she had succeeded in jumping off the cliff, so at least one life had been spared. She now had a future when before she had none. She could actually look ahead and make plans if only she knew what was to happen next. She had just resolved to tackle the red-haired nurse the next time food appeared when the door opened and, instead of the nurse, Madeleine Breuner swept into the room.

In a world of sterile whites and understatement, Madeleine appeared even more overpowering today, dressed as she was in flowing, flowered silk with pearls at the throat and a neat white straw hat, topped with a single ostrich feather. The scent of her perfume filled the room with an expensive fragrance. She gave Sarah a brisk smile and began pulling off her gloves. "*Mon dieu*, the traffic was terrible today. I think that everybody in the world is buying motor cars. At least one knew where one was with the horse. So, how are you feeling?"

Sarah had a ridiculous desire to laugh. It was like a parody of the times she had had measles or mumps and everybody who came to visit always asked the same question. Luckily she did not have to answer because Madeleine went on, pulling off her second glove with a flourish, "I have spoken with the doctor and he says that all is satisfactory and you are free to leave. That is good, no?"

"To leave?" Sarah asked. Was she just to walk out of here

and resume life in the hostel and hospital kitchen? Did she still have a job after several days of absence?

"I've come to take you home," Madeleine said, looking around the room as if she expected Sarah's clothes to be hanging ready to be worn.

"Home?" Sarah stammered. "Home with you?"

"But of course," Madeleine said.

"But . . ." Sarah began, confused by the fact that Madeleine was acting like a guardian angel but did not look like one.

Madeleine held up a slender, red-tipped finger. "No buts," she said, "and no explanations yet. The first thing is for you to recover fully. To get well and strong again and then we can talk about the future. I do not think you will find my house an unpleasant place to recuperate."

She strode across to the wall and rang the bell. The redheaded nurse appeared almost immediately, bringing Sarah's clothes, neatly folded. She helped Sarah to dress, under Madeleine's critical gaze. Sarah's clothes had never been very fashionable and now she was painfully conscious of their shabbiness.

"I'm afraid my clothing is hopelessly old-fashioned," Sarah began as the nurse buttoned up the back of her blouse for her, "and it wasn't even smart to begin with. My father didn't approve of . . ."

Madeleine held up her hand to dismiss the idea. "It is of no matter," she said. "Come, I have an appointment in the city at three. I want to see you settled before then. My chauffeur waits." Then, with a nod to the nurse, she swept out of the room ahead of Sarah. As they left, she thought she detected a look of sympathy, or was it even pity, from the young nurse. She pondered over it for a moment and then dismissed it. Going down the stairs and out into the bright sunlight where the gray Rolls waited, she dismissed any worries. She was alive, when she might not have been, and the world, bursting with color and sound and smell, was still a good place to be.

As she sat in the back of the Rolls beside Madeleine and drove down to the harbor and across on the ferry, she was able, for the first time, to savor the rich beauty of the country she was in. Her first encounters with Sydney had been so fraught with worry, fear, and depression that she had scarcely noticed its beauty. Now she reveled in the shining expanse of harbor, the white sails of yachts, the elegant passenger liners, the green lawns, and the expensive mansions.

The ferry docked at Circular Quay and the Rolls purred through city streets that Sarah had tramped, only weeks earlier. Then the gray buildings had seemed hostile and overpowering. Now the city seemed bursting with life and color, the bright summer dresses of shoppers mimicking the flowers across the harbor. The parks, lined with palm trees, were dotted with picnickers and small children. Further along a small crowd was watching an impromptu cricket match. Sarah stared at it all with wonder and growing excitement, feeling as if she had just emerged, a new butterfly from a long wait in a cocoon.

They left the city buildings behind, climbed a hill through a tumbledown Bohemian quarter, then dropped down through more tree-lined streets, back toward the harbor. Finally they swung in through impressive iron gates to a shaded porchway outside Madeleine's house. Sarah had only the scantiest memory of it before, her senses not having operated fully on that momentous afternoon when she had almost ended her life. Now she appreciated the full elegance of that shaded entrance, the pillars on either side, the stained glass of the porch, the marble hallway inside with its sweeping curved staircase. There were statues of Grecian goddesses in niches along the hallway. A half-open door showed a glimpse of a parlor decorated in rich brocades with elegant European furniture all ornately carved, its floor covered in a Persian carpet. The checkered marble floor stretched beyond the staircase and down a long passage with closed doors on either side. Before Sarah could look further, a maid appeared and, without a word from Madeleine, motioned Sarah to follow her up the stairs.

Twenty-one

SARAH PACED RESTLESSLY UP AND DOWN HER room. It was two weeks now since she had been led up those stairs, then up a second flight to an attic room. During that time she had seen nobody, except for the maid who brought her meals. She had been told, rather firmly, that it was on doctor's orders that she was to rest quietly until she was quite strong and well again and was not to walk around until pronounced fit. The room was prettily furnished with lace curtains and ribbons on the bedspread, equipped with a bookcase full of books and a desk with writing and drawing materials. A little stone balcony opened onto a view of the gardens, with glimpses of the harbor beyond. Sarah had sat out there in the dappled sunlight, enjoying the warmth on her body, eating the luscious fruits that were constantly placed in her room and reading her way through the shelves. For a few days this had been delightful. She felt like a spoiled child, able to indulge in luxury and indolence. But after a few days the luxury palled. She longed for company and activity. Her room faced the back of the house so she had no idea who came and went. The gardens below were always deserted, except for an old gardener who mowed the lawns. Birds landed in the trees below her window, but even strange birds lost their appeal after being observed day after day. Sometimes she had opened her door to hear voices echoing up from the hallway or muffled laughter, but none of the voices came up this high. So she sat, playing with her hair, trying out new styles and wondering when and if Madeleine would invite her down to be part of the household.

At night, as she tried to sleep in the complete silence, strange worries would creep into her mind. Why was she there? If Madeleine went in for rescuing young girls from ruin, why were there not more of them? At times she even wondered if she was a prisoner, since the maid evaded her many questions with a polite, "That's not for me to say, miss." But why would anyone want to keep a young girl as a prisoner—and least of all an elegant woman like Madeleine? If she wanted Sarah as a servant, why was she housed and treated so regally?

At last she could stand it no longer. She opened her door and stood outside, taking in the silence of the household. Then, very quietly, she walked down the stairs. She crossed the entrance hall and pushed open the door to the parlor. French windows were wide open, letting in the gentle breeze and sweet smell of newly cut grass outside. From a distant lawn came the rhythmic sound of the lawn mower. A grandfather clock against the wall gave a deep tick-tock as its pendulum swung back and forth. Otherwise all was silent, as if a sleeping spell had been put on the household. Sarah crossed the room, her feet sinking into the richness of the carpet and stood at the French windows. She was just about to go outside when there was a stifled gasp behind her. She spun around to see a young woman, no older than herself, watching her in horror. She was dressed, not unlike Madeleine herself, in elegant silks, and her face, like Madeleine's, was touched up with makeup and painted at the lips. Her hair, as flaming red as the nurse's at the clinic, was held with a mother-of-pearl comb in a shining coil.

"You must be the new girl that Madeleine spoke about," she said, in a voice that was upper class English, masking the slightest hint of cockney. "You'll be in awful trouble if she catches you down here."

"Why, I'm not doing anything," Sarah said. "I got bored sitting up in my room. I thought I'd take a look around."

"But not dressed like that," the girl said, eyeing Sarah's clothing. "If Madeleine saw you down here, dressed like that . . ." her voice trailed off.

She walked across the room and escorted Sarah firmly back. "We'll use the back stairs," she said, taking her down the hallway and up a flight of plain wooden stairs. "Just in case."

"Are you one of Madeleine's relatives?" Sarah asked as their feet clomped noisily on the uncarpeted wood.

The girl broke into real amusement. "Her relatives?" she asked.

"Then do you work here?" Sarah persisted.

The girl looked at her with interest. "What has she told you already?" she asked.

"Nothing," Sarah said. "Nothing at all. I've no idea why I'm here or anything."

The girl's face became a mask again. "Best wait until she tells you herself," she said. "She'll get around to it, when the time is right, don't worry."

"But I can't stand being cooped up in that room any longer," Sarah said. "When would be a good time to talk to her? As you say, I can hardly barge into a dinner party or something looking like this . . . but I'm beginning to feel very strange, living here at her expense, eating her food . . ."

The girl broke into a musical peal of laughter. "You're a rum one, you are," she said, this time with more than a shade of cockney showing through. "I wouldn't fret about eating her food, if I were you." They reached the upper landing with Sarah's open door on the far left.

"Do you live in this house, too?" Sarah asked.

The girl lowered her eyes, as if Sarah's gaze made her uncomfortable. "Yes, I live here," she said. "And I'd best be getting back downstairs. I'll be talking to you soon, I expect. When Madeleine thinks it's right. What's your name, kid?"

"Sarah," she answered, thinking it strange to be called "kid" by someone who looked no older than herself.

"I'm Renee," the girl said and gave her a warm smile.

Down on the ground floor the doorbell pealed, echoing across marble. Renee jumped as if stricken. "Oh my gawd!" she muttered. "I'll be for it, if I'm not down there," and she fled down the back stairs, leaving Sarah very mystified.

She was not to be kept in the dark much longer. Clearly Renee had passed onto Madeleine herself that Sarah had been found wandering around the house because the next morning, right after Sarah's breakfast tray had been cleared away, Madeleine appeared in Sarah's room, followed by a large older woman dressed from head to toe in black.

"My dressmaker," Madeleine said, motioning with her hand at the older woman, who bowed very slightly in Sarah's direction. She turned to the woman, "What do you think Claudine?" she asked. Claudine eyed Sarah as if she were a rag doll.

"She 'as ze look of innocence," she said with a strong French accent. "You could make good use of zat."

"Exactly," Madeleine said. "Old-fashioned, but not too old-fashioned. A *la recherche du temps perdu* . . . holding onto memories of things past . . ."

The dressmaker stepped up to Sarah and began to measure her. Sketches were made, swatches of fabric were produced, discarded, or approved of. Never once was Sarah consulted on shades that she liked or disliked, but she understood by the end of the session that a wardrobe of considerable size had been ordered for her. There was even a ball gown, falling in folds from the shoulders like the Grecian nymphs who adorned the niches in the hallway down below.

At least, thought Sarah, *I am not destined for the kitchen!*

"Madeleine," she began, "I wish you'd tell me what you have planned for me . . . nobody tells me anything. I'm very confused. I can't understand why you're being so good to me."

Madeleine threw back her head and laughed. "You don't see me as a simple benefactress, using her vast fortune only to ease the lot of those less fortunate?" Then as Sarah did not answer, but blushed instead, she went on, "But you are perfectly right. One of the reasons I chose you is because you are a realist. You see no reason to stay alive, so you decide to end life. I give you a reason and you take a chance on it because it is better than death. This is the type of person I like to work with."

"You want me to work with you?" Sarah asked.

"But of course," Madeleine said. "I, too, am a realist."

"What sort of work is this?" Sarah asked, "I'm afraid I have no secretarial skills or anything like that."

Again Madeleine laughed and exchanged a comment in French under her breath with the dressmaker who chuckled, too. Sarah was annoyed that their dialogue was too rapid for her schoolroom French.

"All will be made clear very soon, *ma petite*," she said. "You are healthy. You are ready to work, ready to learn. This is good. But first you must be made presentable. These clothes of yours are only fit for scrubbing steps. When my good Claudine has created miracles with her needle, when your hair no longer resembles a haystack—then we will think about putting you to work. But first you have much to learn. I will send you up a tutor."

She rose and walked to the door. Claudine cleared up her designs and fabric and hurried to catch up with her.

Next day the hairdresser came. Sarah had expected to end up with close cropped hair, like Madeleine's own, such as was becoming fashionable, but the hairdresser insisted she had instructions to leave Sarah's hair long. She trimmed a little, then swept Sarah's hair into a cluster at the back of her head, held it in place with pins, and teased little wisps of curls free around her face. When Sarah looked into the mirror, an elegant stranger looked back at her. After the hairdresser, another woman came in for makeup instruction and manicure. The first of the outfits arrived. To Sarah, who had never had anything more than the plainest clothes and had envied every other girl at birthday parties, the dress was beyond her wildest dreams. So was the accompanying silk underwear and even silk stockings.

"I'll never even dare wear these," she confided to Renee, who had brought the package up to her room and was now helping her to try on.

"You'd better not let Madeleine see you without them," she said. "Very particular about dress, Madeleine is, especially when you go out."

Sarah walked across to the window and pulled back the lace curtain. "I was beginning to wonder if I'd ever go out again," she said.

"Go out when you like," Renee said easily. "Madeleine doesn't mind, in fact, it's a good advertisement if you're well dressed."

"Does she run a dress shop then?" Sarah asked, light beginning to dawn. "We are like her mannequins?"

Renee sat on the bed, pushing the tissue-lined boxes aside and patted a space for Sarah beside her. "Madeleine's asked me to talk to you," she said. "I'm supposed to be your instructor, although I'd rather not be."

Sarah walked across and sat. Her back felt suddenly cold in the sheer silk.

"You want to know what's going on here," Renee said evenly. "Of course you do, cooped up in this little room, but Madeleine couldn't risk letting you wander around before you'd been properly instructed. You might bump into clients, you see. Get the wrong idea about things."

"What sort of things?" Sarah asked. "And what sort of wrong idea?"

"You see," Renee said slowly, "What Madeleine does here

is entertain men . . . not just any men, of course, just high-class ones. She's a real snob. Only ambassadors and lords are good enough for her. She's even turned down millionaires if they don't have the proper credentials."

"I don't understand," Sarah interrupted. "You mean she's like a hostess? For parties and things?"

Renee looked at her oddly. "My word, she said you were naive and you really are. Still, that's how she likes them. She doesn't pick anyone who looks like a tart."

"A tart?" Sarah asked. A memory flashed across her consciousness. The little girl who had left the hostel, who stood on the corner with too tight clothes and painted face and walked away with the sailor. That was a tart—someone who sold her body to . . . She looked up, an angry flush reddening her face, and stared hard at Renee. "Is that what happens here?" she demanded.

"Is what?"

"You know," Sarah mumbled. "Men come here . . . for . . . for . . . sex?"

"Not always," Renee said, shifting uncomfortably under Sarah's gaze. "Sometimes they're new in town and they want a pretty escort for the opera or a cocktail party—an escort they can rely on, who won't open her mouth and put her foot in it. Madeleine only chooses high-class girls, preferably English. Like I said, she's a proper snob, but she can rely on English girls. She's on the board of directors for the Church of England home for unmarried mothers. She's always scouting there for the right girl."

Sarah thought with black humor that she would not have escaped Madeleine's clutches even if she had decided to do the right thing. She shook her head, as if shaking might clear it of all she was hearing and did not like.

"Did she find you there?" she asked Renee.

"Not me," Renee said. "I'd have rather died than go to a place like that. I'd already had the baby when she found me. I've got a nice little boy, you see. I pay a lady to take care of him up in King's Cross. He's well looked after and I manage to pop in on him most days. It suits me fine. Men are just rotters anyway. Might as well make a good living off them, right?" She gave Sarah a twisted smile. "I used to be an actress in England. Pretty good one, too. Who knows, I might have been a star by now if I hadn't taken up with a no good lay about. I'm not top drawer like you, you can tell that, can't you? But I can be ever so posh if I have to. I can be French or even Russian. Always good at accents. That's why Madeleine likes me . . . we get a Russian count and low and behold I'm Olga from the Volga! Makes him feel like he's at home."

Sarah shuddered again. "But surely most girls won't . . . I mean, what makes Madeleine think that I'd be interested in something like this? What makes her think I'll stay?"

Renee shook her head as if Sarah was indeed very stupid. "You really are wet behind the ears, aren't you?" she asked. "Madeleine wasn't born yesterday, you know. She really has her head screwed on right and she hates wasting money. You'll stay because you can't leave."

"What do you mean, I can't leave?" Sarah asked indignantly. "She can't keep me here against my will."

Renee was still shaking her head sadly. "You just try it and see. She has her ways, Sarah. She traps us all. Just think what you already owe her: a couple of hundred for the abortion, another hundred on clothes and hair. Where would you come up with that kind of money? You walk out of here and she'd have you thrown in jail for nonpayment of debts."

"But surely a place like this is against the law?" Sarah asked, her voice trembling slightly, even though she fought to keep it even. "She wouldn't dare go to the police?"

Renee laughed. "The chief constable of the state is one of our best customers—so's the mayor of Sydney and even good old Col Murphy, the premier. They're all good customers. No, I'd say Madeleine had the law sewn up pretty well, and I think you'd have to agree that you'd prefer living a life like this to jail. The food's better for one thing!" and she laughed, merrily this time. Then she reached across to Sarah and patted her on the hand. "It's not such a bad life, believe me, kid. And Madeleine's tough but fair. She doesn't allow any kinky types, only good respectable blokes who know how to treat a girl properly and she pays fairly and the perks—well, the perks are not half-bad. If a bloke takes a fancy to you, why he might pop a diamond in a pair of stockings and send it round as a present. Some girls have even married old rich blokes. I remember Maisie and this wool broker went off together. Someone saw her at the Melbourne Cup last year looking a proper toff; and her dad had only been a vicar or something back in the old country. What was your family like, Sarah?''

''My family?'' Sarah asked, thinking painfully of her bedroom at Wickcombe, with lace curtains not unlike these. ''That's all past, now,'' she said with finality. ''I don't have a family anymore.''

''Wrong. You've got us now. They're nice girls here. Your type of girl. You'll like them—and I like you already. So don't worry about things, they're not nearly as black as they seem.'' She got up, patting Sarah's hand again as she did so. ''Don't worry. Madeleine breaks you in gently. We'll show you the ropes and it's not as bad as you're thinking. Some of the old blokes only want some kind words and a cuddle and you get paid just the same. And it can't be worse than lying splattered at the bottom of the cliffs, which is where you'd be now if you hadn't met Madeleine.''

Sarah ran her hand down the smoothness of her silk. It felt cold and lifeless, like the trout her father caught for sport, lying silvery and dead on the kitchen table. She shivered. She recalled jokes she had heard about a fate worse then death whispered at parties and never fully understood. Was any fate worse than death? she wondered. At least there are possibilities in being alive.

She turned to Renee. ''I know nothing at all about any of this,'' she said. ''You'd better let me know what I'm in for.''

Twenty-two

SHE STOOD OUTSIDE THE DOOR, HER HAND AN INCH from the polished brass handle and fought against the panic. The day had finally arrived. After she walked through that door nothing would ever be the same.

''I don't know what you're making all the fuss about,'' Renee had said in exasperation when Sarah had clearly shown her horror and disgust at a teaching session. "It's not as if you're a bloody virgin after all, so stop behaving like one." She had walked across the room, then turned to look back at Sarah. "We were all fallen women in the eyes of the world before we got here. That way Madeleine keeps a clean conscience when she goes to confession."

Sarah had wanted to argue then. She was not a fallen woman. She had fought against somebody stronger than her and lost. She had not deserved the proverbial fate worse then death, and she refused to be classed with the other girls she had met at the house who had taken up with unsuitable men, only to be deserted again. But after she went through that door, of her own will, she would be a fallen woman, by anybody's description—no different from Lily or Rose or Diana, the parodies of English upper-class virtue she had already met downstairs. They all still looked, at first glance, as if they had come straight from afternoon tea at the manor house, or from shopping at Harrods, or a stroll in Hyde Park, but there was something about them that made Sarah realize they were now parodies and not the real thing. Maybe it was the too wide, innocent eyes, the mascara, the clothes that emphasized figures in a way that no girl would have thought proper back home.

She thought of the conversation she had had with Diana the night before. Diana was a classic English beauty with ash blond hair and a perfect peaches and cream complexion. She confided to Sarah that she had been to Cheltenham Ladies College and asked where Sarah went to school.

"Nowhere," Sarah admitted. "My father wanted to keep me at home. He was worried I'd get ideas about normal households if I once got away from him. He hired me the most dreary governesses . . ."

"So your father was beastly?" Diana asked. "What about your mother?"

"I never knew her. She died when I was born."

Diana sighed, a sigh that seemed to come right from the depths of her soul. "My daddy was wonderful," she said. "He was vicar of a small parish in Shropshire and he was the kindest, gentlest man . . ."

"Is he dead, too?" Sarah asked kindly.

A spasm crossed Diana's face. "Not as far as I know."

"Then you could go home again one day," Sarah suggested.

Diana looked at her as if she were crazy. "How could I?" she asked. "How could I ever let them know how I'd let them down?"

After that she changed the subject and they spoke no more about England.

Sarah stared at the door in front of her. It was white, with panels outlined in gold. A very elegant door to an elegant room. Madeleine had furnished the whole house in the style of upper-class France as she remembered it—a miniature Versailles on Elizabeth Bay in Sydney. Inside the door would be a satin-covered bed, with quilted headboard and satin drapes above it, a brocade sofa and a small marble table with its bottle of champagne, or whatever the occupant of the room had ordered. Off the main room would be a discreet bathroom. Sarah had been through the ritual in her training sessions. After every session she decided at least ten times to walk out and risk jail and every time reason won over and she stayed. Could anything really be worse than skinning dead sheep, facing a lavatory with a spider in it, or even stirring evil smelling pots of stew in a hospital kitchen, dragging heavy carts through depressing wards full of coughing people and coming back for the night to a bleak hostel bed? When she weighed up decisions, she found that she could look in from the outside, impersonally assessing the pros and cons of her situation. Never once did she wrestle with the moral implications. It was as if the old Sarah, the Sarah who had good and evil drummed into her in Janet's daily teaching, had really died that day on the cliffs and only the shell of her body had walked back to the car with Madeleine.

You can't stand here all day, she told herself severely. If you don't go in soon, someone will come and then you'll be in trouble. Don't forget the poor old man is paying by the hour and will probably be dying of expectation! This comment even made her smile. At least she was still managing to hang on to her sense of humor! And maybe he's just one of those Renee told me about who only want to cuddle, she went on, determined to boost her morale. Madeleine did promise me an easy introduction, after all . . .

"Lytton Argus is a real gentleman, Sarah," she had said when she summoned Sarah into her office that morning. "In every sense of the word. And very rich. He breeds racehorses and he visits us every time he comes to Sydney. All you have to do is to be yourself—well-bred, genteel, and polite. He will do the rest. And if you please him, you will not find him ungenerous . . ."

Sarah seized the door handle and went in. The man who rose from the sofa to greet her was not what she had expected. She had expected men who visited places like this to look decadent and crude, their vices oozing out of them like Punch cartoons. This man could easily have been a minister of the church. He was slight and not very tall, dressed impeccably in a light suit with matching maroon tie and handkerchief. He had a cherubic pink face and wisps of baby-fine white hair above it. In fact, he looked like somebody's benevolent uncle who always gave gold sovereigns at Christmas. He bowed very slightly as she came in and his face crinkled into a million tiny laugh lines, as if it was fine porcelain that had cracked.

"How delightful," he said in a voice that was Australian rather than British, but not the broad twang she had heard until now. This was the clipped Australian of the elite. He held out his hand to her. "So you are Sarah. Madeleine has already told me a lot about you and I've been so impatient. Come and sit beside me on the sofa." He patted the brocade. "I've taken the liberty of pouring you a glass of champagne," he said. "I always think champagne goes down well on a hot afternoon, don't you?"

Sarah nodded and gulped at the glass. He reached out his hand and put it gently on her knee. "My dear, you are nervous. You don't have to be. Now, let's talk and get to know each other shall we? I always think that's a good idea. I like to visit friends when I come to Sydney. I want us to make friends. So tell me," he went on, "do you know anything about horses?"

"A little," Sarah said. "I used to hunt at home, of course. Everybody did. And we went to the races at Newmarket."

"Newmarket, eh?" Lytton Argus asked. "Yes, I remember. A bit cold and bleak for my liking, but I went there once to see a filly I was thinking of buying. I buy all my bloodstock in England, you know. If you like horses you must come out to my place one day. I'll show you around. I've got a couple of champion stallions—a derby winner whose son won the Melbourne Cup for me . . . "

Sarah listened politely, as she had been taught in the drawing room at home, but again she was fighting with the feeling of unreality. She was sitting next to a strange man, whose interest she had expected to be only in her body, discussing racehorses as if they were taking tea at the Corner House in London. She wanted to laugh out loud, to shout, to grab Lytton Argus and shake him—anything to make this absurd life make sense again.

He looked at his watch. "And now, my dear," he said in that same quiet, cultured voice. "It would give me infinite pleasure to watch you undress."

"Oh, . . . oh yes, of course," Sarah stammered. She got to her feet and began to unbutton the shoulder on her dress. She was glad that all the clothes Madeleine had designed for her were designed with the purpose of sliding off easily with no embarrassment. It would have been awful to have to reach around to the back and fight with unseen buttons in front of a stranger. The feeling of unreality continued. She let her silk dress slide to the ground and stepped out of it.

"Splendid," Lytton Argus said, as if he was watching one of his colts performing. "And now the slip." She slid down the straps from her petticoat and it, too, slid to the floor, leaving her in a brassiere and garter belt, attached to her silk stockings. He got up and came toward her.

"I think now you can do the same for me," he said. "There, I'll start you off by taking off my jacket." He slid it onto the sofa. With nervous hands she eased off his tie, then slipped off his braces so that his trousers began to sag.

"They unbutton," he said. "Three buttons I think it is." Her hands fumbled with the buttons of his trousers, horribly conscious of the warmth of the flesh she was brushing against. The trousers came down and she bent to help him out of them, like a nursemaid. Then she unbuttoned his shirt, sliding it off easily. She noticed that he smelled of baby powder. He was now standing, facing her in his underpants.

"I think we'll finish off the rest on the bed," he said, walking across and lying himself neatly on the satin sheet. "Come, we'll undress each other. I always find that most pleasurable."

With neat fingers he began to undo her stockings as she stood beside the bed, letting them slip down as he unhooked the garter belt. She looked down at his unclothed body lying beside her. His chest and stomach were pasty white and flabby, sagging even though he was not overweight. Incongruously, the flesh reminded her of the dough Cook used to let her make when she was a little girl. For a second she smiled as she was back in that big, drafty flagstone kitchen with its smell of baking.

Lytton Argus misinterpreted the smile. His hand lingered on her breast as he reached up for her brassiere and pulled it off. "Delightful," he said, running his hand around the breast as if it were a fruit he was testing for ripeness. "Now you may remove my underpants!"

She pulled them down, realizing as she did so that she was really observing a male anatomy for the first time. On him the male organs did not seem so frightening as she had feared. As her hand moved down with his underpants he trapped it, looking into her face with the expression of a cheeky schoolboy. She felt his penis move under her hand and had to fight the desire to pull her hand away. She eased off the underpants and he motioned her down onto the bed beside him. She noticed he was breathing heavier now, but that was the only indication of his excitement. He did not even hurry as he eased himself on top of her, one hand still caressing her breasts. She closed her eyes against the expected pain, but was instead hardly aware that he had entered her. She opened her eyes again, watching him as he began to move rhythmically but not urgently, his breathing becoming more of a panting, but displaying none of the violent abandon that she had expected from the act. It was at the same moment both a relief and anticlimax. She was able to lie there, watching the crystal chandelier on the ceiling, feeling that she should be doing more for him than lying like a statue beneath him. She was hardly aware that he had climaxed until he gave a gasp of relief and, almost immediately, pulled away from her.

"Most pleasurable," he muttered, lying back beside her. After a short time he sat up and smiled down at her. "I'm sure you would prefer to dress again in the bathroom. I know that most young women are sensitive about these things . . ."

"You . . . er . . . don't wish to use the bathroom yourself first?" she managed to ask in a voice that sounded almost normal. "Would you like me to dress you?"

He smiled. "That won't be necessary. Our hostess always makes sure that I am supplied with warm water and towels and that is really all I need. Thank you, my dear, it was most pleasurable. The highlight of my trip to Sydney. Now I already look forward to my next visit!"

He helped her up from the bed as if he was escorting a lady

from his car. Sarah scooped up her clothes and retreated into the bathroom. Once safely inside the closed door, she fought with the desire to vomit, pressing her hand to her mouth because she knew it would be insulting to a man who had only treated her with the greatest kindness. Hurriedly she washed and put on her clothes, trying to overcome the disgust and horror that threatened to overwhelm her. The worst thing of all was not that it had been so terrible. It had been an experience she had hardly even felt—so completely removed from Jake's brutal violation that it could have been a different act all together. The worst thing of all was that it had been so easy, as if it was now something that really did not matter very much.

By the time she came out of the bathroom, her hair and clothing both back in place, Lytton Argus had gone. But on the corner of the marble table, beside the half-empty champagne bottle, he had left a golden sovereign. Sarah picked up the coin and drained the rest of her champagne glass.

Twenty-three

THAT EVENING SHE WAS INVITED TO JOIN THE REST of the girls for dinner for the first time. Until that moment her meals had been brought up on a tray and taken alone, or sometimes with Renee, but as she came down from the room she had shared with Lytton Argus, Madeleine was waiting for her in the front hall.

"You did well, Sarah," she said. "Mr. Argus was most delighted. He said it took him right back to his youth . . . now, if we can only preserve that quality of innocence about you, we'll have them flocking to your door."

Sarah didn't know what to say. She smiled politely while inside conflicting emotions raged. Part of her wanted to blurt out she was hardly likely to remain innocent when Madeleine was deliberately corrupting her, while part of her was arguing it really wasn't so bad after all—more like a farce than a tragedy really, and with a golden sovereign tip every time she was not likely to remain Madeleine's slave forever.

Again it was as if Madeleine was reading her thoughts. "So—it was not really so terrible, was it?" Madeleine asked. She slipped a friendly arm around Sarah's shoulder. "I thought that I, too, would rather die, the first time, but one soon learns that living is preferable and living well is most preferable of all."

Sarah looked at her with interest as Madeleine led her down the hallway. It was the first time Madeleine had revealed any feelings at all. Madeleine caught her look and laughed. "You did not believe that I, too, started out like you?" she asked. "You thought perhaps I was born to this life?" She nodded to herself as if remembering. "I began like you, my dear Sarah. A privileged life, a townhouse in Paris, a country house . . . then I met a young writer and lost my head over him. What he wrote was inflaming Paris. He had to escape in a hurry and I went with him to Australia. I thought poverty would be romantic. What did I know, silly young girl of seventeen?" She laughed again at the memory. "I soon learned that poverty is not romantic, and my poor Jean-Jaques, he tried to make extra money without telling me. He got himself mixed up with the drug trade and his body was found stabbed in the Domaine Park. I had nothing but my looks. I owed on the rent and my landlord made me a proposition. I thought, like you, that I'd die . . . but then I decided: if this man pays me five pounds, why not find men who will pay me a hundred pounds?"

They reached the door at the end of the hall and Madeleine opened it. "I have been very successful, Sarah. If you follow my instructions, you, too, can be very successful!"

The door opened onto a long, white-clothed table, laid with silverware and fine china.

"Our dining room," Madeleine said. "We eat together here whenever possible. Just like one big happy family. You will join us from now on. Tonight you will meet your coworkers. They are all very nice girls, very much like yourself. You have already spoken to one or two, I believe." She gave that characteristic flourish with her hand. "I will be dining out, unfortunately, but I wish you *bon appétit*!"

Then she walked out, leaving Sarah alone in the room. Again Sarah fought with unreality. Even this room was a parody—the big happy family gathering for dinner around the table, or the new girl at the seminary being led in by the headmistress, waiting nervously to meet her classmates. The maid who usually waited on Sarah came in with a silver tureen containing a lobster bisque. Sarah smiled to herself. At least the food was better than at a ladies seminary. She felt really hungry for the first time in weeks.

On her way out the maid rang a small silver bell and immediately feet started to hurry from various parts of the house—the boarding school pupils running down for their gruel! They converged, talking and laughing, the ones Sarah had not met, eyeing her with interest. Renee took charge of her. "Over here, Sarah," she said. "You get this place."

"So this is Madeleine's latest find, is it?" a tall dark girl asked, draping herself languidly on a chair. She sounded completely English, but her looks hinted that she might have some genes from east of Suez. Her expression was not altogether friendly as she eyed Sarah.

"This is Sarah," Renee said, motioning to her.

"I'm Sheila, darling," the dark girl said. "I've been here five years, which makes me the old pro around here."

The others laughed at her pun. Renee introduced the other girls quickly as the maid began serving the soup.

"You're the first new girl we've had in a year—since Hettie left," Sheila commented. "I thought she said eight of us was enough. I wonder if she's planning to get rid of me?" She laughed, a deep, throaty laugh.

"You won't have to worry," Renee said. "I bet you've got enough put by."

"I'm not stupid, darling," Sheila drawled. "I'll let Madeleine pay my fare back to good old England and I'll run an exclusive dress shop."

Sarah looked from one to the other with interest. "Why would Madeleine want to get rid of you?" she asked.

Sheila laughed again. "Because I'm over the hill, darling. A lady who's approaching thirty can no longer project the image of virginal innocence."

"You didn't project it at twenty," someone commented and there was general laughter. Sheila raised an eyebrow. "I'm sure I didn't," she said, "but I never met a man who wasn't interested. Sultry beauties always have their lure."

"Would Madeleine really pay your fare home?" Sarah asked.

"Heaven knows, I've earned it many times over," Sheila said. "And she usually gives a little gift for devoted service. She gave Maisie a wedding present, even though she was taking away a good client."

"So she doesn't mind people leaving?" Sarah asked. "I thought . . ."

Sheila's eyes were sharp. "She doesn't mind people leaving with her blessing. But just try walking out on her and you'll find she does not forgive or forget."

There was a silence as the girls attacked their soup, each thinking their own thoughts.

"The food seems very good," Sarah commented to the girl next to her, feeling that she should be making conversation.

"Of course it is," the girl said. "For one thing Madeleine makes enough money out of us, and for another she wants us to be used to eating all the best dishes. She doesn't want to risk taking us to a party and having us say, 'What's this?' when caviar is offered."

"She takes us to parties?" Sarah asked in astonishment.

"Of course. How do you think we get business?" Sheila asked.

"When she's sure of you—that you'll behave properly in public and not put your foot in anything," Renee said, "she'll start taking you out to mix socially.

"Only she has to be very sure of you first," she added, "because she doesn't want to risk another Hettie."

"Hettie?"

"She started speaking to the wife of a client. Told her she knew her husband. Heaven knows what she'd have told her next, but luckily Madeleine came along and saved the situation. Poor old Hettie—one drink and she couldn't stop talking."

"What happened to her?" Sarah asked.

"She left," Renee said, looking down at her plate.

"I hear she went to Perth," one of the girls commented.

"I heard New Zealand," another added.

"I wonder if she didn't go on a long sea trip . . . and accidentally fall overboard conveniently far from land," Sheila said with meaning.

There was an embarrassing pause as each of them digested what could possibly happen to them if they ever broke the rules.

"So you see," Renee said, ultra brightly, "Play your cards right and you go to lots of exciting places—first nights at the theater, even down for the Melbourne Cup."

"Down to Melbourne?" Sarah asked. The scope of the future was becoming brighter. She had almost forgotten how she had to earn these trips. Renee nodded. "We go to embassy parties and race meetings with her and if anyone seems interested in us, she arranges to have a quiet word passed on that we're available. Only if the bloke is suitable, that is. She checks him out better than Scotland Yard first."

Diana leaned across the table. "I hear you met our dear Mr. Argus this afternoon," she said. "How was he?"

"Did he wear you out?" the girl sitting next to Sarah asked and there was general laughter.

"He was . . . very kind," Sarah said hesitantly, wondering exactly what was discussed around that dinner table.

"He is—very kind, indeed," Renee added. "One of the best. I wouldn't mind if they were all like him."

"They're not all kind?" Sarah asked suspiciously.

Renee's face was guarded. "Mostly they're decent enough. Madeleine doesn't let in the really kinky ones, but sometimes they've been drinking too much or they're in a bad mood. Cynthia got a black eye last year, didn't you Cynthia?"

A pretty little blond girl at the other end of the table nodded. "But Madeleine threw him out and told him not to come back."

"Doesn't she ever worry about making enemies of important men like that?" Sarah asked.

"Madeleine—worry?" Sheila asked, looking at Sarah pityingly. "Nobody would be fool enough to cross Madeleine. We had a man in here once from one of the gangs, demanding protection money. Poor man. Madeleine said sweetly, 'But I already have protection,' and the police arrived and escorted him away."

"I don't know what she'll do when we change chief constables," one of the girls suggested.

"She'll make friends with the new one," Sheila said.

A light began to flash above the dining room door. She got up, throwing down her napkin. "Damn, that's my light again. Parliament must have finished early. I hope Col won his debate or he'll be in a foul mood."

She swept out. Sarah could tell from the other girls' expressions that they did not really like or trust Sheila.

The girl next to Sarah, a serious, round-faced girl called Helen, tapped Sarah's arm. "Just be careful what you say to her," she said. "She is Madeleine's favorite and she's a bit of a bitch."

Sarah looked toward the closed door. "Those lights?" she asked.

"We each have one," Renee explained. "Yours will be number nine. When your light flashes, you report to Madeleine's office on the double, or you go right upstairs if you're expecting a client."

"Who was that Sheila was talking about in Parliament?" Sarah asked.

"Col Murphy himself," Renee said. "Only the very best for Sheila."

"I'm sorry. I haven't had time to get into Australian politics," Sarah said.

"Col Murphy?" Diana interjected, surprised. "Don't you ever read billboards? We've just had an election—where were you?"

"Not paying much attention, I'm afraid," Sarah said. "You'll have to educate me."

Diana blotted her mouth daintily with her napkin. "He's the premier of the state of New South Wales. Don't tell me you haven't heard of him? He makes the headlines every other day—he's always fighting somebody. He got in on the union vote and then married a wealthy landowner's daughter. He's still trying to court both sides."

A picture began to form in Sarah's mind: a train stopped in the middle of the night, the special coach, the noisy party, and the man who had winked at her. So much had happened since that she had completely put the incident from her mind.

"Who cares about his politics?" Renee interrupted. "He's a good customer here, even if he does prefer Sheila, which doesn't say much for his taste."

"Poor man, I feel sorry for him, with that dried-up wife of his," Helen commented. "I'd be popping in here all the time if I had to go home to her."

"Ah, but she's got the money," Renee said, chuckling. "He

may call himself a socialist, but I don't think you'd find him wanting to go home to a tenement in Paddington."

"I don't blame him one bit," Helen insisted. "All he's trying to do is find a way for everybody to have a good life, and isn't that what we all want?"

What do I want? Sarah wondered as she looked down at her plate. *I have been only existing for so long now that I've forgotten what dreams are all about. Will I ever find anything worth running toward, rather than away from?*

Twenty-four

THE NEXT DAY PASSED EASILY ENOUGH. NO CALL came for Sarah as she sat reading on the terrace at the back of the house. One of the other girls was writing a letter and Sarah couldn't help thinking how nice it could be to get mail, to keep at least some contact with the real world outside. She had considered sending back to the hostel for her few belongings, then decided against it. There was nothing from the past she wanted to cling onto, except for Jimmy's letters and those she always carried around in her purse with her. The girls at the hostel were welcome to her old-fashioned clothing and Jake Cotrell was welcome to the stuff she had abandoned there. Probably they all thought she was dead by now—vanished without trace, which was not a bad thing. But she did consider writing to Jessie. Letters from Jessie would have been so refreshingly normal. But when she came to put pen to paper, she found that she was ashamed to tell Jessie the truth and even more ashamed to lie to her. She had even invented a situation for herself as companion to a rich family, but when she came to write about it, she tossed the letter into the waste basket in disgust. There was no longer any point in having contact with the real world, since she no longer belonged to it.

The early evening, in contrast to the day, was a whirlwind of activity. Bells rang, girls rushed around begging each other to help finish their hair in a hurry. There was a big cocktail party on a yacht that Madeleine was taking several of the girls to. Sarah, of course, was not invited. She watched them go out, laughing excitedly, feeling a little like Cinderella watching the ugly sisters set off for the ball. When she went in for dinner, only Renee and Sheila were there. Renee had been to see her little boy and was pensive all through the meal, Sheila had had a difficult client all afternoon and was in a bad temper.

"I had to spend an hour with the stupid man while he showed me photos of his life back home," she said with a sigh. "You've no idea how dreary it was—wild boar shoots, pheasant shoots, they seemed to spend their lives shooting everything in sight. Most probably to hide the fact that they weren't any good at anything else. Especially not in the bedroom. I tried everything for another hour just to get the thing up, and in the end even I had to admit defeat. He kept saying it was because of his saintly wife, he felt so guilty, but I get the feeling he couldn't do much more with her either. These bloody foreigners. Why won't they admit that their way of life has gone forever and stop clinging onto stupid photographs. This one was an Austrian, I think, but I had a Russian who was just the same."

Renee looked up from her dessert. "Oh, I remember him—Count Streletski or something? He was the one who thought I understood Russian, and he kept taking my face between his hands and telling me things in Russian and I kept saying 'Da, da' and trying not to laugh!" She smiled at the memory of it. "At least it's nice to get paid for sitting there doing nothing but listening and looking at photos," she added.

"Are you joking?" Sheila asked. "I'd much rather have the wham, bam, thank you ma'am type. They know what they come for. Let them just get it over with. I hate playing the sympathetic ear."

Coffee was brought in. Renee got up. "I think I'll just go on up to my room," she said. "I don't feel like coffee tonight."

She walked out. Sarah watched her go. "Poor Renee," she said. "Is she always depressed when she's been to see her little boy?"

Sheila stirred her coffee forcefully. "Renee is a pain," she said. "All that fuss over a snotty-nosed kid. Thank God I'm not saddled with one, *n'est-ce pas*?"

"I can see you're not the sentimental type," Sarah commented dryly.

Sheila laughed. "Quite right, darling. That's why this life suits me to a T. No ties, lots of luxury, no horrible, embarrassing, emotional scenes . . . just perfect."

"But you said you wanted to go back to England and open a dress shop," Sarah reminded her.

"Only when I'm too old to do this," Sheila said dryly. "There's nothing sadder than an old woman pretending to be a girl. Besides, Madeleine won't keep me forever and I do have a longing to see the old country again. Don't you? Would you go back if you could?"

Sarah shook her head. "I don't think so," she said. "I've nothing to go back for . . ."

A light began to flash on the board. Sheila looked up in annoyance. "Oh damnation," she said. "I've done enough for one day. You go."

"Me?" Sarah asked, horrified.

"Of course you. You're the new girl. You get the assignments I don't want."

"But Madeleine said . . ." Sarah mumbled.

"Heavens above, you've been spoon-fed long enough," Sheila said impatiently. "Go on, hurry up. Madeleine will be very angry if you keep a client waiting."

"What about Renee?" Sarah asked.

"It's her day off," Sheila said. "God knows Madeleine gives us few enough days off. I thought you liked Renee. I thought she was your big sister . . ."

"I do," Sarah said, "It's just that . . ."

"Oh, go on," Sheila said. "There's nothing to be scared of. You're such a frightened little mouse. How on earth did you manage to get yourself pregnant if you're such an innocent little virgin?"

Sarah opened her mouth to say, "I was raped," then closed it again. She did not want this woman's pity. Whatever happened to her, she was determined not to lose the Hartley pride. She strode from the room with her head held high.

"What bloody took you so long?" a sharp voice demanded as Sarah opened the door to suite five.

"I'm sorry, but the girl who was supposed to be here was . . ." Sarah began then gasped as a large, florid man came out of the bathroom. He was wearing a military ginger mustache, a black velvet riding cap, and nothing else. Sarah had never seen anything quite as ridiculous or repulsive. She could not help thinking of the illustrations in Alice in Wonderland back in the nursery. If Tweedledum had been undressed, he would probably have looked very similar to this man.

"Who the hell are you?" he asked, looking at her through beady pig eyes.

"I'm Sarah," she managed to say politely. "I'm new."

"Where's Sheila?" he demanded.

"She's . . . indisposed," Sarah muttered.

"Is she, by god," he spluttered. "Bloody lazy cow."

The way his words slurred reminded Sarah sharply of Jake when he had drunk too much. She looked longingly at the door.

"Well, don't just stand there, get your bloody clothes off," he commanded. "And don't take all day about it. I don't pay to watch you standing there like a bloody statue."

Sarah tried to undress calmly, her fingers trembling violently with each button while he stared at her, playing with the riding whip in his hand. She got as far as her brassiere and panties. "You want me to take it all off?" she faltered.

"Of course I do," he bellowed. "Can't do much through your bloody underpants, can I?"

Sarah closed her eyes to force back the fear and disgust as she pulled down her panties and let her brassiere slip to the floor.

"All right," he commanded. "Now get down on all fours."

"I beg your pardon?" she asked.

"I said get down on all fours. Are you deaf?"

Sarah dropped to her knees and immediately felt something cold and heavy put in the small of her back. Cold metal clinked against her sides and something icy swung to touch the side of her naked breast.

"What are you doing?" she demanded, fear making her forget that she was to be pleasant at all times.

"Putting your bloody saddle on."

"My what?"

"Your saddle. You know what a saddle is?"

"What for?"

"So I can ride you, damn it," he said, easing himself onto her back, "and you won't ask so many fool questions when I get the bit in your mouth." He forced her jaws open, but before he could settle with his full weight on her, Sarah leaped up. Saddle and harness fell to the floor in a jangle of metal. The man fell backward, hard.

She was trembling so fiercely that she could hardly speak and she backed away from him. "No, I'm sorry, but I won't do this," she said. "I won't be treated like an animal."

"You're to do what you're told girl," he said, his face bright puce now as he staggered to his feet and reached for the riding crop. "I paid for you, you're mine for the next hour. Now get back there this minute." The whip flashed out and stung her bare buttock. Sarah let out a shriek of pain and ran to the other side of the bed.

"The hunt is on, tally ho!" he shouted and ran after her. "Got her!" he yelled as the whip came crashing down again, making Sarah stumble. She scrambled to her feet and dodged past him. She could feel the swish of the whip and hear its whistling as it missed her. She reached the door, wrenched open the handle and fled. She could hear him yelling after her, but she didn't stop. Unaware even that she was still naked, she ran across the balcony, making for the next flight of stairs to her attic. She was vaguely aware of a door closing, then Madeleine's voice echoed up through the house. "Sarah!!"

The voice was so commanding, so chilling that Sarah even paused for a moment, as if she had been caught sneaking down after lights-out by a headmistress at a very strict school. From the open door of suite two she heard a man's voice demanding, "Madeleine? Get me that bloody girl!"

She glanced over her shoulder, then resumed her flight up the uncarpeted stairs to her own room. Almost immediately the door was flung open and Madeleine stood there, cold fury on her face.

"How dare you," she said icily as Sarah attempted to pick up her robe and cover herself. She strode toward Sarah who was shaking so hard that she almost dropped the satin robe. "How dare you leave a client and make a spectacle of yourself," she said and she slapped Sarah hard across the face, almost knocking her backward onto the bed. "Now go back immediately and apologize, only put on some clothing first. If anyone had seen someone running naked through my house! What do you think this is—a common bordello?"

Sarah fought to stop tears that were welling at the back of her eyes. "I'm sorry," she muttered through chattering teeth, "I'm sorry, but I can't go back in there. I can't."

"You'll go where you're told!" Madeleine said quietly. "At this moment I own you. You dance to my tune."

"No," Sarah said, suddenly finding strength as her pride was stung. "You don't own me and if that's what you think, I'll walk out of here and go straight back to The Gap and you can watch me jump off knowing that you'll never recover your precious money."

Sarah's fight obviously surprised Madeleine. "Foolish girl, stop talking such nonsense," she said. "Now, pull yourself together immediately. I've invested a lot of money in you, it's true. You'll be no use at all to me if you crack under the least little strain."

"It wasn't a little strain. It was a huge shock," Sarah said, her teeth beginning to chatter again as she thought of it. "There are certain things I just can't do—I'm sorry, but I wasn't brought up . . ."

The clatter of high heels on the uncarpeted stairs made them both look up. Renee came running into the room, flushed with the exertion of sprinting up the stairs.

"Don't be angry at her, Madeleine," she called, even before she entered the room. "It wasn't her fault. It's Colonel Neville and he's in one of his horse riding moods again."

"Neville?" Madeleine asked, her voice sharp with surprise. "Who sent Sarah in to Neville? Where was Sheila?" she demanded.

"She said she was tired and told me I was the new girl," Sarah muttered.

"Mon dieu," Madeleine said under her breath. She motioned to Renee. "Take care of her, I'll have to quiet him down, stupid old fool. God knows what I'll have to think up to appease him or we'll be blacklisted on the front page. I do wish he wouldn't drink whiskey. It really doesn't agree with him."

Then she swept out of the room, leaving the two girls staring at each other. As the footsteps died away, Sarah felt suddenly weak and sank down on her bed. Renee gave her an encouraging grin. "Bit of a shock, old Neville, eh?"

Sarah put her hands up to her face and nodded. "I couldn't . . . I just couldn't do what he asked me to. I had no idea . . ." She looked up at Renee. "I had no idea such things existed . . ."

Renee grinned again. "You haven't seen the half of it," she said, "but Madeleine doesn't usually let the strange individuals in, of course. Only Colonel Neville's a different story."

"Why?" Sarah shuddered at the thought of him. She could still picture the piggy eyes, the rolls of white fat on his belly . . .

"Because he's a dangerous man, of course," Renee said. She sat down on the bed beside Sarah and draped a rug over Sarah's shoulders. "You know who he is, don't you?"

"No, I've no idea."

"Crikey, you really did live in a dream world before you came here, didn't you?" she asked. "How could you be in Sydney and not know Colonel Neville? Didn't you ever read *Neville's Weekly*?"

"It's a newspaper?" Sarah asked.

"Probably *the* newspaper for ordinary people," Renee said. "If he picks up something to expose—watch out. He helped get more police to control the street gangs than there used to be before the war. He helped get the soldier settlement money through when the soldier came home to no jobs. He's a very powerful man. Unfortunately, as you've seen, he can be a rather strange man, too." She began to braid the fringe on Sarah's rug as she talked. "That's why Madeleine doesn't throw him out and doesn't want to offend him. He'd be the wrong person to upset. If he did a big story on this place, he'd get public opinion to close us down in a jiffy."

"Even with Madeleine friendly with the police force and the state premier?"

"If there was a public outcry, heads would have to roll, wouldn't they?" Renee asked. "Besides, he's not such a bad old stick most of the time. Sometimes he comes here and he's as polite and normal as anyone. Other times he's decidedly odd—especially when he gets his horse riding fantasies." She laughed. "I think he must have been thrown by a horse as a child and been trying to get his own back ever since."

"Pity it didn't throw him on his head," Sarah muttered. Renee laughed and patted her hand fondly. "That's right, love," she said, "don't lose your sense of humor. You'll survive just fine if you keep your sense of humor."

Sarah shivered. "At this moment I don't see how I'll survive at all," she said. "I won't ever get used to this. Even a harmless little man like Mr. Argus was almost too much for me. I just haven't led the sort of life . . ."

"Neither had any of us when we got here," Renee said, "Except for our Sheila, maybe. Who knows what her past was? I hope Madeleine gives **her** a dressing down for sending you into the Colonel."

Sarah shrugged her shoulders. "Presumably she didn't want to go in there either."

Renee chuckled. "Sheila? There's not much she objects to, if the pay is right. She's a real pro in all senses of the word, if you get my meaning. I think she actually enjoys sex, for it's own sake."

Sarah shuddered and Renee saw. "I gather you never had a good relationship?" she asked. "You never knew what real love between a man and a woman was like? Well, let me tell you. It was wonderful. You feel like . . . well, nothing like this. I never feel a thing here, although the men like you to fake it, of course. It's good for their masculine pride."

"Are women supposed to feel something?" Sarah asked. "All I ever heard about was duty."

Renee laughed and patted her hand again. "You wait until you do feel something. You meet the right man one day, then you'll know," she said. "You'll wonder what hit you."

Sarah smiled. "I don't think that's likely to happen to me here," she said.

"All the better," Renee said. "Makes it a lot easier if you can feel nothing. You've got to learn to treat it as a business. You're doing a service for a client, just as surely as if you had to cut his hair or wash his clothes. Just think of it like that and it's easier." She got up. "I suppose I'd better go down and see if Madeleine has quieted the Colonel yet. She might have had to have a go herself."

"Madeleine does this herself?" Sarah asked.

"Not usually anymore," Renee answered. "That's why they become madams—because they can let somebody else do it for them. But she's not above doing a favor for an old friend." She gave Sarah a friendly wink. "You get some sleep. You'll feel better in the morning, and you can bet your boots something like this won't happen again. Madeleine will be more careful with you. After all, she doesn't want you to do a bolt, does she? After all that training?"

Sarah began to take out her nightdress and slip it over her head, finally covering her nakedness. "I only hope I can face the Lytton Arguses of this world again," she said. "The way I felt tonight . . ."

"Just don't take it seriously and you'll do famously," Renee said from the doorway. "After all, they do look pretty ridiculous don't they? Their little pink bottoms going up and down—panting and groaning and working up a sweat. If you think that you're being privileged to watch the most distinguished men in the country looking like bloody fools, then you can face any of them. Good night, love."

"Good night, Renee," Sarah answered.

Twenty-five

TRUE TO RENEE'S PREDICTION, MADELEINE TOOK better care of Sarah after the Colonel Neville incident. She did not ever tell Sarah she was sorry for the upsetting incident and it was never mentioned again, but she left clear instructions when she was not present as to which clients Sarah was or was not to see. After two weeks, Sarah found that she could face the door to a client's room without the horrible feeling that she was about to vomit. Most of the men, as Renee had said, were only there for the soft, feminine comfort and warmth they could not get at home. An elderly English peer talked to her about his spaniels for an hour, had tea with her, didn't even demand that she take her clothes off and left her a sovereign tip. Instead of facing one day at a time, and that with dread, she began to let her imagination slip into the future—planning what she would do when the pile of sovereigns in the handkerchief in her top drawer grew to a mound, big enough to spirit her anywhere in the world she wanted to go. The trouble was that her mind went blank when she tried to picture where that place would be. She could obviously not stay in Sydney and risk running into former clients at functions. She tried to visualize herself as a smart lady in London, but every fantasy of herself, climbing into a handsome cab to go to the opera was always tinged with memories of driving rain and biting wind.

At least, with the hope of more sovereigns being added to her secret savings, she could look upon Madeleine as a finite experience, which made everything easier to face. Likewise thinking of her clients as potential suppliers of her ticket to freedom spurred her to be extra charming and warm. She understood from Madeleine that there had been several compliments about her, and Lytton Argus prolonged his stay in Sydney, even though the Randwick race meeting was over, just to see her again. He had a huge bouquet of flowers sent to her and left her a five pound present.

"If you play your cards right, you could wind up as Mrs. Lytton Argus one day," Renee teased, "if his old mother ever kicks the bucket."

"His mother?" Sarah asked in surprise.

"Over ninety but still rules him like he was a schoolboy," Renee laughed. "I think the major reason he comes here is to do something that defies her. That's why he's never married. His mother never found a girl who was good enough."

Sarah was beginning to think that most of the very rich or very aristocratic led very strange, twisted lives. She equated their perfect manners, Madeleine's snobbery, to Jessie's open friendliness and Renee's warmth. At least you knew where you were with the lower classes. They liked you for what you were as a person, not for what you represented in terms of connections or financial gain. As it happened, she was able to test this theory the very next day, when she was summoned to suite one in the middle of the afternoon.

"Col Murphy is here," Madeleine whispered, with a touch of awe in her voice, as if she was saying, the Pope is here. "I don't need to remind you that he is very influential, indeed. The poor man is under a lot of stress. He uses us as a home away from home, so I want you to be as charming and warm to him as possible."

"I thought Sheila always . . ." Sarah began, but Madeleine cut her short with a brisk wave. "Yes, yes, but Sheila's unfortunately gone off to a beach hideaway with an American millionaire for a couple of days. Only don't let Col know that. I wasn't going to turn down that kind of money just to keep an hour free for him. Tell him Sheila is indisposed.''

The words brought back an alarming echo into Sarah's mind. She remembered Colonel Neville's face when she had said them. Why did Col Murphy always get Sheila? ''There's . . . nothing I should know about him, is there?'' she asked warily.

Madeleine laughed. ''I don't think I've yet met anyone who didn't like Col,'' she said. ''Now, make yourself you're prettiest and get up there.''

Sarah knocked then opened the door cautiously to suite one. Unlike most of the other rooms, this was a real suite, with gold-and-white-brocaded sitting room and bedroom beyond it. A decanter with whiskey was on the low white table, along with small finger sandwiches and a pitcher of lemonade. Sarah took in the room for a second before she noticed the figure standing at the window. He was leaning on the sill, looking out over the garden, resting on his elbows like a little boy. A big man—not fat, but big-boned—a Clydesdale rather than a thoroughbred, he had taken off his jacket and tie, throwing them across the back of an armchair, and his rolled up shirt sleeves revealed tanned arms. But the most striking thing about his back view was the mop of iron gray hair—springing in all directions in wild, wiry curls. Sarah remembered that hair from the train window. He continued to stare out of the window, as if he wasn't aware of her presence.

''Good afternoon,'' she said politely. He turned toward her with a surprised look on a face that looked more like a farmer, or even a boxer than a politician. Sarah noticed that under wild, busy eyebrows, his eyes were very bright—an alarming green and piercing—a young man's eyes in an old weather-beaten face. The eyebrows moved up and down, as if they had a life of their own, as he looked at her appraisingly.

''Who are you?'' he asked. ''Where's Sheila?''

In spite of the booming voice, Sarah instinctively did not find him alarming, sensing that this was no Colonel Neville and noting that the eyes had lit up with interest, as if someone had switched on a light bulb.

''I'm Sarah,'' she said politely. ''I'm new here and it's very upsetting to my morale that everybody I meet asks me why I'm not Sheila. I don't enjoy being everyone's last resort.''

Col Murphy's eyes gave a hint of amusement. ''I wouldn't

call you a last resort,'' he said, ''but I always get Sheila. I'm a creature of habit.''

''I'm afraid she's indisposed this afternoon,'' Sarah said, still politely.

He laughed loudly, ''Too bloody right she is,'' he said. ''Indisposed with a better offer. You can't fool a politician with double-talk. You're talking to the master.'' He looked at her appraisingly. ''I suppose you'll do,'' he said. ''Sarah, is it? Well, Sarah, how about pouring me a drink? I wouldn't be surprised if that's all you'll have to do for me right now. I'm too bloody wound up to do anything else, I think. Ten bloody days of this debate—sessions going on and on until midnight until I don't even know what my own position is supposed to be anymore! It's enough to drive a man to drink!'' And, as if to illustrate his point, he took a large swig, draining his whiskey glass in one go.

Instinctively Sarah leaned over and poured him another glass. He shook his head. ''Oh, no thanks, darlin'. I've got to keep a clear head or those bloody country partyites will crucify me. I want to go back and wrap this thing up tonight—I'm exhausting them into agreement. At least, I hope I am. I hope they don't exhaust me first.''

''What's the debate about?'' Sarah asked.

''You don't read the papers?'' he asked. ''It's the Prevention of Profiteering Act.''

''Some people would be against that?'' she asked.

''Too bloody right,'' he said. ''I'm against it, for one.''

''You are?'' she looked amazed. ''But . . .'' she stammered, remembering that she was supposed to be warm and sympathetic to clients.

''But what?'' he asked aggressively.

''But isn't it a good thing to stop people taking advantage of other people. Doesn't profiteering mean that you give kickbacks to get contracts and that sort of thing? That can't be right.''

Col laughed. ''You know that and I know that,'' he said, ''but that's not how politics works. The unions like things as they are, see. They like the closed-shop theory and they certainly like to make their extra quid under the table—and it was the unions who elected me. I'm their champion. But, on the other hand, we have big business—the big construction companies and the transportation giants and they like things as they are, too. And they are the ones with the money who finance me—and I have to like things as they are because I'm the one who gets the under-the-table settlements when the government hands out big contracts."

"But that's terrible," Sarah blurted out.

Instead of looking angry, Col laughed. "Unfortunately that's how things work here. Politics here isn't like good old England with noble people representing honest peasants. Here it's ex-cons representing schemers and you walk over or get walked on. All you can do is to try and make sure every bloke gets his fair share of things. That's all I'm trying to do in a way."

"But if half the people get shut out on contracts, that isn't being fair, surely?" she asked.

"Ah—but it's not that simple, see? There aren't enough people in this state to finance things as they should be financed. We need roads and railways and hospitals. Sometimes we need a little help under the table to get things moving, to attract foreign capital to get projects finished and supply the jobs."

"That sounds like politician talk," Sarah suggested, "for rationalizing why you don't want to turn down any money that's offered, no matter where it comes from."

Col burst out laughing. "You're too damned argumentative," he said. "You must be bloody Irish, too!"

She shook her head. "Very English," she said. "Born in Suffolk. Pure Anglo-Saxon, I'm afraid."

"I wouldn't be afraid if I were you," he said. "It looks good on you—those peaches-and-cream looks. I can tell you haven't gone in for our latest sunbathing craze. Most Aussie beauties look as if they come from the West Indies these days. It's hard to tell the upper class from the Abos, only don't quote me on that!" He laughed easily. "You should see my wife. Spends the whole day toasting herself on a sun-bed, turning herself over and over like a leg of lamb . . . when she's not working on some strange keep fit-and-diet program. She thinks she looks good, but in actual fact she's beginning to resemble a prune—which, incidentally, she makes me eat at breakfast every day now." He looked at Sarah, speculatively. "I bet you don't look the least bit like a prune," he said. As he spoke he moved across until he was standing behind Sarah. He placed his hands on her shoulders and slid down the shoulder straps of her dress. With a rustle it dropped to her feet.

"Mmmm, white shoulders," he whispered. "How long since I've seen a good pair of white shoulders." And he leaned forward to kiss the back of her neck, making Sarah squirm. "You don't like it?" he asked.

"It tickled," she answered with a smile, not wanting to admit that she found it very disturbing.

He looked at her with interest. "You know, you're not a bit like the other girls here," he said. "I come in here, too tense to do anything but pace up and down and, instead of mopping my fevered brow and luring me into bed, you start arguing with me."

Sarah flushed. "I'm sorry," she said. "It's just that I'm new to this sort of thing and . . . and it doesn't come naturally to me."

He turned her toward him, his big hands still firmly on her shoulders. "Don't change a thing," he said. "I find it most refreshing. Sheila would have had my trousers off in two seconds flat and I'd have had to perform whether I wanted to or not, or go back to Parliament House feeling like a failure. I get the impression you don't mind whether we do anything more than this or not."

She was still embarrassed, not sure if this was a veiled criticism that Madeleine would eventually hear about. "I've enjoyed talking to you," she said. "You don't know what it's like, cooped up here. You begin to think the outside world doesn't even exist."

He laughed again. "Come and sit down," he said. "We'll talk some more and maybe even eat those bloody sandwiches. I can't remember when I had a meal last—that wasn't prunes, that is."

He escorted her round to the sofa and they sat. He took a tentative sip from his glass of whiskey. "So what's in the sandwiches?" he asked. She picked one up and took a bite. "Smoked salmon," she said. "They're quite nice." She offered him the plate.

"This is very unnerving," he said, taking a sandwich from her. "I feel like I'm having tea at a bloody English vicarage with an English lady who's only wearing a brassiere."

"I could put my dress back on," she suggested, "if it upsets you."

"Or we could try taking the brassiere off," he suggested,

"just to see if there's any flicker of interest this afternoon or whether I'll have to go back to the chamber a failure."

"You don't strike me as the sort of man who's ever failed at anything," she said.

"You're not wrong," he said. "I bloody hate to fail."

He took her strap and slipped it gently down her shoulder until her breasts were exposed. "Just as I thought," he said, appraisingly, "you don't look at all like a prune. More like a peach melba. I wonder if you taste like a peach melba?" He leaned toward her and speculatively ran his tongue around her right nipple. Sarah was unprepared for the jolt of desire that shot through her, starting deep in the pit of her stomach and sending an electric shock right up through her breasts. Instinctively her hands closed around his head, her fingers entwined in his thick wiry hair as she pulled him to her. He looked up, a challenging twinkle in his eyes. "I think I might be getting interested, after all. Let's go next door."

He took her hand and led her through to the bedroom. This time there was no languid undressing. He peeled off his clothes swiftly, grabbing her shoulders and lowering her firmly onto the bed. Sarah could not have believed that she had such passion in her. She was not conscious of time or place, just overwhelming desire, her whole body throbbing until at last there was a glorious explosion and they both lay still. Col propped himself up on an elbow, looking down at her with a grin. "Hot little piece, aren't you?" he asked. "You certainly had me fooled. And here I was thinking you were one of those prim English virgins."

Twenty-six

LYING ALONE IN HER OWN NARROW BED IN THE ATTIC that night, Sarah went over the afternoon again, not knowing how to handle the feelings that were still racing through her body. Every time she thought of her own abandonment, she felt her cheeks hot with embarrassment. Surely she really was now a fallen women, as described by drawing room gossip back in England. Nice women, well-brought-up women of her class should not react like that to the touch of a man, least of all to the touch of one who was not a husband or even a suitor. Why the one to have woken this passion should have been Col Murphy, she could not understand. He was not in the least the ideal man of her fantasies. He was neither elegant nor refined. He was old enough to be her father and was probably a rogue with moral standards very different from her own. She was not, like Madeleine, the kind of person who would be impressed at such close contact with someone of power. The fact that he was premier of the most important state in Australia did not matter to her one bit.

"Why?" Sarah asked herself, tossing and turning in the warm night. Was it just that Col Murphy was the first experienced man she had met, that he knew how to arouse a woman, just like a car driver knows how to push the correct buttons to get the motor to start? She hoped it wasn't just that. She hoped her body did not respond, independent of her feelings, to the right stimulus, so that any man, any future client could make her behave in that way again. She was therefore very relieved when she was assigned new clients and lay there watching the chandelier, feeling nothing but mild contempt, her brain filled with speculation about the size of the tip they would leave her.

She didn't see Col again for more than a week and was afraid that he had come to call and asked for Sheila instead of her. But he arrived, very late one night, and Renee woke her to tell her that Col was in suite one, and he was pacing impatiently.

"I suppose you're happy now, aren't you?" he demanded as soon as she closed the door. "Your bloody bill got through. Or, at least, a compromise version got through. I've just signed it."

"Not a compromise to your satisfaction, I gather," she asked with an inquiring smile.

He snorted. "No good will come of it, but the small-minded buffoons can't see that. No more closed shop in the building trades, no more fixed tariff on transportation. Just wait until the people out back-o'-Bourke find that nobody's willing to deliver goods to them on unprofitable routes!"

"No more money under the table for Mr. Murphy?" she

asked sweetly. He stepped forward and grabbed her, crushing her very close to him.

"Do you know what you are, you're a teasing little minx," he said, "and damn it, I've been thinking about you all week!"

"I'm flattered," she said, feeling herself relax in his arms, "but I hope I wasn't a distraction and responsible for making you lose the debate."

"You probably were," he said. "More than once I was about to say something and I heard your prim little voice saying it was political double-talk."

Sarah laughed. "I didn't realize I had the power to effect the political future."

"I think you know bloody well what power you have," he said. "Do you drive the other men crazy, too?"

"The other men haven't interested me."

"I bet you say that to each of them in turn?" he teased.

She shook her head seriously. "I always say what I really mean," she said.

His eyes held hers for a moment. "I believe it," he said.

"I've been thinking about you all week, too," she said quietly. "Don't ask me why."

"Have you, by Jove?" he asked. "And what have you been thinking? How you're going to reform an old reprobate and turn him into an honest man and make Australia a green and pleasant land?"

She shook her head embarrassed to her confession that he attracted her so wildly. "Nothing so lofty."

"You do have one fault," he said, eyeing her critically.

"What's that?"

"You talk too bloody much," he said, and kissed her full on the lips. Their encounter was a repeat of the first time, leaving them both lying, side by side, laughing to each other, as if they now shared a secret joke.

Col stirred first. "And now I suppose I'd better be going home, to the prune lady," he said, attempting to rise and put on his underclothes.

"Why do you come here?" she couldn't help asking. "Why don't you do this with your wife at home?"

His face clouded for a second before he grinned. "Have you tried making love to something with two inches of cold cream on its face? It takes that woman two hours to prepare for bed and by the time she's finished, you wouldn't recognize her as a human being.'' He looked down at Sarah with something approaching tenderness. ''It's more than that, of course. There never was what you'd call love between us. She had money and I had potential. She likes being Mrs. First Lady of the state and I need her money so that I don't have to live in a dreary slum with my constituents. We don't even share a bedroom anymore—not that she was ever interested to begin with. She's an Allcott, you know, of Allcott and Co.—the biggest overland transport company.''

Sarah laughed. ''Now I fully understand why you didn't want the freedom from protectionism!''

He dropped a pillow down on her face. ''Like I said, a teasing little minx,'' he said. ''Next time I come here, I think I'll ask for Sheila again. All she wants is a quick poke. She doesn't try to wrestle with my conscience.''

Sarah sat up, holding the sheet up to her breasts. ''No, don't ask for Sheila,'' she said quietly. ''I won't even open my mouth again.''

He turned back and ruffled her hair. ''Strangely enough, I enjoy your little sermons,'' he said. ''Much more fun than going to confession. Who knows, you might end up making an honest man of me before I die. Although I doubt it. I've already got my ticket down to the firey furnace.'' And he laughed as he finished dressing.

After that he visited Sarah at least once a week, sometimes more often, always unpredictably—midnight after a late meeting of Parliament, mid-afternoon during a boring debate . . .

''You'll be pleased to know that we're now moving on to the Fair Rent act,'' he said one day. ''I know that will please someone concerned with social justice like you.''

''Surely even you couldn't object to fair rent, could you?'' she asked, pouring him a glass of whiskey and putting it down beside him. ''Or do you secretly own tenements?''

''I just don't like being tied down with all these laws,'' he said. ''I can see too many possibilities. What if the cost of living goes up and the poor bugger can only charge a pound a week when the pound will only buy a loaf of bread? It's happened in other countries. It happened in Germany and France, didn't it? I like supply and demand to take care of themselves, only I have to go along with this damned rent bill because the working classes want it.'' He drained his whiskey in one gulp. ''I know that I claim to be a socialist,'' he said, ''because that's what this country needs. But between you and me, I have a feeling that if you try to stop the rich being rich, the whole of society turns into a shambles. Look at Russia. It will take them years to get out of that mess and all they want to do is be equal!''

Sarah decided that Col was not the blustering, loudmouthed Irishman he had seemed at first. Underneath that rough exterior lurked a very shrewd and deeply thinking brain. She began to understand his success: he could be all things to all people. To his followers in the unions he was a rough, no-nonsense sort of bloke who'd shout you a pint in the hotels. To his wife's family and their sort he was a person who knew what to do with money to make the most of it. To her he was fast becoming the cynical observer who tries his best against all odds to make sense of an absurd world. She also began to understand why he had struck such a chord of response in her. The response had been initially intellectual—he had treated her as an intellectual sparring partner and not as an object-woman. When she analyzed their relationship, she realized that he was the first man who had not automatically talked down to her or wanted to dominate. Even sweet, mild Jimmy had only wanted to protect and provide for her. Col enjoyed her company, not only in a sexual way. He was as happy to sit arguing as he was to carry her across to the bed afterward. She reveled in his companionship, feeling fully alive for the first time since Jimmy left England, almost three years ago.

She realized that her relationship with Col Murphy would not go unnoticed or uncommented on. Sheila accosted her one night in the dining room, when they were the last two to leave.

''I haven't seen Col in weeks,'' she said. ''I understand that he's coming to see you instead?''

Sarah tried hard not to smile. She decided it might be wiser to be tactful with someone as acid-tongued as Sheila. ''You were away with your American millionaire,'' she said. ''I had to fill in for you.''

Sheila gave her a critical stare. ''I can't think what he could see in you,'' she said. ''Maybe the poor dear just needed a rest. I do tend to exhaust them, the way any real woman would.''

''That's probably it,'' Sarah replied sweetly. ''Mostly he comes to talk to me.''

"I knew it had to be that," Sheila said, giving a condescending smirk. "I've never yet found the man who would turn down the chance of going to bed with me for the chance to go to bed with someone else. I should think making love to you is like eating cucumber sandwiches compared to . . ."

"Curry?" Sarah could not resist asking sweetly as she left the room.

She couldn't wait to tell Col about Sheila's reaction. It was wonderful to know that there was someone in the world that she could finally share things with. Renee was kind, but they were not on the same wavelength. Sarah could tell that she was bitter about men, and her own experiences had led her to dismiss them all as no good. In fact, the only male in her life was her little boy, whom she worshiped. Sarah secretly felt that she could never feel like that about a child and was thankful that her maternal instincts had not, after all, had a chance to be tested.

Instead she reveled in her first tastes of freedom. Madeleine was not generous in time off and not very trusting about letting her girls wander around the city, but as the weeks turned into months, she allowed Sarah more and more freedom. Sarah began to make the most of the fall weather, wandering through the botanical gardens and delighting in the flowers and shrubs, the tree ferns and palms. She visited the art galleries and rode the harbor ferries, content to feel the wind in her face and the salt spray in her hair. From the ferry she could look at Madeleine's house on the bay thinking that from the water it did not look imposing at all—just one small unit in one large, sprawling city.

With Renee as guide and companion, she had also discovered the pleasures of shopping. For the first time in her life she had money of her own and freedom to spend it. Although the hidden pile of sovereigns had been sacred—her ransom from slavery, she had thought it, she now felt the urge to escape less urgently and could be persuaded by Renee to accompany her to a sale at one of the big stores in town. At Renee's urging, she opened a bank account with her savings, because, as Renee put it, "I wouldn't trust some of those girls farther than I could throw them—Madeleine neither!" She could even be persuaded to indulge in frivolous items: a new hat in the latest cloche design, or even a pair of silk stockings, which cost an average person a whole day's pay! It was fun to realize that you needed nobody's approval to buy or wear things. Madeleine, of course, encouraged the shopping expeditions because they got rid of money and kept her girls dependent on her. As far as salary went, Sarah found that it would take six months to pay off her debts to Madeleine before she saw a penny of her own earnings. Perhaps the customers realized this and were therefore generous with tips.

One day she was shopping in David Jones's department store with Renee. The winter collection was in and the girls were admiring the jackets trimmed with fur. Sarah was skeptical that it would ever get cold enough to warrant the expense of a fur-trimmed jacket and Renee was trying to persuade her that she looked the "cat's whisker" in the red fox, when there was a commotion behind them and assistants desperately ran for chairs as three women came into the department. Sarah glanced at Renee in amusement as the assistants nearly fell over each other, scraping and bowing as if royalty had just entered. Renee did not smile back. She glanced nervously over her shoulder, then tried to draw Sarah's attention back to the virtues of the fox fur.

"Something in a dark mink, maybe?" she heard an authoritative voice ask, and an assistant's groveling answer, "Oh, a very wise choice, indeed, Mrs. Murphy. We have a consignment of beautiful minks, just arrived from London."

Sarah could not resist turning round. It was obvious who Mrs. Murphy was out of the three women, since the other two were buzzing around her like bees around a jam pot. The first thing Sarah noticed was that this woman in no way resembled a prune. She had a perfect, ageless face, eyebrows plucked and clearly defined, merest hint of red lips, hair that was a shining blond cap of neat waves and clothes that shouted Paris in their cut and fabric. Suddenly the woman was aware of her stare. Her cool gray eyes met Sarah's, she gave a quick appraisal of the girl's appearance, then she looked away.

"And maybe a silver fox might be interesting," she called after the disappearing assistant.

Sarah pulled off the coat. "Let's go, Renee," she whispered. "I don't like this at all."

"You're going to have to learn to act normally around client's wives," Renee said, taking Sarah's arm as the latter hurried out of the store. "It makes them suspicious if you panic. You'd better get used to treating them as if you don't know them or their husbands from Adam, or you won't get taken to any nice functions with Madeleine. You've no idea the funniest things wives have confessed to me about their husbands, never realizing for a moment that I probably know the old man better than they do.'' She laughed and squeezed Sarah's arm affectionately. ''Don't worry. It's always a shock at first, but you'll get used to it. She's quite a looker, isn't she—Marjorie Murphy? Of course she spends enough to keep looking that way . . .''

Renee chatted on happily as they walked down the stairs and out into the bright sunshine. Sarah heard words but was not conscious of their meaning. She realized that Renee had no idea at all why seeing Marjorie Murphy had affected her deeply. Renee had assumed that she was only embarrassed. She had not realized that Col Murphy had taken possession of Sarah's life until she had really come to believe that he belonged to her. Seeing that gorgeous, self-assured woman had reminded Sarah sharply that Col did not belong to her and never could.

''Let's go home,'' she said to Renee. ''I really don't feel like shopping in this heat.''

Twenty-seven

SOON AFTER SARAH SAW COL'S WIFE FOR THE FIRST time, she was invited to her first party with Madeleine.

''I think it's a little soiree you would enjoy,'' she told Sarah after she summoned her to the parlor one afternoon in April. ''Lots of English people. Sir Hubert Townsley is giving it for Nellie Melba, the opera singer, you know. He always gives a big party when she visits her homeland.''

''Will it be evening dress?'' Sarah inquired.

''Of course. Make sure you look your prettiest because all of Sydney will be there.''

''Including the premier?'' Sarah almost asked, then stopped herself. She wondered how she would handle meeting Col officially in public. She would be able to hide in a corner and ignore him, but she wondered if he wouldn't deliberately seek her out, enjoying the joke of making her embarrassed.

"Stay close to me," she whispered to Renee as the Rolls swung into the driveway of a North Shore mansion, "because I won't know anybody and I'm not used to big parties."

"Didn't your family have parties like this, back in England?" Renee asked, surprised. "I imagined you coming from the sort of family where they were always having hunt balls and that kind of thing."

Sarah snorted. "My father did not like people. We had relatives to stay occasionally and he let me go to a few Christmas parties and hunt balls, but they were always rather pathetic and I had to be home by ten anyway."

"And I thought the upper classes always lived such glamorous lives," Renee commented. "I imagined someone sipping champagne out of your slipper!"

This made Sarah laugh. "I don't remember anything like that. I have vivid memories of sitting like a wallflower, looking around hopefully for a good-looking man to appear and ask me to dance, but instead it was always some horrible, awkward son of a friend, asking me out of duty. He'd tread on my feet while he talked nonstop about whatever sport he was interested in or the latest hunt. Usually there were never enough men to go around and I sat with the other girls in wallflower groups while the few men there talked sports or politics."

"Sounds charming," Renee said. "Of course, I went to a few wild parties when I was an actress. I even had a couple of young peers interested in me. Just think, if I'd played my cards right, I could have been Mrs. Viscountess by now instead of this."

The chauffeur came around to open the door and the girls followed Madeleine in through the entrance hall. The whole house seemed to be milling with people, laughter echoing off the marble floor and high ceiling. French doors were open and the party spilled to the beautifully manicured lawns, now adorned with strings of chinese lanterns and white-clothed tables laden with food and drink. It was the sort of party one had read about in books—iced bowls of caviar, a whole salmon glistening under aspic, buckets of champagne, an orchestra playing discretely in the background, beautiful women and handsome men who all acted as if they were bosom friends.

They had hardly progressed down the hall when a distinguished-looking man in tails came up to embrace Madeleine. "My dear, what delight," he said. "How good to see you again, and looking so young. These two beautiful girls must be your sisters?"

"You flatter me, as usual, you old charmer," Madeleine answered with a delightful little laugh. "Sir Hubert, may I present my two nieces from England, Renee and Sarah . . . er, Hartley."

Hands were shaken and polite words murmured. The girls were swept out into the garden and introduced to the liveliest group. Again a feeling of unreality came over Sarah. *This can't be me, standing with a glass of champagne in my hand, making small talk as if I belonged here,* she kept thinking. She managed the polite answers expected of her. How did she like Sydney so far? Had she had time to go to the beach yet? How long was she planning to stay? Beside her she could hear Renee giving a good impersonation of herself. She had never had a chance to see Renee, the actress, at work, but hearing her now, she had to admit she was very good.

"And the hunt balls," Renee was saying in a voice as upper crust as the royal family's, "weren't they always so dreary? You remember how it was always the son of family friends who was forced to dance with one and he always stepped on one's toes and talked about sports?"

The group she was talking to broke into appreciative laughter. Sarah, now outside the circle of conversation, moved away. *I could never be like that,* she thought, half-critical, half-envious. *I have to be myself. I could never switch into a role, just to impress people.*

Behind her she heard a loud laugh and she turned in time to see Col Murphy, with Marjorie at his side, escorted across the lawn by the host, coming straight toward her. Col had not given any indication of having noticed her, and she looked around to see how she could melt into the shadows. Before she could move, however, Sir Hubert's eyes fastened on her, standing slightly apart from the noisy group around Renee.

"Ah, my dear Miss Sarah," he said, leading his charges toward her. "I know this is somebody you will want to meet during your stay here."

Sarah fought to keep the blushes from her cheeks as she met

Col's gaze. There was an amused flicker at the back of his eyes, but other than that his expression had not changed.

"Miss Hartley, may I present our state premier, Mr. Colin Murphy and his wife Mrs. Murphy. Miss Hartley is from England," he went on.

"How do you like Australia so far, Miss Hartley?" Col asked, nodding his head slightly in greeting.

"It's been interesting, thank you," she managed to answer calmly.

For a moment it seemed as if he was going to behave himself and she would be able to pass with pleasantries, but he addressed Sarah again. "And do you find us Aussies as wild and uncouth as you thought?" He was teasing as she had dreaded he would. She could see his eyes laughing at her. She had a sudden desire to show that he was not going to get away with this treatment. She wondered what he would do if she answered, "I gave you my answer to that in bed last week, have you forgotten?" Would he laugh that off or be angry? Then reason told her that such a reply would mean the end of his visits to her, and that was the last thing she wanted. If he was playing a game with her, she had to play along.

"On the contrary, Mr. Murphy," she answered, "I have been amazed at the standard of culture here. I trust you will be going to hear Miss Melba sing in her opening concert on Saturday?" She saw that she had scored a point without initially meaning to, as she remembered he had told her that he hated opera and was always being dragged to it by his wife.

"Unless I have unexpectedly pressing business in Parliament to take care of," he said smoothly, his eyes giving her the compliment of a touché.

"Are you intending to stay long, Miss Hartley?" Marjorie Murphy added with such emphasis on the word "long" that Sarah wondered if there was any more than politeness intended from the question. Did Marjorie Murphy have spies out so that she knew what was going on in her husband's life? The cool, elegant face did not betray any emotion, but Sarah noticed her eyes, wary as a snakes, dart from one side to the other.

"I'm not sure of my plans at the present," she answered, then as they gave no intention of moving away, "if you will please excuse me, I think I see my cousin summoning me over at that seat."

"And we must get ourselves a drink. Come my dear," Col said. He took his wife's elbow and began to steer her in the direction of the drinks' table. "I hope you enjoy the rest of your stay here, Miss Hartley," he added with a final nod in her direction.

"I intend to, thank you," Sarah replied, and walked with dignity until she was swallowed up in the shadows at the edge of the garden. Once safely away, she found that her heart was beating furiously. *How dare he!* she thought. *He actually enjoyed that. I'm just a source of amusement to him, that's all. He didn't stop to consider my feelings once.* Then, as she calmed down, alone in the sweet-smelling darkness among the trees, she realized that he could not have behaved any differently toward her without arousing suspicion. Probably he flirted with any young girl he met. If he had made an instant excuse to leave or been extra polite, it would have been more obvious that she was someone he did not want his wife to meet. She looked longingly across the grass. Col and his wife were now standing in the middle of a group of admirers. She could hear his uninhibited laughter and watched the animated faces of those around him. She was unprepared for the stab of jealousy that shot through her, angry with herself that he had come to mean something to her. For him she was nothing more than a way of passing the time, an alternative to a game of billiards. She turned her back on the scene and began to walk through the gardens, down toward the black waters of the harbor.

A voice nagged in her head that Madeleine had brought her because she expected her to socialize and that if she disappeared, someone would come looking for her, but she did not want to risk facing Col and his wife again. Surely Madeleine would understand that? She could hear the lap of water below her, louder now than the bright voices and snatches of music that floated across from the party. As she stood above the rocks, she watched a dark object float past, borne on the crest of a wave.

If I hadn't met Madeleine, she thought, *that could have been my body floating through this water and I wouldn't be worrying about anything anymore.* She considered the idea, then dismissed it. *And I would never have met Col either. For that alone it was worth staying alive.* Across the harbor the lights of the city were reflected in the water. A ferryboat passed—a moving finger of light across the blackness. She breathed in, enjoying the heady mixture of frangipani flowers and salt water. However strange life might be at this moment, it was worth being alive, after all. She began to walk on, wandering down the sandy path and out onto the jetty where two large yachts were bobbing. As she passed, a figure moved and she saw that somebody was sitting beside one of the pilings, a figure in evening suit, legs dangling over the edge, like a little boy fishing. He scrambled to his feet, a tall, gangly young man with light hair flopping across his forehead.

"I'm sorry, did I startle you?" he asked in a cultured English voice.

"A little," Sarah admitted. "I didn't see you until you moved. Your jacket blended in with the piling."

"It's very lovely down here," the man commented politely. "Did you come down to get away from the party or to admire the view?"

"A little of both," Sarah said.

"You're English, aren't you?" he asked. "Are you just a visitor here, too?"

"That's right," Sarah said uncertainly.

"I'm staying with Sir Hubert—our host. He's a friend of my father and he insisted I be here at this bean feast. I insisted I didn't know a soul, of course, but he said I'd enjoy it. Of course I was right. I didn't know a soul and the Australians are terribly parochial, aren't they? They are introduced to you and say 'How do you do' politely, then go right back to talking about the price of wool and other dreary matters."

They had walked together as they talked back to the edge of the jetty. He stepped down first and offered Sarah his hand to the sandy path. She accepted and nodded her thanks.

"Did you also wander down here because you didn't know anybody?" he asked. Sarah fought with the smile, wanting to say that it was just the opposite. She was here avoiding people she knew too well.

"I don't feel very at ease in big crowds," she said. "All that laughter and music at the same time was a little overpowering."

"I say," the young man said, "I know we haven't been introduced or anything, but I am sort of connected to the host. Would you allow me to get you a glass of champagne? I'm dying for one personally."

"Thank you, that would be very nice," she answered with a gracious nod, comfortable with the formalities of her youth. The path came out into the open, above the trees, and they walked up onto the springy turf of the lawns, among the swinging lanterns. The young man turned toward her and she was able to see his face for the first time—the boyish hair, flopping forward a little too long, the straight features, the slightly hollow cheeks, and the innocent eyes with eyelashes too long for a man—an exact copy of so many boys she had met and danced with and forgotten.

"I really should introduce myself," the young man said. "My name is Simon Bowyer, and you are?"

"Sarah Hartley," she answered, almost breaking off in mid-speech. "Did you say Simon Bowyer?"

"I thought you looked familiar," he said, a huge grin spreading across his face. "You're little Sarah, from Wickcombe, correct? We used to meet at all those dreary parties at your cousin Hugo's house."

"And you're Lord Belbrooke's son!" she answered delightedly. "I thought you looked familiar, too."

"I hope I've grown a little since then," he said, still smiling at her. "If I remember correctly, I only came up to the girls' shoulders at those dances. It was most embarrassing. For the girls, too, I should imagine." He looked at Sarah, analyzing her in the light of the swinging lanterns. "And you—you have certainly grown up a lot since those days. You're an elegant young lady. What a marvelous coincidence to meet you again. Are you staying here long?"

The question brought Sarah back to reality with a bump. Of course, it would be most awkward to meet him again. "I . . . , I'm not sure how long I'm staying," she said. "I plan to see as much of Australia as possible. I have an introduction to a family in . . . Perth." Her brain raced to think of the farthest point away from Sydney.

"Perth, really?" he asked. "I might also be going in that direction. I have an introduction to a sheep farm near there, or is it a gold mine? My geography's so vague."

"What would you be doing in a gold mine?" Sarah asked with interest.

"I'm supposed to earn my living by the sweat of my brow,

and in the process learn about Life, with capital *L*,'' he answered amiably. ''My father has sent me out here to make a man of me, in his words, of course. He was very annoyed when I enlisted for the war and got put in intelligence rather than fighting and dying in the trenches like a real man.''

''At least you are alive, which says a lot for intelligence,'' Sarah commented and Simon laughed appreciatively. ''How delightful you are, Miss Hartley,'' he said. ''You have certainly grown up. If my memory serves me correctly, you were a snobby little thing at those parties, hardly saying a word to anyone and sulking in a corner looking bored with the whole thing.''

''That's because I was bored,'' Sarah confessed. ''Everything seemed so stilted—you know, the conversations about last Sunday's hunt and the weather and everyone pretending they were having fun when they weren't. Anyway, there was no point in my enjoying myself because my father always whisked me away at ten, or earlier if I looked as if I was actually smiling!''

Simon nodded. ''Oh yes, I remember your father. Very objectionable type, wasn't he? Always had to be right.'' He realized that his comment might have gone too far and nodded to Sarah hastily, ''So tell me, Miss Hartley, what brings you to Australia?''

Again hesitation. He would obviously find out the truth when he was back in England, but he wasn't due back for a long while. ''Isn't travel supposed to be broadening for the mind?'' she asked. ''And sunshine is good for the health. I was always rather delicate.'' The last remark almost made her laugh out loud as she said it. She had been anything but delicate—a sturdy little thing who hardly ever came down with a cold and went out without gloves in midwinter. But it was the sort of phrase you always heard about women in England . . . ''Of course, she's always been rather delicate, poor thing. She needs some sunshine.''

Simon accepted it without query. ''But we must find some time to see Sydney together before we move on, I insist,'' he said firmly. He stopped a passing waiter and reached for two glasses of champagne. He toasted her silently. ''How long have you been here, Miss Hartley? Long enough to know your way around the city?''

"A little," she confessed. "I have enjoyed walking in the parks and gardens."

"And the art galleries? I am very interested in art," Simon suggested.

"There's a good art gallery and a good library," Sarah answered.

"And I'm dying to take a trip up to the Blue Mountains," Simon went on enthusiastically. "Have you seen them yet?"

"Er, not really," Sarah answered, not wanting to get into the details of her journey to the outback.

"Then we must hire a car and go together," he said. "What fun. Things are much more satisfying when done with a companion, don't you think?" he asked. Sarah smiled, thinking that such a remark would have Col rolling about with mirth. Then the smile faded as she began to think of the complications of seeing Sydney with Simon Bowyer. For one thing, Madeleine would probably not allow her the time off; for another, she could easily be recognized by somebody who would let Simon know what she really was now and could lead to his embarrassment as well as hers. It really would be fairer to both of them if she did not see him again . . . and yet she was loathe to let him go again, this specter of her former life, addressing her with all the correct formalities, making her feel that she was once again in her proper station.

"I, really can't tell what my hosts have planned for me, I'm afraid," she said. Out of the corner of her eye she noticed Madeleine, watching her as she talked. Would Madeleine approve of her standing alone, talking to a young English boy? Maybe it would be better to rejoin a group. "Have you tried the buffet spread yet, Mr. Bowyer?" she asked. "Everything looks so delicious."

Twenty-eight

"LET ME GET YOU A PLATE, MISS HARTLEY," HE REplied, springing into action immediately, like an obedient retriever. They walked down the table, discussing the merits of Australian oysters, Australian lobster, how good the fruit was.

"I always find lobster a little frightening, with all those legs waving at one," Sarah confessed.

"Go ahead, try it—sweetest flesh in the world!" a large man next to them commented.

"Better than the English lobsters, sir?" Simon asked politely.

The large man made a noise that was halfway between a cough and a growl. "Those puny little things?" he sneered. "Put two of them on a piece of toast and eat them as an appetizer. I take it you're newly arrived? I thought we'd met before somewhere?"

As he asked this, Sarah looked at his face for the first time. There was something horribly familiar about him. Suddenly she recognized him. This time he was not wearing only a riding cap, but he was, in his elegant dinner suit, unmistakably Colonel Norman Neville, the infamous newspaperman.

Her first instinct was to flee, then she realized that he hadn't quite placed her. As long as he thought that she was attached to Simon, maybe she was safe.

"We've only just arrived, haven't we, Simon?" she asked, turning to him, so that her face was not fully visible to the colonel.

He gave her a speculative glance, wondering why she had used his first name after her earlier formality, but went along with it. "Came out just before Christmas, sir. At least, I did. Which ship did you come out on, Sarah?"

Lie, Sarah commanded herself. *Bluff it out. Don't give yourself away.*

"I came out on the *Ormonde*," she said, noting that she had seen the ship docked at Woolomoloo just recently.

"You did? So did I," Simon said enthusiastically. "How come I never saw you on board. Were you hiding in your cabin, seasick for six whole weeks?"

"I . . . er must confess I was a little . . . I'm not a very good sailor," she stammered, praying for the ground to swallow her up and waiting for doom to fall as the colonel finally recognized her and boomed it out to the world.

"Then I won't take you on a ferry over to Manley," Simon said kindly.

"So where are you staying?" the colonel asked. He was now being the Australian ambassador, jovial to visitors. Sarah sipped at her drink, head down, desperately wondering how she could exit gracefully from this scene.

"I'm staying with our host," Simon said, not aware that anything was wrong. "Sir Hubert is an old friend of my father. They went to Eton together."

"Eton, eh?" Colonel Neville said, somewhat aggressively. "Know where I was educated? The school of hard knocks, that's where. Worked my way around the country, but it made a man of me!"

"I rather think that's what my father has in mind for me," Simon commented dryly. "He has furnished me with introductions to sheep farmers, gold miners, and deuce knows what else."

"Do you good, young man," the colonel said heartily. "But I take it the young lady will not be accompanying you on this expedition?"

"The young lady?" Simon asked. "Oh no, you see . . ."

Before doom could strike a miracle happened in the large form of Col Murphy, this time minus Marjorie. He flung a jovial arm around Simon and Sarah, asking loudly, "Are you boring these young people to death or hogging the lobster or both, Neville?" Then laughed loudly at his own joke.

The colonel's piggy eyes narrowed. "Surprised to see you here, Murphy," he barked. "Didn't know you went in for culture."

"I don't, but I can hardly refuse to welcome home one of Australia's greatest exports, can I?" he said. "As head of the state, it's only right."

"I'm glad to see you do something that's right occasionally," Colonel Neville said with a snort. "And I'm glad to see my Fair Rent bill is finally up before Parliament. Don't try to vote that down, or you'll be sorry." He looked around. "Where's your wife, or did you come out on the prowl alone this evening?"

"My wife's in the powder room, doing the hourly repair to her face," Col said good-naturedly, "but where's *your* wife, or did you come alone on the prowl? If so, you're prowling in the wrong neck of the woods here." Sarah felt a gentle squeeze on her shoulder, "because this young lady already clearly has a highly suitable escort."

"In which case the same goes for you," Neville said coldly.

"Me? I'm just an old friend of the family," Col said with his big laugh.

"Your trouble, Murphy, is that you have no class, no breeding," Colonel Neville snapped. "You can never sense where you're not wanted—which is in most of this state, as I think you'll find out next election."

"Do your damnedest, Neville," Col answered easily. "There's nothing I fear about that puny rag of yours."

"You'll find out one day, Murphy," Colonel Neville said icily. "You'll see which has more power over the people—my puny rag or your wife's money!"

Then he pushed past them and strode off in the direction of the champagne.

"Pretentious bastard," Col muttered.

"Watch your step, Col," Sarah answered, without thinking that she should not be talking to him here. "I wouldn't think he was a good man to have for an enemy."

Col laughed again. "There are no good men who are enemies, Miss Hartley," he said. "It's bad men who are enemies—don't you watch those cowboy and Indian pictures that Hollywood sees fit to inflict on us?" And he patted her affectionately on the shoulder before walking through into the house.

Simon looked at her with interest. "That was the state premier?" he asked. "He's an old friend of the family?"

"The family I'm staying with," Sarah answered, looking away from his intense gaze.

"And the other man?"

"He owns *Neville's Weekly*—the popular newspaper," she answered.

Simon shook his head. "I have a feeling that this country is not run in the same way as England," he said.

He took her arm. "There seems to be a seat free under that large tree. Shall we go and sit down, then we can compare notes in private about all the barbaric Australians!" Sarah allowed herself to be steered to the secluded seat, conscious of Madeleine, following her movement across the lawn.

Twenty-Nine

AFTER THE PARTY SARAH TRIED TO PUT SIMON Bowyer out of her mind. She did not want to admit, even to herself, that meeting him had had a disturbing effect on her. It had been like a mirror into the past, like remembering the steps to a formerly learned dance. He had asked the right questions and she knew the right responses, taking her back to a time when her security had been absolute. She had been shielded and protected by a domineering father, by a rigid society, by a loving housekeeper so that her whole life was one of little things—little duties, little pleasures, little longings. It was a life of the utter security of knowing that tea would always be on the table at four o'clock precisely every afternoon. She had chafed against it at the time, but talking to Simon had made her look back on it with nostalgia. It had been nice to belong somewhere and to know where one belonged.

At the end of the party she parted with formality from Simon, shaking his hand in very British fashion, hoping she would see him again while at the same time regretting that her schedule was very full and she might be embarking on a long tour any day. His eyes, as he took her hand, were hopeful and Sarah worried that she might have encouraged him more than she should. She realized that she had reversed roles from their last meetings. At the hunt balls it had been she who looked hopefully at departing faces, wanting one of those tall lanky boys to speak of calling on her soon. Perhaps they worried then that they might have encouraged her more than they intended. In any case, Simon's face still resembled her own face of six months earlier—innocent, trusting, and hopeful, and she could not be the one to disillusion him whatever happened. She told herself very firmly that however pleasant his company might have been, she would make excuses and not see him again.

The fact that Sarah had spent the evening with him had not gone unnoticed. Madeleine managed to corner her in the powder room, shortly before they were about to leave the party.

"So, Sarah," she said, calmly peeling off her gloves as she watched Sarah in the mirror, "you managed to snare the most eligible bachelor at the party."

Sarah tired to gauge from her voice whether she was pleased or displeased, and, as usual, could do neither. "He's an old friend I bumped into," she said, watching Madeleine as she brushed her hair. "I was not attempting to snare him. I've known him most of my life. He didn't know anybody at the party . . ."

"He's Lord Belbrooke's son, I understand?" Madeleine asked. "Our host has been telling me . . ."

"Yes, Lord Belbrooke's son."

"An eldest son?"

"Only son. He has three sisters."

"Ah . . ." Madeleine's sigh was very expressive, so expressive that Sarah had to turn around and laugh.

"Don't worry, Madeleine, I'm not getting any ideas in that direction," she said. "As I say, I grew up with him and lots of boys like him. It was like stepping back in time . . . It made me feel . . . comfortable."

"And the young man . . ." Madeleine asked, moving to push a curl into place, although it was perfectly in place already, "he pleases you?"

"He's pleasant, Madeleine," Sarah insisted, "which is not the same thing."

"But he would like to see you again?"

Sarah's face flushed. "I hardly see how that can be possible. You give us so little time, for one thing, and if he's seen with me, he runs the risk that someone will know where I come from and whisper a quiet word in his ear—which will be embarrassing for both of us."

"But you would not object to seeing him again, showing him the city, if this were possible?"

"Of course I wouldn't object. I could almost pretend I still belonged to such a world as his, couldn't I?"

Madeleine detected the bitterness in her voice, which surprised Sarah as much as it surprised Madeleine. She looked at Sarah, then smiled. "But you rejected such a world yourself, when you ran away," she said, "which must have been because it did not have enough merits to hold you."

Sarah smiled, too. "Too right, as Col would say," she said. "All the time I was there, I longed to be free of it."

"And with me you have the best of all worlds," Madeleine said.

"But belong to none of them," Sarah said calmly.

"Which might be the best thing, *n'est-ce pas*?" Madeleine asked. "Less heartaches all around."

"Maybe," Sarah answered thoughtfully. She put her tortoiseshell brush back into her silver purse. "Do you want us to tell the chauffeur we're ready to leave now?"

The next day she worried that he would call her and planned what gentle lies she could give him. But he did not call and she thought with amusement that he was like all the other boys of her past who showed interest while dancing and never called again. Had they all been too shy to call or had dancing stimulated awaking male hormones that had subsided after a good night's sleep and a shower? She hoped that Col would find time to stop by so that they could laugh over the party together, but the day drew to a close with no word from him. It was a very slack day. The girls sat around in the parlor, the French doors closed against the light rain that was falling. The doorbell hardly rang. They sat together at dinner.

Around nine Sarah's light flashed. She got up, conscious of the other faces watching her.

"How come she's so popular all of a sudden?" Sheila asked.

"Maybe it's affairs of state," Diana teased.

"It's not, I looked at Madeleine's book," Sheila said firmly. "It has to be someone we don't know about and why she should be called when the rest of us are sitting idle, I don't know—unless it's somebody else come to talk!"

One or two of the girls giggled. Renee gave Sheila a withering look. "Shut up, you lot," she said. "Sarah can't help it if she's called, can she. You know very well she doesn't hang around Madeleine wheedling for favors. You go along and good luck to you, Sarah love."

Sarah closed the door behind her, thinking how strange it all was. She was still new enough to all this that what seemed like a special favor to them, was still something she would rather avoid. She knew the money was important to all of them. They all, even Sheila, were counting on buying their way out one day. She wanted to buy her way out, too, but she still wished it did not have to be this way.

Madeleine met her in the hall. "A special client, Sarah, *ma petite*," she said with one of her rare smiles. "Make sure you look your prettiest. He's very rich . . . the negligee, I think."

"Is he up there already?" Sarah asked.

"He arrives shortly. Be waiting for him. Suite three, I think."

"Not suite one, if he's very rich?"

Madeleine laughed. "You will not need the sitting room."

Sarah went up and changed, taking extra care with her appearance. She held her hair in place with one or two pins, as she had been shown, so that it would cascade over her shoulders with the least little caressing. The men liked that. The tumbling down of hair signified the tumbling of inhibitions to them. She had picked up Madeleine's excitement. Madeleine never gave any outward hint of emotion, but Sarah could sense that she was pleased to have snared this particular client. Perhaps a visiting millionaire, Sarah thought. She recalled stories that were passed around the parlor until they acquired the characteristics of folk legends: stories of girls long past who were given yachts, set up with penthouses in New York, palaces in Paris, married oil tycoons or gold barons. Even a string of pearls or rubies would not be unwelcome, Sarah thought. Strange how one's outlook on life changed. Money had never been important to her before she arrived in Australia. Now money seemed to be the only thing that mattered—the one straw to grasp at in a sea of uncertainty. She had learned a bitter lesson over the last months: that the only true way to be free of other people is to have enough money.

There was a light tap at the door and Sarah called, "Come in." At least the new client would be polite. Most of the men would not think to knock first. The door was closed quietly and Sarah turned to look at the new arrival.

"I hope I'm in the right place," he stammered, "I was told that . . ."

He broke off and he and Sarah stared at each other in disbelief.

"Simon?" Sarah demanded. "What are you doing here?"

"What are *you* doing here is more to the point?" he demanded back, his cheeks almost radish color. "This can't be the family you are staying with. Your father would never have let you come to a place like this . . . but, perhaps, you don't even know . . ." He babbled on, trying to hide his acute embarrassment. "There's obviously some mistake. I've come to the wrong room. I got the directions wrong, or do you think this is somebody's idea of a joke?" He began to back toward the door again. "I'm awfully sorry to have disturbed you, Sarah. Most stupid of me . . . I don't know what you can think . . ." His hand reached the door handle. For a while Sarah was very tempted to let him go, to let him think he had somehow made a mistake, or that someone had played a trick. Then he would never know the truth about her and at least one person in her life would still think of her as the young girl from Wickcombe . . . Then reason took over. Why should it matter what anybody thought of her anymore? she asked herself. She could never go back to Wickcombe, so it really didn't matter if they heard about her there. Let her father hear. Maybe he'd enjoy knowing that she had ruined her life, or maybe he'd even suffer with guilt because of it.

"Don't go, Simon," she said. "I don't think you're in the wrong place."

"What do you mean?"

"I work here. I have a feeling that Madeleine fixed you up with me deliberately."

"But you don't understand," he pleaded, his face still beet red. "I came here to meet, I mean, Sir Hubert thought that I should . . . you see I've never . . ."

"Simon," she interrupted. "I can guess why you came here. Someone thought it would be a good idea if you got some experience with the right sort of girl . . . isn't that right?"

"You mean you're one of them?" he asked, the disgust and confusion showing on his face.

"I'm afraid so."

He sank down on the bed, his head in his hands. "I just can't believe it, Sarah. You poor thing. I've heard about it, of course. I've read all about the white slave trade. I suppose you were alone in a little café . . . they slipped a Mickey Finn into your drink and you woke up to find yourself a prisoner, destined for a place like this."

Sarah couldn't help smiling. "Not exactly," she said, "but believe me, I did not go into this from choice. It's a long story and I won't bore you with it, but I had nowhere else to go at the time."

"Couldn't you have written to your father if you were out of money?" he demanded angrily.

"My father told me I was no longer his daughter when I left Wickcombe," she said. "If I'd had somebody to turn to, believe me, I would have turned."

"But this is terrible, Sarah. I must get you away from here. I'll speak to Sir Hubert . . . something must be done . . ."

Sarah shook her head. "There's nothing you can do, Simon, unless you happen to have a few thousand pounds to pay my debts to Madeleine and set me up in a little cottage somewhere . . ."

Simon's face flushed an even deeper red. "You know I don't get my hands on any money until my father kicks the bucket," he said.

"And even if you did," Sarah said kindly, "it wouldn't be good for your reputation to rescue a lady of doubtful morals."

"Don't say that, Sarah . . . I can't even bear to hear it. You know you don't belong here. Are you being kept here against your will? I could talk to Sir Hubert, you know. I'm sure he could do something for you . . ."

"Simon," she interrupted, "Sir Hubert is one of Madeleine's good friends. He supplies her with clients, just like you. She also has many other good friends, like the chief constable and various politicians. I don't think Sir Hubert would want to risk getting mixed up in anything unpleasant. He likes his life the way it is . . ." She leaned across and touched his arm. "Simon—it's not nearly as terrible as you think. I thought I couldn't do it to begin with, but now it doesn't seem any worse than a lot of other jobs—no worse than stirring horrid smelling pots of stew in a hospital kitchen, which is what I was doing before this, or even skinning dead sheep on a station, which is what I was doing before that. At least I live very well here—I have lovely clothes, I go out shopping and to theaters, I eat only the best, and I meet some very pleasant, charming men." She smiled at him. "You can't have thought this was such a terrible place or you'd never have come here."

Simon coughed in embarrassment. "Let's just say that I wasn't very willing to come," he said. "It was a sort of coercion between my father and Sir Hubert. They both thought it was unheard of that a man could reach the age of twenty-one and still remain a . . ." he coughed again, rather than say the word.

"A virgin?" Sarah finished for him. "It's all right, Simon. You can't say much that would offend me anymore. I'm a fallen woman, remember?"

"I wish you wouldn't joke like that, Sarah," he said stiffly.

"I wasn't joking," she said, "and I agree it's not very funny, but we both have to face facts. I've learned to. I'm not Henry Hartley's daughter from Wickcombe anymore. I'm a high-class call girl, whether I like it or not, and someone has paid good money for you to visit me for a specific reason."

Simon's face had almost resumed a normal color, but he flushed scarlet again as he looked at her. "Sarah, I couldn't. Not with you."

"Wouldn't it be easier with someone you know?" she asked. "I wouldn't laugh or get impatient."

"I know, but . . . I just couldn't," he stammered. "It would be like being with my sister or something."

She smiled. "Last night, at the party, you didn't look at me as if I was your sister," she said softly. "When we were dancing, you held me tightly and you looked at me as if you'd like to do more than dance, wasn't that right."

"Yes, but . . ."

"I'm still the same person, Simon," she whispered. She walked over to him and put her hands gently on his shoulders. "But if you like, I can call in Renee. She's a nice person and very experienced . . . shall I ring for her and explain?"

"No, don't," Simon said, holding her arm as she began to walk across the room. "I'd much rather stay and talk to you. I've thought about you so much since last night. It was like . . . like a vision seeing you in a place where I didn't know anybody, and you're so beautiful now, Sarah. Couldn't we just sit and talk?"

Sarah smiled. "It will be an expensive talk, I'm afraid, and won't Sir Hubert and your father be disappointed if you don't achieve what they sent you for?"

He grinned like a little boy conspirator, about to raid the food cupboard at midnight. "They need never know unless you tell them," he said.

Sarah grinned back. "Then they'll never know," she said. "I'm afraid they gave us the suite without the sitting room, but come and sit on the bed and talk to me." She laughed as she saw his face. "I promise I won't attack, Simon," she said.

He laughed, too. "You must think me an utter idiot," he said. "It's just that I've never been in a bedroom alone with a girl before. My father already thinks I'm a useless pansy."

"You're not, are you?" she asked.

"A pansy?" he echoed. "I don't think so." He laughed nervously. "I really think I like girls—it's just that there has never been any opportunity, apart from the good-night kiss at the end of the ball. I've always lived at home, or school, or in army barracks during the war and, quite frankly, there's never been a girl who's seemed special enough to mean anything to me." He looked down at his hands. They were long-fingered, elegant hands for a man. He sighed. "My father—he's exactly the opposite of me, of course. He'd got a housemaid pregnant while he was still at Eton. He loves killing foxes and he adored killing blacks in the Boor War. He's that sort of man. I'm not."

"We can't all be like our fathers, Simon," Sarah said gently. "Thank heavens I'm not like mine or we would have killed each other long ago. Imagine two bad-tempered bullies in one house!"

Simon slid his hand across the satin spread and took hers. "You're so sweet and nice, Sarah," he said. "You've had a rotten deal, haven't you? I remember your father—he used to talk to you as if you were the dog."

"Not true," Sarah said with a light laugh. "He loved his dogs. He used to talk to his spaniel as if she was a baby."

"No, don't laugh," Simon insisted. "What I was going to say was that you're not bitter about anything. You can still smile and be pleasant."

Sarah stared down at the hand he was holding. How long ago

it seemed since a boy wanted to hold hands with her. Not since . . . she remembered walking down country lanes with Jimmy, feeling his big, warm hand covering hers. How special it had felt then, safe and protected by that big hand. Simon's hand reminded her sharply. "I'm a realist, Simon," she said, looking down at their hands intertwined. "There's no point in longing for something you can't have. I've always been a realist. I never allowed myself to dream of a home with warm, caring parents, just as I'm trying to accept the life I have now. Bitterness is a waste of time and energy. It just eats you up for nothing. Some of the girls here are bitter about men that deserted them. They hate all men because of what happened to them. I think that's silly."

Simon squeezed her hand. "I think you're wonderful, Sarah," he said. "Would you mind very much if I kissed you?"

"Why should I mind?" she asked.

"You might think it was—oh, I don't know, juvenile of me."

"I wouldn't think that, Simon," she said, moving her face toward his. He brushed her lips hesitantly at first, then took her in his arms, his lips surprisingly firm and warm against hers. Sarah could feel his heart hammering through the flimsy silk of her gown. His weight began to press her backward onto the bed. Then suddenly he broke away from her.

"I have to go," he mumbled, rising hurriedly from the bed and backing across the room. "I just can't . . . you have to understand." With that he fled from the room, leaving Sarah staring puzzled at the door.

Thirty

BACK IN HER OWN ROOM AFTER SIMON HAD GONE, Sarah wondered exactly why he had rushed out at the moment when his interest in her seemed to have been aroused. Had he remembered that she was "that sort of woman" and decided that he did not want her after all? Had he suddenly been overtaken by nerves or shyness, or was he really a pansy after all, trying to overcome his repugnance at touching a woman? She wished she knew and felt let down when she realized that she had probably seen the last of him. It had been so refreshing to be with him, with a young man who still behaved like a nervous suitor and did not expect to take her straight to bed. He was the very opposite of the average Australian: he was sensitive and gentle when they prided themselves on their bluntness and masculinity. Also there was something very appealing about Simon's boyishness—the way his hair flopped across his forehead so that he was continually pushing it back, and the way he blushed when any intimate matters were mentioned.

She sat at her dressing table, idly running the brush through her shining hair, wondering if things might possibly have turned out differently in her life, if only she and Simon had had a proper chance to get to know each other earlier. If only she had had a chance to know him better when they were both in England, maybe she would not have been so attracted by Lieutenant Jimmy. Maybe she would have made a suitable marriage by now and both families would have been happy—she broke off and smiled ruefully at her reflection—if her father had ever allowed her to marry anybody! He would have been loathe to let an unpaid housekeeper slip through his fingers, and his desire to dominate would probably have dictated that he picked out a husband for her.

I wonder if I would have been content with Simon? she asked her reflection. Her face, elegantly touched up with a hint of coloring, stared back at her. Her skin had lost its English whiteness and was a healthy light gold. Her hair was also gold-streaked from the sun. She had a hint about her of that healthy colonialism, which had made Jimmy Alison so attractive to her when she first saw him in that English lane. Would she really have been content with Simon and tea parties and the Women's Institute, or was there a part of her makeup that would have been lured by the open friendliness of someone like Jimmy? After all, there was a certain similarity in Col's bluntness that must have attracted her . . .

She finished brushing her hair and put the brush down on the table. *It's no good worrying about it*, she told herself, getting up and walking across to her open window, *because I no longer have the luxury of choice. My only choice now is to make the best of things or not.* Outside, the breeze on this fall evening still carried the scent of unseen flowers. She turned away from the window and got into bed.

She was glad that Col turned up, unannounced as always, the next evening, bringing things back to the reality of the present.

"Thought I was going to have to fight a duel for you at the party the other night," he said, laughing easily as he sat on the sofa, pulling her down onto his knee. "I thought young Lochinvar had come from England to claim his long lost bride."

"Oh, you mean Simon?"she asked, trying to sound unconcerned, as if she had almost forgotten the incident. "Wasn't that funny? He was one of the pimply youths I used to be forced to dance with at hunt balls and things."

"He didn't look very pimply to me," Col said, "and you didn't seem to be finding him very repugnant either—standing there in the darkness gazing into each other's eyes!"

"We were not gazing into each other's eyes," she said indignantly. "I was merely renewing an old acquaintanceship with a former neighbor."

"Oh, is that what it was?" Col asked. "It looked to me as if he wanted to undress you right there on the lawn."

"You sound as if you're jealous!" Sarah commented with amazement and secret delight.

"Of course I'm bloody jealous," he said, wrapping his arms around her.

"I could hardly have spent the evening hanging around waiting for you, when your wife was there, could I?" Sarah demanded. "Madeleine would have killed me, if your wife didn't first. And you were very naughty as it was, asking me all those stupid questions!"

Col laughed loudly. "You should have seen your face!"

"It was not funny! It was highly embarrassing," she said. "In fact, it's time somebody taught you a lesson—you're too bloody smug!" She tried to wrestle herself free of his grip. His grip tightened and the wrestling match ended predictably when they both slipped from the sofa to the floor.

"Now, what lesson were you going to teach me?" he asked with a grin, lifting his face just far enough away from hers to look down into her eyes.

"I hate you," she muttered, making him laugh again.

"No you don't," he said contentedly. "You're crazy about me, which makes it all very nice."

"You flatter yourself, sir," she said, holding his gaze. "I only do this because I'm paid to."

"Like bloody hell," he whispered. "If you come on to the other men the way you come on to me, you'd be an exhausted old hag by now."

"Get off me, you're heavy," she complained.

"Only if you tell me you're mad about me and you prefer me to that skinny, chinless English boy."

"He is not skinny and chinless," she insisted, "but I do prefer you to him. Not that I've had the chance to compare . . ."

"You're too bloody cheeky. You want me to start all over again?"

"I wouldn't mind," she answered.

"You know bloody well I can't," he said, lifting his body from hers and sitting beside her on the floor. "That's one thing a chinless boy can do that I can't and it's bloody annoying."

"I wouldn't worry about it," she said, smoothing down her clothes as she sat up. "One time with you is probably worth several with him."

"You're learning the tricks of the trade," he commented dryly. "You don't have to bloody win me with flattery."

"I wasn't flattering," she said, resting a hand gently on his shoulder. "I meant it, Col. When I'm with you I feel wonderful."

He turned to face her. "Feeling's mutual, darling," he said. "I only wish sometimes that things were different, you know. Marjorie tolerates this, but anything more . . . and bastards like that Neville, he'd have a hay-day if he could pin anything on me. He can't pin this place because I know that he comes here, too." He paused and looked up sharply. "He hasn't touched you, has he?"

"And he won't, don't worry," she said firmly. "He is one of the most repulsive individuals I've met, but I don't think you should antagonize him the way you do, Col. He is powerful, after all. He can sway public opinion."

Col laughed. "He doesn't really want me out of office because the opposition's full of bloody no-hopers and he knows that as well as I do. Country party la-dee-dahs who know the back end of a sheep but not much else. No, let's face it. This state needs me right now, and I have the feeling it's going to need me even more in the next few years."

"What do you mean?" she asked.

Col sighed and laid his hand over hers. "Everybody's too optimistic, Sarah. It can't last. The war to end all wars, they called it, but there's no sound basis for prosperity, that's the problem."

"And you can make one?"

"No. I can't do that. We're too dependent on England and America, and they're both in a bloody shambles, but I know I can do a damn sight better than the country boys. If they get in, they'll allow speculation and then boom and bust. At least I can keep a tighter rein on things and make sure the poor little bastard who came back from Flanders or Gallipoli manages to keep a bit of what he fought for."

"I'd no idea you were a philanthropist at heart," she said.

"I'm not," he said bluntly, "but it makes common sense. If one part of society crumbles, it crumbles for everyone. Any fool can see that. And it doesn't hurt me to stay in power either." He gave her thigh a resounding slap. "Come on, help me get dressed. I'm due at that bloody rent act debate in half an hour."

She watched him go, smiling fondly as he waved from the door, thinking how grateful she was for Col. At least Col was a dependable, real part of her life. At least he cared about her in a way, even though she knew that he could never mean any more to her than he did right now. It was good to have something to cling onto in life, something to look forward to. She knew that most of the girls who worked for Madeleine did not have that. Sheila didn't seem to mind. She enjoyed being with men and she enjoyed the luxuries that she received along the way. Renee had her little boy to live for, but the others seemed to have become smiling masks, shutting out their real selves. Sarah realized that she had never had a real conversation with any of them. She never knew what they really thought or were really feeling. She had no idea if they were consumed with loneliness or futility or despair. Sometimes she saw Diana sitting in a corner, staring up from a book with such emptiness in her eyes that it was frightening. But if Sarah ever tried to be friendly or ask her to join her on a shopping expedition, Diana declined politely—the vicar's daughter turning down an invitation to a tea party with gentility.

Sarah had never mentioned Simon to the other girls and had managed to put him out of her mind. He was merely an incident, best forgotten and she was obviously not going to meet him again. She was therefore very surprised to find a letter waiting for her on the hall table later that week. She had received no mail for so long that it was strange to see her name on an envelope. She was even more surprised to find that the letter was from Simon.

"I've rented a car," he wrote, "and wondered if you'd like to do some sight-seeing with me. I can't leave Sydney to do my grand tour of Australia without seeing all the things tourists are supposed to see first. I've cleared this with Madam Breuner, by the way."

Madeleine came into the hall at this moment. Sarah showed her the letter. "You don't mind?" she asked.

"Why should I mind?" Madeleine said smoothly. "Do you think I'm an ogre or something? Should I want to stand in the way of a blossoming friendship between two young people?"

"Why, thank you," Sarah mumbled, wondering if she would ever understand how Madeleine's mind functioned.

"Why don't you telephone him and tell him that you'd be delighted to accept?" Madeleine suggested.

Two hours later she was sitting beside Simon in an open topped car, driving along the esplanade at Bondi beach.

"I can't get over this," she said, smiling delightedly at Simon. "I never thought I'd see you again, and I certainly didn't imagine Madeleine would let me go driving with someone who wasn't even a client."

"I was a client, remember?" Simon commented, swerving to avoid a young man who dashed across the road clutching a long wooden surfboard, "and why shouldn't you have some time off? You girls should form a union. I understand they are very popular in Australia. Mr. Murphy was going on about the virtues of them the other night."

"Mr. Murphy was going on about a lot of things the other night," Sarah said.

He turned to look at her. "I take it you two know each other?" he asked.

"We have a slight acquaintanceship," Sarah said, staring

straight ahead. "Oh, look at the beach. Doesn't that look like fun?"

Simon brought the car to a halt and they watched as rows of bathers braved the large waves, being tumbled, or riding them in to be swept onto the sand. Several of them had boards and were riding the waves, hurtling effortlessly past their neighbors.

"You want to try it?" Simon asked.

"Only two slight problems," Sarah commented. "I don't have a bathing suit and I can't swim."

Simon laughed. "I don't think swimming comes into it in those waves. It's more a question of holding breath and keeping balance . . . and you could always buy a bathing suit."

Sarah continued to watch. "You know, people are so free here, aren't they?" she asked. "Can you imagine my father letting me do something like this in England. Everyone is so full of life here . . ."

"So you wouldn't want to go back to England again?" Simon asked cautiously.

"I can't go back to England again," she said shortly. "Let's go for a walk on the sand."

Thirty-One

OTHER AFTERNOONS FOLLOWED THAT FIRST OUTING. They drove up to the Hawksbury River and ate oysters at a little fishing shack. They spent a whole day driving up to the Blue Mountains, standing on the edge of the world looking down into silent valleys.

"I have to leave next week," Simon said casually as he poured her tea at a little mountaintop café. "I gather my father thinks it's about time I stopped loafing and started learning about Life, with capital *L*."

"Your father sounds as domineering as mine," Sarah said,

taking the teacup he offered. "Do you have to obey him half a world away?"

Simon shrugged his shoulders. "He's the one with the money, unfortunately. I'm completely dependent on him. I don't like it, but it's the truth. If I weren't so dependent . . ." he looked up at her and broke off in mid-sentence. "Sarah?" he asked, "you do like me, don't you?"

"Of course I like you."

"I thought you did. And you must know how I feel about you, too."

"Your family would call it boyish infatuation," Sarah said, fighting to keep the conversation light.

"I don't care what my family calls it," he said. "I hate to leave you at that place. I hate to think of you . . . isn't there any way I can get you out of there until I come back? Couldn't I find you a little cottage on the beach—you'd like that, wouldn't you?"

"Simon . . ." she said gently, "even a little cottage costs money and I have to eat. I still have about three months before I'm free of debt to Madeleine and can start saving. Don't worry. I'll get out eventually. Sheila has lots of money saved, but she's not anxious to leave. She likes it there."

"I can't believe that," Simon said with a look or horror. "Do you think you'll come to like it if you stay long enough?"

Sarah smiled. "I'm not like Sheila," she said. "I couldn't ever imagine living this way from choice."

Simon's face colored. "I feel so powerless," he said, crumpling his napkin in his hand. "If only I could do something for you."

"You have," Sarah said gently. "You've made me happy. I've enjoyed this time with you more than any time I can remember. I've never been so free, so relaxed, in my entire life. I've done so many things I've never done before, and you've been a perfect companion."

"Sarah," he interrupted. "If I make my fortune—I mean, if I can make enough money working in the goldfields or something—will you come back to England with me? I'm sure I could make my family understand—I'm sure they'd like you."

Sarah smiled uneasily, "What exactly are you proposing, Simon?" she asked.

He flushed even deeper. "I want to marry you, of course, but

I'd have to present it as a fait accompli. If we arrived home married, they couldn't do anything about it, could they?"

"Disinherit you the way my father disinherited me?" she suggested.

"I wouldn't mind," he said. "If I had enough to support you without my family, we could live quietly somewhere. I could get a job . . . You wouldn't mind doing without luxuries, would you?"

"Simon, let's not talk about the future," she said. "There are too many ifs."

Simon reached across the table and took her hand. "I will make something of myself, I promise you," he said. "I'll be back and take you away from that awful house."

She squeezed his hand. "You are very sweet," she said. "You're the one man I've ever met in my life who qualifies completely for the word gentleman."

All the way home she tried to behave as usual, making light, pleasant conversation and giving no hint of the turmoil going on inside her head. She kept thinking of one Christmas when she was about five years old. A friend of the family had given her a big china doll, almost as big as herself. It was by far the most wonderful present she had ever had in her life and she could hardly believe her good fortune. Then, the day after Christmas, her father's spaniel, returning excited from a snowy walk, had bounded into the drawing room and knocked over the doll. The china face smashed beyond repair and her father's only comment was that she should never have stood it in the way. This was exactly how she felt at this moment, the same bleak despair—that a wonderful present she had never expected in the first place had been offered and then taken away again, almost within the same breath. She hadn't intended to get so attached to Simon, and she certainly hadn't intended to think about a future with him. But he had brought up the subject—he had opened that forbidden door and now it would not close again.

Madeleine let her have the evening off before he left.

"I expect you'll miss him, won't you?" she said casually. "It's not often you find a man who is pleasant and rich and young all at the same time."

"Not rich, unfortunately," Sarah said.

"Maybe not he personally, but his family," Madeleine said.

"His father is Lord Belbrooke, *n'est-ce pas*? Now, if only you could land that fish . . ."

"You wouldn't mind losing me?" Sarah asked.

Madeleine laughed. "There are plenty more where you came from, *ma petite*."

They had dinner together at a little fish restaurant, overlooking the harbor, in the village of Watson's Bay, then they drove along the coast, past deserted beaches where waves gleamed in the moonlight. Simon stopped the car and climbed out. "You said you wanted to go swimming and we never did," he said.

"I still can't swim and I still don't have a bathing costume," she replied.

He laughed. "I don't think either of those will matter now," he said. "There's nobody to see except me."

They undressed down to their underclothes in the darkness of the car. The wind was chill as they ran over the sand, but the first water that rushed to meet them was warm. Simon took her hand as they walked in deeper. The waves were strong and the first almost swept her off her feet. She gasped, Simon's grip on her tightened and she laughed with delight as the wave passed.

"Let's go deeper," she yelled. They walked out, hand in hand, turning their backs on each wave, staggering as it knocked into them.

"Is it as much fun as it looked?" he shouted to her.

"More!" she answered. "Now I wish I had one of those boards and could come riding into shore."

Just as she said this, a wave, bigger than the rest, rushed upon them, knocking them both off their feet and snatching them apart. Sarah gasped as her head went underwater. Water was everywhere—in her nose, eyes. She was bowled over and over like a rag doll, unable to tell whether she was up or down, feeling the scrape of sand one minute and the roaring tumult of the water the next. Just when she felt she could hold her breath no longer, she was flung up onto the sand and the wave rolled her one last time as it receded. Coughing and retching, she fought her way to her knees.

Simon ran to her side. "Sarah—are you all right?" he asked, dropping to his knees beside her.

"I think so, if I can just breathe again," she stammered, panting as she pushed her hair out of her eyes and attempted to smile up at Simon's concerned face.

"You gave me such a scare," he said. "I managed to let the wave get past me and I couldn't see you. I was terrified you'd be swept out again."

"I'd no idea . . . water could be . . . so powerful," she said, shaking the drops from her hair and beginning to laugh.

"Do you want to go back to the car?" he asked.

"I've just realized," she said, laughing uncontrollably, "we don't have a towel!"

Simon began to laugh, too. "We'll have to run up and down to get dry!"

"And fly our underwear out of the car window like flags!" Sarah agreed.

He touched her, suddenly serious. "I adore you," he said. "You're not like any girl I've ever met. Other girls would be in hysterics by now . . . nothing phases you, does it?"

Your going does, she thought, but she continued to smile at him.

"You never asked me," he said slowly, "why I ran out on you that afternoon. It wasn't that I lost my nerve or anything. It was that somebody had paid for your time and that would have cheapened something that wasn't cheap. Do you understand what I am saying?"

She nodded. His eyes were very bright in the moonlight. "I wanted it to be perfect," he whispered.

"Like now, you mean?" she asked.

He moved toward her. "Like now," he whispered before he kissed her. His hands moved to pull her soaking undergarments from her body and she helped him, not feeling the urgency he was displaying, but wanting him, too. Their union had none of the exploding fire of her first encounter with Col Murphy, but seemed like the proper conclusion to their relationship, as if they were putting the final stroke of paint on an artwork they had created together. When he said good-bye to her in the car, she found it hard not to cry.

"I will be back, Sarah," he said as she climbed out, her still wet hair sending droplets down her face and neck, as if her whole being was crying. "I promise I'll be back for you."

"Take care of yourself, Simon," she said, thinking of the outback—the harsh red land where men fell from horses and stepped on snakes. Simon would belong there even less than she had and yet his face, in the glow of the street lamp outside the gate, was excited and hopeful.

"Don't worry about me," he said. "You take care of yourself."

"I will," she said. "Good-bye Simon. . . ." She was about to say more, then changed her mind and ran lightly up the marble steps and in through the frosted-glass front door.

After he had gone, she returned cheerfully to work, trying to put Simon and his promises out of her mind. She did not allow herself the luxury of daydreams about his returning to marry her. There were so many obstacles to be overcome before that miracle could happen, and, as she had experienced already from her time in Australia, obstacles were not overcome easily. So she tried not to be fatalistic and denied, even to herself, that his parting had left an aching void inside her.

She was doing very well until Col came to call:

"So finally I have you to myself again," Col said when she told him that Simon had gone. "Did you really see something in him or was it just that he was prepared to pay for a lot of your time."

"That's a hateful thing to say!" Sarah exploded. "My relationship with Simon was pure and wholesome."

"You mean he didn't touch you? After all that? Then there must have been something wrong with the boy . . . his dad won't be pleased."

"What do you mean?" she demanded.

"Why—that he wasted good money to get the boy deflowered and it didn't work."

"How dare you!" Sarah said, stepping away from him. "To bring any relationship down to your level!"

"Hey, listen," Col said. "Why the hell do you think Madeleine gave you so much time off? She's not a charitable institution, you know that. You must have known that Sir Hubert was paying for your time. The boy's father was determined he wasn't going to leave Sydney a virgin and you were the perfect person. It's just that nobody could believe it would take so long. Was the boy really a pansy?"

Sarah gripped the back of the chair, trying to control her anger. "Just go away," she said flatly.

He came up and put big hands on her shoulders. "Come on, Sarah," he said, more gently now. "I just don't want to see you upset. It doesn't pay to get yourself involved with a lad like him. You know there's no future in it."

"There could be," she said.

"How could there, Sarah?" he asked.

"He said he'd be back for me," she said, staring out ahead of her, "and I believe him."

"And you want to go with him if he does come back for you?" Col asked. "What do you think Lord Whatsit will say when he brings you home to meet the family? I don't think things would be too pleasant for you, and I don't think you're in love either. You're just in love with the idea. He's not man enough for you—you wouldn't want to find yourself saddled with a bloody pansy boy."

"Why are you being so hateful!" she yelled, spinning toward him. "You're just jealous because I like him better than you—because he's a gentleman and you're not, and because I might leave this place and leave you!"

He drew her to him, holding her tightly. "Let go of me," she said, pummeling at his shoulders. He laughed, holding her even tighter.

"I'm not going to let you go, Sarah," he said, "not without a fight, and you know how our fights always end. Go on—admit he doesn't make you feel the way I do. You don't want him the way you want me—the way you want me right now . . ." His lips were nuzzling hungrily at her mouth and throat as he talked. She strained against him, trying to hold him away with the flat of her hands as his lips moved down her neck, pushing aside her thin shoulder strap to reach her breasts. He felt the shuddering sigh go through her and laughed as he half carried her across to the bed.

He laughed again as they lay together panting, drained by their frenzied lovemaking.

"You see," he whispered, "you do still want me, don't you?"

"Damn you, Col," she said, but she laughed, too.

Thirty-two

AFTER SIMON HAD GONE, LIFE RETURNED TO ITS former pattern for Sarah. She got up late, she read, and went for walks when Madeleine did not need her, and she waited for the postman's whistle every day at noon to see if there was a letter from Simon. The letters came—not too frequently, but they were all from inaccessible places. Simon was a jackeroo on a cattle station, rounding up yearlings and sleeping at night in a bedding roll under the stars. Then he signed on for a cattle drive across to Alice Springs and she heard nothing from him for several weeks. When his letters finally arrived, they hinted at terrible hardships—not enough water, a disease called sandy blight, which turned one of the crew blind, another man having a foot crushed in a cattle stampede—and yet Simon kept referring to Madeleine's as "that dreadful place" that he longed to get Sarah free from. Sarah found this vaguely amusing and ironic, since she would be hard put to describe her present life as dreadful.

In fact, some days she found it most pleasant. At public functions, she had proven herself to be an asset, behaving with tact and decorum, and Madeleine began to send her out more, to accompany ambassadors to the opera, to nightclubs with a Texas millionaire, even to a country house party with a sheep baron's son, recently returned from England. As she gained more experience of mingling with high society, she enjoyed these outings more and more. She got over the horror of bumping into clients at a function and found that Madeleine's girls were widely known and accepted. More than once a stranger would draw her discretely aside. "Aren't you one of Madeleine's young ladies?" he would ask. The fact that most of these evenings out ended in sex had also ceased to worry her. Most of the men were older and could hardly be described as demanding. The fact that they seemed to get so much satisfaction from so very little amused her and gave her a feeling of power. She remembered a line from Milton's poem "Comus": "Thou cannot touch the freedom of my mind." Whatever the men wanted her to do with them, it was up to her whether she was involved at all, or if her mind was soaring far away.

She saw Col Murphy occasionally, but not nearly as often as she would have wished. The Prince of Wales visit was approaching and he was very involved in the frenzy of preparations, even though he privately confessed to her that he felt the whole thing was a waste of the taxpayer's money. When she saw him, their meetings were as explosive as ever. She also ran into him frequently at public functions and never got entirely used to the effort of maintaining composure as they sat one row apart at the theater, or the stab of jealously she always felt when Marjorie slipped her arm through his and led him away.

Sarah's other steady visitor and loyal customer was Lytton Argus, the elderly racehorse owner. He came into town at least once a month and was always delighted to see Sarah. She had also grown fond of him, thinking of him more as a favorite uncle whose visit always ended in a generous present. The presents had, indeed, become more generous, but Sarah was not prepared for his parting gift when he left one evening in September.

"When you're free, I want you to drive out to my farm," he said, patting her hand as he walked toward the door. "I'd like to give you a little present. I'd like you to choose yourself a colt."

"A colt?" Sarah sounded amazed. "But where could I keep a horse?"

Lytton Argus laughed, a dry, cracked little laugh to match his looks and personality. "You would not have to keep it," he said, his eyes twinkling with amusement. "You merely choose it, then it's yours. I'll continue to train it with the rest of my stable. If you choose wisely and it wins races, you could find yourself a very rich woman one day."

Sarah laughed excitedly. "What a wonderful present," she said, "but I really should refuse. It's far too generous."

"Nonsense, my dear," he said, smiling fondly at her. "It would make me happy." He paused to consider, then spoke again. "Just one thing, though. Please do not call on my mother while you are out there. I don't think she'd be very understanding,'' and he smiled that cheeky boyish smile again.

A week later Col drove her out to the Argus stable. Sarah had told him of Lytton's generous present and commented that she would have no idea how to choose, since she did not know a good racehorse from a bad one. ''I'll just have to go on its pretty face'' she said, ''and I'm sure the pretty ones don't win the races.''

''I know a bit about racehorses,'' Col said. ''But I hardly think Mr. Argus would be pleased to see me accompanying you.''

Sarah grinned. ''As a matter of fact, he's not going to be there,'' she said. ''He's down in Melbourne for race meetings. I've an introduction to his stable man.''

''Tell you what then,'' Col had said. ''I have to be out Riverina way next week, making a speech for the local labor party gathering. Why don't you drive out with me and we'll take a run over to the farm together.''

''Are you sure you want to be seen with me in the car?'' she asked.

He laughed. ''I'll tell them you're a party agent from headquarters,'' he said. ''They don't know their arse from their elbows out there—they believe anything you tell them!''

The drive with Col was delightful, the countryside bursting with the first glimpse of spring—bright yellow wattles in flower in the gray-green bush and fruit trees in a shimmer of pink and white blossom on the farms.

''I didn't realize how dreary the winter had been until today,'' she commented to Col. ''Australians fool themselves into thinking they have no winter, but it has definitely been dreary.''

''Usually I'm too busy to notice what season it is,'' Col answered. ''I wish I had more time to spend out here. I think I could be content on a little farm.''

Sarah laughed. ''You on a little farm? I don't see you in big boots striding through the muck–and up at five to milk the cows.''

''Not that little,'' he said grinning. ''It would have to be big enough to employ a bloke to milk the cows and walk through the muck for me . . . like the farms Marjorie's family owns: a few thousand acres close to civilization. That's my sort of farm.''

''Or like the one we're going to now?''

"I wouldn't say no to that either," he said. "You play your cards right and maybe he'll leave it to you in his will, then I'll quit politics and come out and live there with you."

"Maybe he'll ask me to marry him and he'll live to ninety-nine," Sarah said, her eyes holding Col's. "Then you'd be completely out of the picture."

She saw the flicker in his eyes. "You wouldn't do that, would you? Marry an old fogie like Argus just for his money?"

"I might. He's a gentleman."

"I'd rather you married young Cyril or whatever his name is."

"You know perfectly well that his name is Simon," she said, "and stop acting so damn possessively about me. If someone wants to marry me one day, I shall probably accept. Especially somebody rich and pleasant, too." She looked at him seriously. "You must see that my present life is not ideal," she said. "I need something more than meeting a man like you when he has time, and a lot of boring, stupid other men in between. I'm only human, Col. I'd like to belong somewhere."

"I suppose so," he said. "I just don't like the thought of you not being around when I need you."

"Typical bloody male," she said and he laughed, putting a big arm around her and drawing her to him.

Lytton Argus's trainer showed them around and helped them select a spindly chestnut with huge brown eyes whose official name was Golden Sovereign and whom Col immediately called Buster.

As Col made his speech, Sarah sat at the back of the hall. She had never had a chance to see Col at work as an orator before and was rather amused by his fiery rhetoric. She could see, however, that he knew exactly how to rouse an audience. These farm people were listening to him openmouthed, with expressions of rapt awe on their faces, applauding and shouting out agreement as he promised to make sure wool prices stayed high for the next year.

"The old rogue," she thought with a smile and let her gaze wander around the hall. Her eyes fell on a calendar on the wall. She realized with a shock that she had sailed from England exactly one year ago this week. How strange to think how much had happened in one year—that now she was sitting in a hall, listening to the state premier, who was also her lover, while in a field nearby, a colt called Buster would race one day under her colors. *And yet if my father heard, he would still only think of me as a fallen woman,* she thought. *Strange because that isn't how I think of myself at all. Right and wrong don't seem to exist anymore—at least not in the way that Janet taught them to me. I don't feel guilty about what I do. I don't even feel guilty about accepting a racehorse or even sleeping with another woman's husband. I suppose I must be corrupted beyond hope, but I really can't feel unhappy about any of it.*

But later that month, something happened to shake her acceptance of her present life style. Diana took a walk with her one day, along Rushcutters Bay where the yachts bobbed capriciously in a brisk spring wind. It was unusual for Diana to accompany her, since Diana was always very aloof.

"Do you like it here?" she asked Sarah as they stood looking down on the water.

"It's pleasant enough," Sarah replied thinking that this was nothing more than a polite question to make conversation.

Diana looked down at the water, her hands gripping the stone balustrade. "I hate it," she said. "I'll never stop hating it."

Sarah looked at her in surprise. "Then why don't you leave?" she asked.

"Madeleine won't let me," Diana answered.

"But surely, you've been here long enough . . . you don't owe her anything anymore?" Sarah asked.

Diana looked at Sarah's face and laughed. "You know nothing, do you?" she said bitterly. "You don't have an idea how anything works in this place. Madeleine owns us. She owns us forever, or until she lets us go."

"I'm sure that's not true," Sarah replied. "She even suggested that I'd be lucky if I married Simon."

"Because she'd get a big kickback from that transaction," Diana said. "If somebody wants to take you away, they have to pay for it. A dowry, you see. But you try telling her that you want to leave . . ."

"But I don't want to leave," Sarah said. "I quite like things as they are. It's not a bad life. We're treated well . . ."

"It is a bad life," Diana said bluntly. "We are sinning every day of our lives. We are damned to hell—surely you must know that."

"I don't think I'm damned and neither are you," Sarah replied strongly. "I think you've been brooding too much. It's that vicarage upbringing of yours." She attempted to smile, but Diana's eyes were cold.

"I thought you might understand how I feel," she said. "Let's go home. The wind is too cold."

The next day she killed herself. She was found by the maid with an empty bottle of sleeping pills beside her. Sarah was consumed with guilt that Diana had obviously been crying out for help and Sarah had failed her. She tried to talk to the other girls about it, but the general consensus was that Diana was a "silly bitch" and that Madeleine was about to throw her out anyway because she wasn't any good at her job. It was at times like this that Sarah wished Col had a private telephone number she could reach him at. He would have understood what she was going through. But the Prince's visit was about to take place and Col never had time for even the briefest visit. So Sarah kept her feelings about Diana to herself, wondering in the early hours of the morning when she returned to her own room, who was really right. Was Diana correct to feel that she was sinning? Was she correct to have taken the only way out of an intolerable situation? In past ages saints and martyrs were made of such actions, choosing to face lions rather than submit their bodies. Perhaps Diana had been right, perhaps she was damned after all and didn't even know it.

It was into the middle of this turmoil that Simon returned. She was up in her room, writing a letter to his last known address, when Renee banged on her door excitedly.

"There's someone to see you in the parlor," she called.

"Col?" she asked, opening the door and instinctively tidying her hair as she went to follow Renee.

"What would Col be doing in the parlor?" Renee shouted back, already running down the stairs.

Sarah slowed her pace. She was not anxious to face a client right now, even a nice client like Lytton. Renee melted into the office and Sarah pushed open the parlor door. Simon rose to his feet from the sofa where he had been sitting.

"Hello Sarah," he said shyly.

She took in the tanned face, the open shirt. "Simon!" she shouted, running toward him delightedly. "What an incredible surprise!" She flung her arms around his neck, laughing up into his weather-beaten face. "I thought you'd be gone for two years! The last I heard you were over in South Australia . . . I never expected . . ." She sighed, gazing up at him happily. "I still can't believe you are here. You said you'd come back for me, but I never really thought . . ."

"Sarah," he interrupted. "I'm here because I have to go home to England. Things have changed."

"You've already made your fortune?" she asked, then she noticed how serious his eyes were. "Something's happened?"

He nodded. "My father is very ill," he said. "I've been called home. They don't expect him to live . . ." he laughed uneasily. "I might be Lord Belbrooke before the year is out."

"Oh Simon, I'm sorry," she said, "but you weren't very close, were you?"

"He's the only father I have," Simon said, simply. "You think of things differently when you realize you might never see somebody again." He slid his hands into hers. "Look, can we go somewhere to talk . . . out into the gardens perhaps?"

"Of course," she said. "Come outside and tell me everything . . . I still can't believe you are here."

Simon went to say something, then bit his lip. She sensed his uneasiness. "You do still . . . care about me, don't you? Your letters, they were wonderful. All those nice things you said . . ."

"I still care about you," he said, smiling down at her gravely. "I'll always care about you, Sarah." On the raked sand pathways the wind was stirring up fallen leaves. The palm trees rattled overhead. On a branch above, a white cockatoo gave a sudden harsh squawk. They walked on. Sarah shivered suddenly in the wind. "It's cold out here," she said, realizing as she said it that she was echoing Diana's words. "When will you be sailing for England?"

"I've managed to get a passage on the *Ulysses*. She leaves tomorrow," he answered. He picked up her left hand, playing with the fingers. "It's all so sudden, Sarah. I know I wanted to take you with me, but now wouldn't be the right time . . . I don't want to cause a major upset with my father dying. You do understand, don't you, darling?"

"Of course I understand," she said, sounding more confident than she felt.

"And I will send for you, I promise," he said squeezing her fingers as he spoke. "As soon as things sort themselves out, I'll find a way."

Sarah smiled. "When you are Lord Belbrooke, you'll be able to do what you want, I imagine. Even cut off a few heads."

He looked down at her tenderly. "I do love you," he said. "I'll always love you. I'll carry around the image of the way you look right now—the way your hair blows out in the wind and those adorable freckles on your nose."

He reached into his pocket and brought out a parcel wrapped in paper. "I wanted to give you a ring," he said, "but there hasn't been time, so I thought that this might do instead."

Sarah took it. It was very heavy. She opened it curiously. "It looks like a rock," she said in surprise.

"It is a rock," he said. "I mined it myself. It's a piece of raw opal to remember me by—the only thing I did here that was worth anything. You should have seen the opal fields—I lived in a hole in the ground, just like a rabbit! And it was hotter than Hades, but finding this made it all worthwhile. They told me it was quite valuable. They were surprised that an idiot like me could strike anything except his own fingers."

She turned it over cautiously. Sparks of iridescent fire shot from the gray surface as the sun caught them. "It's beautiful," she said, "but oughtn't you to take it home, to prove to your father that you did make something of yourself, after all?"

He looked down at her with infinite tenderness. "I want you to have it," he said.

A head poked out of the French windows. "Sarah? Madeleine's asking for you," a voice called.

Sarah put her hand on Simon's shoulder. "I have to go," she said.

Simon slipped his arms around her waist, pulling her close to him. "I hate to leave you like this," he whispered, "but it won't be long. Things will sort themselves out soon. I'll tell the family about you—I'll make them accept you and I'll send you a ticket home as soon as I can. Don't forget me, will you?"

She looked at him steadily, taking in every feature on his young, tanned face—the clear, light blue eyes, the absurdly boyish, hopeful look, the hair flopping across his forehead. "How could I ever forget you?" she whispered. "Don't you forget me."

"As if I could," he said with a bitter laugh. "Will you come and see me off tomorrow?" he asked.

"I don't think so," she said. "I might make a fool of myself. I hate crying in public."

Simon looked as if he was about to cry at any moment. "I don't want to leave you, Sarah," he said, gazing at her with such intensity that she felt his eyes burning into her. "Not here."

She smiled, reaching up to touch the worried frown lines on his forehead. "I've survived this long. I'm sure I can manage a little longer. Don't worry about me, Simon."

His arms crushed her to him. "I'll do everything in my power to bring you home soon, I promise," he said.

"You take care of yourself," she whispered, "and don't let your father bully you."

"I won't," he said.

They stood there, frozen like two statues, staring at each other as if they both wanted to memorize every detail of the other's face. The cockatoo squawked again, breaking their concentration and making them both look up.

"I really have to go," Sarah whispered again. "Madeleine doesn't like to be kept waiting."

"I love you," Simon whispered.

"I love you, too." She reached up to kiss him gently on the mouth, then rushed away from him.

She began to walk toward the house without looking back. She had almost reached the French doors when he ran after her.

"I can't let you go," he cried and crushed her into his arms, kissing her on the mouth, nose, eyes until finally their lips came together and they remained without moving, locked in each others arms. Sarah was the first to break away. "I have to go," she said again and this time she could not hide the pain in her voice. "Good-bye Simon."

"Not good-bye. *Au revoir*," he insisted.

"*Au revoir* then." She turned and hurried into the house, leaving him standing in the dappled shade.

When the boat sailed the next day, she watched it from the garden. She watched the great white ship, its decks lined with black specks of people, glide past toward the Heads. And, although she knew he couldn't see her, she stood waving her handkerchief until the ship was lost from sight.

Thirty-three

WHEN COL CAME TO VISIT NEXT, SHE SHOWED HIM the rock. It was mostly gray but when you scratched the surface, veins of fire glinted through.

"It's pretty, isn't it?" she asked.

"What's that—the consolation prize instead of the ticket to England?" he asked.

"That's a horrid thing to say," she said. "He obviously couldn't take me with him right now."

"Obviously."

They stood looking at each other like two boxers in the ring. "You don't think he will send for me, do you?" she asked at last. "Well, I think you're in for a surprise. Simon's learned a lot during these last months. He's gotten tougher. He mined this in a hole in the ground."

Col grinned. "He could hardly mine it up a bloody tree, could he?"

She turned away. "You really don't care one bit about me, do you? I'm just something you hire for an hour at a time, like a hack at the riding stable."

"You're a lot more fun," he said, then he came up behind her and put his big hands on her shoulders. "I'm sorry, love. I can see you're hurting, but there's nothing I can do about it for you. I should say I hope your young man comes up trumps and you go to England and become Queen of the May or whatever bloody title it is—"

"Lady Belbrooke," she said, laughing.

"Lady Belbrooke, then," he said, "but I wouldn't count on it. England's a hell of a long way away. It's half a world away from here."

"I know," she said, "but he promised . . ."

"Then, for your sake, I hope he keeps his bloody promise,"

Col said gently. "Although I'll turn into a doddering old wreck if you leave me."

She spun around to face him. "Now one thing I can't see is you as a doddering old wreck. You'll still be pinching the maids bottoms when you're ninety."

"Only if you stay around to keep me young," he said. He picked up the opal. "Look, do you want me to get this thing of yours valued? It might be worth a lot."

Sarah looked horrified. "I couldn't sell it," she said. "It was a present."

"It's no bloody use the way it is," Col said. "Have it made into something if you're going to keep it—a nice necklace or something."

Sarah looked down at it. "No, I think I'll keep it as it is," she said. "Then every time I look at it, I'll think of Simon mining it for me."

Col shook his head. "And I always thought you were a realist," he said. "Don't tell me you're turning into a romantic?"

She looked at him seriously. "There has to be something in my life that is not reality," she said. "I need dreams and hopes, too, you know."

"As well as me?" he quipped.

She smiled. "There is nothing romantic about you, Col Murphy."

Col laughed and the next time he came to see her, he showed up with a bouquet of red roses. Sarah was very glad for Col. Even though his visits were sometimes sporadic, he was the one thing she could look forward to from day to day. He was real and tangible when Simon was very far away. Letters began arriving from distant ports, funny postcards of Egyptian pyramids and camels. Then a long letter from England, then nothing for a long while. Life went on as before. Sarah went to operas and races and parties. She drove out to watch her colt frisking in the field beside his mother. She saw Lytton Argus regularly and heard that her selection had been a good one and she tried not to think about England at all.

Christmas came and went with many parties, picnics, and beach celebrations. Sarah bought a bathing costume and worked on a tan with the other girls. Col gave her a Christmas present of an opal ring—"Just in case you decide not to touch that bloody great rock." She received other presents from other men and no longer thought it either strange or degrading. Then, in January, the long awaited letter finally arrived. It was the first of the very hot weather and Sarah carried the letter out into the garden, to read it in the shade of the big magnolia tree. She was disappointed to note that, when she opened it, no ticket fell out.

"Dear Sarah," the letter began. The formal greeting made her shiver in the heat of the afternoon. "I know I have not written for a while, but things have not been easy here. My father made a miraculous recovery and is now considered to be over the worst. He is not allowed to do any strenuous work, however, so the day-to-day running of the estate has fallen to me. It's a good thing I got all that training on the cattle stations as the work here seems never ending. Although he is still weak physically, he has lost none of his mental strength and tries to run everything from his bath chair. It seems as if I'm to be saddled with the estate for good, though. I'm getting used to the idea.

"What I want to say next will not be easy, which is one of the reasons I've put off writing for so long. I always was a bit of a coward, I'm sure you knew. The fact is that my family has been putting a lot of pressure on me to get married. They want to see me settled before father dies, which, I suppose is understandable. Did you ever meet Henrietta Stanley? The Stanleys own property up in Norfork and Lincolnshire and there is no male heir, which would mean a considerable property settlement, so I suppose she is an ideal match, looked at that way. She is a pleasant enough girl, too. Our engagement was announced last week in the *Times* and I thought I'd better write and tell you in case you saw a copy of the paper.

"I want you to know that I'll always love you. If things could only have been different . . . if I hadn't come from one of the great families and had the burden of tradition and responsibility hanging over me, I'm sure we'd have been very happy together. But, unfortunately, I am a future peer and I can't let down all those generations who preceded me. I realize I'm sounding pompous and I don't mean to. I just want you to understand that I loved you best. I wish every happiness in the world to you, Sarah. Don't think unkindly of me, will you. I hope you can find it in your heart to wish me happiness, too.

With fondest regards, Simon.

P.S. If you decide to sell the piece of opal, I think you'll find it is worth enough to get you free of that place.''

She showed the letter to Col, who arrived shortly afterward. ''I won't say I told you so,'' he said, looking down at her with compassion.

''I think I always knew I wouldn't see him again,'' she said.

''Spineless little twerp,'' Col commented. ''Only wrote because he thought you'd see it in the *Times* first. You're better off without him, Sarah. You'd have had nothing but misery if you'd married him.''

''Maybe,'' she said, looking out past him into the garden. Another ship was passing down in the harbor. More people sailing to England, more hearts being broken by partings.

''No maybe about it,'' Col said firmly. ''He was weak, Sarah. He crumbled under the first bit of pressure his family put on him. He chose conformity and property settlements over you.'' He walked across to her desk and picked up the opal. ''I think you'll discover in the long run that the rock was better value than the chinless wonder.''

''You may be right,'' she said. ''I don't know what to do with it now. I was planning to leave it whole and use it as a paperweight . . .''

''Bloody expensive paperweight,'' Col replied, picking it up and turning it over in his hands.

''It really is worth something then, you think?''

''A few thousand maybe? I'm not an expert of course.''

''Thousand?'' she echoed.

''I'd think so. Look at the color in it. You've got yourself half a pound of black opal there. I'll take it and get it valued for you if you like,'' Col suggested. ''I know a good bloke in the jewelry business.''

''I could buy myself a little house, as he suggested,'' Sarah said, half to herself.

Col looked amazed. ''A little house—what on earth for?''

''I can't stay here forever,'' she said firmly. ''I don't want to stay here forever. I need a place of my own somewhere in the world. Simon wanted me to get out.''

Col smiled. ''I said the rock was worth a couple of thousand, not half a million,'' he said. ''You could buy your nice little cottage, but what then? You've got to live on something.''

"I could take a job. I'm not helpless. I'm well educated—a governess or something."

Col laughed out loud at this. "I can just see you as a governess," he said.

"I'd make a very good governess," she said haughtily.

"I don't doubt it, love," he said, reaching up to fondle her hair, "but not in this town. We're a small society and you're getting to be well-known."

"Then I'll go back to England," she insisted. "I'm not well-known there."

"What for, for Christ's sake?" he demanded. "Who do you have in England? What you need to be happy is people and life, not a bloody cottage and a couple of cats. Do you really want to get out of here so badly?"

"Not really," she said thoughtfully, "but I do have to think of the future. I can't stay here forever."

"Then open your own bloody house—that's a much better idea than a cottage and crochet."

She laughed. "I don't know why you think I'd take up crochet!" she said, "and I don't think that a couple of thousand is going to set me up in a house like this."

"Then start small," he said.

Sarah kept laughing. "A cottage on the beach catering to navvies and fishermen at sixpence a time?"

"Now you're making fun of my perfectly good suggestion," he said, looking wounded.

"Only because it's not a good suggestion," she said. "I could never be another Madeleine. I wouldn't want to be. I'm not hard like that."

"You don't have to be like Madeleine," he said, "and it seems to me like you've got it made. You've already got a solid circle of admirers—save your money for a while, start small with one or two girls."

"You are determined to send my soul straight to damnation, aren't you?" she asked.

"No, I'm determined not to let you slip away from me," he said, drawing her into his arms.

"Then you set me up in a nice little house," she said, her eyes teasing him.

"I was elected by a very narrow margin, lady," he said seriously, "and much as that sounds like a very appealing proposition, my wife and the opposition would crucify me in a couple of weeks."

"Then it will have to be the cottage, crochet, and cats," Sarah said. "Maybe I'll even sell the crochet!"

Col squeezed her to him. "You wouldn't survive," he said. "You've got too much of a taste for good company, good food, and good living."

"Me? I'll have you know that my ancestors lived on turnips for three months when they were besieged."

"But why live on turnips when you don't have to?" he asked. "You can try it, if you like, but I guarantee you'll be back. Now, do you want me to get your opal valued for you? I'll put it in a safe place now, because I may forget it afterward."

Col took the stone with him and Sarah lay alone in bed, considering what to do with unexpected wealth. Pay off Madeleine, to begin with. It would be a good feeling to know that she was free to leave whenever she wanted to and that any money she earned now went into her account. She thought of Col's suggestion of setting herself up in a house and laughed. "Madam Sarah," she muttered out loud, and laughed again. On the other hand, leaving Madeleine would mean no more Col, and he was the one element in her life that gave it spice and meaning. *And what point would there be in going back to London?* she asked herself. *I know nobody there and I have no means of entry into society there. There's only Cousin Hugo and the girls and I'm sure they'd be no help. They wouldn't want to displease my father, for one thing, because they are obviously his beneficiaries now.*

Lying there, thinking of the last, painful scenes with her father before she left England, her mind drifted on to Jimmy. She had not thought of him for several months, having kept him out of her waking thoughts with a conscious effort. She had never dreamed about him since the day she arrived in Ivanhoe, but on this night she did dream. They were out together on Jimmy's farm, and Jimmy was attacking the rock-hard red soil with a pickax.

"This ground is good for nothing," he was saying. "I don't know why I ever brought you out here. If we sold it, maybe we could buy a little cottage in Sydney . . ."

She opened her eyes, staring at the tree shadows on her wall, moving in the night wind. She remembered her helplessness when she stood looking at Jimmy's farm, knowing that she had been cheated out of it and knowing that she was powerless to do anything. Well, now she was not powerless. She had money and she had friends . . .

Col stopped by with the opal the next afternoon.

"He says it's a fine piece and the fire runs true right through it," he said, placing it reverently on her table. "He'll offer you fifteen hundred pounds for it himself."

"Fifteen hundred . . ." Sarah said thoughtfully. "Do you think that would be enough to hire a really good lawyer?"

Col looked surprised. "A lawyer? What do you need a bloody lawyer for? You're not going to sue that spineless twerp for breach of promise?"

"Heavens no," she said. "What would be the point of that?" She walked across to the window, playing with the tassels on the blind. "I want to get my land back," she said.

"I never knew you had any land," he said, coming to stand behind her.

"I didn't tell anybody before because I thought there was nothing I could do about it, and it was all too painful," she said, "but I came out here to get married. My fiancé was killed a week before the wedding. When I got there, I found that his neighbor had already taken over his land and everything in payment of a small debt and because there was no next of kin. I had no way of proving that I had any claim, and yet I know Jimmy had already taken out the marriage license and bought the ring."

"So you think somebody quietly nicked them?" Col asked.

"I'm almost positive. I searched all through his things, but I couldn't find them. And the speed with which the local constable rushed it all through. It was all highly suspicious." She turned and slipped her hands onto Col's broad shoulders. "Do you think I'd be wasting my money to hire a lawyer? Do you think I really have a case?"

"Oh, you have a case all right—but what's the point of it? Is the land valuable?"

"Pretty bloody useless," she confessed with a laugh.

"Then why bother—you're usually a realist. Is it worth a lot of hassle just to settle an old score?"

"It was a very big score," Sarah said.

"So it means a lot to you to win your case?"

"Yes, Col. It would mean a lot to me."

Col smiled. "All right, he said. "Where did you say this land was?"

"Out past Ivanhoe," she answered. "I doubt if you've even heard of it. It's beyond the back-o'-Bourke as they say here."

Col looked at her steadily. "As a matter of fact, I know exactly where it is," he said. "I have a friend—Ralph Johnson, who has a big spread out there and I've been keeping tabs on that area myself." He grinned. "It might just be very interesting . . ." He paced up and down then abruptly turned back toward her. "I'll get you your lawyer, darlin', and we'll get your land back for you. Only promise me that you won't go and live on it. I'm not riding out to bloody Ivanhoe to see you!"

Sarah laughed. "Nothing in the world would make me live out there," she said, "and I might even sell the land back to the man who tricked me, but I'm damned if he's going to get the better of me."

Col looked at her appraisingly. "You're beginning to sound more like a bloody Aussie every day," he said.

"It must be the corruption of being around you too much," she suggested.

He laughed, his big, rich laugh, and pulled her toward him. "That's my favorite sport—corrupting sweet, young things like you," he said.

She saw nothing more of him for a week or so. The opal was sold and she had the satisfaction of paying Madeleine her debt. She also refused to satisfy Madeleine's curiosity about where the money came from. "I came into an unexpected inheritance," was all she would say.

A few days later a letter arrived from Col.

"I'm writing this in the conference chamber," he had scrawled. "Some old cove is going on and on about the need for preservation of the habitat of the lesser bandicoot or something equally ridiculous. I'm appearing to take furious notes, but instead I'm writing to you. I have your lawyer for you. He's the best there is for your sort of case—fast talking and crooked as hell. I've given him the background and he sees no problem in wrapping it up quickly. So you don't need to worry about a thing. All you need to do is give him a call and arrange a time when you can both drive out to the farm together."

He proceeded to give an address and added as a postscript:

"no monkey business with the lawyer. He's a damned good-looking bastard and I wouldn't trust him an inch!

"P.S. Don't take too long. I'll miss you."

Sarah smiled down fondly at the letter. *There's no way I'd stay away from you too long, Col Murphy,* she said.

Thirty-four

COL MURPHY LOOKED UP FROM HIS DESK IN ANswer to the light tap on his door. He called, "Come in," and his secretary, Jack Hemmingway entered the room. The young man was still impeccably dressed, with high-starched collar and gold studs, but over a year with Col had changed the rigid ideas on political science with which he had come down from Oxford. His sharp brain was now beginning to think like a younger, more polished Col and Col was beginning to find him very useful, indeed.

"Jack," he said, leaning back in his leather armchair. "I want you do to something for me."

"What is it?" Jack asked, already opening his notepad.

"Two things really," Col said. "First I want you to get Sam Tanksley on the phone. I've got a little job for him—case of landownership . . ."

"Landownership?"

"Yes, a young friend of mine, who shall be nameless, has a piece of land that she was cheated out of. I want to make sure she gets it back again."

"And the other thing?" Jack asked, wisely not delving into Col's possible "young friends."

"The other thing is I want to see those geologists reports on uranium that we had done."

Jack's eyes looked at his boss with speculation. "Something tells me that these two subjects are not totally disconnected," he said.

Col chuckled. "Too bloody right," he said.

Jack appeared moments later with the file under his arm. "It didn't look too hopeful on the uranium, did it?" he asked Col as they spread open the map on the desk.

"Not too hopeful, I agree," Col said. "According to this geologist bloke, the big deposits are over the border in South Australia. Still, that gives me an excuse to hold up the rest of that bloody railway, doesn't it?"

"And where is this land you were talking about—your young friend's land?"

Col's stubby finger pointed around Ivanhoe. "Out there," he said. "End of the bloody world."

"But you think there might be deposits on her land?" Jack asked excitedly. "It's not too far from the mines at Broken Hill."

Col looked at him as if he were not too bright. "I don't think in a month of Sundays that there will be anything of importance on her land," he said, "but I just wanted to check whether the land comes within the area we designated for future mineral exploration." He checked the map and looked up with a grin. "And what do you know—it seems to sit inside that little red line. Now, isn't that nice and convenient."

"I still don't understand . . ." Jack began. Col shook his head. "You don't need to, my boy."

"I need to know what's going on, Col," Jack insisted. "You need someone to keep you in check, or one of these days you'll commit political suicide."

Col grinned. "It's very simple really. I'd like to do this young friend a favor. I can't give her as much as I'd like to, but I'd like to see her with an income. Now, if this land's inside the exploration area—the area we officially voted on, then the government can lease it for exploration, right?"

"But there has to be some expectation of minerals being found," Jack insisted. "People would question. It would be bound to come out who owned the land . . ."

Col looked up. "That uranium report. It doesn't exactly state that there is no uranium on our side of the border, does it. I don't see any reason why the veins, or whatever uranium runs in, should not extend a few more miles in our direction."

Jack smiled. "Possibly not," he said. "You'll have to get it approved by the committee, though. Take a few months."

"It's okay. We can wait. I just want her to have something for the future, without looking as though I've given it to her."

Jack closed his notebook. "Are we talking about Sarah Hartley?" he asked.

Col looked surprised. "How the hell?" he asked.

"I'm your secretary," Jack said. "I'm supposed to know everything. There were too many times when you were at your club, but you weren't. One had to find out where you actually were, just in case Russia declared war or the king decided to pop in."

Col laughed. "We've already had the Prince of Wales. Now we're safe for the next few years. Boring little fart he was, too . . . left me to pay his debts at the races." He stared speculatively at Jack. "You're pretty sharp, aren't you. I hope you aren't too sharp for your own good."

Jack's gaze did not waver. "I think I know exactly how sharp to be for my own good," he said.

After he left the room, Col stared down at his papers again. He drew a doodle in the margin, a doodle that turned into a tall, lanky youth. Underneath it he doodled a big question mark.

Thirty-five

THE LONG OPEN PIERCE-ARROW ROADSTER BUMPED along Ivanhoe's deserted main street. It was just as Sarah had remembered it—the dusty eucalyptus trees, the tin roofs glinting in the setting sun, the peeling white paint on the Australasia Hotel, a couple of horses tied outside, a lone car parked next to the post office and general store, but no people, no sign of life at all except for the smoke rising from chimneys and a flock of bright parakeets that dipped, twittering, down into a backyard.

For the past hour Sarah had sat silently beside Samuel Tanksley, the heavy jowled, dark-suited lawyer, as the car bumped and skidded over the rutted track. Sam was driving fast and speech was almost impossible without the risk of biting ones tongue. He had not been particularly chatty since the journey had begun and Sarah had been able to retrace her route westward, lost in her own thoughts. Before she began the journey, she had felt excited but detached—as if she was about to move her queen into checkmate in a game of chess. Now she was finally about to confront Jake Cotrell again, she began to feel more and more alarmed. Would she really be able to remain calm and dignified when she saw him, to give him no hint at all of the anxiety he had caused her? She was determined that he should see no emotion at all on her face, and yet, as the first buildings of Ivanhoe appeared in the dusty evening haze, she felt her throat constrict with panic.

What am I doing here? she asked herself. *I don't even want the land and I don't want to confront him.*

For Jimmy, she reminded herself. *You are doing this for Jimmy because you owe it to him to settle things the way he would have wanted them settled.*

Sam Tanksley coughed as they hit a particularly dusty patch.

"Bloody god-forsaken hole," he muttered. "You don't really want land here, do you?"

"Only because it's really mine," Sarah answered, holding onto the dashboard to steady herself.

"But you're not planning to live out here?" he shouted back over the protesting roar of the engine. "Just going to lease it and get out?"

"I'm not even sure what I'll do with it," she said. "I'm not sure anyone would want to lease it . . ."

She thought she detected a grin from under that droopy mustache, but he said nothing more until he had brought the car to a stop and switched off the engine.

"I suppose the first thing is to get a room for the night," Sam said, eyeing the hotel with distaste. He sighed. "Ah, the things I have to suffer in my line of work! Ten to one it will be lumpy beds and boiled cabbage."

"Not far wrong," Sarah agreed, "and a dragon of a landlady to go with them."

Sam came around to help her out of the car. "You fix up the hotel," he said. "I'll pay a visit on the police and have a message sent to this Mr. Cotrell. You think they were definitely in this together?"

"I'm fairly sure of it," Sarah said. "Of course, it will be hard to prove in court, I should think."

Sam's face twitched in a smile. "Who said anything about court?" he asked. "The way I work, it won't ever need to come to court. Nice, simple little case like this—we should get this settled in one day—or I'll become so expensive you won't be able to afford me!" And he gave her a wink as he headed across the street toward the tin-roofed bungalow.

The wink reassured Sarah. It said clearly that Sam Tanksley was on her side. She took a deep breath and walked into the hotel. This time she did not make the mistake of going into the wrong bar. She walked into the Ladies Lounge and, because there was nobody in sight, rapped on the counter. Mrs. Gallagher, looking not quite as formidable as Sarah remembered her, came out of the kitchen door, wiping her hands on her apron.

"Yes?" she asked.

"Good afternoon Mrs. Gallagher. I'm back on a visit . . . you do have room?"

The woman took in Sarah's tailored silk costume, the sleek hair, the tiny feathered hat, crowned with a hint of a veil. A puzzled look came over her face.

"I'm sorry, madam—but do I know you?"

"I was here a year ago," Sarah said, details of that first entry into this room flashing through her mind like frozen frames from a moving picture. "I came out here to get married, do you remember? You were kind to me . . ."

Recognition, mixed with wonder, spread across the woman's leathery face. "The young lady who stopped on for a while out with Jake Cotrell?" she asked. "Well, I never. You're looking a deal better than when you left here last—a proper elegant lady—I'd never have known you. Back on a visit, are you?" Her eyes strayed out through the open door to where Sam Tanksley could be seen crossing the street toward them. "Is this the new hubby?" she asked.

"My lawyer," Sarah said, conscious that she was role playing and finding it hard not to smile.

"Lawyer—fancy that." The woman's face looked anxious. "Nothing serious, I hope?"

"Very straightforward, Mrs. Gallagher. Merely a question of documents proving my rights to some land here."

Sam entered the bar, removing his hat and giving the slightest of nods to the landlady.

"Mrs. Gallagher—this is Mr. Tanksley. He's a very famous Sydney lawyer."

"Pleased to meet you, sir," she said, not taking her eyes from him for a second. "And you'll be wanting rooms for the night?"

The way she phrased it made it clear that she was asking whether they wanted one room or two.

Sam Tanksley nodded again. "At least for the night, maybe two nights—your two best rooms, if you please, dear lady—I can't abide lumpy mattresses. I suffer from a bad back, you know—and if you can possibly find a good bottle of claret to go with our dinner, we shall be most grateful."

The landlady left, bowing backward from the bar as if exiting from royalty, with promises of the very best rooms and every possible comfort that Ivanhoe could provide.

"You've certainly managed to charm her," Sarah commented as they walked out into the open air again. "I thought she was made of stone and afraid of nobody, but you had her bowing and scraping."

Sam smiled. "Getting people to eat out of my hand is part of the trade, dear lady," he said. He took her hand and patted it. "Now, don't you worry about a thing. This matter is as good as concluded already. One word from me and they'll be begging you to take back the land."

"You really must be a genius, Mr. Tanksley," Sarah said. "I don't know how you managed to find the copy of the marriage license so easily . . ."

He patted her hand again. "Let's just say what my old mother always said to me, 'Them who asks no questions don't get told no lies.' " And he laughed loudly at his own joke.

Sarah spent a restless night. Following Mr. Tanksley's request, the bed was not too lumpy and there had, indeed, been a bottle of wine to accompany the meat pudding and boiled cabbage, but Sarah was too tense to sleep and every little night noise—the whine of a mosquito, the barking of a distant dog, seemed magnified enough to keep her awake. When she did half doze, disturbing images of Jake Cotrell played themselves out until she shook herself awake again. A year ago, pure survival instinct had kept her going and kept her from the full impact of what had happened to her. Now, twelve months later, here by choice and with leisure to think, she allowed herself to go over that last night once again. Having shared the sex act with many men since that time, she realized more than ever that Jake Cotrell had behaved like an animal and that no amount of drink could ever excuse what he did. She wondered how he thought about his behavior when he woke next morning to find her gone. Did he ever worry that she would bring the police? After twelve months, he surely never expected to see her again. Was he, too, lying awake worrying about their meeting the next morning?

Knowing Jake, he'll be snoring soundly, thinking that no helpless English miss could ever get the better of him, she thought. *Well, he's in for a shock tomorrow because this English miss is no longer helpless . . .*

Thus comforted, she finally drifted into dreamless sleep and awoke to the crowing of cocks at first light the next morning. Sam Tanksley met her in the dining room. He was dressed impeccably, his clothes showing no hint of dusty travel, his white collar gleaming, and a heavy gold watch chain draped across his waistcoat. The image he presented was perfect: he was prosperous and formidable. He had already been seated at the oilskin-topped table and was halfway through a huge plate of steak and eggs.

"Not bad at all," he said jovially, indicating his plate. "Have some, you might need staying power."

Sarah shuddered. "No thank you," she said. "One thing I never learned during my brief stay in the outback was to face meat for breakfast." She poured herself a cup of tea and sipped at it. Sam studied her.

"You're worried," he said. "You don't need to be. Confidence, that's what you need. When I have a confident client, the battle is already half won. You must have thought you had a right to this land, or you'd never have taken this up again. Now's the time to assert your rights."

He smiled at her before dipping a thick slice of bread into a pool of egg yoke and cramming it into his mouth. Sarah got up again. "If you don't mind, I think I'll wait outside," she said. "A little walk to blow away the cobwebs wouldn't be a bad idea."

"Suit yourself," Sam said. "Meet you in half an hour. Let's hope that fellow Cotrell gets here. I don't want to have to go out to him. The suspension would never take it, neither would my old bones.''

''I can't see that he would come to us,'' Sarah said. ''It would be like Jake to make us come out to him.''

''I think he'll come,'' Sam said, turning back to attack his breakfast again, ''for the simple reason that he's scared.''

Sarah hurried out before she could witness the sight of Sam mopping up the last of the congealed egg yolk. Outside she stood blinking in the fierce light. She had forgotten how unnaturally bright it was—a land full of unreal primary colors where people perpetually scowled against the brightness. She walked the length of the porch and turned the corner to find a figure blocking her way. He was just a harshly defined shadow against the sun until he spoke to her.

''Well, if it isn't Sarah?'' he asked. She stepped back to the safety of the shaded porch where she could view him without squinting.

Now that she was actually facing Jake Cotrell, actually staring at that slightly mocking smile, she found that she was not nervous at all. She was wonderfully calm, calm as all Hartleys on the eve of battle.

''Good morning, Mr. Cotrell,'' she said. ''I don't think you expected to see me again, did you?''

''Too bloody right,'' he said, pushing his hat back on his head as he examined her. ''Don't think I'd have recognized you either. You're all gussied up—did all right for yourself then?''

''Very nicely, thank you,'' she answered, ''now that I'm moving among people of culture again.''

''My oath,'' he muttered. ''Found yourself a high-class bloke then?''

''On the contrary,'' she said evenly, ''I have established myself in my own profession. Now, if you'll excuse me, you are holding me up in my morning walk.''

She swept past him. She heard him go to follow her. ''Hey, hold on, Sarah,'' he ran to catch up. ''This land business. You don't really want the land out here, do you? It's useless bloody land. You sound like you're nicely set up in the city . . . what would you want land out here for?''

She turned back and looked at him frostily. ''Because it's mine, Mr. Cotrell, and you stole it from me and I now have the power to get it back.''

He raised an eyebrow, his smile still mocking. "You really think so?"

She continued to stare at him without blinking. "The one thing I've learned since I came here for the first time is that money is power, Mr. Cotrell. When you saw me a year ago, I was powerless because I was penniless. Now I can afford to pay for the best lawyer in the state, I can afford friends in the highest places. I don't think you stand a chance against me—but let's not discuss it further until my lawyer is present." She began to walk on down the street and this time he didn't try to follow her.

They met a half hour later in the dingy little police station with its flypapers hanging from the ceiling and its dirty brown walls. The police constable was a flabby, florid man who continually mopped his perspiring forehead even though the day was not yet warm. Sarah took an instinctive dislike to him and was glad that she had never gone to him for help. That he was clearly on Jake Cotrell's side was obvious by the frequent glances he gave Jake as he spoke.

"Yes, I went out with him to inspect the deceased man's cabin," he said, glancing at Jake, but not meeting Sarah or Sam's eyes. "We turned it over good and proper, we did, but nothing came up about next of kin or we should have contacted them right enough. No one in the neighborhood knew a thing about the boy, see? So Mr. Cotrell here being owed a debt for the sheep, it seemed only right and proper that he should get it."

"And you say there was no marriage license?" Sam Tanksley asked, leaning back in his chair so that it creaked. "Strange when my client was to have married him the day she arrived."

The policeman grinned. "You know how it is sometimes, sir," he said. "Young men don't always come through on their promises, do they. They don't always mean what they say in letters . . . It's my belief he had second thoughts and he intended to tell the young lady to her face, being an upright young lad . . ."

"And if we could prove that he intended to go through with the marriage as stated?" Sam asked, leaning forward again suddenly so that the chair creaked alarmingly. "You'd agree then, would you not, that the young lady would have rightful claim? There are several precedents in English law I can quote to you of the legal rights of the affianced."

The policeman looked at Jake Cotrell again, then smiled. "Ah, but there you have it, don't you sir? What can we take as proof? You're a legal man yourself—you must know what would stand up as proof in a court of law and the testimony of a young girl, plus a few love letters just won't do it."

"I agree with you there, my man," Sam said. "What would stand up in court is a copy of the marriage license, which I just happen to have with me, plus an entry in the books of the catalog company who sold the young man the ring, which unfortunately was also never found . . ."

The change in the policeman's face was noticeable. He darted a glance at Jake. His normally florid face was darkening as they watched. "A copy of the marriage license? I don't believe that . . . I mean, how could there have been a copy when the original . . ." his words trailed off as he realized he was well and truly caught. He could not denounce the copy as a forgery without admitting that he had knowledge of an original.

Sam acknowledged his meaning. "I see that you understand the position perfectly," he said politely nodding to both Jake and the policeman. "Now, as I see it, we have two alternatives: we can wait until the traveling magistrate comes around again—I'm not sure when that will be, but the young lady and I both have time, although it will be a sacrifice to stay at that hostelry across the street . . . where was I? Ah yes, as I was saying, we can wait and take this thing to court. Who knows, the traveling magistrate may be able to find flaws in my evidence and deny this young lady's claim. Not likely, I hasten to add, since my reputation in this state is for only taking on impeccable cases I can't lose . . . or, we can settle this thing here and now, amicably, between ourselves." He leaned back again, as if stretching. "Oh, I might just mention," he said, "that if the magistrate rules in favor of my client, there will be a question of costs and our prolonged stay at the hotel could run pretty expensive. Still, don't think I'm trying to pressure you for one moment. You must do what you think is right." He wagged a finger at Jake. "If you genuinely feel that you have the best and only claim on this land, then you must fight for what you believe to be right."

"There's the question of my sheep," Jake muttered.

"Ah yes, the debt," Sam said, consulting his notes. "My client, of course, would settle any debt owing at the present rate of thirty shillings per sheep."

Jake looked once at Sarah, then down at the floor. "The land's not worth a brass farthing anyway," he muttered. "She's bloody well welcome to it."

Sam nodding approvingly. "Then if you'll just sign these papers I've had drawn up, acknowledging Miss Hartley as legal owner and agreeing to accept the compensation per sheep as established by the state agricultural commission, then we can all go home and I can have a decent bottle of wine with my dinner tomorrow night."

He spread a document on the table in front of Jake. Jake read it through, then signed it. "There—you've got your bloody land," he said to Sarah. "I don't know what you think you're going to do with it, though. There's not enough water on it for sheep and I don't think you'll find anyone around here who's willing to buy or lease it from you."

He looked straight at Sarah, his eyes challenging, his smile almost mocking again. Sarah opened her mouth to speak, but Sam Tanksley spoke first.

"I don't think that will be a problem, Mr. Cotrell," he said. "I understand that there might already be an offer to lease the land . . ."

"There is?" Sarah and Jake both asked together.

"I understand," Sam said, folding his papers as if he had finished checking his notes for the day. He got to his feet. "Now, if we have nothing further to discuss . . ." he began to stuff papers back into his briefcase. "Come, my dear lady," he said, taking Sarah's arm. "We have a long drive ahead of us."

He steered her outside into the bright sunlight. She looked up at him in wonder. "Col said you could fix everything," she said. "I still can't believe it. That copy of the marriage license . . ."

He held up a warning finger. "Remember what my old mother used to say!" he said.

"And you said somebody might want to lease the land?"

"I understand," he said dryly, "that the government of New South Wales has recently allocated monies for expansion in the field of mineral development. I understand that this is one of the sites under consideration . . ."

"The state government . . . you got the government to lease my land?"

"I can't take credit for that," he said, smiling. "The state government has to decide where to spend money on exploration . . ."

"So that was Col's doing?" she asked, beaming delightedly. "How can he get away with that?"

"He's not getting away with anything," Sam said smoothly. "Your land does, I believe, fall within the boundaries of the designated area marked for future exploration. Now that the war is over and Australian industry is expanding, it is most important for the future of our country that we make the most of our valuable mineral resources."

"Mr. Tanksley, you are an old rogue," she said, beginning to laugh.

"No more than your friend Mr. Murphy, Miss Hartley," he said, smiling back at her. "Now, I think I'll just pop inside and settle up the bill. I'll have your things brought down for you in a jiffy and we can be out of here for good."

As he left, Jake came out of the police station and walked right past her to his tethered horse. He untied it and led it past her again.

"So you've got your land," he said. "Satisfied? Aren't you going to take a look at it? There's not much to see anymore. We had a bushfire come through in the spring that leveled the cabin . . ."

"I don't want to see it, Jake," she said. "Any ghosts there have moved away long ago."

"You've changed," he said, looking at her critically. "You're . . ."

"Less vulnerable?" she asked. "You're right. I've learned to fight for myself. I don't think you'd find me such an easy target anymore."

"You never were," he said. He went to go on, then lingered. "When I heard you were coming back, I hoped for a moment . . . things could have been different, Sarah . . ."

She looked at him in surprise. "How could you ever have thought that I'd come back here, after . . ."

A spasm of anguish crossed his face. "Do you think I haven't thought about that?" he asked. "I've gone over and over that night in my mind. I'd do anything to change what I did . . . it was the bloody pain, you see—I was half crazy with pain and all I could do to numb it was drink . . . I'm a decent bloke usually, you know that. I had hoped that maybe you and I . . ."

She almost laughed. "How can you have thought that, Jake?" she asked. "What did you ever have to offer that I might have wanted?"

"So there's nothing I can say that would make you change your mind?" he asked.

She laughed now. "Determined to hang onto that land by fair means or foul?" she asked. "No, Jake, there is nothing that would make me change my mind, but I'm glad I came out here today. I find that I don't hate you anymore."

"That's one thing then," he said. He pushed at his hat brim. "Well, I'd best be riding. How soon will you want my sheep off your land?"

"My lawyer will let you know," she said.

He nodded gravely. "Right oh," he said. He took the reins and swung himself up into the saddle. "Good-bye Sarah," he said.

"Good-bye Jake," she answered. Then, as the horse walked past her, "Oh, and I thought you'd like to know—they told me your baby would have been a boy."

Then she turned away and walked into the hotel before she could see his face.

Thirty-six

SAMUEL TANKSLEY REAPPEARED SOON AFTER WITH a smile on his face.

"Right," he said, "let's get back to civilization, shall we?"

He opened the door of the car for her.

"I'm suddenly hungry, after all," Sarah said. "I think I'll pop into the store and get some provisions for the journey. Anything you'd particularly want?"

"Yes, but they would not stock it," he replied, smiling at her. "Never fear, dear lady. I shall suffer the deprivations of the journey with the anticipation of the good dinner you and I will have tomorrow night in Sydney."

"Then if you'll wait a moment for me," Sarah said. "I will not spurn their biscuits and lemonade."

She hurried into the store. The store was also just as she remembered it, smelling of vegetables and polish and piled with unlikely combinations of rat poison and English biscuits and socks and sweets and yards of unbleached calico. In one corner was the post office counter. Sarah chose gingersnaps and humbugs and several bottles of lemonade.

"You're the young lady from Sydney who was visiting?" the woman behind the counter asked. "They say you was here before?"

"I came out here to get married a year ago," Sarah said, putting a coin on the counter to pay for her purchases. "You might remember my fiancé was killed."

"Oh yes, I do remember," the woman said. "What was the name again?"

"My fiancé's name was Jimmy Alison. He was tall with a lot of blond hair . . ."

"Alison?" the woman said. She appeared to be going into a trance. "Now, what does that remind me of? Alison? Jimmy Alison?" Suddenly she nodded excitedly. "Of course. Well, blow me down. It must have been meant for you, mustn't it? Mrs. James Alison—They said you'd come out here to get married and gone again. What a bit of luck, you popping in here like this. I'd never have got it to you otherwise. Didn't know where to send it on to, see?" While she was talking, she walked into the post office and came up with a crumpled letter.

"This come a month or so back," she said. "We didn't know where to send it on to, seeing that you'd left, and there was no address to send it back to, so it's just sat here. Lucky it did, eh?"

Sarah was turning over the crumpled letter as she spoke. She took in the English postmark and Janet's neat copybook writing before she ripped it open.

"News from home, love?" the woman asked. "Always nice to get news from home, I say."

Sarah was skimming down the page as the woman babbled on. She finished the page and looked up. "Er, thank you for your trouble,'' she said. She put another coin on the counter and walked out.

Sam had driven the car and was now parked outside the store. He smiled to Sarah. ''Got what you wanted?'' he asked.

''Oh—oh yes,'' Sarah answered. He looked at her. ''Something wrong?''

''I've just found this letter,'' she said. ''It was written back in September and it's just been lying there. I'm not sure what to do about it. It's from our old housekeeper—my father has had a stroke. He's paralyzed and he keeps asking for me apparently.''

''Oh, that's too bad,'' Sam said, starting up the big car and beginning to ease out of Ivanhoe. ''It's not easy to be so far away from family when things like this happen. So you'll be rushing back to England now, will you?''

''I don't know what to do,'' Sarah answered. ''England's a terribly long way away and . . . do you think I should go back to England to see him?''

''It's up to you, I suppose,'' Sam said, staring straight ahead as he steered the car past an extra large pothole.

Sarah sighed. ''I really don't know what to do. This letter is already three months old. He might have died by now and I would have gone all that way for nothing.''

Sam turned to glance at her. ''Were you fond of your father?'' Sam asked.

''Not in the least,'' Sarah said forcefully. ''In fact, he disinherited me the last time I saw him.''

Sam grinned. ''Then that would be a good reason to go, wouldn't it? Dying father forgives erring daughter and reinstates in will. I take it he's worth a lot?''

''Quite a bit, I should think,'' Sarah said.

''Then I'd go,'' Sam suggested. ''Never turn down a chance for ready cash.''

''You are very heartless, Mr. Tanksley,'' Sarah exclaimed. ''Doesn't guilt and making peace before you die come into it at all for you?''

Sam laughed. ''Good lawyers have to be students of human nature. There are not too many people who will go halfway across the world to make peace, in my experience, but most people will go to the ends of the earth to inherit a fortune.''

''You're very cynical.''

''Only realistic,'' he answered. ''And I might remind you

that you've just chased all the way to the back of beyond to get back something you thought you were entitled to.''
Sarah smiled. ''Maybe you're right,'' she said, ''but you don't know my father. If he disinherited me, he would rather die than go back on it.''
''But I thought you said he'd been asking for you? That shows a remorse to me. Illness does strange things to old people.''
''So you're telling me to go?''
Sam grinned. ''If that were me, it would be worth the gamble. You've no strong ties here, have you—and you have a hell of a lot to lose if he leaves the fortune to someone else . . .''
''When you put it like that . . .'' Sarah said. ''I'm just not used to zooming around the world at a moment's notice.''
''The bright young things do it all the time, so I hear. There is a positive traffic jam across the Atlantic these days of people coming and going. And I understand one can already travel between Sydney and Adelaide by aeroplane . . . You can afford the trip, can't you?''
Sarah smiled. ''I'll have to wait and see your fees first.''
Sam chuckled. ''Nonsense—you've just got yourself a mineral lease. Ask the government for a first payment on that. I understand you have some influence at the state level?''
Sarah smiled. ''Col has been too good to me already,'' she said. ''I'm sure that mineral lease was highly irregular.''
''And yet I don't see you turning it down,'' Sam said smoothly.
Sarah stared out at the countryside. There was no more sign of habitation, just red earth, patches of brush, purple smudges of hills. Such a big, bright land. ''I've learned that you're a fool if you don't take what you can get,'' she said. ''Especially in a country like this where so much is waiting to be taken.''
''Too right,'' Sam said. ''God's own country, Australia is, and it doesn't need too much in the way of brains to get more than your share of it.''
They bounced and skidded onward, clouds of red dust obscuring the way behind them. Sarah sat in silence, thinking of England for the first time in many months. The thought of confronting her father was not appealing. Did he really want to see her or was that just Janet's way of getting her back home again? She played through the last terrible scene with her father—his puffy face apoplectic with rage as he pointed at the door. Was

the chance of any amount of money worth going through another scene like that? And yet, as Simon had said when he left to go home, you only have one father, and knowing he is about to die does change the way you think about him. Her father had brought her up believing he was doing his best for her. The fact that his "best" stifled and dominated her and would even have crushed her if she hadn't inherited his own Hartley spirit, was irrelevant. And if he was really waiting for her forgiveness to die in peace . . .

A smile flashed across her face as she pictured Col Murphy. "What a load of old codswallop," Col would say. "It all boils down to whether you want someone else to get his hands on your inheritance or not."

Then she pictured her cousin Hugo—her boring, pretentious cousin Hugo, striding around Wickcombe, dismissing Janet, upsetting the tenants.

"I think I have decided to go home after all," she said to Sam. "I'll catch the next boat out, only I'd be grateful if you wouldn't tell anybody until after I'm gone."

As soon as she made mental plans to leave, she realized she might have problems with Madeleine. Would Madeleine understand that she had to go to a dying father? Probably, if money was involved, Sarah thought. But somehow she did not want to risk the encounter. She decided to pack up essentials and leave a note behind explaining everything.

Three days later, on January 30th, 1922, she was on the P and O ship, *Mooltan*, bound for England, a note addressed to Madeleine on her dresser, another to Col beside it. The first class journey back was nothing like the cramped little cabin in the bowels of the ship that she had shared with Jessie. She ate at the captain's table, played endless games of shuffleboard and deck tennis, and fielded two proposals of marriage. She realized with some astonishment that her year with Madeleine had groomed her into a young society woman, capable of mixing and conversing at the highest level. She was almost sorry when they docked in Southampton and she caught the boat train for London.

It was raining, a thick, sleety rain, as she emerged from Waterloo station. She stepped out into the worst of it to hail a taxi to take her across to Liverpool Street and the train to Suffolk and was immediately tapped on the shoulder.

"Back of the queue's down there," a sharp-faced woman told her, eyeing her with distaste. Obediently Sarah made her way to the back of a long line, standing under the station awning, which was just not wide enough to keep the rain from stinging at her legs.

"Welcome to England," Sarah muttered to herself. Crowds of gray, drab people hurried into the station, scowling as the Australians had done against the sun. Everywhere there were queues—queues for buses that appeared as bright splotches of red in an otherwise colorless landscape, disgorged passengers, filled up again and left, queues for taxis, queues even to buy evening newspapers—patient lines of tired-looking faces, never talking to each other, all lost in silent worlds of misery. Sarah wrapped her fur around her but could not keep out the cold.

"Think of roaring fires, chestnuts roasting," she kept telling herself. "Think of quilted beds, thick soups, sheepskin slippers." But still she shivered. She noticed the faces in the patient lines watching her with interest and realized that with her tanned face and bright colors she represented something strange and foreign to them.

At Liverpool Street she found herself an empty first-class compartment and turned the heat up to full. The train pulled out, passing through gloomy inner suburbs—row after identical row of soot-streaked houses—backyards full of soot-streaked, wet washing, puddles and dustbins. Nowhere a single splash of color to brighten the grayness. Her mind drifted to red earth, blue sky, yellow wattles, bougainvillea, bottlebrush, frangipani—the heady smells that she had come to take for granted. The tenements gave way to outer suburbs—semi-detached houses, squares of lawn, bird baths and low brick walls—red brick houses, red roofs with bare trees and gray streets. Then finally the last of the suburbs fell away and the flat fields of eastern England melted into the distance in varying shades of gray. Stands of skeleton trees broke the flat monotony of fallow fields and the only movement was the clouds of rooks which rose and circled in the copses.

At Ipswich station she first heard the familiar Suffolk accent—the slow ponderous country speech of her childhood.

"You want a taxi all the way out to Wickcombe?" the driver asked in surprise.

"That's right," Sarah said. "Are you free?"

"Don't know about that," the young man said, scratching his head as if that action might speed up the inner workings of his brain.

"Well, are you free or aren't you?" Sarah insisted.

"Cost you a pretty penny that will. Petrol's not cheap anymore, you know."

"Nevertheless, I have to get to Wickcombe this afternoon and I am prepared to pay," Sarah said, impatient now to be so close to her journey's end and to be confronted by a slow-moving native. "Do you want the job or shall I find another car?"

"Didn't say I wouldn't take you, did I?" the young man asked. "This your luggage? Don't think we'll make it to Wickcombe before dark. Roads not too nice on a day like this." Muttering to himself, he carried her bags to the waiting taxi and halfheartedly helped her inside.

"Come from foreign parts, have you?" he asked as he went to close the door.

"From Australia," Sarah said.

He looked delighted. "Aghhh! I said to myself that you was foreign the moment I set eyes on you."

Sarah smiled to herself as the car moved off, headlights shining in the closing twilight. How strange and amusing to be taken for a foreigner in her own town. She hadn't realized how very much she had changed until she noticed the reactions this afternoon. She wondered what the reaction would be at Wickcombe.

"Do you know Wickcombe Hall?" she asked the young driver.

"Arggh," he replied, which she took for a yes.

"Do you know Major Hartley, who owns it?"

"Arggh . . . old bugger, ain't he?"

"So he's still alive, is he?"

"Far as I know."

At least this was a relief. To have arrived after such a long journey to find her father dead and herself disinherited as ever with nowhere to go was not a cheering thought. They were passing through familiar territory now. These dripping, leafless lanes were where Sarah had ridden her ponies as a young child, had gone to tea with neighbors in the gig, or into Ipswich to do occasional shopping with Janet. She peered through the trees for the first glimpse of the Orwell—that broad, winding river that had inspired Jimmy to name his station. They came around a bend and there it was, full to overflowing with rain, a red-sailed coal barge making its way placidly with the current down to the mouth. Even in the rain-washed twilight it was as beautiful as she remembered and a lump came to her throat. For the first time it really dawned on her that she was coming home.

There were lights in the upper windows at Wickcombe Hall as the taxi turned into the driveway, gravel scrunching as they drove past the gatekeeper's cottage and up to the main house. Sarah, who had sailed halfway across the world with the same matter-of-fact attitude that had taken her out to Australia in the first place, now experienced a moment of panic. What if the Hall had been sold, if the door was opened by strangers? The taxi driver was unloading her bags, carrying them up the flight of stone steps, and depositing them outside the imposing studded front doors. She paid the driver the money he asked, even though she suspected that she was being overcharged for being a foreigner, and rang the doorbell. After what seemed like hours, the door opened and Janet's pinched little face looked up at her, first suspiciously, then in astonishment, and then pure delight.

"Hello Janet," Sarah said, her voice choking with emotion.

"God be praised, you've come back," Janet answered. "And look at you—you've turned into a beautiful young woman. I'd never have known you, and you don't look like you've been slaving on many farms either. Come away in with you out of the cold. This is better than Christmas!"

She closed the front door behind Sarah. "I'll have Ellen take up your bags to your room while I'm fixing you a nice cup of tea," she said, bustling ahead of Sarah down the hall and into the big kitchen. "I never thought I'd see you again. I hoped you'd come, but I never thought . . . ach, but it's grand to see you lassie."

"My father?" Sarah asked, pausing to stare up the wide staircase to the dimly lit gallery beyond. "Is he still alive?"

Janet followed her gaze with distaste. "Oh yes, he's alive all right, the crotchety old fool, but only just. The doctors didn't expect him to hang on this long. It's my belief he was waiting to make his peace with you."

"So he really has been asking for me?"

"In his sleep he murmurs your name over and over: Sarah, Sarah, Sarah. It's uncanny to hear it, it is."

"You said he had a stroke," Sarah said, accepting the tea that Janet had poured. "Is he still paralyzed?"

"Aye—can't move a muscle, except his eyes and his mouth, and he slurs something terrible when he tries to speak. You'd think he'd be extra grateful that someone had to wait on him hand and foot, but not him. Curses every time he speaks. It's only when he's asleep and running a fever he talks so gentle and always your name. That's why I was hoping you'd come . . . I've been with the old fool so long I'd hate to see his black soul go straight down to hell, that I would. If he could only make his peace first, it's my belief he'd die happy."

Sarah took a sip of the scalding liquid and put the cup down again. "Do you think I should go up and see him right away? Will he have heard me come in?"

"You sit you down and finish your tea first," Janet instructed. "Like as not he's sleeping. He does most of the time. I'd be taking his dinner up to him at seven and he'll wake for that. Still hasn't lost his appetite, although I can only get liquids down him—lots of soups and milky puddings, that's what he's been living on and that's strain enough to get him to eat. Poor housemaids have to prop him up for me and he growls at them till they're terrified!"

Sarah finished the cup of tea and watched Janet preparing a tray.

"Where's Cook?" Sarah asked.

"Ach, she upped and left us a couple of weeks back after he complained again about her cooking," Janet said. "He's scared almost everyone away. He never was the sweetest man in the world, but after you left, he turned terrible mean and nasty. Ach, but it does my heart good to see you looking so bonny. Married life agrees with you then, does it?"

"That's a long story, Janet," Sarah said. "Let's wait until we have time before I tell it to you. I'd rather see my father and get it over with now. I'm getting more nervous by the second."

"Very well, I'll take you up then," Janet said. "I can't guarantee how you'll find him, but he's a stubborn old thing. Even if he's delighted to see you again, don't expect him to show it right off."

"Don't worry, I won't," Sarah said. "I know him too well for that."

She followed Janet out of the warm kitchen and up the dim

drafty staircase. An oil lamp was burning in the farthest bedroom and the lamp threw eerie shadows on the walls. Sarah held her breath as she tiptoed in. Her father lay propped in his big bed. He had always been a big man, but now his considerable size made him look like a deflated balloon. His heavy jowls sagged against the white pillows, his mouth hung open at a strange angle, and his eyes had sunk into hollow sockets. Sarah took a half step back and touched Janet's arm. "He's . . . he's not dead, is he?"

Janet gave him a swift appraisal. "Ach, he's looked like that for months. No, he's just sleeping. We'll wake him up for you." She stepped briskly up to the side of the bed. "Major Hartley, sir. There's a lovely surprise for you. You'll never guess who's come home to visit her sick papa!"

The sunken eyes twitched open and closed a few times.

"What the devil are you babbling about woman?" he demanded through crooked lips. "It's not time for my dinner yet, is it?"

Sarah stepped up to the bed. "It's me, Father, I heard you were ill and I've come home to see you."

"Who are you?" he demanded, peering at her.

"I'm Sarah, your daughter. Don't you recognize me?"

"Sarah?" he demanded and the word came out clearly. "Sarah? My daughter?"

"Yes father," Sarah said.

He tried to raise his head to see her better, making a gurgling noise in his throat as he did so. Sarah stood patiently beside him. Then he formed the words clearly, "I . . . don't . . . have a . . . daughter."

Sarah recoiled from the venom of his words. "I understood you might want to see me, Father," she said.

The words came out in a slurred torrent, barely intelligible: "You have the nerve to come back here? I thought I told you never to come back—do you hear me, miss? Never to darken my doors again, that's what I said."

"I know that Father, and I didn't come back because I wanted to," Sarah said calmly. "I came back because I understood you wanted to see me—you were asking for me!"

"Never!" he bellowed, twitching his head as he tried to move. "Never! You came crawling back because you wanted to get your hands on my money. Well, you never will, miss. Understand me! So you wasted your time. You came all the way back for nothing because I'll never forgive you, never as long as I . . ." His jaw jerked as he tried to form the words, then he gasped and his jaw went slack. He slumped back onto the pillow. Janet rushed up to his side.

"Lord have mercy," she mumbled, "He's dead."

Thirty-seven

SARAH STARED DOWN AT THE SAGGING FACE IN horror. "Are you sure he's dead?" she asked.

"Aye, he's dead all right," Janet answered. "We'd best send for the doctor."

Sarah continued to stare. "I came all this way, and I killed him," she said with a shudder, "and the worst thing is that I don't feel any remorse."

"Why should you?" Janet asked, pulling the sheet over the body in a matter-of-fact way. "Not one scrap of love did he ever show you. He drove you out of this house, that he did. And now he's gone with that load of hatred still in his heart . . ."

"He told me I'd come all this way for nothing," Sarah said thoughtfully, "and it looks like he was right. He couldn't forgive me and I suppose I couldn't forgive him either, and I'm just as disinherited as I ever was."

Janet put an arm around her. "Come away with you out of this place," she said. "Come down to the kitchen where there's a nice warm fire. There's nothing you could have done that you didn't do. You tried and the stubborn old fool was not willing to bend."

Sarah allowed herself to be led to the kitchen. "So I suppose Cousin Hugo inherits all this now," she said. "Pity. I don't like to think of Wickcombe in the hands of someone like him."

Janet's face became alert, almost sly. "Well, he may inherit, or he may not," she said. "I never saw your father's original will . . . but I don't think you'll be too disappointed."

"What do you mean?" Sarah asked. "My father cut me out of his will. He wrote a new one."

"Aye, that he did," Janet said. "He called in me and Cook to witness it, which we did. Then he had me take it to the mail, which I didn't."

"Are you saying that you didn't post his will?" Sarah asked incredulously.

"That's right," Janet said. "Cutting off his only daughter without a penny. That was a downright shameful thing to do."

"So the new will never got to the solicitors?" Sarah demanded. "And my father never found out?"

Janet sniffed. "He took it for granted that it was away and filed safely." She smiled. "All this time he was laughing, thinking that he'd taught you a cruel lesson, and all this time I was smiling behind his back because I knew he hadn't."

Sarah gave an incredulous smile. "Janet, you old rogue," she said.

Janet managed a guilty look. "I know that what I did was wrong, in the eyes of the law, too, I suppose," she said, "but I couldn't let him get away with that. It was monstrous. Your poor mother, God rest her soul, she would have wanted it this way."

Sarah actually laughed. "You ought to meet Col Murphy," she said. "You two would make a splendid pair."

"Who is this Mr. Murphy? An Irishman? You know what I think of the Irish—thieving Papists the lot of them."

"An Australian crook," Sarah said, "who also happens to be the premier of New South Wales."

"Well, fancy that," Janet said. "Don't tell me you've been hobnobbing with prime ministers."

"I suppose you could call it that," Sarah said with a smile. "Col Murphy is a good friend of mine. He'd appreciate what you've just done." As she spoke, a great longing for him came over her. She shuddered as she felt the touch of his lips on her bare shoulder . . . *So far away,* she thought.

Janet misinterpreted the shudder. "You poor wee soul, traveled halfway around the world and now a nasty shock like this. What you need is a good bowl of Janet's soup. Sit you down now, and then I'll be putting the hot water bottles in your bed and have a nice fire going in your room."

Obediently Sarah allowed herself to be seated at the kitchen table, then put to bed like a little girl again. She fell asleep without giving hardly a thought to the dead man in the room down the hall.

Mr. Fergus McKenzie, the solicitor from Colchester, and Sarah's cousin, Hugo Hartley, arrived on the same day later that week. Hugo exhibited surprise at her presence.

"You certainly have a nerve to show up here again," he said. "Still, I suppose I should thank you, since you obviously helped the old boy meet his Maker sooner than he might have done and thereby made me master of Wickcombe sooner than I might have expected."

Sarah looked at Hugo with distaste. She had never liked him. When they had played together as children, he was a bullying older cousin who teased in an underhanded sort of way, who led the younger ones into mischief, then melted away when punishment was meted out. With his hooded eyes, his cold handshake, and extra pale skin, he had always struck her as vaguely reptilian. Now, with the image of healthy Australian men still fresh in her mind, she decided that he resembled nothing more than a toad. She managed a polite smile. "I wouldn't be so sure, if I were you."

The hooded eyes raised a flicker. "You, my dear, do not get a bean. The old man told me himself. I don't know why you bothered to come all this way."

"You obviously do not consider filial affection and family ties sufficient reason?" she asked haughtily.

Hugo laughed. He had a thin titter that matched his pale exterior. "Come now, my dear," he said. "You disliked the old man as much as we all did, and don't pretend otherwise."

Not a toad, she thought, *a fish!* She gave him a cold stare. "Then let's just say that I came over to make sure you don't get your hands on my dolls. They were a legacy from my mother, and, as such, not part of the estate."

He looked at her with interest. "I must say, peasant life obviously agrees with you. You look disgustingly healthy and not at all as if he beats you three times a day."

"That's because I haven't been living as a peasant," she said.

"Why not? Did farmer Joe strike it rich?"

"I didn't marry, after all," she said, moving through ahead of him to the library where Janet had already seated the solicitor.

"Why not? He wouldn't have you or he already had a wife nd kids?"

"None of your damn business," she said, glancing back over er shoulder. She noted with satisfaction that he was shocked nd remembered that ladies in England probably did not swear. he watched him as he took a seat in one of the big leather ibrary chairs. He was twitching with anticipation, as a toad vould if a fly landed near it.

The solicitor cleared his throat officiously and glanced down t the papers. "You are Miss Sarah Elizabeth Hartley," he sked, "and you Mr. Hugo Wolverstone Hartley? Good. I am amed executor of the will of the late Major Henry Francis Hurst Iartley of Wickcombe Manor in the county of Suffolk."

"Yes, yes, we know all that, get on with it," came Hugo's lipped interruption.

The solicitor peered at him over the top of spectacles. "As I vas saying," he said, clearing his throat again, "of Wickcombe Manor in the county of Suffolk." He produced a sheet of parchnent and held it close to the light of the lamp. "I Henry Hartley, eing of sound mind, do bequeath my worldly possessions and states as follows: to my groom, Thomas, the sum of one hunlred pounds. To the gardener, Frederick, likewise one hundred ounds. To my faithful housekeeper, Janet, the sum of one thouand pounds . . ." Intake of breath heard from Janet at the back f the room. Sarah was conscious of every noise—the rustling f the parchment in old arthritic hands, the ponderous tick of he grandfather clock in the hall outside, the moan of wind in he chimney.

"To my only child, Sarah Elizabeth Hartley, I leave the sum f fifty thousand pounds," the man read. Sarah was conscious f the explosive, "What?" from Hugo.

"To my only child . . ." the solicitor tried to repeat.

"But this is preposterous," Hugo spluttered, half rising from his seat. "The old man disinherited her. He cut her off without a penny. This is the wrong will!"

"This is the only will lodged with McKenzie, Stroud, and Pearson," Mr. McKenzie said. "I know of no other."

"I will most certainly protest this in court if no other will is found!" Hugo blustered. "The old man definitely told me . . ."

"Mr. Hartley, will you let me continue," the solicitor went on. "To my only child, Sarah Elizabeth Hartley, I leave the sum of fifty thousand pounds to be held in trust for her until such time as she shall marry or turn twenty-nine years old, whichever shall come first. Until the time when she passes into her inheritance, she shall receive the interest on the said sum as an annual allowance and further amounts may be advanced at the discretion of the trustee.

"To the only surviving male Hartley relative, Hugo Wolverstone Hartley, I leave Wickcombe Hall, with its accompanying estates, farm buildings, equipment, and livestock. The conditions of this bequest are that he does not sell it during his lifetime and that it is passed on to his son or nearest male heir; also that he provide a home for Sarah Elizabeth Hartley for as long as she remains unmarried and act as trustee for her estate."

The solicitor looked up, peering first at Sarah and then at Hugo. "That, ladies and gentlemen, is the will. If another will materializes when the deceased's papers are gone through, it should be brought to me immediately and this will shall naturally be revoked."

Hugo had already risen to his feet. "There has to be another will," he said. "I'm going through the papers right away."

"I don't know why you are so upset," Sarah said, blocking his way out of the room. "You get Wickcombe. I should have thought that was enough for anyone."

"Wickcombe?" Hugo almost spat. "What use is a crumbling old manor house without the capital to run it? And that, my dear cousin, apparently goes to you."

"Yes," Sarah acknowledged in delight. "It does appear to."

Although Hugo searched fervently all evening and all next day, no other will came to light. He finally departed in disgust, leaving Sarah and Janet alone.

"Well, my dear, it appears that you are now quite a wealthy woman," Janet commented.

"Not until I marry or turn twenty-nine," Sarah answered, "and I don't like the thought of Hugo being my trustee. And I certainly don't like the thought of living under the same roof as him. Do you think that is a condition of the will? It almost sounded like it."

"You don't want to stay on at Wickcombe? Where else would you go?"

"I'd rather be independent," Sarah said. "I don't want to be anybody's ward."

Janet sniffed. "Ach, the world is not an easy place for an independent woman," she said. "There are always men waiting to take advantage, but then you'd know nothing of that . . ."

Sarah had not told Janet the details of her stay in Australia. Somehow she did not think that Janet would understand, and she needed an ally at this moment. It was much easier to let Janet think that she had lived with a wealthy family and acted as companion, which was not too far from the truth.

"I might want to go back to Australia," she said.

"Australia? Why would you want to go back there?" Janet demanded. "You've no need to go back into service and you've no ties outside that . . ."

She's right, Sarah thought, I have no ties outside that. Col enjoyed my company, but that was all. He has probably already found a replacement, so has Madeleine . . . I've no real reason to go back at all. The trouble is that I don't seem to belong anywhere anymore . . .

Thirty-eight

LIFE WENT ON AT WICKCOMBE FOR SARAH AS SHE waited for the will to pass probate. It was a strange life, lived from day to day, but not unpleasant. Janet waited on her more than she had ever done when Sarah was a child. Spring came, turning the gray countryside into a colorful pageant of wild flowers and blossoms. On fine days she went out riding. Former neighbors called. She went through her father's things and gave away his clothes to grateful tenants. She kept his gold cuff links and watch for herself and did not tell Hugo. Hugo himself showed up from time to time with his horse-like wife, Patricia, to plan alterations and modernize bathrooms. Patricia and Sarah fought almost immediately when Patricia wanted Sarah's bedroom for her podgy three-year-old son, Hengist. Sarah thought that Hengist was one of the most objectionable children she had ever met and refused to turn over her room to him.

"You seem to forget that this is our house now," Patricia said in her sharp upper-class voice.

"Not until probate is granted," Sarah said sweetly, "and then only as long as you give me a home."

"There are plenty of other rooms," Patricia said.

"They would not seem like home to me," Sarah answered.

"Hugo will just have to hurry up and find you a husband," Patricia snapped, "although at your age, it won't be an easy task."

"I'm afraid I am very choosy," Sarah said smoothly, "and I do think that twenty-nine is an ideal age to marry, don't you?"

In a way she enjoyed baiting Patricia, but only as long as she looked on her present situation as temporary. In May, Hugo and Patricia moved in, although the house was still technically not theirs for another month. Hengist was put in the room next to Sarah's and his bad-tempered nursemaid in the room next to him. Sarah could hear him wailing and whining through half the night. She overheard Patricia saying to Hugo that at least they would not need to hire a governess, as they had one right on the spot.

The situation turned into an instant battle of wits with Patricia. She was determined to break Sarah's haughty pride and turn her into dependent relative status. She invited over important county families to dinner or tea and then introduced Sarah as "our poor unfortunate cousin who has just lost her father and is making her home with us." Then she would attempt to gush over Sarah in a patronizing sort of way.

"We must get our heads together, mustn't we, Cecily?" she would ask at tea. "I'm sure we'll be able to come up with an eligible young man for poor, dear Sarah."

Sarah smiled and said nothing, which infuriated Patricia all the more. She sat listening to the local gossip, the racing tips from the men, the scandals, and the baby talk from the women as if she were a being newly arrived from a distant planet. Now that she was back among them, she remembered how boring she had found her neighbors before. The cozy tea parties, the flower arranging, the Sunday walk to church—all the things that she had yearned for during her exile in the outback were now reduced again to meaningless rituals. She remembered how the genteel manners were used to disguise cattiness and snobbery. The world for these women did not even extend as far as London. It finished in a neat barrier somewhere on the other side of Ipswich and anything outside that barrier was primitive, uncultured, uncivilized, and not worth discussing.

"You were in Australia, my dear? How madly interesting," they would all say when first introduced to Sarah. Then, with the next breath they would all make similar comments. "Wasn't it just too, too primitive for words? I hear they don't even have bathrooms and, of course, they haven't even heard of culture."

Having dismissed Australia with one sentence, the conversation would swing back to the tennis club, the planned summer holiday in Cornwall or Bridlington: "We always go there. Martin's nanny took him when he was three, and he's been back every year ever since. The air is so bracing," or the current topic—that of the rising middle class: "My dear, you can't imagine who wanted to join the pony club? Those new people who bought Archie's old house. The man is a grocer."

"Oh, come now, Caroline (this from one of the men). He does own a chain of large stores. They say he's worth a mint."

"He can own every shop from here to Timbuktu, but he's still only a grocer," the woman replied and everyone nodded in agreement, all joining in with similar examples of how the lower classes were getting above themselves and progressing from there to the terrible servant problem. It seemed that after the war, nobody wanted to be servants anymore.

"I knew it was a mistake, letting them work in factories and things. The money has gone to their heads. My groom demanded Sundays off. Imagine that? Who does he think would rub down the horses when we hunt?"

General laughter. Sarah looked down from face to face around the room. Particularly she examined the men's faces. *Imagine being married to one of them,* she thought. *And yet I have to do something about my future. I want to settle down someday—but where? And with whom?*

Probate was granted and Sarah took her first allowance to go straight up to London, returning with an expensive new wardrobe that she wore to the next dinner party. The dress was of the Grecian design, popular that summer and against the remnants of her Australian tan, the colors glowed. She noticed that every man at the table was looking at her with admiration, every woman with envy. Although Patricia tried to steer the conversation back to pony clubs and early strawberries, it always managed to find its way back to Sydney and kangaroos and surfing beaches.

After dinner, Sarah went out obediently with the other ladies before the port was served, but would not join them for gossip in the powder room. Instead she wandered out into the soft June night. She stood on the terrace, looking up at the familiar lines of the house, the black shapes of the clipped yew hedge and the climbing roses around the trellis. It had all been dear to her and now it was spoiled. She was not conscious of footsteps behind her until a voice spoke, almost in her ear.

"Admiring my house?" She turned to eye Hugo with dislike. He smiled and the smile was even more repulsive than his normal stare. "It must grieve you to know that you are only here by my grace and favor," he said.

"On the contrary," she replied smoothly. "You are only here by my grace and favor. You fail to give me a home and the will is null and void."

"The situation is an impasse, my dear, because I hold the key to your money. Your allowance is hardly enough to buy clothes like those you have appeared in this evening, and any advances on capital have to come through me. What a pity . . ." He continued to gaze at her. "Of course, there is a compromise that could suit us both . . ."

"There is?" she asked suspiciously.

"A very obvious one," he said, moving one step closer. "You have grown into a very desirable woman. My wife is . . . not a very desirable woman. I could arrange to move my son out of the bedroom next to yours and no one need ever know . . ."

Sarah almost laughed out loud. She attempted to play the affronted lady. "Are you suggesting that I should become your mistress?" she asked.

Hugo recoiled a little. "What would be the harm in it? You don't seem like the sort of woman who'd want to spend the rest of her life in a convent and I . . . I am a man of experience, a man of the world. I could instruct you in the delights of the flesh . . ." He stepped toward her and made a clumsy grab at her, his hands running over her breasts and down her body as he gave a little moan of desire. Sarah caught the hands before they could explore any further and pushed him away from her.

"Hugo. Are you crazy? You have guests just inside those windows."

He was panting. "Later then, when the guests have gone . . . I'll come to your room."

"You will do no such thing!" she said, stepping back to a safe distance.

"But can't you see that I want you?" he said, the words coming out as gasps. "I desire you. I want to possess you!"

"But I don't desire you, Hugo," Sarah said. "That's the problem."

"That's because you are young, you are inexperienced. I could arouse you until you were mad with desire for me . . ."

A smile twitched on Sarah's lips. "I doubt it," she said, "but unfortunately you won't have the chance to try."

She had felt completely secure, knowing that one scream, floating through the open windows, would bring help. But suddenly Hugo grabbed her wrists, his nails biting into her flesh, drawing her close to him. "You listen to me," he hissed. "Either you be a good little girl or you'll be very sorry. I can hold up every penny of that money until you turn twenty-nine, and that's a long time from now. I can make you dance for every penny, and I can come into your room anytime I want to and there is nobody who would stop me!"

"Let go of me, you're hurting," she said, alarmed and surprised by his sudden strength. She realized that what he said was true. He could come into her room and there probably was nobody who could stop him.

"Then I shall leave this house," she said, "if you insist in making silly threats."

He laughed. "Where would you go? Where would you live on the allowance you'd get?" He twisted her arms up until her face was inches from his. "No, my dear, you are trapped here for as long as I want you to stay, and you'll just have to face that fact." Then he kissed her savagely, his teeth crushing her lips, before he released her and walked back into the house, leaving her somewhat shaken in the darkness.

When she came back to join the women, only Patricia watched her with interest, her eyes calculating as Sarah sat down to drink her coffee. After the guests had gone, alone in her room next to the wailing Hengist, she sat at her dressing table and stared out into the clear English night. Through the window came the sweet summer smells of the English countryside—roses and apple blossoms and newly cut grass. A bird was twittering in the woodland, and the moon streaked the formal gardens with bands of silver. Sarah put her hands to her head to shake off the feeling of unreality.

"What am I doing here?" she asked herself, staring at the elegant reflection in the mirror. "Somehow I've got to get my hands on that money and escape."

Next morning she went out for a long ride, and by afternoon she had made up her mind that she had to act now. There was no way she was going to bed with Hugo and if Patricia found out he was trying to bed her, she would be all the more venomous. She cornered Hugo in the library. "You and I have to do some serious talking, Hugo," she said, closing the door and sitting in her father's old leather chair before Hugo could do so.

He walked across and perched on the arm of her chair, looking across at the closed door and then at her. "You've come to your senses," he said. "I knew you would."

"Precisely," Sarah said. "I think it's time you and I faced facts. I have the money and you have the house—both rather useless without the other, don't you think?"

"Absolutely," he agreed. "There was no way you should have got the money. I don't know how you managed it, but I want you to know that I shall certainly find some way to get my hands on it before too long."

"I thought you might," Sarah said, "which is why I've come to make you a proposition."

"You have?" he looked interested.

"It's this: we split the fifty thousand between us, twenty-five each. I get all my share now and get out of your life. You don't have to give me a home and I'm not dependent on you."

He nodded, still not taking his eyes from her for a second. "Interesting," he said.

She got up and began to pace impatiently. "Oh, come on, Hugo, see sense. There is no way you're going to get me into bed with you. Do you really want me hanging around here, tempting you all the time? And you could certainly use the money. Twenty-five each is a useful amount for both of us. I can buy myself a little house—you can run Wickcombe the way you'd like to—we both end up happily ever after."

He walked over to her, trapping her between himself and the writing table. "I'll agree to it if you let me make love to you now, just this once, right here in the library."

He was already pawing at her again, pushing her backward across the desk, his hands feeling her breasts like ripe oranges, making animallike moaning noises.

Why not just let him do it? The thought flashed across her mind. *What is it to you? It would mean nothing, just like the others. What is one more?*

Then the answer came so forcefully that she found the strength to push herself upright and to hold off those grasping hands. *If I do it with him, then I'll always be a whore.*

"Hugo, hold on a minute," she begged. "Whoa—cool down! Just listen to me. I'm not the innocent little virgin you think I am . . ."

"All the better," he said, reminding her ridiculously of the big, bad wolf. The situation was rapidly developing into a farce. *How Col would have laughed,* she thought.

"Listen to me," she insisted. "You can't have me, because . . . because I have syphilis."

It was a touch of inspiration, but it had an immediate effect. He leaped backward in horror. It was all she could do to keep a straight face.

"Oh . . ." he stammered. "Oh . . . that explains it. That explains everything. You're right. You must get away from here. It wouldn't be healthy . . . for my son . . . My wife must never know. She's led a sheltered life . . ."

Sarah smiled politely. "So you'll agree to my proposition?" she asked. "We'll split my money, fifty-fifty and you'll never see me again?"

He kept nodding. "Yes, that would be best. That would be the best thing."

It was only after she had reached her own room that she collapsed onto the bed in delighted laughter.

Thirty-Nine

COL MURPHY STOOD UP TO HIS ANKLES IN WATER, staring out across the breakers. Every now and then a wave rushed in, sweeping up to his thighs, wetting his shorts, and almost throwing him off balance, but he didn't stir. Jack Hemmingway came out of the house and stood on the terrace watching Col before he walked across the sand to join him.

"What are you looking at?" he asked.

"Japan," Col said, without turning around.

"Japan?"

"Yeah. Must be vaguely in that direction, mustn't it? Sort of north eastish?"

"I suppose so," Jack said. "A couple of thousand miles in that direction. Why are you looking at Japan?"

"I was thinking that they wouldn't have many sheep up there, would they?"

"I don't think so."

"And lots of people to feed?"

"Definitely."

"And no woolly sweaters to keep them warm in winter? It does get cold in winter in Japan, doesn't it?"

"Pretty cold, I should imagine."

Col nodded and went on staring.

"Were you thinking about exporting to Japan?" Jack Hemmingway asked hesitantly.

"Just toying with the idea," Col said.

"I wouldn't if I were you," Jack advised. "You know what Aussies think about the yellow peril."

Col laughed. "I don't want to let them into the bloody country, just sell them our wool," he said.

"People haven't forgotten what happened when we let the

Chinese in,'' Jack reminded. ''They'll see one or two traders as the foreguard of an army.''

''Then they're bloody stupid,'' Col growled. ''It makes all the sense in the world to trade with Asia. They're our closest neighbors, for Christ's sake.''

''But they don't look like us,'' Jack said with a smile. ''The farmers wouldn't want to sell their wool to clothe slit-eyed people.''

Col shook his head, smiling. ''I said I was just toying, Jack. Just imagining, you know. It's this Imperial Preference debate, Jack.''

''You don't like the way things are going?''

''I don't like it and neither do any of the boys who got dumped on a beach at Gallipoli by the wrong orders of the English,'' Col said. ''They figure they've done enough for king and country without supplying them with cheap goods.''

''But it has plenty of advantages for Australia, as well as England,'' Jack insisted. ''Protected tariffs, guaranteed market.''

''I know,'' Col said. ''It all looks good on paper, but what it really boils down to is keeping the British empire going just a little bit longer.''

''Most people feel that England is the mother country and it's only right to export our goods to her,'' Jack said.

''Not most people,'' Col said. ''Those people who have subsidiaries in England and who get in on both sides of the deal like it. The farmers won't be so much in favor when England dictates their wool prices or won't buy their meat because they've already bought it cheaper from New Zealand. It's just not healthy to depend on one market.''

''But we get preferential treatment in return,'' Jack insisted. ''English motor cars . . .''

''What's wrong with our own bloody motor cars, for Christ's sake?'' Col demanded. ''I know they're not as fancy as the English ones, but you've got to start somewhere, haven't you? There's the Summit—that's coming along, so I hear. Maybe we'll outdo Henry Ford!'' And he grinned, his cheekily boyish grin. Then his face fell serious again. ''It really sticks in my craw to rely on imports for everything,'' he said. ''We could do everything here. We have the raw materials, for Christ's sake.

We just need the know-how. It doesn't make sense to import bloody English motor cars."

"We have a guaranteed market for our products, that's important, isn't it?" Jack asked.

"And when that market gets wiped out in another war? What then?" Col asked.

"You're turning into a bloody pessimist," Jack insisted. "I always thought you were in favor of the easiest way out, and this seems to be it. In addition to which, my dear Col, if the federal government goes along with Imperial Preference, and it looks as if they are going to, there's not too much you can do about it, is there?" Jack asked. "The states will just have to go along with government policy and do what they are told."

"Maybe not," Col said. "But I never was a good little boy who did what he was told."

"That might not be wise, Col," Jack said.

Col grinned again. "I know that. Marjorie has already warned me that the moment I'm out of favor with the electors, I'm out of favor with her, too. She also keeps telling me to be a good little boy and eat my prunes . . ." He gave one of his big laughs. "She's also been nagging me about exercise. She says I don't do anything. Had me up at dawn this morning for a swim . . ."

"Good for you, I expect," Jack said.

"I don't know," Col sounded suddenly weary. "I'm so tired right now. I could just sleep all day. And I've got this god-awful pain in my chest. I must have pulled a muscle the last time she had me playing tennis." He paused and rubbed his chest reflectively. "I came up here for a rest, not bloody exercise. I used to get plenty of exercise . . . it doesn't seem to matter any more."

He turned back to staring at the ocean. Jack said quietly, "I was wondering, when I saw you here, whether you were looking out toward England?"

Col continued to stare. "That would be bloody stupid, since England's in the other direction. Besides, there's too much land in the way—Himalayas and things, you can't see through those."

The two stood in silence, then Col said, "Besides, there wouldn't be much point in looking at England, would there? Nothing there now."

He came out of the ocean. "I think I'll take a nap before dinner," he said. "I'm feeling bushed. Think I'll ask Doctor

McClean to take a look at me when he comes to dinner tonight. Make him work for his supper.'' He looked across at Jack with the ghost of a smile before he set off slowly up the beach.

Forty

THE MAGIC WORD, "SYPHILIS" WORKED LIKE A charm. When Sarah had recovered from the absurd humor in the situation, she realized, a little more soberly, that the last time she lived in this room, she did not even know that such things existed; also that she was lucky that she had not had to face such problems in real life. Madeleine was always ultra careful in screening her clients and checking on their backgrounds, but the risk of disease was always there. It was only now that she was free of that life that she began to appreciate the risks that went along with it. In the lurid Sunday papers, prostitutes were always being murdered or dying from drugs. She appreciated for the first time also that Madeleine's strict rules had protected her girls. It was strange to look back on that episode in her life—almost as if it was a chapter in a book she was reading about another life long ago and far away. How surprised Hugo and Patricia would have been if they had seen her sipping champagne at an embassy ball or riding to the opera in the Rolls!

Hugo could not get her out of the house soon enough. The money was withdrawn and a check made over to her. He was even generous about letting her choose favorite objects from around the house, and it was eventually a whole cart load of possessions that made their way to the station in Ipswich while Sarah and Janet followed in a taxi. Janet was crying into her handkerchief. Wickcombe had been her home for forty years. Sarah could feel no such remorse. She looked back at the gray stone facade, the rose gardens, and the orchards, then she turned back again, feeling that this chapter of her life had, in reality, closed two years earlier.

In London they took two rooms in a quiet hotel on one of the better squares. Janet looked around them critically.

"Not enough room to swing a cat," she said.

"But I don't have a cat," Sarah laughed, "and they are big enough for our present needs."

"So how long are you planning to stay here?" Janet asked.

Sarah sat on the neat hotel bed and stared out of the window. "I wish I knew, Janet. That's the whole problem. I don't know where to go from here. I don't even know what I want out of life."

Janet sniffed. "You need to find yourself a good man and settle down. Have some bairns before it's too late. You've been on your own too long."

Sarah smiled. "Maybe you're right, and don't think I wouldn't like to find a 'good man' as you put it, but where? Not those boring idiots out in Suffolk. I was hoping to meet some interesting people in London. There must be some in the world."

"Your money will soon be eaten up staying in a place like this," Janet, the thrifty Scot, commented. "I've never heard the likes! Ten pounds a week! It's robbery, that's what it is."

Sarah reached out and took Janet's hand. "Look, Janet, you don't have to stay with me if you don't want to," she said. "You've inherited some money. You could buy yourself a little cottage back in Scotland with that, and put some away to live on. I'd make sure you didn't go short . . ."

Janet drew her hand away. "And what would I want, living in a bleak place like that?" she asked. "I don't know a soul in Scotland. I went into service in your dear, departed mama's house when I was fifteen and she a wee babe in arms. That's the only life I've known. But if you don't need my services anymore . . ."

Sarah got up. "Of course I need you, you silly old thing," she said. She went to hug her, but realized at the last minute that this would not be appreciated. "You're the only person I know in London. Of course I need you."

"You need to meet some young people your own age," Janet said. "Go to parties and things."

"Yes, but how?" Sarah said.

"Ach, these things take time," Janet said.

"I seem to spend my life waiting for things," Sarah said,

absently picking up her coat and hanging it in the wardrobe. "And most of them don't materialize."

The next weeks she made an effort to become part of London life. She went to Wimbledon for the tennis championships, to Lords for a cricket test. At each of these events she was conscious of the tanned Australians who seemed larger than life against the thin, wiry British. She sat in the stands and spoke to no one. No one spoke to her. One day in Harrods she commented on a hat to a woman who was trying it on. The woman froze her with an icy stare. "I don't think we've been introduced, have we?" she asked and went back to her mirror as if Sarah didn't exist. *I want to meet people, but how?* she wondered.

Janet, on the other hand, soon loved London. She would come home excitedly from Fortnums or Harrods. "You'll never imagine what they've got there," she would relate. "Pâtés and pies all ready made and pheasant already cooked and salmon already under aspic. A body could live here and never need a kitchen!"

Sarah laughed at her. "And you were the one urging me to economize. Those items are expensive, or didn't you notice?"

Janet nodded. "Now if you'd only get out of this place and buy yourself a nice wee house in a good neighborhood, I'd not feel guilty about getting us a nice wee pheasant."

"But which neighborhood?" Sarah asked. "I don't know where I want to be. I don't know if I can ever settle in England . . ."

"You're not thinking of going back to Australia, are you?" Janet asked.

"Maybe," Sarah said. "I miss a lot of things about Australia, but some things would be very hard for me . . ."

She changed the subject before Janet tried to cross-examine her. How could she ever tell Janet that she was a marked woman in Sydney and that it would be too painful to be in the same town as Col Murphy and never be able to see him? He had made it perfectly clear that he would never be allowed to get in touch with her outside of Madeleine's and that part of her life was behind her.

I've got to give this place a fair chance first, she told herself. *After all, London should be a city where someone could find enough to keep them occupied!*

Then, the next day, it was as if a good fairy had heard her. As she was walking through the lobby after lunch, a smartly dressed woman approached her hesitantly. "I really must apologize for coming up to you like this," she said, "but the manager tells me you are a charming, unattached young woman, and I wondered if you might do me the biggest favor?"

Sarah extended her hand. "Sarah Hartley," she said. "How can I help you?"

"Veronica Bridges," the woman said, returning the handshake. "It's my daughter Amanda. Perhaps you've seen us together in the restaurant. She's seventeen and we're up in town together for the first time. We very rarely come down from Cumberland, where we live, so it's a big treat for Amanda. I'd promised to take her to the tea dance at the Savoy today, but I know that I'm coming down with one of my sick headaches and I simply couldn't stand the music of a dance. I wonder—and I'm sure it's very impertinent of me—if you would consider accompanying her to the dance. I'd never dare suggest such a thing, but we know nobody here and every day is precious to a young person like Amanda."

"I'd be delighted," Sarah said. "As a matter of fact, I know nobody here either, so it will be a treat for me."

Amanda turned out to be a stunningly pretty seventeen-year-old who talked breathlessly and nonstop. She danced almost every dance at the tea dance and ended up with a large circle of male admirers around her. At the end of the dance she flew up to Sarah. "We've been invited to a party tonight—in Eaton Square! Isn't that too, too thrilling? An absolutely dishy young man and he's the son of an earl or something, so I'm sure Mama will approve. Do say you'll come with me or I won't be allowed to go."

"I'll come," Sarah said. "I haven't been to a good party in ages."

Amanda turned stunning blue eyes on Sarah. "Yes, I suppose it must be very dreary when one becomes older . . ." she said.

Amanda babbled excitedly all the way to the party. "Allistair gives such ripping parties, so I've heard. Last time they had a scavenger hunt and they drove around collecting policemen's helmets and things like that. And another time they all bathed in the serpentine. I am so looking forward to it!"

Sarah began to feel very old. She couldn't see the excitement in childish stunts. She found herself wondering how the policeman would explain his missing helmet to his sergeant.

She sat at the party, listening to the loud jazz music, watching the frantic dancing, feeling like an elderly chaperon. The participants were all so young. In fact, Sarah had noticed everywhere in London a singular lack of men her own age. Most of them didn't come home from France, she thought. What a terrible waste—and for the women, too. How many young women there are who will never have the chance for a husband and family . . .

She was sitting, sipping champagne, lost in thought about the husband and family she might never have, when she felt herself being watched. She glanced up and looked across the crowded dance floor. A pair of eyes met hers and opened wide with surprise. Then the fair face flushed with pleasure and Simon Bowyer fought his way across the wildly gyrating couples to her side.

"Sarah! It *is* you!" he exclaimed. "I thought I must have had too much champagne."

"Hello, Simon," she replied guardedly. "How nice to see you."

"But what are you doing here?" he asked. "You are the last person I expected to see."

"I'm staying at the Clarendon Hotel for the moment. My father died recently. I expect you saw it in the *Times*."

"No, I didn't. I'm not the greatest newspaper reader," he said, "and I've been run off my feet working on the estates. Unfortunately my father did not die and he's a positive slave driver. He has a horrible fear that I'll let everything go to pot the moment he pops off, so he's giving me a crash course in estate management, from the pigstys upward." He laughed, his eyes holding hers with obvious delight. "I can't get over seeing you here," he said. "It's so good to see you again."

"I'm surprised to see you, too," she replied. "I wouldn't have thought this was the right environment for a young married man. You are already married, aren't you?"

He made a face. "Not yet. Henrietta's family believes in long engagements. Next spring, I understand, is when the ax falls."

"And Henrietta is here tonight?"

He flushed. "Good Lord, no," he said. "She doesn't go in for things like this. She's very much the country girl."

"But she doesn't mind you being here?"

"She doesn't exactly know," he said, looking around as if a spy might be hiding behind his chair, "but I don't think she'd care too much. Henrietta's not . . . well, we don't know each other very well yet."

"I see," Sarah said. Simon continued to beam at her. "So you finally got out of that place," he said. "I'm so glad for you. Now you have a chance for a normal life here, where nobody knows about you. Would you like to dance?"

Sarah looked up. "Yes, but not to this. I don't know any of these new dances," she said. "It seems to consist entirely of flinging the arms around."

"Then would you like to come for a drive in my new car?" he asked.

Sarah looked around. "I'm supposed to be chaperoning Amanda," she said, "and do you think it would be right for me to drive with you? After all, you are engaged to someone else."

Simon's eyes were earnest. "I'm sure nobody would begrudge me a meeting with an old friend," he said.

"But I can't leave Amanda," Sarah said hesitantly.

At that moment Amanda, surrounded by young friends, came rushing up to her. "We're going to paddle in the fountains in Trafalgar Square!" she shouted.

"Are you sure you should?" Sarah asked. "What would your mother say?"

"Oh, don't be such an old stick-in-the-mud," Amanda said, pouting prettily. "You have to let young people have fun, that's one of the rules! And Allistair has promised to take good care of me, haven't you Allistair?"

"Cross my heart!" the boy beside her said. The whole group burst into noisy laughter.

Simon took Sarah's arm. "That settles that, I think," he said. "Your services are no longer required as chaperon and you wouldn't fit in their car if you tried. Besides, you don't really want to paddle in fountains, do you? It's very tame after Sydney beaches." His look said plainly to her, "You remember what happened on a Sydney beach, don't you?"

Sarah got to her feet. "I suppose there can be no harm in a car ride," she said, "unless you plan to steal policemen's helmets."

Simon laughed. "I'm a little past that stage," he said.

"I'm glad," Sarah commented. "I must confess I've been feeling very old. We were never as crazy at seventeen, were we?"

"That's because there was a war when we were seventeen," Simon said gently. "Nobody let us be crazy, even if we wanted to. Everyone is catching up for lost time now. The whole of London is crazy these days—the music and the new fashions and a new craze every few days. Pleasure is all that matters."

"And up on your estates?" she asked.

"Very sober," Simon said. "My father is still pretty much an invalid and goes to bed at nine. No parties up at Waverly, I'm afraid."

"So you come down here to escape?"

"This is the first time—and I must say I'm enjoying it," Simon answered. He led her to a white Daimler parked outside. "Go on, tell me it's a spiffy car," he said.

Sarah laughed. "I'm afraid I don't know much about cars," she said, "but it certainly seems pretty."

"My father bought it for me—for being a good boy," Simon said flatly as he opened the door. "He's training me like a dog—reward versus punishment. So far it seems to be working."

He climbed in beside her and they drove off through darkened streets. They sped past dignified monuments and historic buildings. They drove through the West End where shop windows were still illuminated and night clubs were spilling out late revelers, down Whitehall, past the Houses of Parliament, and across Westminster Bridge, its line of lamps throwing pools of light into the black waters of the Thames beneath.

"It's very beautiful," Sarah said, looking back at Big Ben, glowing from its tower. "There are so many beautiful things in London that one takes them for granted."

"Until one is in a place like Australia where the oldest building has only been there a hundred years and is most likely a monstrosity," Simon said, laughing. "Doesn't it feel good to be back in civilization again?"

She smiled but didn't answer.

"I can't believe you are here," he said again. "I thought I'd lost you forever."

They were driving along the embankment with the river at their right. Here there was no sign of life, except for a solitary policeman, plodding his beat. Simon pulled the car to a halt in the darkness between street lamps.

"You have lost me forever," Sarah said. "You are going to marry Henrietta, remember?"

Simon let out a big sigh. "I wish things could be different," he said. "I'm sure she'll make a splendid wife and all that. She's very efficient and strong and I'm sure she'll be very good at having babies, but . . ."

"But?" Sarah asked.

"She's cold," Simon said. "It's like kissing an icicle—when she lets me get close to her, which is very seldom. She says it's not proper to be alone until we are married." He sighed again. "Not that it matters much. When I touch her, I feel nothing. When I was with you, Sarah, everything felt right."

"Don't go on," she said shortly. "You'll just upset both of us. No good can come of sitting brooding about what might have been. Maybe you should drive me back to the party."

He turned and took her into his arms. "There must be a way, mustn't there? If two people love each other—they should be able to find a way to be together." He kissed her lightly and she didn't resist, then he wrapped her into an embrace and began to kiss her more and more hungrily. "Oh Sarah," he moaned, "how can I live without you?"

Sarah fought to keep control of her senses. "Simon," she said firmly. "Simon, please drive me home. Please don't do this to both of us. You are engaged to marry somebody else . . ."

"But I don't want her," he said passionately. "I want you. You are the only one I've ever wanted. We'll find a way. We must . . ." He held her away from him and looked into her eyes. "Tell me that you still want me, too, Sarah."

"It's no good wanting what I can't have, Simon," she said.

"Don't you believe in fate?" he whispered excitedly. "It must have been fate that brought you back to me. I'm not going to let you slip away again."

"Oh Simon," she said as much with pity for herself as for him. "What do you think you can do? As long as your father is alive, you are at his mercy, and he has already arranged for you to marry Henrietta. You wrote me that long letter about your duty to your family and your heritage."

"I know," he said, "and I do feel a duty to my family and my heritage, and my father for that matter, but I won't be penniless and dependent forever. If you can just be patient—my allowance is raised when I marry. It ought to run to a flat for you in town, to keep you comfortably enough—not extravagantly—you'll have to wait for that until the old man dies, but I'd come down and see you whenever I could . . ."

Sarah continued to stare at him, trying to digest what he was proposing. "You want to keep me in a little flat in London?" she asked, almost wanting to smile at the irony of it, "while you live a respectable life with Henrietta?"

He swallowed hard, clearing his throat. "Yes, well, there are certain things one has to do," he said, "and I can't get out of the marriage without the old boy disinheriting me—but . . ."

"But you'd like a bit on the side, is that correct?"

"Don't put it like that," Simon said in horror. "I don't think of you that way at all. I love you, Sarah. I cherish you."

"But you still want me to be a kept woman in a little flat?" She laughed. "And you were the one who kept begging me to escape my sordid life in Australia. What difference would there be—except that the food was better there, and the climate, too."

"You don't understand!" he insisted.

She drew away from him. "Oh, but I do, Simon. I understand very well. You love me, but not enough to run any risks for me. Did you ever stop to think what sort of life a little flat in London might be for me? Did it ever occur to you that I might not enjoy waiting around for you to visit me every few months? Did you never think about possible babies? That obviously never entered your mind after our last encounter."

Simon looked at her sharply. "I didn't . . . I mean, you weren't, were you?"

Sarah smiled. "Don't worry, Simon. They teach us how to take care of that sort of thing in my profession."

He winced. "Don't—don't torture me, Sarah. I only wanted—I only wished that we could be together."

"So did I, Simon," she said, "but I want more than you are prepared to offer me. Wherever I end up, I want a proper life—not the remnants of somebody else's. Now, would you drive me home?"

"There is only one difference between men in Australia and England," she told Janet at breakfast the next morning. "The men in England are more genteel about it, but they both want the same thing in the end."

"Ach, you've just had bad luck so far, lassie," Janet said, putting bacon and eggs in front of her. She glanced over Sarah's shoulder at the paper, lying open on the table, as yet unread. "Oh look—isn't this the man you were talking about once? Mr. Colin Murphy, premier of New South Wales?"

"Yes," Sarah said, snatching at the paper. "What does it say?"

"The poor man's just had a heart attack," Janet said as Sarah grabbed the paper from her. "Where is it?" she demanded.

"Hold your horses," Janet clucked. "There—little paragraph at the bottom."

Sarah read it. "It doesn't say that he died, does it?" she asked. "It would have said if he had died, wouldn't it? That must mean that he recovered . . ."

Janet looked down at her, folding her arms. "It says that he was holidaying in Queensland with his wife," she said firmly. "That was all it said."

Sarah continued to stare at the paper. "I wonder if they'd know more at Australia house?" she asked. "I have to know if he's going to be all right."

Janet continued to look disapprovingly. "It seems to me that you are a mite too interested in the well-being of a gentleman with a wife," she said.

"I know I am, Janet," Sarah said, "but I can't help it. I tried to stay away from Australia because of him, but it's no use. I have all the same problems in London and the sun hardly ever shines here."

"You're not thinking of going back to that place?" Janet asked in horror.

"That's right. I'm going right down to P and O and booking passage on the next ship. Will you come with me?"

"To Australia?" Janet asked. "All the way to Australia? For a visit, you mean, or for good?"

Sarah shrugged her shoulders. "I have nothing to keep me in London," she said. "I see no reason to come back here."

"You want to settle there? Is it not a heathen country with a lot of half-naked men and women running around?"

"Yes, I suppose it is," Sarah said, laughing, "but I think you'd like Australia, Janet. Lots of good food—fresh fish in the markets, oysters, shrimp, and good fresh air. I'm quite determined to go, but that doesn't mean you have to come with me.

I'd like it more than anything if you came. You're the nearest I have to family, but if you'd rather not come, I'll understand.''

Janet pursed her lips. ''Ach, what do I have to keep me in England?'' she asked. ''I've no family here and I'm far too old to take on a new position at my age.'' She pointed at the paragraph in the paper that Sarah was busily cutting out, ''And there's no knowing what you get up to if I'm not there to keep an eye on you!''

Ten days later the *Mooltan* sailed for Sydney with Sarah and her companion on board.

Forty-one

THE GOOD SHIP *MOOLTAN* WAS BARELY OUT OF Southampton when she ran into one of the famous Biscay squalls. For two days she heaved and tossed, sending china flying in the dining rooms and making Sarah's robe swing like a pendulum on the back of her door. In the end she had to crawl from her bunk and take it down because watching it made her more seasick than ever. Having enjoyed every moment of two previous voyages, the seasickness caught her by surprise and made her very angry at her frailty. She lay on her bunk, facing the wall and refusing to look at the broth and crackers her stewardess offered her at regular intervals. She saw nothing of Janet and understood that she was similarly stricken, as were at least half the passengers on the ship. As Sarah lay there, wanting only to die, she wondered whether the sickness was a bad omen. Perhaps the fates were warning her that going back to Australia was not the right course of action. To this she told herself firmly that a large liner was hardly going to turn around just for her in mid Atlantic, so she had better make the best of things.

On the third morning the ship had sailed through the Straits of Gibraltar and into the Mediterranean. Sarah awoke to a perfectly stable cabin door, feeling terribly hunger. She wolfed down the toast and tea her stewardess brought for her, then ventured up on deck, where she found Janet, looking like a walking ghost, coming to check on her.

"Ach, but the sea is a cruel thing," Janet said. "I thought I'd never leave that bunk alive."

"Find yourself a deck chair and let the stewards bring you some broth," Sarah said. "I had some and it's done me the world of good."

Janet looked skeptical. "And we have three more weeks of this, you say?"

"The rest is all plain sailing," Sarah said. "We've passed the stormy bit. From now on it's good food and deck tennis."

Janet groaned. "My legs will hardly carry me up the steps," she said. "I think I'll find that chair as you said, if you can do without me."

Sarah patted her on the arm. "There are enough stewards to cater to my every whim," she said. "You go and find your deck chair. And don't forget that broth."

She watched Janet stagger back to second class, then she took a brisk turn around the deck. At lunchtime she presented herself in the dining room and was shown to the purser's table. The purser was a jolly-looking red-faced young man, who rose to seat her beside him.

"So you're the mysterious Miss Hartley," he said, beaming at her. "We have all been speculating about you. The other gentlemen at the table will be delighted to find that you are not an elderly spinster, after all. Let me introduce you, Miss Hartley: I am Peter Pierce, your purser and opposite you are Mr. and Mrs. Barclay, going out to visit their daughter in Sydney, Mr. Campion, who is in the wool business-correct, Mr. Campion? And beside you is Colonel Neville, who is a famous newspaperman down under. You have to watch what you say to him, or you'll find it reported in next week's edition, eh Colonel?"

Sarah found herself looking into Colonel Neville's shrewd, piggy eyes. He inclined his head politely to her. "Miss Hartley?" he said. "This is your first voyage to Australia?"

Lie! Make him think he has never seen you before! raced through Sarah's brain. She fought to keep composure on her face. "Er, yes, Colonel. My first voyage."

The piggy eyes did not waver. "Strange," he said. "I could

have sworn I'd seen you before somewhere. Did we meet in London? I was staying at the Savoy."

"I was there once for a tea dance," Sarah said, relaxing slightly as he seemed to be off target. "Maybe we passed in the lobby, unless you go in for tea dances, Colonel?"

There was a gentle titter from the table companions. Colonel Neville smiled, too. "I? I fear I'm a trifle old for such frivolities," he said. "Can't see the sense of dancing at teatime, anyway."

"I agree with you, Colonel," Mrs. Barclay chimed in, mercifully taking his attention from Sarah. "Dancing belongs with candles and moonlight. How can one take a stroll from the dance floor and find oneself in the middle of rush hour?"

"Ah, but you have to understand the origins of the tea dance," her husband instructed. "They grew out of the war, when we all had to blackout our houses at sunset. It was too dangerous to allow young people out in the dark."

"But not too dangerous to allow them in the trenches?" Mr. Campion asked.

"That was a sad necessity, which you, coming from a far away country, can't really appreciate," Mr. Barclay told him.

Mr. Campion flushed. "I can appreciate it very well, Mr. Barclay. My own small town in New South Wales sent thirty boys over to Europe to fight and only ten of them came back. Two thirds of our youth is a generous sacrifice for the mother country, wouldn't you say?"

"Would you have willingly sold your wool and meat to German buyers?" Mr. Barclay asked.

"Not all Australians think like him," Colonel Neville said. "There are still some of us who think of England as our mother country and accept the loyalties and responsibilities that go along with it—including mutually beneficial trade."

"If Australia is to survive in the future," Mr. Campion said, "we must learn to loosen our ties with the mother country, and we need to develop our own industries, not rely on an exchange on raw materials for finished products. I understand our government is considering Japan as a trading partner."

"Japan?" Mrs. Barclay exploded. "Those horrid little yellow men making horrid cheap imitations of everything? I should have thought they were the last people in the world to trade with."

"I agree with you, old girl," her husband echoed. "Completely untrustworthy. Australia ought to learn on which side her bread is buttered and stick with it!"

"I agree with you wholeheartedly," Colonel Neville said forcefully, "although I don't think of England as doing Australia the favor, rather the reverse. You'd have starved after the war without our lamb . . ."

The purser sensed that tempers were rising and prudently began to pour wine, thus switching the topic of conversation to the quality of Australian wines. Sarah sipped her Riesling with relief. She was just somebody the colonel remembered seeing somewhere. He had not placed her, and, as long as he thought she was newly out from England, he never would. She would have to be very, very careful what she said for the rest of the voyage and eat as many meals as possible in her cabin!

By the time the meal was finished, they had docked in Gibraltar and she enjoyed an afternoon's sightseeing with Janet, coming back onto the ship laden with Moraccan leather. Before dinner she took a bath and washed her hair. She was in the middle of towel-drying it, when there was a tap at her door.

"Come in," she called, expecting Janet to help her dress. She heard the door close softly and pulled the towel from her face to see Colonel Neville, sitting on her bed.

"What are you doing here?" she demanded.

"I came to pay a friendly visit," he said, smiling amiably.

"I hardly think it's accepted practice to visit a young lady in her cabin," she said, eyeing him frostily and wrapping her big bath towel more tightly around her. "Kindly leave before I ring for the stewardess!"

"I don't think you'll do that," he drawled, leaning back on the bed.

"Are you crazy?" she asked. "You can't burst into a strange woman's cabin and get away with it. Kindly leave at once." She walked across to the bell on the wall.

He leaned across and grabbed at her towel. "I wouldn't do that, love. Seeing that you don't want anybody to know who you really are."

"What are you talking about?" she demanded, trying to hold onto the towel. "You've made a terrible mistake. I am Miss Sarah Hartley from Wickcombe Manor. Now, leave before there is a terrible scene."

He grinned at her discomfort. "No mistake, girlie," he said. "You see, I remembered where I'd seen you before . . . you're one of Madeleine's girls, aren't you?"

"I don't know what you are talking about," she said haughtily.

"Oh yes you do. I remember you quite clearly now. I've seen you at enough functions with her . . . And you said you'd never been to Australia before! Didn't your mummy teach you it was naughty to tell fibs?"

Sarah wriggled away from him. "Colonel Neville," she said. "That was one brief, unfortunate period in my life. It is over and forgotten."

"Not by me," he said and grinned again. "Very embarrassing if I chose to remember it to other people, what?"

She took another step toward the wall. "I'm going to ring this bell right now," she said, "and have you thrown out of here. Anything you care to tell, I shall deny and you will be the one who comes across in a bad light."

The colonel actually laughed. "Feisty little thing, aren't you?" he said. "But I don't think you will ring that bell. You see, I checked with your maid before coming here. She told me you'd only been back in England a few months, and I'm well-known on this ship. I make this journey regularly. The captain has been my guest in Sydney. Trust me, my dear—enough people will believe what I say to make you the subject of a lot of gossip. Passengers on ships love a good gossip . . . Do you want tongues to wag wherever you go on board?"

"Why are you doing this?" she asked. "Are you trying to blackmail me?"

He smiled. "Not for money. I don't need your puny money. I have all I want. But your nice little white body. I wouldn't mind that . . . it would pass the time on the ship very nicely. I always find sea voyages so boring. How about you?"

"You are disgusting," she said, "and if you think I'm going to let you . . ."

He got up and walked toward her, taking the wrist that was nearest the bell. "You're going to do exactly what I say," he whispered, "because if you don't, you'll never have a chance of a respectable life again. I'm known all over Australia. Try to live a respectable life in Sydney, in Melbourne, even in Perth, and I'll spread the word about you. There won't be a decent home you'll be welcome in." With one move he ripped the towel from her body. She gasped and tried to flee, but he held onto that one wrist, twisting her under him. "So what's it going to be, Cinderella?" he asked. "Me now, or back to Madeleine for the rest of your life?"

He laughed and threw her backward onto the bed, then calmly began to unbutton his trousers. "I think you were the only girl I never did manage to screw at Madeleine's," he said as he climbed onto her. "I aim to make up for that now."

At that moment there was a light tapping at the door. Sarah stiffened and tried to sit up. He held her down. "Send them away," he hissed.

"Miss Sarah? Are you in there? I've come to help you with your hair," came Janet's voice. The locked door was rattled.

"No . . . you go on down to dinner, Janet," Sarah called. "I have a bit of a headache. I'm resting. I'll join you later."

"Smart girl," the colonel whispered. "I can see you know what's good for you, after all."

Sarah turned her face toward the wall as he forced her legs apart.

Forty-two

COLONEL NEVILLE WAITED IN HER CABIN, WATCHING her while she dressed for dinner, then escorted her upstairs as if nothing had happened. The touch of his hand on her waist as he steered her into the dining room was enough to make her shudder, but she mastered herself enough to sit at the table and answer remarks addressed to her. While her body went through the motions of eating and conversing, turmoil was raging inside her head. She kept hearing his low, drawling voice, before he let her out of the cabin. "And to think we've got three more weeks of this. I am going to enjoy this voyage . . ." She had never felt so trapped before. Even in the outback there was a place to flee. On a ship there was nowhere to hide. *I'll leave the ship at Cairo,* she thought. *I'll take the next ship, or even a boat back to England . . . and be running away for the rest of my life?* she answered herself. *If I run away, he'll hunt me down. He's that kind of man. He won't leave me in peace wherever I go, unless I play along with him now . . .*

She picked at the Dover sole on her plate and nodded politely to Mrs. Barclay's comments. *Janet must not find out!* she thought desperately while her face maintained a composed smile. *Above all else, Janet must not find out . . .* wild, absurd plans began to go through her mind. She would lure him up on deck and push him over the side . . . she would take a bread knife from the table and stab him, claiming that he came to her cabin to rape her. *But what if I did not succeed?* she reminded herself. Colonel Neville was a very powerful man. The price of failure might be a life in jail, or, even worse, a life as his mistress . . . *I've got to get to Sydney,* she thought. *I've got to see Col. If anyone can get me free of this man, he'll know how . . .*

Dinner finished and they stood up. The young purser turned to Sarah. "Might I escort you to this evening's waltz party?" he asked.

Before Sarah could answer, Colonel Neville had already taken her arm. "Miss Hartley has already agreed to come with me," he said. "Better luck next time, old boy. Come, my dear."

I'm never going to be free of him . . . never, she thought in desperation.

The band was already playing a Strauss medley. Colonel Neville did not wait to ask her permission. He swept her onto the dance floor and began to waltz. Around and around they went until the room seemed to be going around and around. Tension, combined with the days of fasting and seasickness, made her head sing. Lights began to dance and flicker in front of her eyes. There was a roaring, as of a mighty tide. . . . Without warning Sarah fainted.

When she came to, she was lying on a sofa beside the dance floor and a woman in white was waving something foul smelling under her nose.

"That's better, miss," the woman said. "You gave us all a nasty scare. Now, I'm going to have these two nice young sailors carry you down to the infirmary for a doctor to check you over." Sarah noticed Colonel Neville standing in the background, but he did not attempt to intervene as the sailors picked her up and carried her discretely out and down to the infirmary.

The ship's doctor was a distinguished-looking gray-haired Englishman. He took Sarah's pulse and made clucking noises. "We can't have you fainting all over the place," he said seriously. "It scares the other passengers into thinking we've got an epidemic on board." And he gave Sarah a friendly wink. "Of course, if you will go dancing right after getting up from seasickness, I suppose you are asking for trouble, but I'd better give you a thorough examination, just in case it's something more serious."

He stuck a thermometer under her tongue, then wandered through to his office next door. A sudden inspiration struck Sarah. She leaped off the table and ran the thermometer under the hot tap. If she were really sick, maybe she could be kept in here, or quarantined—saved from that dreadful man. She leapt back onto the bed as she heard the doctor returning and stuck the thermometer under her tongue. He took it out and examined it, then walked across and closed the door firmly between her room and his officer where the nurse could be heard bustling around.

"Okay, what's up?" he asked, perching on the bed beside her.

"I . . . er . . . fainted," she stammered. "I don't feel very well. I think I have a fever . . ."

He nodded, smiling as he watched her face. "I mean—what's really up?" he asked. "Because if your temperature was really that high, you'd have died long ago."

"I would?"

"There's no documented case in medical history of anyone living with the mercury right off the top of the thermometer. Which makes me suspect that you want to appear sicker than you are—and yet you really fainted. That was genuine enough. Your pulse is still erratic. Is there a logical explanation to all this?"

"Doctor?" she asked cautiously. "If I were really ill, would you keep me in here for the rest of the voyage?"

"If you were contagious or required constant medical attention, yes." He paused, looking down at her with interest. "Why would a pretty young girl want to be confined to an infirmary for a whole voyage? You'd miss out on seeing all those exotic ports, doing all that lovely shopping . . ."

"I'd be willing to forgo those things," she said. "It's more important to me right now to be considered seriously ill."

His eyes appraised her. "Is there someone or something you'd like to avoid? Is that it?"

"Yes," Sarah said. "Someone."

"I see . . . You must want to avoid them pretty badly to make you faint at the sight of them," he said. "This sounds like the stuff of spy novels. Are you a beautiful Russian countess fleeing from Bolsheviks?"

Sarah managed a smile. "Just an ordinary girl fleeing from unwanted attentions," she said.

"Then why don't you tell the young man that you are not interested?" the doctor said, laughing.

"He's not the sort of man that takes no for an answer," she said.

He walked up and down, rubbing his hands together. "You could cost me my job," he said, "if anyone found out. Who are you traveling with—your family?"

"Just my maid."

"And she can't protect you from the unwanted suitor?"

"No."

"I see . . ." he paused at the end of his pace and looked back at her. "You could always have measles, I suppose, or we could go one stage worse and make it typhoid . . . no, we don't want to make it too bad, or they won't let you into Australia. A childhood disease would be best—which do you fancy?"

"Chicken pox?" Sarah suggested. "That is pretty repulsive, isn't it?"

"I don't think you could fake the spots," he said slowly. "and it would be over too quickly. Mumps might be a better idea—less easy to detect and gentlemen are very scared of mumps, too. I'll have your maid bring down your things and spread the word around the ship that you are stricken with mumps. No guests allowed."

Sarah beamed at him. "Doctor, I love you," she said.

He paused on his way to the door. "You shouldn't go saying that to too many men," he said. "It might get you into trouble!"

Sarah watched, triumphant and delighted as a room was made up for her in the infirmary and Janet brought down her things.

"You poor wee thing," she said, clucking around her. "I thought you had the mumps when you were six or seven, did you not?"

"You're thinking of measles," Sarah said quickly. She longed to explain to Janet, but every time she got up enough courage, she remembered remarks Janet had made—describing a décollete beauty as "Damned to the fires below," and a young girl with a much older man as "might have well as married Old Nick himself"—told her that Janet surely would not understand. Sin to her was what she had been taught in bleak childhood Sunday schools. Having never experienced love between man and woman, she had never modified her views to include tolerance.

Sarah enjoyed a few days of peace and rest, her confidence rose and she was feeling ready to tackle anything when she got to Australia. She wrote down lists and plans on paper. Then, one afternoon, she answered a light tap on the door, without even looking up from manicuring her fingernails. The doctor came in and smiled at her.

"Glad to see you looking so bonny, my dear," he said. "I thought it might be boring for you down here all alone, so I've brought you a visitor." He stepped back and allowed Colonel Neville to come into the room. "Colonel Neville tells me he's an old friend of your family. He was very concerned when he heard that you had been taken sick and he very kindly volunteered to come and cheer you up. He tells me he's definitely had mumps,"—he winked at her conspiratorially—"and he thought you'd enjoy a little chat."

Neville's eyes were holding hers, daring her to say something, to bluff her way out of this one. "How are you feeling, my dear?" he asked. "Silly time to go and get mumps. Missing all the best of the fun up on deck." He strode over and perched himself on the end of her bed.

The doctor moved to the door. "I should be getting back to my office," he said. "Nurse is in the next room if you need her."

Sarah tried to make her eyes plead with him to see that something was wrong, but he was not even looking in her direction. He was rubbing his hands together, in true doctor fashion, and already closing the door behind him.

Colonel Neville smiled at her, much as a spider might smile

hen it noticed a fly had blundered into its web. "I expect you ought you were pretty clever," he said. "Did you really think ou could avoid me for the rest of the trip?"

"I hoped to," she said. "I still hope to."

He rested his large podgy hand on her thigh. "No such luck, y dear. I don't like people getting the better of me."

She tried to outstare him. "At least there's not too much you an do here. The nurse is in the next room. I've only got to call ut and she'll hear."

"Now she is," he said easily, "but I happen to know she oes off duty at night. I just wanted to let you know that I can ome down and visit you whenever I want to . . . it's better at ight, isn't it? The dim lights, the quiet corridors . . ."

"I don't understand you," she said. "Why are you doing this when it's quite apparent that I find you repulsive? It can't give ou much pleasure to force somebody who's completely unwilling, surely?"

A crooked smile spread across his face. "Ah, but it does," e said. "I'm a military man, remember. I miss the thrills of attle. I like conquering . . . and I like danger. I can assure you t will give me infinite pleasure to creep in here at night, undeected, and have sex with you—especially if someone is in the urgery next door. That makes it all the more spicy." His hand lid up her thigh, very slowly. "Yes," he drawled on, "I find it ery enjoyable doing it with you . . . you're my little captive, ren't you? I'm the conquerer and I've carried you home as part of my spoils, and I can have you whenever I want and you can't lo a damn thing about it."

His hand was moving up her body, pressing into her flesh ntil it almost hurt, spanning both her breasts beneath his big ingers. "As a matter of fact," he went on in the same, quiet voice, "I'm begining to think it might be rather fun right now, after all—to see if we could do it without the nurse hearing anything, because I don't think you'd cry out . . ." He went to pull down the sheet that was covering her. Without thinking, Sarah grabbed at her nail scissors and dug them into the back of his hand.

"Don't you touch me again," she hissed. "Don't you dare ever touch me again!"

He pulled his hand away with a half cry, sucking it to his lips to stop the blood. Sarah stared, half-appalled, half-delighted a what she had done.

"You bloody little minx," he muttered.

"You deserved it," she said breathlessly. "You're an animal that's what you are! You think you're civilized, but you're not If you ever try and touch me again, I'll go for your heart, I swea it."

"Don't talk such bloody nonsense," he said, still with hi hand to his lips.

"You think I wouldn't?" she demanded. "I'll get a scalpe from the doctor's office and I'll keep it under my pillow. If yo ever come near me again, I'll claim it was in self-defense—tha you were drunk and you attacked me and I reached for th nearest object!" Suddenly she laughed. "I've just realized, yo can't hurt me anymore! You can tell whatever tale you like t the captain or the passengers about me, and it doesn't matter because I'm not up there to listen! What a joke!"

He stood up, backing away as if she was a dangerous animal "I suppose you think you've been very clever," he said, "bu what do you think will happen to you when you get to Sydney?"

"Meaning what?"

"Where do you think you will go?" he asked. "I'm still a very powerful man there, you know. You'll have to go straigh back to Madeleine because there won't be anywhere else—and when you do—I'll always ask for you . . ."

"You forget, I also happen to know a powerful man," she said. "I'm sure he'll take good care of me. He hates bullies."

"Murphy, you mean?" he asked, and laughed. "Murphy's had a heart attack, didn't you hear?"

"Yes, I heard," she said. "But he's strong. He'll recover."

Neville shook his head. "He might even be dead by the time we land. And even if he recovers, he was on the way out. His policies aren't what the masses want anymore." He reached the door of the room. "No, my dear, don't count on Col Murphy for anything. He won't be able to do a thing for you anymore." He opened the door. "See you in Sydney, my dear—suite two, I think, don't you? I always liked the way you could see the gardens from the bed . . ."

He went out, closing the door quietly behind him. Almost immediately the nurse came in.

"Had a nice chat, did you?" she asked. "You're looking

much better. Quite pink around the cheeks. Maybe we'll ask the doctor if you can go up on deck soon."

"No, don't do that," Sarah said, sinking back on her pillows. "I still feel very weak. I'm sure it's better for me to rest, but do you think a camp bed could be put in here for my maid? I hate taking up so much of your time."

The next days passed without incident and it was only when the ship was just outside Sydney Heads that she came up on deck, looking very pale and wrapped in a big shawl. She stood at the rail, watching the sandstone slabs come nearer and nearer.

"Looks a right heathen sort of place," Janet commented. "As wild as Scotland, too."

"The town is on the other side of the headlands," Sarah said. "You wait until you see the harbor. It's so beautiful."

Janet looked at her critically. "The first time I've seen you smile in a long time," she said. "I'm glad to see you're on the mend. I thought I was stuck with an invalid for the rest of my days."

"I can't wait to get off the ship," Sarah said excitedly. "I can't wait to find out . . ."

She froze as Colonel Neville came up to her, in the company of two other men. He nodded gravely.

"Ah, Miss Hartley, I see you have made a miraculous recovery, just in time for our landing. I trust you are now well?"

"Thank you," Sarah said, inclining her head in turn. "Very fortunately there were no complications."

"And you think the complications will not show up later?" he asked.

"I don't plan to stay in Sydney, where I understand the climate may not be too healthy," Sarah said. "In fact, I may return to England, or even go on to America. I understand America is a very big country."

"I see," he said slowly. "I wish you luck, Miss Hartley."

"And I wish you the success you deserve, Colonel Neville."

The group strolled on.

"Who the dear was that gentleman?" Janet whispered when they were safely far down the deck. "He came to your door once during the voyage, inquiring after your health. He seemed to hint you were old friends. I didn't let him in, of course."

"That was Colonel Neville," Sarah said, staring out at the rugged sandstone bluffs.

"The man they were talking about, the big noise who owns a newspaper?"

"That's the one," Sarah said.

"My word," Janet said. "They say he's a very powerful man in Australia."

"He is."

"There's a lot I don't understand here, Miss Sarah," Janet said. "And I suppose it's not my business to ask, but there's something going on that I don't know about. You go out to Australia to marry a poor boy and live on a farm and you take a post as governess when he dies, but it seems you know half the important people in the country. How does a governess meet people like that?"

"It's a small country," Sarah said, "and one day I'll tell you all about it, but not now."

She was busy staring out at the familiar features of Sydney. The lighthouse above the South Head, the red roofs of the seaside townships, the big hospital up on the hill, and, nestled in between the cliffs, the famous Gap, where she had almost jumped, half a lifetime ago. Would it have been better if her life had, indeed, ended then? It seemed that she had been sucked into a downward spiral of destruction ever since—a spiral from which it did not seem to be possible to break free. All I ever wanted was a normal life, she thought, but it doesn't seem that I will ever be free of Madeleine unless I go and bury myself in the depths of the country—and what would I do there? Fight off farmers instead of colonels. A women alone has no chance in this world, and yet I don't want to marry the first oaf who asks me, just for the protection he could offer me. I want to do something that makes me strong enough to protect myself. I want to be a person who matters enough to be left alone . . . .

She turned back to Janet, who was still talking. "I'm sorry," she said apologetically. "What were you saying?"

"Same as all your life," Janet scolded. "Never would listen to a thing anyone told you. Always thought you knew better—and where's it got you, I'd like to know?"

Sarah grinned. "Let's go down to our cabin," she said. "We have to make sure everything is packed before the medical inspection and the customs men."

"I'm not having any heathen medical man inspecting me," Janet called forcefully to Sarah's disappearing back.

"They'll only look at your hands," Sarah said, turning back laughing.

"My hands? Do they want to see if I've washed my finger-nails or what?"

"If you've had smallpox," Sarah replied.

"And what about you?" Janet asked in a softer voice as they walked together down the passageway. "Will they not find out that you haven't really had the mumps?"

"What do you mean?"

Janet looked scathing. "Ach, you must think I'm daft or something. You had the mumps, clear as clear, when you were four years old and the doctor told me then that it's not possible to get it twice in your lifetime. So whatever you had, it was not the mumps!"

"I think I'll leave you to make sure the cases are all shut," Sarah said, turning around abruptly. "I'll get us a place in the medical line in the salon."

Two hours later they finally disembarked in Sydney, having gone through the frustrations of officialdom.

"If I never see another man in a peaked cap again, it will be too soon," Janet said as Sarah shepherded her down the gang-plank. "And one of them had the nerve to call me ducks! Is there no respect in this heathen country?"

"Not much," Sarah said. "They all believe that every man is as good as the next one, but not every woman. They believe she belongs somewhere down the pecking order beside the dogs."

"Then I wouldn't have thought this was the sort of place you'd choose," Janet said in surprise. "I've never noticed you being particularly meek where men were concerned. If you'd only behaved like a young girl should, way back when you were seventeen, we'd have had you happily married off by now. Instead you insisted on telling all the young boys what you thought of their dancing and you never saw them again!"

Sarah laughed happily. "Thank heavens," she said. "I might at this moment be sitting around a tea table, gossiping about the tennis club, instead of this!" and she spread out her arms to face the shining waters of Sydney Harbor.

"Ach, it's pretty enough," Janet said, "but do they have decent drains?"

Forty-three

FROM THE SHIP SARAH HAD THEIR THINGS TAKEN to the Grosvenor Hotel nearby and found out from the bellboy that Col had not been heard of since his heart attack, but had not, as he put it, "Kicked the bucket as far as he knew." The news boosted Sarah's spirits, which had already risen at the sight of Sydney's clear air and sparkling water. Janet was amazed at the daffodils growing in pots on their balcony.

"How do they manage to keep them still in bloom in September?" she asked.

"Because we're just coming into spring here," Sarah said, happily. "The season's are upside down, remember I explained?"

"Well, I never," Janet said. "And it looks like quite a pretty town after all, after you get clear of those horrible docks. They even have big department stores and churches. So what are you planning to do with us now? You told that colonel man that you were not staying here. You're not thinking of taking us to America?"

"Of course not," Sarah said. "That was just to get rid of him. I'm planning to live quietly—maybe get a little house down by the beach, maybe even go into some sort of business."

"Business? What sort of business?"

"I don't know. A dress shop? Something respectable." She leaned over the balcony and looked down George Street. "I don't know what's going to happen, Janet. I just know that I feel alive again and excited about things. Right now I'm going to wait and see what happens."

As if her statement was prophetic, she had three visitors the next day. She had been torn between getting in touch with people and leaving her past life firmly behind her. If she moved up the coast and bought a little shop, she decided, nobody need ever know that she wasn't Sarah Hartley, fresh out from England and starting a new life in Australia. The only disadvantage to that was that she would have no chance of seeing Col again—and she had to see him. Just to see that he's getting well, that he'll be alright, she told herself, trying to ignore the ache of longing she felt in the pit of her stomach whenever she thought of him. She was sorely tempted just to pick up the telephone and call him, but she had no idea how sick he still was or whether he'd even want to see her. She wondered if she could survive without the hope of running into him casually at functions and whether the hope of running into him was worth the risk of running into Colonel Neville. Three times during the morning she got out the hotel notepaper to write to Col, and three times she put it away again.

Then, around noon, she had her first visitor. There was a tap on the door and, when Janet opened it, Madeleine swept in, without waiting to be asked.

"My dear, welcome back," she said, seating herself on Sarah's sofa and taking off her black kid gloves.

"How did you know I was here?" Sarah asked in a not too friendly voice.

"Have you forgotten what a small town this is?" Madeleine asked. "We always look at the passenger lists of every ship. We always know who comes and goes. Otherwise one would feel so isolated down here." She pulled off the second glove and dropped them onto the coffee table. "You left without telling me."

"I left a note," Sarah said. "My father was dying back in England. I had to go straight away."

"And he did die?"

"Yes."

"My condolences. So you are now the rich heiress?"

"Not exactly rich, but rich enough to lead my own life."

Madeleine took out a cigarette and put it into a gold holder. She turned to Janet. "Is this your maid?" she asked Sarah.

"My companion," Sarah answered.

"Then I wonder if you'd be kind enough to have her run down to the chemist's shop in the lobby for me," Madeleine said. "I broke a nail on the wretched car door and it is so noticeable." She handed Janet a half crown. "Bring me up a bottle of Rich Ruby nail polish, would you be so kind?"

Janet gave Sarah an inquiring look, then dropped a half curtsy and left the room.

"Now, my dear," Madeleine said, smiling confidently at Sarah. "We can really talk."

"Did you come here just to say welcome back, Madeleine?" Sarah asked frostily.

"But of course. It would only be polite to greet an old friend and colleague." She peered at the door. "Your . . . companion . . . and old faithful retainer from the past? How touching. Does she know about you?"

"There's nothing to know, Madeleine," Sarah answered. "I've closed that chapter of my history."

"I see," Madeleine said, drawing on her cigarette and sending a spiral of smoke upward as she exhaled. "The girls all send their regards."

"Is everyone well? You still have the same people? How's Renee?"

"Everyone's there, except Renee. She had problems with her child. You knew she had a child, of course? Most inconvenient. She had to leave—but I have a splendid new girl, a dancer from Paris. Very acrobatic . . ." She paused to study the effect of the rising smoke, as if thinking. "Have you returned to stay?"

"I'm not sure," Sarah said. "I intend to look for a suitable place to settle. I'm not sure where that will be. I only plan to live quietly."

Madeleine tapped ash into the ashtray. "And you really believe that you can put your past behind you and live a simple life, unknown and unnoticed in a backwater?"

"I plan to."

"With some country yokel, no doubt," Madeleine said. "Will that satisfy you? A husband who gets up at dawn to milk the cows or goes to a dreary bank? Is that what you want?"

"I want to be free, Madeleine," Sarah said. "To be dependent on nobody."

"My dear, how naive you are," Madeleine said with a smile. "In this world any woman who lives alone is suspect—especially a beautiful young woman."

"Then what would you have me do? Marry the bank clerk or the milkman?"

"Come back to me, of course," Madeleine said.

"Why would I want to do that?" Sarah asked with an aston-shed laugh. "Surely you can see that from my point of view it s not an ideal way to live?"

"There are plenty worse," Madeleine said. "You were ne of my most desired girls. Lytton Argus was ecstatic when e heard you were back. The old bear is positively panting. He can't live much longer and he has a very large fortune to eave . . ."

"How mercenary you are, Madeleine. Don't you think hap-iness comes in somewhere?"

"Frankly, no," Madeleine said. "I don't think happiness, as ou seek it, is obtainable. Only security."

"I want to make my own security. In a respectable way," Sarah said.

"And what will you do for sex in your respectable, indepen-lent life? You don't need a sex life anymore?"

"Nuns survive perfectly well without one."

Madeleine laughed. "You, my dear, are not nun material—and I rather think that you enjoyed many of the advantages of he life you led with me. You liked the parties and the theater and the opera, didn't you?"

"Yes, I did, but I'm very prepared to do without them. I don't hink there's anything you can say that will entice me back."

Madeleine looked at her shrewdly. "I could get you back omorrow, if I wanted to," she said. "One word to the police constable in the town where you decide to settle and I do not hink he will be happy to know that an ex-call girl has landed in nis community. I think you would have to go very far away to escape me."

"Why are you talking like this?" Sarah asked. "I've done nothing to you. Why would you want to punish me?"

"You walked out on me," Madeleine said. "That is another hing I do not find easy to forgive. I say who comes and goes. I give the permission."

Sarah walked across the room. "I paid you back my debts, Madeleine," she said. "You don't own me anymore. Just let me go. Leave me in peace."

"If that's really what you wish," Madeleine said. "I'll say *au revoir* for now. But I have a feeling we shall meet again soon."

Janet knocked before coming in with the nail polish. "They

only had the crimson lake, madam. The assistant said that was almost the same.''

''Thank you,'' Madeleine said, taking it. ''I was just leaving. Good-bye Sarah, my dear.''

And she made a grand exit. Janet looked after her in wonder. ''And who the dear was that?''

''My ex-employer,'' Sarah said.

''How very nice of her,'' Janet answered. ''She just came to say hello?''

''She came to offer me my old job back.''

''But you're not going to take it, of course?''

''Of course not. Why would I want to work for somebody else?''

''You were obviously good at it, or she'd never have asked you to return,'' Janet commented, making Sarah smile.

''I'm beginning to think,'' she said thoughtfully, ''that you and I should go and dig for opals and live in a hole in the ground, like a friend of mine once did.''

''You're not serious?''

''Why not—it seems less complicated than living anywhere else . . .'' Sarah came over and put a hand on Janet's shoulder. ''No, of course, I'm not serious. We'll find a nice little house in a nice little town with a good butcher shop for you to buy your meat and we'll be very, very happy.''

She picked up her hat and gloves. ''I'm going out for a walk. I need fresh air. Go and look at the shops. They're not as primitive as you think.''

She walked briskly through the town, down the length of Hyde Park, had tea in a parkside café, and returned much later to find a second visitor waiting for her. Janet met her at the door with a nervous look on her face.

''There's a lady here to see you,'' she whispered. ''She insisted on waiting until you came back . . .''

Sarah took a look at the figure lounging elegantly in the armchair, reading a magazine. The woman looked up and her eyes met Sarah's.

''Mrs. Murphy,'' Sarah said in astonishment.

''So you remembered who I was,'' the woman said. ''I wondered if you would.''

''How could I forget?'' Sarah asked. ''Would you like me to ring for a cup of tea or something?''

"I think a gin might be more in keeping with our little chat," Mrs. Murphy said.

Sarah walked across to the telephone. Janet moved uneasily toward the door. "If you don't need me, madam, I'll be in my own room."

"Thank you, Janet," Sarah said gratefully. She placed the order and came to sit facing the older woman.

"You were surprised to see me?" Mrs. Murphy asked.

"Very. I didn't think you even knew who I was."

Marjorie Murphy laughed. "My dear, I'm not a complete fool and I'm certainly not blind. I knew perfectly well who you were, all the time."

"How is . . . your husband?" Sarah asked cautiously. "I read that he'd had a heart attack."

Marjorie Murphy played with her silk scarf. "You know Col. He was warned to take it easy a couple of years ago. He doesn't listen to anyone. He'll kill himself eventually if he goes on the way he is. The doctor said he was lucky to survive this time."

"But he is recovering?"

"Much too well," Marjorie Murphy said shortly. "He is supposed to be on a strict diet and no alcohol and I find he's slipped out to the neighborhood pub for meat pie and beer."

Sarah grinned. Marjorie saw the grin and her face became hard again. "And having you back here is a complication I certainly don't need at this moment. You are only on a visit, I take it?"

"I'm not sure," Sarah said.

"What did you come back for?"

"I came into some money and I decided I liked Australia better than England."

"That was the only reason?"

Sarah played with the ring on her little finger. "Mrs. Murphy, if you are trying to ask me whether I came back to renew my friendship with Col, you need not worry. He made it very clear to me that once I left Madeleine he couldn't see me again. I understand that."

"I'm glad you do," Marjorie Murphy said, "but I don't think you realize what an influence you had on him. After you left, he went into quite a depression. He was unbearable to live with—not that he was ever the most pleasant man in the world. I don't want him to hear that you are back again because I don't know if he could keep away from you.''

''I see,'' Sarah said, trying to keep her voice from shaking. Inside her a voice was shouting that Col had missed her. It seemed like the best news she had had in years. She had an absurd desire to smile. Marjorie Murphy was watching her closely.

''I wanted to see you as soon as possible,'' she said, ''before you had a chance to get in touch with my husband. I wanted to make several things very clear to you: if he is involved in a scandal, his career is over. Everyone knew about his visits to Madeleine and they were a sort of community joke—in fact, they endeared him to people—made him seem like one of the boys. Just another woman is a different matter—his backers would never tolerate that. Absurd, but true.''

''And the other things you wanted to make clear to me?'' Sarah asked.

''The other thing is me,'' Marjorie Murphy said, fixing Sarah in a steady gaze. ''I do not intend to compete for my husband with another woman, and I do not want myself to be involved in gossip. I think you are intelligent enough to know that I control the purse strings. If I and my family stop supplying the money, Col stops being premier—as simple as that, and Col would be very miserable if he couldn't be in the limelight. I don't see him pottering around a rose garden, do you? I think that would kill him more quickly than anything else.''

''That sounds to me like a genteel sort of blackmail,'' Sarah said. ''If I see your husband and he has another heart attack and dies, it's my fault, is that what you are saying?''

''What I am saying,'' Marjorie Murphy said sharply, ''is that I do not intend to negotiate with you. I am not giving you a choice. I want you out of Sydney immediately.''

''Mrs. Murphy—I am no threat to you. I have already said that I am not going to try and see Col . . .''

''But he might try and see you. What would you do if he shows up on your doorstep? Turn him away?''

Sarah took a deep breath, trying to fight against the image of Col standing on her doorstep, looking at her with that cynical little smile of his . . . She closed her eyes to shut out the image. ''Look—I happen to care about him too much to want to ruin his career," Sarah said. "I've come back here to live quietly and mind my own business. I just want to be left in peace."

"Not here," Marjorie Murphy said shortly. "I don't want you within reach of my husband."

"And if I don't go?"

"My dear, where do you think you would be welcome? I am the most important woman in this city. If I spread the word, there isn't a civilized household to which you would be invited. You would be a social outcast. You would have nobody." She got up and began to walk up and down. "Just because Madeleine is socially accepted, do not think that most Sydney-siders are not prudish. She is an exception. Apart from her, ladies of your profession belong in the slums of Balmain and King's Cross."

There was a knock on the door. The waiter entered with a tray and two cocktails.

"Ah, drinkies," Marjorie Murphy said, taking hers from the tray. "Let us drink to your rapid departure and your future success—elsewhere!"

Forty-four

"AND WHO WAS THAT LADY, MIGHT I ASK?" JANET said as she came back into the room after Marjorie Murphy had left. "Another old employer?"

"That," Sarah said with a pensive smile, "was Mrs. Murphy."

"Mrs. Murphy? Mrs. Colin Murphy?" Janet asked.

"That's the one," Sarah answered.

"Oh." Janet considered the fact. "And she came to welcome you back?"

"She came to tell me to go home again."

"Well I never," Janet said. "It seems to me that half of Sydney is to-ing and fro-ing to your door and I suspect that I don't know the half of it. Still, I daresay you'll tell me about it in your own good time. I just wonder who on earth will come calling next?''

The next caller was, in fact, Renee. She arrived late that evening and Janet looked at her very suspiciously as she let her in. Sarah could see why Janet was so suspicious. Renee looked more like a tart than Sarah had remembered. Her dress was just a little too revealing, her makeup a little too bright. It was fairly obvious that she had been drinking.

''Sarah!'' she yelled, flinging her arms around Sarah's neck even before the door was closed. ''I just heard you were back and I had to come right around to welcome you. Sorry to show up this late,'' she added, ''but I've just come from the theater . . .''

''You're working back in the theater?'' Sarah asked. ''Madeleine told me you'd left her.''

''Is that what she told you?'' Renee said, perching on the edge of the sofa. ''She threw me out, that's what she did—after all the years of work I put in for her. Miserable cow!''

Sarah glanced across at Janet. ''Er, Janet . . . would you like to see if you could find us some hot cocoa maybe?''

''Make it something a bit stronger for me, if you don't mind, love,'' Renee interrupted. ''I could do with a good, stiff brandy.''

''You want me to go and get you a brandy?'' Janet asked in polite horror.

Sarah smiled. ''No, that's all right, Janet. I'll have one sent up. Renee's an old friend—why don't you leave us to talk?''

''An old workmate,'' Renee chimed in. ''We both used to work for the same old cow . . .''

''Both governesses in the same place?'' Janet asked icily.

''What?'' Renee asked, a smile spreading across her lips.

''Not exactly,'' Sarah interrupted with a warning look at Renee. ''Renee was more like the nanny . . .''

''The what?'' Renee asked, then nodded, ''Oh yes, I was the nanny. That's it.''

Janet gave a disapproving sniff. ''Then I'll be in my room, if you two want to talk in private, Miss Sarah.''

''Who was that?'' Renee asked as Janet closed the door firmly behind her.

"Our old housekeeper. She's sort of attached herself to me," Sarah answered.

"And I take it you haven't filled in any details of your life here?"

"She's a strict Presbyterian, how could I tell her anything?" Sarah asked. "I had to think of something, so I said I was a governess."

"To Madeleine—that would be a laugh," Renee said bitterly. "Any child of hers would have been drowned at birth because it interfered with her way of life." She seated herself more firmly on the sofa and studied Sarah. "So you managed to get out—more power to you. You might have let your friends know."

"I didn't want anyone to know until I'd sailed in case someone tried to stop me," Sarah said. "I gather she wasn't too pleased that I left without telling her."

"Pleased?" Renee asked. "You should have seen her. She was bloody furious. I heard she's already paid a call on you—what did she say?"

"She invited me to come back and join the happy family," Sarah said with a grin.

"Or else?"

"Not a real 'or else.' Only that she wasn't very pleased with me."

"I'd watch it, if I were you," Renee said. "She hates someone to get the better of her. It really pissed her, pardon my language, that you'd managed to slip away to England right after she'd broken you in. You're not planning on staying around here, are you?"

Sarah laughed. "What is this? It's like being in Macbeth—a procession of weird women keep coming into my room saying, 'Beware, go back!' All I want to do is find myself a nice little house and settle down somewhere. Is that too much to ask?"

"Sounds pretty good to me," Renee said. "It's what I've wanted all my life. Question of money, ain't it?"

Her face reminded Sarah that Madeleine had thrown her out. "So what's happened to you now? Did you say you were working in the theater?"

"No such luck," Renee said. "I just filled in at the burlesque show for a couple of nights because this girl I know's hurt her foot. But work's not too easy to find. I have to pay the rent for me and Billy and sometimes I don't work in weeks. It's hard times coming here now. You'll see lots of folk out of work and begging. Respectable folk, too. Lots of farms failed and the price of wool dropping all the time. I tell you, it's a worry. Sometimes I think I'll be forced to go on the streets . . . really on the streets, I mean. I really hate to do that—getting mixed-up with pimps and taking God knows what to bed with me, but it pays better than scrubbing floors . . ."

Sarah moved across to sit beside her on the sofa. "Look Renee, if it's a question of money."

Renee took her hand away as if Sarah were holding a firebrand. "Look, I didn't come to see you for charity," she said. "I don't want a handout. Just wanted to see you again. See how you were doing . . ."

"I'm doing fine," Sarah said, "and I'd like to help you if I could. You were always good to me. What happened between you and Madeleine, anyway. I thought you were one of her favorite girls. Why did she throw you out?"

"It was on account of Billy, see—my little boy—well, he's getting to be a big boy now. Soon be ready for school!" Renee said. "The woman I boarded him with found herself a new husband and he made a fuss about having Billy living with them. She came to me overnight and said I'd have to take him. Well, I didn't have anywhere to go with him, did I? I smuggled him up to my room and thought I could keep him safe there until I found someone else who'd look after him. Then Madeleine had a client for me and Billy woke up all alone up there and got scared and wandered down the stairs and started opening doors, looking for me. Of course, you can imagine what a fuss there was—a little kid looking in on everybody and crying, 'Mummy, where are you?' Madeleine nearly blew her top. She told me to get rid of him right away. I asked for time and she wouldn't give it. What could I do? My little boy comes first, doesn't he?" She played with the long string of jet beads at her neck. "So here I am—respectable and starving."

"Have you got a place to stay now?" Sarah asked.

"Of a sort. It's not ideal—terrible neighborhood and the woman who keeps an eye on him—well, I don't really trust her. I've found bruises on him that I know weren't made by falling down. Still, it's all I can afford until I find something better."

"What are you looking for?" Sarah asked.

Renee laughed. "What's anyone looking for? A nice rich man

to take care of me and love little Billy like his own. That would do—it's just that I don't think men like that exist. If they're rich, they're spoiled and selfish and old. And speaking of that—old Lytton, bless his heart—he wasn't half sad that you'd gone. He said you were the one thing that kept him young."

Sarah smiled. "And Col?" she asked. "What did he say?"

"I can't tell you that," Renee said. "He got your note and he stormed out and we haven't seen him again. You heard he had a heart attack, poor bloke? Mind you, I'd have a heart attack if I was stuck with that bitch."

"She came to see me, too," Sarah said.

"Mrs. Murphy?"

"That's right. Told me to get out of town or there would be no respectable door open to me." She laughed. "It's nice to know my arrival has created such an impression. I was in London a whole month without talking to anybody."

"So you're not going to leave town?"

"I don't see why I should," Sarah said. "It's a free country, isn't it—and it's not as if I'm going to be mixing in the same circles as Mrs. Murphy, or Madeleine for that matter."

"You want to set yourself up in a nice cushy job," Renee said. "Open a school, maybe, then I can come and give elocution lessons. I can speak terribly, terribly proper if I want to—real actress elocution."

Sarah laughed. "No thanks," she said. "Not to your elocution lessons, but to the idea of a school. I don't think I like children that much—and besides, can you see what would happen if one parent at the school recognized us?"

Renee laughed. "Bit of a giggle, eh?" Her face grew serious again. "You're right, though. When you've got a certain reputation, you can either face it or move right away. Of course, you could always set up in opposition to Madeleine."

"Open my own house, you mean?" Sarah said, laughing at the thought of it.

"It's what I'd do if I had the money. Cushy job being the madam. Your girls do all the work and you keep the cash. Not a bad life at all."

Sarah continued to laugh. "Col suggested I do that once, but I think he was only teasing."

"I don't think it's so funny," Renee said. "Do Madeleine

good to have some competition. She's been the big wheel too long. But you need money to set up right."

"How much money?" Sarah asked.

Renee looked at her steadily. "A really nice house. Good clothes, good furniture. Same standard as Madeleine if you want to attract the best—of course, you could always start small with two or three girls, then expand with the custom."

Sarah laughed uneasily. "Renee, are you really suggesting that I should use my money to open a whorehouse?"

"Not really," Renee said. "You're out of it. You stay out of it. It's not the right life for a nicely brought up girl like you with her whole life ahead of her. For me, it's different. I want to make something for Billy one day . . . I was just saying that somebody could do very well for themselves if they set up in opposition to Madeleine. I know several of Madeleine's girls who'd come across like a shot, for example, and think of the clients who would come with them . . ."

Sarah pushed back her hair from her face. "I wanted to start a small business," she said, "but I was thinking more in terms of a little shop."

"That's right," Renee said. "A nice little shop in the suburbs, that's what you want. Give yourself a chance to meet a nice, ordinary man and be happy. I wouldn't say no to that."

They were interrupted by a knock as the brandy was brought in. Sarah handed Renee a glass and raised hers in a toast.

"I wonder if there are any nice, ordinary men?" Sarah said, more to herself than to Renee.

"Got to be somewhere in the world, haven't there?" Renee said with a laugh. "They can't all be blighters and rotters can they?"

"But the ones who aren't are so boring," Sarah commented. "I think I'd be more scared of being stuck with a boring man than a rotten one."

"If you'd got your own house, you wouldn't be stuck with any man," Renee said. "You only have to let in the ones you like the look of. Be your own mistress, not somebody else's."

Sarah took a gulp of her brandy. "Judging by the number of men who have suggested I become their's in the last few weeks, that might not be such a bad idea . . ."

"So you're really considering it?" Renee asked.

"I've got to do something," Sarah said. "I have the money

to invest in a business and, as dear Madeleine said, a single woman, living on her own is always suspect. I don't want to be a defenseless female, always at the mercy of some man—it would be rather nice to decide who came to visit and who didn't."

"You bet it would," Renee agreed.

"And I'd really like to stay in Sydney, but it has become fairly obvious that nobody's going to let me forget about my past history." She laughed, shaking her head at the absurdity of it. "They do say, 'If you can't beat 'em, join 'em,' don't they?" she said.

"That's what they say all right." Renee began to laugh, too. She raised her glass. "Here's to Madam Sarah!" she said. "God bless her!"

Sarah perched on the arm of the chair, becoming serious again. "You really think this could work?" she asked. "What would Madeleine do if we took some of her girls, do you think?"

"I don't see what she could do," Renee said. "A person can hardly go to the police and say that girls who she blackmailed into becoming tarts have now left her, and as long as we have the right sort of men as clients—men who can pull strings, so to speak . . . have you got in touch with Col Murphy yet?"

"No," Sarah said, looking down at her glass.

"I'd have thought that was the first thing you'd do—straight from the dock."

"Have a heart," Sarah said with a smile. "I've only been here two days. Besides, I'd heard he'd had a heart attack. I wasn't quite sure how to go about seeing him again. And now his wife was around here threatening . . ."

"But you want to see him again?" Renee asked. "I always thought that you two were something special—you know what I mean?"

Sarah nodded. "I thought so, too," she said. "I can't wait to see him again, and if I'm going to run a house of ill repute, then Mrs. Murphy's threats can't harm me anymore, can they?" She began to laugh delightedly. "I can't believe that I'm actually sitting here, discussing this seriously," she said. "I must be going out of my mind, Renee. I have a chance to live a respectable life—why do you have to put ideas like this into my head? It's absurd. Why would I want a life on the fringe of society if I'm not forced into it?"

"Maybe because you like excitement," Renee suggested,

"and you like all the nice things that lots of money can buy . . . and . . . you like the chance to see certain gentlemen again."

Sarah jumped up. "You're right," she said. "I do like all those things—and I like being in control. I'm going out to look at houses tomorrow, do you want to come with me?"

"Of course I'll come with you. Wouldn't miss this for the world," Renee said.

"And you will come and work for me, if I find my house?" Sarah asked. "I wouldn't mind if you brought Billy . . ."

"I would," Renee said. "I don't want him growing up around things like this. I want him to have a good life, go to a good school—that's the only reason I'm not working as a waitress."

"Then we'll look for a place that has a gardener's cottage, apart from the house, and find some nice old woman to live in with him, and you could pop down to visit in your spare time."

"It does sound wonderful, doesn't it?" Renee asked. She got up. "Almost too good to be true. I'd best be going now. They lock the door on me if I'm not back by midnight."

She picked up her gloves and walked toward the door. "I'll see you tomorrow, then, Madam S," she said with a cheeky grin and closed the door behind her.

As soon as the door closed, Janet's door opened and she came through from the adjoining room. "She's gone then?" Janet asked, sniffing in disapproval as if Renee's perfume and the brandy offended her. "Who on earth was that person? Surely not a friend of yours."

"A good friend," Sarah said. "In fact, the only person who was kind to me at one point in my life. I owe her a lot."

Janet folded her arms. "She looked like a tart," she said. "I don't know what your family would have said if they'd seen you mixing with people like that."

"My family threw me out," Sarah said. "I've had to make my own life without them."

"But not mixing with riffraff like that person," Janet insisted. "You'll not tell me that she was ever a nanny, looking like that?"

Sarah patted the seat of the sofa. "Janet, sit down," she said. "I think there's something you should know."

Janet sat, her arms still folded.

Sarah took a deep breath. "It's about my life here before," she said. "You said Renee looked like a tart, and you were right.

She was a tart—but not how you were thinking. She worked in a high-class house—it was all society people, very top drawer, very respectable people.''

''Don't excuse her,'' Janet interrupted. ''A tart is a tart and you should have had more sense and more decency than to go talking to women like that.''

''So you'd condemn her, just because of what she did for a living?''

''A living, you call it?'' Janet's voice rose. ''A living—making it sound like a respectable, God-fearing job when what she does is an abomination!'' Her expression softened a little. ''Ach, but then maybe you led too sheltered a childhood, maybe you didn't even fully realize . . .''

''I realized, Janet,'' Sarah said, ''because I worked with her.''

Janet rose to her feet. ''No . . . what are you saying?''

''I'm saying that Renee and I worked together. We were both 'tarts' as you put it.''

Janet backed across the room as if she was getting away from a newly dangerous animal. ''No . . . I don't believe it. Not you . . . not after the way I brought you up . . . you wouldn't.''

Sarah got up, too, and came toward her. ''Janet,'' she said softly, ''it wasn't a question of choice. I didn't tell you until now because I thought it would upset you, but you have to know sometime if you're going to live with me. Most girls go into that profession because they have nowhere else to go.''

Janet was still shrinking away from Sarah. ''Anything is better than that,'' she said. ''Anything—a Salvation Army hostel is better than that.''

''Some of us didn't even have the choice of the Salvation Army, Janet. We were all pretty desperate . . . and it's not as terrible as you think,'' Sarah said. ''We were treated well, we lived very well and the men—they were mostly very nice—charming, cultured, high class. I went to theater first nights and operas and receptions . . .''

''And then to their beds?''

Sarah had to smile at her horrified face. ''No, mostly they came to my bed,'' she said, ''but at least they paid me well for it, which was more than my dear cousin, Hugo, wanted to do for the privilege.''

''Don't joke about such a thing,'' Janet said. ''I thought you might have been not too wise while you were here—some hanky-panky with that Mr. Murphy, maybe, but selling your body to men . . . no . . . no." She shuddered as if she were being forced to take bitter tasting medicine.

"Janet," Sarah pleaded gently. "I'm still the person you've always known, aren't I? Look at me! I haven't turned into a monster . . . it's been a shock to you, I know, but go to bed now. When you get used to the idea . . ."

"No!" Janet said firmly. "I will never get used to the idea. What you have done is the most terrible kind of sin. When a woman is forced by a man, that is one thing, but when she offers her body freely . . . that is damnation! That is damnation to the fires of hell and only the most bitter repentance can save you now."

"You really think I'm damned to hell?" Sarah asked.

"Aye, I do," Janet said. "And I'm very, very sorry for you."

"Then I don't think you should stay with me any longer," Sarah said hesitantly, "because I'm thinking of going back to a life of damnation, at least for a while."

Janet turned and walked toward her door. "Then I'll be packing my bags, miss," she said. "I'll not stay in a house of sin and sorrow."

"I'll pay your fare back to London, of course," Sarah said, "but I'm sorry you feel like this about me. You raised me and took care of me. I'm closer to you than anybody. I've always thought of you as my real mother, and I know I'm not a bad person."

"Maybe not bad," Janet said, her voice cracking with emotion, "but misguided, and damned just the same. I'll pray for you, that you receive the light of guidance from the Lord."

"Do you want me to find you a new hotel tonight?" Sarah asked, "or can you bear to sleep in the room next to a scarlet woman for one more night?"

"It's not a joking matter," Janet said, giving Sarah a frosty stare.

"Of course it's not," Sarah said. "I'd hoped that you'd spend the rest of your life with me, but I see now that it never could have worked. Your religion wants to send everyone down to the fires, and I believe in a God who wants to love everyone, in spite of their failings. I don't think what I do is wrong because I don't harm anyone . . . but I don't think I'd ever be able to convince you of that."

She and Janet stared at each other for a long while, then Janet turned away. "I'll be going to my bed now, Miss Sarah," she said, "and you'd maybe be good enough to look into passages back to England for me in the morning."

Forty-five

THE HOUSE THAT SARAH FINALLY SETTLED ON WAS a big white colonial style with green shutters and porch, perched at the end of Darling Point—farther out from town than Madeleine's house in Elizabeth Bay, but having the advantage of being more secluded and possessing a fabulous view from most of the rooms. In true colonial style, it was built around a big square hallway with a balcony running around all four sides upstairs. The rooms were all high-ceilinged and spacious and an attempt at modernization had already been made. Sarah got to work right away, completing modernization, adding bathrooms to the four main bedrooms on the first floor and redecorating with the most elegant silks and brocades she could find.

She was delighted with the way the whole project was going and took over the direction of all remodeling herself, much to the annoyance of all the craftsmen who wanted to work at a much slower pace. When they queried why it was so important to finish plastering by a certain date, a tip slipped into their pocket convinced them that they were, indeed, able to work much faster. If they guessed what the house was to be used for, none of them said so. The nearest one man came was to comment, "What you going to do—wash yourself in a different bathroom every night?" The general opinion was that Sarah was going to open a luxury bed and breakfast establishment and Sarah did not disillusion them on this.

In fact, her one disappointment at this time was that Janet would not change her mind and stay. Sarah had felt herself so close to the old woman and really hoped that a good night's sleep would make her see things in more perspective. She tried to reason with Janet but Janet remained unmoved.

"I'm sorry, Miss Sarah," she said. "You were a fine, wee girl and there's no denying I was fond of you—but you should have known better. I'd brought you up to know right from wrong and I'm fair ashamed that you turned out the way you did."

She packed her bags and moved the next day to a small Christian hotel nearer to the docks, waiting for the next ship back to England. Sarah watched her from the window as she climbed into a waiting cab and swallowed back the lump in her throat. Not since seeing Jimmy's grave had anything managed to get through the thick veneer of self-protection she had built up. All the while she watched Janet pack, she longed to encase the old woman in her arms and tell her how much she loved and needed her. But Janet's world was an undemonstrative one. Sarah did not remember any hugs during her whole childhood. She had always shaken hands with her father and Janet had patted her when she cried or fell down—but a real, honest-to-goodness, bone-crushing hug was outside their sphere of experience and Janet would have fled from it. So Sarah stood in silence and watched her go, realizing that the last element of her past life had now left her. She was, finally, completely alone in the world.

This made her throw herself even more fully into the preparations of her house. She wore Renee out rushing from furniture stores, to wallpaper shops, to tiling specialists, and curtain makers.

"I can't walk another step," Renee complained one afternoon as she staggered after Sarah, her arms laden with wallpaper pattern books.

"Then you take a cab from here," Sarah said. "I'll send you on straight to the house and I'll just swing by David Jones and see if the satin quilts I ordered are in yet."

"Don't you ever get tired?" Renee complained. "I've never met such a slave driver."

"You can always go back to Madeleine," Sarah quipped laughing. Renee made a face. "Sometimes that doesn't sound like such a bad suggestion. At least she let me sleep late in the mornings."

"I want everything to be ready as soon as possible," Sarah said. "I'm spending all this money. I need to start making some soon. That reminds me—this evening you and I will need to go rough our plans—how we get in touch with the girls and the ients most tactfully. I'll want your ideas on that."

"Like I said, bloody slave driver," Renee muttered. "Aren't ou even hungry? We haven't eaten since breakfast."

"I'm a little thirsty," Sarah said, "but don't worry. I'll stop or a cup of tea at that little café round the corner from David ones. That will keep me going."

She stepped out into the traffic and hailed a cab. Renee limbed in and drove away, leaving Sarah to turn in the direction f Pitt Street and the big department stores. It was late afternoon nd rush-hour crowds were beginning to build, hurrying in the pposite direction from Sarah, to the railway station or the newly uilt subway station on Macquarie Street. As Sarah stepped aside o prevent herself being mowed down by two large women laden vith parcels, she almost stumbled onto a beggar woman, sitting n the corner of an alleyway at the back of David Jones, a sleeping baby clutched to her in a shawl.

"Spare a copper for the baby, miss," she called, holding up er hand to Sarah. Instinctively, Sarah reached into her purse nd was about to put the coin into the woman's hand when she roze. The woman was Jessie. Jessie with whom she had shared cabin and secrets. She looked at her again, wondering if she ad made a mistake, because the beggar women still showed no igns of recognizing her. The woman, instead, was looking at he size of the coin.

"God bless you, ducks," she said. "You're a proper toff," nd her accent convinced Sarah that she hadn't made a mistake.

"Jessie?" she asked. "Is that really you?"

The woman's eyes opened wide and focused on Sarah's face or the first time. "Blimey, it's Sarah," she said. "They said ou was dead. You don't look like a ghost to me."

"I'm very much alive and kicking," Sarah said kindly, "but 'm really distressed to see you like this. Why don't you come nd have a cup of tea with me and tell me what happened."

Jessie's eyes were wary. "Me? Come and have a cup of tea vith a posh lady? You wouldn't want to be seen with me."

"Don't be silly—of course I don't mind," Sarah said. "You aven't changed the kind of person you are just because you're lown on your luck. Come on—I know this nice little place round the corner. They do very good toasted tea cakes."

She helped Jessie to her feet and the baby whimpered and

opened big brown eyes. "It's all right, love," Jessie whispered "We're going to get drinkies." She looked up at Sarah and smiled as the chubby little one wrapped arms around her neck "My little boy," she said proudly. "He's a good little kid, but it's hard for him to sit still for long at his age."

Sarah observed him, thinking for a moment that she could easily have been in Jessie's place with a sturdy one-year-old by now. She led them down the block and into the cosy café. The hostess gave Sarah an inquiring look as she seated the ragged couple at her table, but Sarah nodded and she said nothing. She watched them wolf down tea and buns before they even started conversing.

"Now Jessie," she said, "do tell me what happened. You seemed so settled and secure in your little cottage—I couldn't imagine anything going wrong for you."

"You never know, do you miss?" Jessie asked, holding the cup steady so that the baby could drink from it. "Everything was going really nice. Little Tommy here was born fine and healthy and his dad was so proud of him. Took him around the stables like he was a prize turkey." She smiled at the memory of it. "I was beginning to settle in real nice, too. Getting along and starting a little garden, then it happened. My Tom was so keen to start riding as a proper jockey and he was doing just fine. He'd got so they let him exercise the horses in the mornings and this one morning the horse threw him. He went right down on his head, miss. Hit his head on a rock. Well he was out for a month or more. They never thought he'd wake up again, but he did wake up—only he isn't the same anymore. He just lies there—can't talk, can't feed himself, nothing. Sometimes I think it would have been better if he hadn't woken up again. It fair breaks your heart to see him . . . you just keep hoping, you see. Some days he almost seems to recognize me and be about to speak, but then the next time he's just like always. Doesn't even turn his head when his little boy cries for him."

Sarah reached out her hand and covered Jessie's. "I'm very, very sorry for you, Jessie," she said. "What a terrible thing to happen. Where is he now?"

"In the mental hospital, miss. Out Liverpool way. I don't like to leave him out there with all the loonies, but someone has to look after him. He needs feeding worse than a baby, you see and I didn't have anywhere to put him."

"They wouldn't let you keep him at home in the cottage?" Sarah asked.

"Them?" Jessie's voice was sharp-edged. "When they found out he wasn't going to get better again, they said they needed the cottage for Tommy's replacement. We had to get out. They gave me five pounds for compensation. Have you any idea how long five pounds lasts these days? I've had to sell most of my furniture and things just to buy food."

"But where are you living now?" Sarah asked.

"Sometimes in the church mission, miss," Jessie said, "but they don't let you stay there—only a couple of nights, then you have to leave again. I've been looking for a job, but once they see you've got a baby, you can forget it. I've even talked to the adoption people, to see if he'd have a better chance with someone else—but I can't yet bring myself to give him up—just in case his dad gets well again one day."

Sarah opened her purse and put down money on the table for the tea. "I'll offer you a job right now, Jessie," she said. "I've just bought a big new house and I need a maid right away. It's even got a separate gardener's cottage at the back where another little boy is going to come and live. You could take care of both of them and he'd be a companion for your Tommy. Come and see it right away. I was going to David Jones, but that can wait until morning."

Jessie stared at her in wonder. "I just can't believe it, miss," she said. "I was almost ready to give up Tommy and jump off the Gap, I was getting that desperate. Are you sure this is all right? I'm not going to cause a row between you and your husband?"

Sarah laughed. "I have no husband. The house is all mine and I say you are more than welcome. Of course," she said, pausing at curbside to wave at a passing taxi, "when you hear about it, you may not want to come."

"What do you mean, miss?" Jessie asked as the taxi screeched to a halt beside Sarah. Sarah paused before opening the door. "It's a brothel, Jessie. I'm going to be running a high-class brothel."

Jessie's eyes shot open with surprise, then she burst out laughing. "Lord love us, miss. Who would ever have thought it? You of all people. No wonder you look so prosperous."

"So you wouldn't mind?" Sarah asked.

Jessie continued to laugh. "What I say is get money out of the buggers any way you can," she said. "Good luck to you, miss."

Jessie settled in quickly and speeded up their preparations by working nonstop at a furious pace. She refused to slow down, even when begged to by Sarah and Renee. "I feel better when I'm busy," she always said.

One day she was scrubbing the newly laid hall tiles and Sarah was upstairs in the best bedroom, trying to decide which wallpaper would go with the pink satin drapes and thick white carpet. Sarah was conscious of voices raised down below and thought, to begin with, that Jessie was only arguing with one of the carpenters who had just walked across her clean floor. But then Jessie's face appeared around the bedroom door. She looked pink and flustered.

"If you please, ma'am," she said, "there's a gentleman downstairs and he's very insistent. I told him we weren't open yet and the rooms weren't ready, but he says he's not fussy and someone bloody well better hurry up!"

Sarah pushed back a stray wisp of hair from her face. "Thank you, Jessie," she said. "Don't worry, I'll handle this. I expect we'll have to get used to handling all sorts of strange people . . ." She walked out onto the balcony.

"Can I help you?" she called down to the hatted figure who was standing in the shadow of the front door.

"Too bloody right!" the voice boomed back. "What sort of an establishment do you call this? No bloody service and I hear the owner's off-limits to the clients."

Jessie gave a little gasp of horror, but Sarah flew down the stairs. "Col!" she shouted in delight. "Oh Col!" and she flung herself into his arms.

"Hello, Sarah," he murmured, wrapping her in a big bear hug.

"I can't believe it's you," she said, gazing up at him in sheer delight. "I've missed you."

Col held her by the shoulders so that he was still looking down into her eyes. "You left without saying good-bye," he said.

"It all happened so quickly. I wrote you a note, explaining."

"That's not the same thing at all. You didn't even say good-bye to me. I thought I'd never see you again." His eyes searched hers.

"I didn't dare come and say good-bye, if you want to know the truth," she said simply. "I was really in two minds about going in the first place. If I'd had to go through a good-bye scene with you, I'd never have left."

"So you missed me, then?"

"Every day," she said. "Then, when I read that you'd had a heart attack . . ."

"In England?" he asked. "You read that in England?"

"It made the *Times*," she said, laughing, "right below the riots in South Africa."

He beamed like a little boy. "How about that. I made the same page as Gandhi. I must be moving up in the world."

She slipped her hand into his. "Come into the parlor," she said. "We're not really ready for guests yet, but we do have a carpet and a couple of chairs. Shall I get Jessie to bring you a cup of tea?"

"Cup of tea?" he asked. "What do you think I've turned into. A whiskey would go down better."

"But I understood you were strictly not to drink—or do anything else harmful."

"That's what my bloody wife keeps telling me. But I say, if I'm going to go, I'm going to go happy."

Sarah slipped an arm around his waist. "Don't talk like that," she said. "You're not going to go anywhere. Who else have I got in this town who's pleased to see me. Everyone else told me to get back to where I came from."

"Including my wife, so I hear."

"Including your wife. She told me that there would not be a respectable house in Sydney where I would be welcome."

"So you decided to open an unrespectable one?"

"Exactly," she said. "I decided if I was going to be a social outcast all my life, I might as well enjoy it."

Col looked serious for a moment. "The only difference between you and those bloody bitches is that you're open about it," he said. "If we pinned up a list of the men my wife has been to bed with, we could use it as a bridge across the harbor . . . only she's been very discreet about it." He smiled at her again, not taking his eyes from her face for a second. "I think you're going to be very successful."

"I hope so," Sarah said. "I'm taking a big risk, of course. As of this moment I have no girls or clients . . ."

"They'll both come easily," he said. "I wouldn't worry about them. There's only one thing wrong with this business as far as I can see."

"And what's that?" she asked, looking at him anxiously.

"Stupid rule they always have that the madam is off limits to the clients," he said. "I don' think I'll bother to come here after all."

She slipped her arms around his neck. "There is no rule about the madam being off-limits to her friends," she said.

He gave a low chuckle and pulled her toward him, kissing her down the throat. "Does this establishment have any pieces of furniture bigger than those pathetic chairs?" he whispered, nuzzling at her ear.

She laughed. "The beds are still on order," she said. "I've a couple of circular ones coming that might interest you."

"I'm more interested in right now," he said, bending to kiss her bare shoulder while his hand was toying with the button at the back of her dress.

"Col! Not here," she whispered, holding him away half-heartedly. "There's nowhere we can go . . ."

"What's wrong with right here? The carpet's soft . . ."

He had managed to undo the button and was sliding the dress from her shoulder, following its progress with a line of kisses. He sank to his knees as he pulled the dress down, running his lips between her breasts and down to her bare waist. He put pressure on her, trying to pull her down beside him.

"My maid's in the house and liable to come in at any moment," she whispered, sinking down beside him in spite of herself, her head dizzy with longing.

"Give her a taste of what she's going to be in for if she works here," he said, his eyes laughing as her panties slid away in a rustle of silk. "And you'll have to forgive me but I just can't wait to get myself undressed, too." She heard herself laugh at the back of her throat as he grabbed her urgently. She arched her back toward him, digging her fingers into his broad back with a moan of desire.

Forty-six

CHRISTMAS THAT YEAR WAS THE FIRST TRULY happy celebration Sarah ever remembered. There was no father waiting in the wings to criticize, no one to decide what she should be doing. Five girls had come across from Madeleine and the house was in full operation. Sarah understood that more girls might want to follow them, but she prudently decided that putting Madeleine out of business would not be a wise course of action. She had sent out Christmas cards to all the old clients she and Renee could remember, saying simply, "Should Auld Acquaintance be Forgot?" and signed simply Sarah. Between the cards and word of mouth, they had quite enough clients by the end of December.

As Sarah could have predicted, Lytton Argus was one of the first to appear, looking completely unchanged, so that Sarah wondered at his true age. He could have been anywhere from sixty to eighty. He was so delighted to see her that she had to bend her rule and accompany him personally to her best room where they had their usual polite session of very restrained passion. Afterward Sarah had dinner sent up for them and they chatted as if they were in a London drawing room with Lytton filling her in on all the events that had happened during her time away.

"And you must come out and see your colt," he said, smiling at her shyly.

"My colt!" Sarah exclaimed. "I had forgotten all about him. How is he?"

"He's a sturdy little fellow. Very strong as a yearling. I think you might have yourself a Melbourne Cup winner."

Sarah laughed. "And to think I chose him because of his eyelashes!" she said.

Lytton Argus did not laugh. "After fifty years of breeding

horses, I've come to the conclusion that hunches beat skill every time in picking future winners," he said. "Maybe you have a flair for this sort of thing. You might want to invest in your own stable when you have money you want to put somewhere."

"I can't see that day happening in the near future," she said. "I have to earn back my capital first. If you are going to be my only client, that might take a while."

"Nonsense, my dear," he said. "I am sure you will be very successful. You have class, and that's what counts."

As Lytton had predicted, the clients did remember and come back—some because of Sarah and others following Renee or the other girls. Christmas day Sarah held a big garden party and barbecued a whole sheep. The party finished with a swim in the harbor.

"You must build a swimming pool," Renee suggested. "Have something in to heat the water—imagine what a selling point that will be over Madeleine when we can invite our clients for a sexy moonlight swim."

"I'll have to learn to swim first," Sarah said. "I only just learned to splash in the waves."

"It's easy," Renee laughed. "If I can learn, anyone can. You want to take private lessons in an indoor pool. They've got one at Col Murphy's place. Get him to teach you."

Sarah chuckled. "Can you imagine his wife letting me come for swimming lessons?" she asked. "I told him to drop by to-day, but you'll notice he hasn't. When it comes down to it, she still pulls the strings."

"The purse strings, you mean," Renee said. "It's too bad he doesn't have his own money, independent of her."

"Yes," Sarah agreed. "It is too bad."

She wandered down to the edge of the water. She could hear the squeals of bathers who were being pursued by young men or splashed by each other. Everyone seemed to be having fun—but I feel so old suddenly, Sarah thought. As if life has passed me by. She picked up a pebble from the rocks and threw it out into the black waters, watching the rings spreading in the glow of lamplight. I suppose I'm learning to face the fact that Col will always belong to her first, that he can never be free of her . . . The rings reached the shore and ran into the sand with soft lapping. Would he every marry me if he could? Sarah wondered. Of course he wouldn't. A public man like Col could never risk being associated with a person of doubtful reputation. Maybe I should be glad that things are the way they are. At least I see him sometimes . . .

But at that moment, standing alone in the velvet darkness of a summer night, sometimes did not seem to be enough.

The next morning she was awoken by Jessie, bringing in a tea tray with an excited look on her face.

"Sorry to wake you so early, ma'am," she said, "but the gentleman's downstairs again."

"What gentleman?" Sarah sat up and reached for the teacup.

"The one that came that afternoon—the very impatient one . . ."

Sarah jumped out of bed, almost spilling the tea and reaching for her robe. "Tell him to wait in the parlor and that I'll be right down," she said.

"I take it he's not the usual gentleman caller then?" Jessie asked as she reached the door.

"You take it correctly," Sarah called after her. She rushed through her toilet and hurried down to the parlor. Col was standing by the window, his back to her, looking out toward the high buildings of the city and the sparkling water. "It's a grand town, Sydney," he said as she came in. "And it's going to be even grander still. I've got such great plans—streets of high-rise buildings, a bridge right across the harbor . . . if only I manage to stay in office long enough to accomplish them."

"You mustn't talk like that," Sarah said, reaching out to stroke his cheek. "You are going to stay fit and healthy forever. My orders."

He took her hand and kissed its palm. "Anything to please you," he said. "But I wasn't meaning only my health. If the heart doesn't get me, the voters will. Only a matter of time. You always get fed up with what you've got and want a change. And there's a lot of vultures sitting on the fence right now, waiting for their moment."

"I don't want a change," Sarah said.

He looked at her tenderly. "Merry Christmas," he said. "Sorry I couldn't say it yesterday, but you know how it is. The whole house was full of Marjorie's relatives. My word, that family breeds like rabbits—nieces and nephews crawling out of the woodwork. Did you have a nice Christmas?"

"It was pleasant to take a day off. I've been so busy that haven't stopped running for three months."

"Any plans for today?"

"Not really."

"Want to come for a drive?" he asked. "Marjorie's departe with a load of her friends and I've got my car and driver. W could go out into the country."

"I don't know if I should really leave for a day," Sarah saic

"Of course you should. You won't get any customers on Box ing Day. The poor bastards are all stuck at home trying to pu together clockwork train sets, wearing ridiculous paper hats o their heads and trying to face cold turkey."

Sarah laughed. He slipped an arm around her shoulders "Come on," he said. "How often do you and I have more tha ten minutes alone together?"

"It would be nice," she said. "I've been meaning to driv out and see that racehorse I chose. I gather he's going to be promising two-year-old now."

"Let's do that then," Col said, "and afterward we can pay visit to that new winery I heard about. A big German calle Fritz has come out of a prisoner-of-war camp and opened it They say the wines are excellent and he has picnic tables unde the trees . . ."

"Sounds wonderful," Sarah said. "Let me get my hat an tell Renee I'm going."

They drove through almost empty suburban streets, out int the country. Everything was so peaceful and serene. Home steads stood in pools of deep shade under spreading Europea trees. Jacarandas created bright spots of purple among the green

"Peaceful, isn't it?" Col commented. "It's hard to believe that I've got to go back to that bloody place in a couple of weeks and start all that yelling and screaming again. I must be getting too old."

"Getting too old!" Sarah said with a snort. "You know very well that the greatest statesmen often came to the peak of their power when they were over sixty. The Duke of Wellington lived to eighty and remained the royal adviser, so I believe."

"You're right," he said. "I just feel old sometimes when I'm with you."

"Thanks a lot. You certainly know how to flatter a woman," she replied laughing.

''I didn't mean it like that and you know it,'' he said, putting his hand on her knee. ''I meant that I keep thinking of all the young bloods you should be thinking of settling down with, not wasting your time with a forty-five-year-old has-been.''

''I don't think I'm a very hopeful runner in the settling down stakes,'' Sarah said. ''I haven't a very good track record. Besides, wine, I believe, gets better with age. So does whiskey. They become richer and stronger.''

He laughed and pulled her close to him. ''I don't know what I'd do without you around, young Sarah,'' he said.

''You'd find another young Sarah,'' she quipped, trying to keep the conversation light.

''I'm afraid I won't be seeing too much of you in the new year,'' he said. ''I'm going to be up to my eyes in this Japanese trade visit. You might have read about it. I've invited a delegation to New South Wales to explore the possibilities for further trade between our countries.''

''Sounds like a good idea,'' she said.

''You might think so, but there's certainly enough opposition to it,'' Col said. ''Most Aussies are very suspicious of anything Oriental. They look upon the Japanese as treacherous little yellow bastards who'll pretend to talk trade, bow prettily, and then steal all our industrial ideas.''

''And won't they?'' she asked.

''They have a reputation for doing so,'' Col admitted, ''but I aim to keep them so bloody busy that they won't have time to blink inside an industrial plant. And we have to be realistic. We've just been through a war that almost wiped out Europe. It is naive to think that we can always count on mother England to protect us and buy our raw materials. Japan is a growing power. They are going to need meat and coal and steel and automobiles and there is no reason why we shouldn't be the ones to supply them. Of course, some people think that sounds like sacrilege. In my position you just have to do what you think is best in the long run and take the knocks if it turns out to be a bad idea.''

''Or hope that the opposition is in by the time it turns out to be a bad idea,'' Sarah said.

''You be quiet, or I might bring some little Japs to visit you.''

''That might be interesting,'' she said. ''I don't think any of the girls has ever had an experience with Oriental gentlemen. Doesn't legend have it that they are very small where it counts?''

"I won't have to worry about you joining in then, will I?"

"You don't ever have to worry about me, Col," she saic "My interests are purely business ones."

"Except for old men who give you racehorses."

She grinned. "Don't tell me you are jealous of Lytton? He i such an old sweetie I could hardly say no to him after he'd give me a racehorse, could I? And between you and me, I hardl know whether anything's happened or not."

They stopped outside the white-painted gates of the stable and waited for the chauffeur to open them. The head stable ma met them with a smile of recognition. "Come to see the littl fellow, have you?" he asked. "He's turning out just fine—an frisky? Sometimes he streaks up and down that field, just fo the hell of it." He led them through the stable yard to the lus green fields beyond. "There he is, that's little Buster." H laughed. "You see, the nickname stuck. He's still Buster to al the grooms."

The colt had grown into a sleek two-year-old and put on display of friskiness for them, galloping from one end of th field to the other.

"Lytton says he might be a Melbourne Cup winner," Sara commented, leaning on the white fencing to watch him.

"That wouldn't be bad. You could retire and keep me in m old age," he said, running a hand along her shoulders as h spoke. She shivered as his hand touched her. "Don't say thing like that when you know they can't happen," she said and move away. "You'll grow old being waited on by Marjorie and a whol hospital full of nurses who will feed you prunes and never le you out to come and see me."

He walked up behind her and slipped both hands around he waist. "You should never have got yourself involved with me," he said. "I'm no use to you."

"You're right," she answered, looking out into the blue distance. "I never should have let myself. But it's too late now. I am, and there's nothing I can do about it."

He leaned over to kiss the back of her neck. "Come on, love We've seen the bloody horse. Let's go and get ourselves a nice lunch. Let's not get broody over the future. Who knows if I'l be here next week."

She turned to face him, burying her head into his chest. "Oh Col. I can't help it, but I love you. It's stupid, isn't it?"

"Bloody stupid," he said, then, as she looked up in anger, he threw back his head and laughed. "Anyone who loves me has to want their brains tested," he said. "I'm a bad-tempered, conniving old bastard. But I'm glad you do, because that means it's reciprocal." He kissed her lightly and tenderly on the lips. "Let's go and get that lunch."

They drove through wooded-hill country where yellow dust rose in a cloud behind them, then dropped to a sheltered valley where giant tree ferns overlooked a sluggish, dark-pooled stream. Before them were meadows with horses in them, and the slopes beyond had been terraced for grapes. The house was a replica of a Bavarian chalet, with a carved balcony and checkered-cloth tables under the trees. When they got out of the car, the air smelled of eucalyptus, mingled with the heady smell of fermenting new wine.

"Grab a table," Col said. "I'll go and let someone know we're here and we need service. Some cold sausage and white wine do for you?"

"Perfect," she said, beaming at him. He was just returning with a tray of wine and food when a noisy party came up from the stream below. They were carrying big wicker picnic baskets and disappeared out of sight on the far side of the building. Sarah could hear them noisily setting up for their picnic.

"Wine! I'm dying of thirst!" one of them shouted and there was loud repartee.

"I have to find the little girl's room, if there is one in this godforsaken place," a woman's voice said.

"Don't be so damn proper, Marjorie! Use the bushes like the rest of us!" the first voice yelled after her. Col and Sarah both froze as the figure came around the building toward them. It was Marjorie Murphy. She saw them at about the same time they saw her. Her perfectly made-up face flushed with a spasm of anger. She went up to Col and grabbed his arm, making the wine glasses rattle on the tray.

"What the hell do you think you are doing?" she hissed. "Are you out of your mind? Flaunting yourself in public with that floozy?"

Col was clearly embarrassed. "Come on, Marjorie. We were minding our business. You mind yours. Go over and join your friends. We'll move on."

"You'll do no such thing," she murmured, keeping her voice

to a well-bred modulation. "I'm not risking having you spotte
as you drive through Sydney, although God knows where you'v
been already. Probably around Luna Park for half the world t
see."

"We went for a drive in the country, Marjorie. We wanted t
be alone. We still do."

"Don't be ridiculous," she said. "Send her home right away
You're not driving back with her. You might have given som
thought to my feelings . . ."

"Sarah has feelings, too," Col said. "Did that ever occur t
you?"

"She was told to stay away, cheap little tart. She deserve
everything she's got coming to her," Marjorie said in a ven
omous undertone.

"Marjorie, I won't have . . . ," Col began, but Sarah got up

"It's all right, Col," she said quietly. "It's obviously bette
if I go now. I'll get your chauffeur to take me home, unles
Marjorie would rather I walk." Then she picked her way daintil
over the rough ground. Before she reached the car, she hear
Marjorie's voice ringing loudly, "Look everybody. Guess wh
I found! He thought he could slip off for some wine tastin
alone, but we won't let him be alone on Boxing Day, will we?'

The general loud laughter drowned any answer that Col migh
have given as Sarah got into the car.

After that she didn't see Col for some time. She read in th
paper about his negotiations with the Japanese. Some of th
headlines seemed to hint that if the five members of the delegation were let in, they would take over the country in a matte
of days, or go home with the secrets of every Australian-made
automobile hidden under their kimonos.

As Sarah's list of clients grew, she had a not-unexpected visi
from Madeleine.

"I must say that you have a nerve," Madeleine said, flinging
down her gloves as she took in the furnishings of the parlor.
"You let me teach you all the tricks of the trade, then you steal
my best girls away."

Sarah picked up a cigarette and put it into her gold-tipped
holder. "I didn't ask you to teach me, if you remember, Madeleine," she said. "You forced me to learn, whether I wanted
to or not. The girls came to me of their own free will. They
came because they were tired of having their lives ruled for

em. With me they can work when they want to and go where ey want to in their spare time, just like any other job. And they don't like the look of a man, they are not forced to go rough with it either. Can you wonder that they prefer to work re?"

"You don't think you will be allowed to remain in business, you?" Madeleine asked.

"I don't exactly see who's going to stop me at the moment," rah said. "Certainly not you. I understand that the rest of ur girls want to join me as soon as I give the nod. Except eila and your little French acrobat, that is. I hardly think you n satisfy all tastes with just them."

Madeleine's eyes narrowed as she observed Sarah. "I should ve let you jump," she said. "I saw at the time that you were o damn strong-willed. I had a hard job convincing you then, dn't I?" She picked up her gloves again and began to cross e room. "Just remember one thing, though. I had to fight to tablish myself in this town. I'm prepared to fight again to keep hat I have, and I'm a very dirty fighter."

"I don't doubt it for a moment," Sarah said.

"And another thing, mademoiselle," Madeleine snapped as e reached the door. "You are only in business because of Col urphy. We all know that he can pull any string he wants to. hen he goes, you go—and, strictly between ourselves, I hear s days are numbered."

"What's that supposed to mean?" Sarah asked, but Made- ine had gone. Sarah took a long, nervous pull at her cigarette. aybe she had been naive to expect that she could open in pposition to Madeleine without much trouble. The whole ques- on was, would Madeleine have the power to ruin her? I could ose down Madeleine tomorrow, she thought, but it sticks in y throat to ruin anybody. I just hope I won't live to regret it.

Forty-seven

SARAH HEARD NOTHING MORE FROM MADELEIN after that visit. She refused to take more of Madeleine's gir and hoped that Madeleine would look upon this gesture as desire to coexist, not to rule. The running of the house on Da ling Point seemed all too smooth. There was always a steac stream of clients, the girls were content, and the clients re ommended their friends. When Sarah took down the money the bank each morning, she had a hard job of not feeling guil about the rapid way her bank account was growing.

A few years of this and I shall be rich enough to retire an live my own life, and not even people like Marjorie Murphy wi be able to stop me, she thought.

But every time she thought of the future, she could not hel including Col in those thoughts, and she knew that was a dar gerous thing to do. She had hardly seen him since he was es corted away by his wife on Boxing Day. She read in the pape that the dates for the trade delegation had been fixed and hope it would soon be over with so that she could look forward to hi visits again. In fact, her spirits rose tremendously when Jessi knocked on her bedroom door very late one night.

"Miss, there's a gentleman downstairs, says he has to see yo and nobody else," she whispered.

Sarah jumped out of bed, slipped on her robe and hurrie down the stairs. A hatted figure was standing in the dim light c the parlor.

"Col?" she whispered.

"Afraid not," the voice said. It was a voice she had neve heard before—low and rasping as if it's owner was about t cough.

Sarah walked across to turn up the lamp. "I'm sorry, but don't think I know you," she said, taking in the man's poorl jacket and lack of tie. "I must ask you to leave and return the morning if you have business to discuss. It's far too late receive callers."

"Not if the callers have the right amount of money in their ckets, eh?" the man said and gave a sort of laughing cough.

"I don't know what you are talking about and I find your tone her offensive," Sarah said in her best upper-class manner. Jow, please leave before I have to summon my gardener and auffeur and have you thrown out."

"Gardener and chauffeur, eh?" the laugh continued. "Not ing badly at all, eh? That's what Joey thought. That's why he at me. Shame if this little lot had to come to an end . . ."

"I don't quite understand," Sarah said icily, "but is this some ad of threat?"

"Listen ducks," the man growled. He walked up to Sarah d grabbed her by the front of her robe, pulling her close to n. "Joey controls the crime in this town. He decides who erates and who don't, and those who want to operate have to y for the privilege. Maybe you're too new to know that. That's right. Joey's a big hearted sort of bloke. I'm sure he'll over- ok the fact that you ain't paid until now, if you starts paying gular . . ."

"I don't think I understand," Sarah said, glaring at the man d attempting to wrench her arm free from his grasp. "Exactly hat are you suggesting I pay for?"

"For protection, lady. That's what you pays for—for protec- on," and he laughed, showing a mouthful of missing and ackened teeth.

Sarah managed to twist her arm free. "Tell your Joey, who- er he is, that I don't need his protection," she said.

The man continued to laugh. "Oh, but I think you do, issus. Otherwise some nasty little accidents might start to hap- n."

"Such as what?"

"Small things at first—little robberies, a few windows nashed, one of your girls beaten up on her way home . . . and en if you don't get the hint, the accidents will get bigger. nash up the whole bleedin' place if we want to and take a zor to your lily white cheeks, too."

"You think I'm afraid of a few hoodlums?" Sarah asked, unding less concerned than she really was.

"Who would you go to—the police?" the man asked a gave that coughing laugh again. "Nah, lady. I don't think yo go to the police somehow."

Sarah weighed this thought. The police had not bothered h so far, but she had to admit that she did not have Madelein influence where police hierarchy was concerned. "How mu does this friend of yours expect me to pay?" she asked.

"Now you're talking," the man said. "Now you're showi sense. And all it's going to cost yer is fifty quid a week."

"Fifty pounds?" Sarah asked. "Don't be ridiculous."

"Come of it, lady," the man said. "We know you take in lot more than that."

"Yes, but I have a house to run, a large staff to pay."

"Then you might have to cut back on that gardener and chau feur of yours. Pull a few weeds yourself like ordinary folk ha to."

"You can tell your hoodlum friend, Joey, to do his worst, Sarah said haughtily. "I will not be scared into paying him penny. And if he tries anything, he might have an unpleasa surprise, because I happen to have quite enough friends in hig places."

"You mean Murphy?" he asked. "He won't be here fo ever."

"Get out," Sarah said.

"I'm going," the man answered. He began to walk towa the door. "You know what the sentence is for running a hous of prostitution?" he asked. "I don't think you'd enjoy jail to much. Don't have no gardeners and chauffeurs in jail, yo know." Then he went out, slamming the front door behind hi and leaving Sarah standing in the empty parlor, trembling a over.

The next morning she broke her usual rule and sent a messag round to Col at his office. He came over immediately.

"What's wrong?" he asked. "I knew it had to be pretty se rious or you'd never have called me."

Sarah found herself shaking again when she thought of th man. "I had a visit last night from a gang member of a protec tion racket," she said. "I was told to pay up, or else."

Col nodded. "That's always a risk you run in a business lik yours. Did the bloke say who he was working for?"

"He talked about a Joey."

"Ah. That will be Joey Tarrantino—nasty little dago thug. He runs the drug trade. I'm surprised he didn't try to sell you some cocaine at the same time."

"You don't seem to be very concerned," Sarah said angrily. "The man threatened to cut me up with a razor and you're standing here discussing it as if it wasn't anything important."

Col came over to her and slipped her into his arms. "Come on, Sarah," he murmured. "You mustn't let things like this get you down. You've got to be strong enough to sail right over them. I have to. I get threats all the time—even death threats. I don't let them worry me because once they see you're scared, they've won."

"But what am I going to do, Col?" Sarah asked, nestling her head against his shoulder and feeling the reassuring scent of his jacket. "I don't have Madeleine's in with the police. If they should raid, I'd go to jail. I feel so vulnerable. When I opened this business, I felt so proud of myself. I thought I'd finally proved that a woman could run her life without any man bossing her around, but now the first really bad thing's happened to me, I come running to you for protection."

"That's what I'm here for," he said. "And you don't have to feel weak because you ask someone for help. I do it all the time. I'd be out of office if I didn't continually ask for favors."

"Can you really do anything against this Joey?"

"Oh yes. I can buy him off all right," Col said. "He and I have a little arrangement about letting his cocaine in through customs. If he wants that little racket to go on working, he has to be prepared to give in some other areas, doesn't he?"

Sarah wrapped her arms around his neck, like a little child with a favorite uncle. "You are marvelous," she said. "I don't know what I'd do without you."

"Lead a boring life," he said.

"Have you got time for a little light lunch in my private sitting room?" she whispered.

"I'm sorry, but I have to get back. My Japs arrive in a couple of weeks. I want everything to go perfectly smooth. If I play this right, I can break the English hold over the wool market and put up the price of wool again, keep a few more farmers in business."

"So I suppose I won't see you for a while longer?" she asked sadly.

"I might bring my Japs round for an evening's entertainment, if they're the right sort of blokes," he said with a wicked little grin, "and maybe you and I can slip away for a weekend when they've gone. I've got a friend with a boat on the Hawksbury. Nobody could spy on us there, could they?"

"Sounds wonderful," she said with a sigh. "Only I just can't see it happening. Something always gets in the way . . ."

"Keep your chin up," he said, kissing her lightly on her nose. "Stiff upper lip, like they say in good old England!" He squeezed her tightly. "Don't worry my dear, it will all work out all right. You'll see."

"I hope so," she said, releasing him. "Good luck with your Oriental gentlemen."

Col did not go straight back to Parliament House. Instead he went back to his own office and rang for Jack Hemmingway.

"What are you doing here?" Jack asked. "Isn't Parliament still in session?"

"Too right, but I need something done right away and I thought you'd be the man to do it," Col said.

"Col—pardon me, but you can't afford not to be in that chamber at the moment. You know what a fine line you are walking with that Japanese delegation coming. Half of Australia is scared silly about a few Japs coming in. You're lucky McKinnon is such an ineffectual little man. An orator could have whipped up the opposition too string you from the nearest tree by now."

"I'm doing what I think best," Col said. "I'm doing it for them, the silly bastards. Trade with Japan will be the start of better prices for their wool and meat and wheat, too. Don't they realize that?"

"They see the other side of the coin, which apparently you don't," Jack said bluntly. "They see that letting in a few Japanese on the excuse of trade will open the door to a flood of Orientals and bang goes white Australia."

"They they're blood silly, aren't they?" Col blustered.

Jack shrugged his shoulders. "Keeping your territory to yourself is the strongest instinct in humans. That's what every war has been fought over—not religion, or anything else. You know that."

"But I don't want the little yellow bastards to come and live here," Col shouted. "I just want to make sure we have trading options. Look at America! Look how it's booming! It can't last, you know that. What happens when it crashes? England will go, too—their economies are too tied up together for it to survive alone. I want to make sure we keep our heads above water in bad times. The federal government is totally blind or apathetic—which is what happens if you have the country party in power, of course—and I feel it's all up to me, Jack."

Jack looked at him earnestly. "So you see yourself as the savior of Australia?" Then as Col didn't answer. "Isn't that a little over ambitious for a man who used to brag about his life in the slums?"

Col turned away and began to pace the room.

"You know, Col," Jack said softly, "this heart attack has affected you more than physically. You were better when you just thought about lining your own pocket and staying in power. Wanting to save the nation just isn't going to work for you. You need an image like Abe Lincoln or The Duke of Wellington to get away with it."

Col turned back and flashed a grin. "You think I should grow a beard?" he asked.

Jack did not smile. "I just think you should realize that the people liked you the way you were. They don't trust you as a do-gooder. They think there's something behind it—that you've done a secret deal with the Japs, maybe. I'm warning you, Col. This could bring you down."

Col shrugged. "Bloody pessimist," he said. "What do you know of real politics, anyway? Just because you've got a degree from bloody Oxford doesn't make you an expert. I've fought for what I know."

"And you're about to blow it all because your judgment's clouded—and I think it's because you're infatuated with a girl."

"That reminds me," Col said, spinning around with agility. "That's why I called you here. Joey Tarrantino's man has been to see Sarah. He wants protection money."

"What do you want me to do?" Jack asked.

"I want you to pay Joey a little visit," Col said. "Remind him who lets him bring his cocaine in. Tell him if she has one more visit, I tip off the customs to his warehouse and close him down."

Jack looked at him impassionately. "I hope you know what you're doing, Col, sticking your neck out like this."

"What do you mean, sticking my bloody neck out?" Col shouted, banging a fist on the desk and making a pile of papers slide to the floor. "Who runs this bloody state anyway? Who does Joey Tarrantino think he is? A sniveling little dago worm, that's who he is."

"I'm just saying," Jack said evenly, "that it might come down to a question of who is more powerful—and right now, I'm not sure you'd win."

"So you won't see him?" Col said. "You want me to see him myself?"

"I'll see him," Jack said. "After all, I'm still in your employ, aren't I?"

"The way you're talking right now, I wouldn't be surprised if you were working for the bloody opposition."

"Because I can see clearly and your vision is distorted?" Jack asked. "I'm only telling you the truth, Col, for your own good."

"And what should I do for my own good," Col asked, "since you seem to have the bloody answer for everything?"

"You should cancel the Japanese and stop seeing Sarah," Jack said, "if you really want to know what's going to keep you in power."

"Like hell," Col said.

"Then you might lose everything."

Col looked at him steadily. "I always was a man who enjoyed a good gamble," he said. "I'll take my chances."

After Col's visit, Sarah heard no more of Joey's gang and she began to relax again. She did take the precaution of hiring an extra man to be a night watchman and insisted that her girls went everywhere by taxi, but Col's influence really seemed to be working. The house slipped back into its peaceful routine. The Japanese delegation arrived and Sarah saw pictures of them touring sheep stations and coal mines. She also read headlines proclaiming, "Japs caught spying at auto plant." The most vociferous came from *Neville's Weekly*, she noted. She had put Colonel Neville out of her mind and did not expect to see him again. But one evening a flustered Renee, who had been running the office downstairs, appeared at Sarah's door. Sarah was in the middle of dressing for a concert and came to the door in her robe.

"What's the problem?" she asked.

"I'm not quite sure how to deal with it," Renee whispered. "Colonel Nevile is here . . ."

"Oh Lord," Sarah said. "That was all I needed right now. Is he here for the usual or does he want an interview?"

"He wants a girl," Renee said, "and from what I gather, he wants Jessie."

"Jessie? How did that happen?"

"She opened the door to him. I've been trying to placate him, but I think you'd better come down."

"I suppose I must," Sarah said. "I can hardly not admit him without causing trouble. Is Joline available? Maybe I can persuade him to try her . . ."

She slipped on a dress and came down the stairs. Colonel Neville was seated on chair in the parlor. He had a terrified Jessie on his knee.

"Colonel Neville?" Sarah asked in her most formal manner. "What a surprise. Welcome. I understand that you'd like to make use of our facilities. We have a delightful new girl I think you'd like to meet . . ."

It was obvious the Colonel had been drinking heavily. His eyes were bloodshot and he was exhaling pure alcohol. "I want this girl," he said. "Nice buxom little piece."

"I'm sorry, but she's only the maid," Sarah said. "You wouldn't want her and she's not available anyway."

"Then make her available," he said. "What's the problem? She a virgin or something? Doesn't matter—it's got to go sometime hasn't it and better to go with a man like me than with some butcher's boy down behind the shed."

Jessie let out a little sob. "Oh, Miss Sarah, I couldn't. Don't make me," she whimpered. "I just couldn't."

"Of course you couldn't, Jessie," Sarah said firmly, "and nobody is going to make you. You are employed here as a maid, that's all." She faced the colonel. "Colonel Neville. I am delighted you have decided to patronize our establishment, and we have several girls at your disposal, but my maid is not one of them. Kindly let her go and I'll bring the girls to meet you."

"I don't want them," he said belligerently. "She's the one. Nice round little titties . . ." Jessie screamed as he felt her. Sarah intervened. She yanked Jessie from his knee.

"If you are going to be abusive, I'm afraid you'll have to leave," she said. "Maybe you should go back to Madam Breu-

ner's. That seems to be more your style. We only cater to ge
tlemen here."

The colonel staggered to his feet. "Bloody tart," he sai
leering into her face. "Bloody cheap little tart. Think you ca
throw me out? I can ruin you. I can put you out of busine
tomorrow."

"I don't think so," Sarah said calmly, "because I have thre
witnesses in this room to the fact that you came here as a client
I think your rival newspapers would love that piece of news
Please leave quietly. I'm sure you wouldn't want to be throw
out by the large watchman I keep for such occasions."

The colonel's piggy eyes flamed red. "You think you've go
the better of me, don't you?" he slurred. "You think you coul
hide from me on that ship? You think you are smarter than me
You think you are safe because bloody Col Murphy can protec
you? Just you wait girlie. You made a big mistake when yo
didn't play along with me." He lurched to the door, grabbin
hold on the doorpost for support, then launched himself off int
the hallway. Renee held the front door open for him. He turne
back to Sarah. "Right at this moment I am the most powerfu
man in this state—just you wait and see." Then he stagger
out into the night.

Jessie was still sobbing quietly. "Thank you, Sarah," she
said. "I hope I haven't fouled things up for you, but it was such
a shock, see."

"Of course you haven't fouled things up, Jessie," Sarah said.
"Go and make yourself a nice hot cup of tea and go to bed. We
are much better off without that man. We don't need him as a
client."

"All the same," Renee said pensively, "he can be very dangerous. I hope Col can get you out of this one."

Forty-eight

A WEEK LATER, COL PHONED ONE EVENING. "GUESS what?" he asked, jovially. "I've just had a pleasant dinner with my Japanese gentlemen, and, if I understand them correctly, they were hinting that they'd like to round off the celebrations with a little hanky-panky. Can I bring them around?"

Sarah laughed. "How many of them are there?"

"Five."

"By all means, come on around. I'll have five girls ready, although I don't have kimonos!"

Col's rich laugh reverberated down the line. "I don't think they care about the bloody kimonos," he said. "It's what's underneath that counts. See you in an hour!"

Sarah bustled around excitedly, making the place as luxuriously peaceful as she could, putting fresh flowers in rooms, since she had read that Orientals liked fresh flowers, and making sure the baths were well stocked with towels and bath oils, since she had also read that baths played an important role in their society.

The men arrived, almost indistinguishable from one another, small, thin middle-aged men looking ill at ease in Western business suits. Sarah served drinks in the parlor and they all accepted Western scotch, conversing politely until the girls were brought in and introduced. Then they needed no urging to shed politeness and be led upstairs. Col winked at Sarah. "Randy little bastards, aren't they?" he asked. "Did you see old Noritaki's face when you brought in Joline?"

"I suppose it makes a change from geishas," Sarah said.

Col glanced toward the stairs. "Now that everyone else seems to be occupied, how about you and me slipping up to your room?" he asked. "It's been so long I've almost forgotten how."

"Well, just for a few minutes then," Sarah said. "I reall should be available in case there are problems."

Col slipped an arm around her shoulders. "You won't se them again for hours," he said. "They've been drinking whiskey with me all evening, and now more here. They'll probabl fall straight to sleep."

"It would be very nice," Sarah said, reaching her own ar around his waist so that they went up the stairs entwined aroun each other. It only took them seconds to undress.

"You might have to teach me again," Col whispered, pullin her naked body toward him. "It's been so long, I've forgotten."

Sarah laughed, writhing her breasts seductively across hi chest and wrapping her leg around his thigh. "When you finall turn senile," she whispered back, "this will be the last thin you forget." She lay back, opening her arms to him, laughin in delight as he aroused the passion in her. Then suddenly among the exploding fireworks in her head, there was another louder sound. The door was kicked open. A blinding light shon in their faces.

"Here they are, in here," a voice shouted.

"Police raid!" a second joined in, and then, triumphant abov all the other voices, "Smile!" and a camera flash popped wit an overpowering smell of sulphur.

"Do you know who this is?" Sarah demanded, angrily reaching for her robe while young policemen grinned.

"Of course we do," a man in a raincoat, obviously a reporter, said with a smirk. "That makes it all the better. Mak a great headline tomorrow: Premier hands over Aussie secret to Japs in whorehouse!"

"What are you talking about, you cretin?" Col roared, attempting to struggle back into his trousers while another flash bulb went off in his face. "And get that fucking thing out o here before I smash it over your head."

"Violence won't help your case, sir," the senior policeman said. "I suggest you finish dressing and come down quietly to the station."

"On what charge?"

"On the charge of using the services of a prostitute."

"You'd find that hard to prove," Col said. "The lady and I are very old friends. What we do in the privacy of our own bedroom does not involve the exchange of money."

"That may be so, sir," the policeman said. "Nevertheless, you were found in the middle of an indecent act with a known prostitute and that's good enough for us to arrest you."

Downstairs girls were screaming and the Japanese were protesting loudly, half in English, half in Japanese.

"I've got important foreign visitors here," Col said to the senior policeman. "You arrest them and you'll create a second world war."

"That's for the judge to decide, sir," the man said. "I'm just doing my job. I had orders to raid the place and arrest everybody I found here."

"Orders from whom?"

"My superiors, sir."

"What bloody superiors?"

"I'm just doing my job, sir. I don't know where the orders came from. I'm sure you'll find out everything down at the station."

"Too bloody right I will," Col stormed. "Heads will roll when I get down to your bloody station!"

"If you'll just come along quietly now, sir," the policeman said, taking Col's arm firmly.

"We've been set up," Col murmured to Sarah as they were both escorted out and half pushed down the stairs.

"By whom?" she asked.

"Give you one guess."

Sarah's gaze went down to the front hall. Colonel Neville was standing there, talking to another photographer and reporter. "That's it," he called out, "get a good one of them being bundled down the stairs!"

"You bastard," Col yelled. "I'll fix you."

"On the contrary," Colonel Neville said as they were swept past him. "I've fixed you. Good and proper this time. Let's see you get out of this one, Murphy!" His voice carried out through the open door as they were bundled into the back of waiting police vans, women in one and men in the other. Sarah did her best to comfort the crying, frightened girls.

"Don't worry," she said. "You can just plead guilty and I'll pay your fines for you. They won't send you to jail, I'm sure."

"But what about you?" Renee asked.

"I'm not so sure about me," Sarah said. "It looks like he's

done it this time, Renee. I'll need a lot of luck to get myself out of this one."

The van bumped and lurched over cobbled streets to the central police station, where they were dragged out and brought before the desk sergeant. He seemed to be expecting them.

"Put them down in the cells for the night. I'll talk to them in the morning," he said, hardly looking up from his clipboard.

"Just a minute, sergeant," Sarah said, stepping out of the line and assuming authority. "There is no reason to keep any of us in here overnight. State your charges now and then I'll pay the bail."

"I'm sorry miss," the sergeant said, looking as if he was secretly enjoying Sarah's discomfort, "but charges will be brought in the morning."

"Then we'll come back in the morning," Sarah said impatiently. "What is the bail for us?"

The desk sergeant eyed her steadily. "I can't accept your money," he said. "I have orders. Your assets are all frozen, miss. Proceeds of ill-gotten gains."

"This is ridiculous," Sarah said angrily. "Let me talk to a lawyer."

"In the morning, I said," he growled impatiently. "A night in the cells won't hurt any of you. Maybe teach you what being a criminal is all about!"

"You are going to be very sorry for this treatment," Sarah said frostily. "I have many friends in high places in this state."

"Like your friend Mr. Murphy?" he asked. "I wouldn't count on it. I think Mr. Murphy is about to find himself in pretty hot water as well. There are some pretty serious charges against you and Mr. Murphy, I understand . . ."

"Such as what?" Sarah demanded.

He leaned across his desk toward her. "I don't think you realize how serious this is," he said. "Running a house of prostitution is enough to send you to jail, but passing secrets to the Japs? Selling cocaine? They'll put you away for life."

"What are you talking about?" Sarah demanded. "There was never any question of passing secrets to the Japanese, and I have never allowed drugs on my premises. Never."

"Then how did my men manage to find a big packet of white powder, that appears to be cocaine, hidden quickly behind your sofa?" he asked. "And the plans for the new Summit motorcar were found in Mr. Murphy's overcoat pocket. I think he'll have a hard time convincing the jury he wasn't planning to sell them to the Japs, particularly because I understand one of the Japanese gentlemen had a large sum of money on him."

"This is preposterous," Sarah said. "Can't you see the whole thing has been set up to frame us? I demand to see a lawyer."

"Demand all you like," he said. "You ain't getting one until the morning. Now, if you'll be good enough to put your valuables into this here envelope and sign for them, I'll have Charlie here escort you down to your cell." He took the envelope from her and motioned to the policeman. "Okay Charlie, take them away."

They were half dragged down a white-tiled corridor, past jeering male prisoners who called out lewd comments and finally shoved into an already crowded cell containing streetwalkers, drunken old women, and a couple of fierce-looking young girls.

"Step aside riffraff, it's her ladyship come to call," one of the girls said, mockingly. The inmates crowded around them. "Think you're so bloody stuck up," one said spitting in Sarah's face. "Just because you make ten quid a time. You want to try it standin' up in an alley, for a shilling a go, because you need the money to stop yourself from starvin'."

One of the tough girls grabbed Sarah's arm. "Just watch yourselves," she growled. "You get that space in the middle. Step out of line and you'll be sorry." She gave Sarah a shove that sent her ricocheting into the other girls. Sarah opened her mouth to say something, then closed it again. There was nobody they could call to protect them down there in the locked cell.

The night seemed to go on forever. There was hardly enough room to sit, let alone lie down, and all night Sarah was trodden on as people made their way across to the open toilet in the corner, from which a fearful stench began to arise. For the first time Sarah began to feel really frightened. The desk sergeant had talked of jail for life. She pictured living in a cell like this for the rest of her life—no windows, no sunshine, no hope forever and ever.

Janet was right, she thought, smiling grimly. She said I'd come to a bad end and I have. Maybe it would have been better if I'd jumped off the Gap and Madeleine had never found me . . . but then I'd never have met Col and everything was worth it, just for that alone . . . I hope he's all right. He has enough friends who can pull strings for him. They'll clear him, won't they? They won't believe this absurd charge of passing over industrial secrets?

In the middle of the night, with the naked light bulb glaring overhead, this wasn't too easy to believe. If Col went to jail, she thought, he wouldn't last long. His heart condition would kill him. Not seeing him again would be the hardest thing of all to bear.

Forty-Nine

EARLY IN THE MORNING A TERRIFYING-LOOKING woman appeared with a tray of tin mugs of tea and some huge hunks of bread. The other inmates ate theirs hungrily, but Sarah could take no more than a sip of tea. She wished she had her purse with her so that she could at least do her hair before facing what she had to face today. As it was, she felt very vulnerable, dressed as she was in only part of her underwear and a hastily pulled on dress.

Warders began coming to the cell, removing occupants one or two at a time. Sarah's girls were taken out and did not return. At last only Sarah and the two rough girls were still in the cell. Each time a jailer appeared, Sarah demanded her rights to see a lawyer.

"Won't do no good," one of the girls said. "I've been screaming me bleedin' head off for days and they keep me here. They want to make sure they've got the case against you first, before they let you out on bail. They wouldn't even give me bail, even though me old man could have paid it, on account of I hit a bloke over the head with a bottle and killed him. I was only goin' for his wallet, too. Silly sod should never have tried to struggle . . ."

Sarah tried not to shudder. *I'm going to be left here with urderers,* she thought.

Then finally feet approached again and the door was un-cked. "You're wanted upstairs," the sour-faced man said and otioned to Sarah to come out. Her heart was pounding so udly that Sarah felt surely it must echo back from the tiled alls as she made her way up the stone steps. This time she was ot brought before the sergeant, but was shoved through into a oom down another long hall. She blinked in the bright daylight nd found herself staring straight at Sam Tanksley, her old law-er friend.

"Hello, Sarah love, in a spot of bother, are we?" he asked ith a big smile.

Sarah looked around the room. It was clearly an outer office r another room, through a frosted glass door. The sound of a pewriter could be heard inside.

"How did you know I was here?" she asked, delighted to e one friendly face. "They wouldn't let me call a lawyer."

"Col sent me over this morning," Sam said.

"How is he?" she asked. "Have they got him in jail, too?"

"He's out on bail," Sam said, "and I think we've a good hance of getting them to drop the charges. The Japanese have aimed diplomatic immunity, of course, and are leaving the ountry today. They have hotly denied any notion of buying ade secrets and nothing actually changed hands, so I don't ink they've got a case."

"Thank heavens," Sarah said.

"Doesn't matter if they do or don't, poor bastard," Sam said. You should have seen the headlines in this morning's papers—nd they had to censor the pictures! They've got dirty great black rosses all over them except for your faces. The poor bastard's een crucified all over the front page. Public outrage that an lected official could behave like that. I understand they're going call a special meeting of Parliament this afternoon and de-and his resignation."

"Poor Col," she said. "What a stupid way to end a career. e had such high hopes for this Japanese trade mission, too. He eally thought it would benefit Australia."

"He's been walking a tightrope for too long," Sam said. "It as bound to happen in the end. It's you I'm more concerned bout now, my dear. They can't prove charges against Col, but they've got enough on you to make it very unpleasant for you. That cocaine really makes it serious."

"I don't allow drugs, Sam," she said. "Someone must have planted it."

"Any idea who?"

"Several: Colonel Neville for one . . ."

"Probably not. He got all the story he wanted from the Japs. And he got the trade mission sent home in disgrace which he wanted, too."

"Then both Madeleine and Marjorie Murphy wanted to put me out of business, I'm sure . . ."

"It's not the sort of thing a respectable lady does," Sam said, scratching his head. "Besides, just the police raid alone would have been enough to put you out of business. They could have called the police any time they wanted, and Marjorie Murphy was not likely to do so when her own husband was there."

"Then it must have been those thugs," Sarah said thoughtfully.

"What thugs?"

"Oh, I had a visit from a protection racket awhile back. I think Col said it was Joey Tarrantino . . . I turned them down."

"That sounds most likely," Sam said. "I'll send out word to my men in the underworld, to see if anyone boasted about it. They usually do, you know, then we'll get the bloke and make him squeal. In the meantime, I'm trying to arrange bail, but they are being stubborn. I'm also trying to arrange a meeting with the chief constable. I think he might be a little more flexible. So don't worry. I'll do my best and I've never had a client hung yet." He laughed when he saw Sarah's face. "Come on, that was a little joke. You're going to be out of here, one way or another, although I'm afraid it's going to cost you . . ."

Sarah sank back into despondency as she was marched back to her cell. Her two murdering friends were a little more friendly, now that they didn't have to put on a show for a crowded cell and told her tales of their past exploits and how they had managed to get off on technicalities. Somehow Sarah did not find these comforting either.

It wasn't until the next day that Sam Tanksley came back. He looked pleased with himself.

"I've arranged a meeting with the chief constable," he said.

This may be your best chance, so don't say anything until u've thought it over carefully.''
''Should I admit guilt and plead for mercy, you mean?''
He smiled. ''That won't be necessary. Just play your cards ght and you could be out of here by tonight.''
She was escorted up broad stairs and along more polished-ored corridors until at last she was shown into a large, elegant fice. The police constable recognized her as she came in.
''Ah, my dear Sarah, come in,'' he said. ''Most unfortunate siness, I'm afraid. Do take a seat. Cigarette?''
Sarah took it and allowed him to light it for her. ''Thank u,'' she muttered.
''As I said,'' the constable went on, ''most unfortunate busi-ss. Need never have happened either. The problem is now w to get you off without making us appear like crooks or fools. e've got a man onto the cocaine problem. I think you were ite right in your hunch and we pretty much know that you ere not selling the stuff from your establishment. But that still aves us with the charge of operating a brothel. I think we'd anage to get the judge to commute the sentence if you showed at you were a reformed woman . . .''
Sarah had to laugh. ''You want me to join the Salvation Army d walk up and down with a flag?''
''No need to go to those lengths. I was thinking more in terms the police benevolent fund . . . a small donation . . .''
''How small?''
He smiled. ''We'd really like to open a boy's club in Surrey ills. Lot of crime there. Good idea to get boys off the streets. think we could buy the building we want for five hundred ounds.''
''Five hundred pounds?'' Sarah stammered. ''That's almost l I have in my bank account.''
''I know that,'' the constable said, laughing. ''In fact, I hap-en to know that the small donation, plus the fine I'm going to vy, will clean you out. But it's your choice. Jail or no jail.''
''I don't have much choice, do I?'' she asked.
''Not very much,'' he said.
''And what's to stop me going back to my house and opening up again, making sure I pay the necessary bribes to the right eople this time?''
''Only one thing. You don't have a house. We've confiscated

it—evidence of criminal activity . . ." He smiled again. Th thought flashed across Sarah's mind that her life seemed to be series of men smiling at her when they were being anything bu pleasant.

"So if I agree to go along with you, I have nothing?" sh asked, tossing back her hair which had fallen across her face.

"And if you don't, you still have nothing," he said. "I ca take over your bank account anyway. It just helps to get you o if you donate willingly."

"And what guarantee do I have that the poor little boys o Surrey Hills will actually get any of this money for their clu house?" she asked sarcastically.

"None at all," he said. "But then you're not in much of bargaining position now, are you?"

"It seems not," she said. "Very well. I have to accept. I you'll let me go back to my house to collect my personal be longings, I'll write you a check for the five hundred."

"Sensible girl," he said. He got up and came around th table. "If you'll take my advice," he said, "I'd go to anothe state. Maybe down to Melbourne, and start up again there. You' make yourself another good living. You're pretty good at i from what I hear, although I never got the chance to try yo personally . . ."

Sarah slipped past him. "And you won't, either," she said "I've become more choosy in my old age."

Col Murphy came out of the chamber and stood in the quie at the top of the stairs, breathing heavily. Over his heart was dull ache again. Somehow it didn't seem as frightening as th time before, when the dull ache had spread into a burning clutching pain that had landed him in an ambulance. He exam ined the feeling dispassionately, as if nothing really mattere anymore. Light from the stained glass windows threw a rainbov of colors onto him and reminded him of church as a boy. Hov long ago and far away that all was. Maybe he would have don better to have followed his father into the docks, and not let hi head get swelled by the scholarship to Saint Ignatius gramma school. Maybe he would have been quite content as a docker working his shift, drinking beer with his mates, wife and kiddie waiting at home . . . He blinked and stepped out of the rainbov light back into shadow. Sarah—he wondered what had happene to her. At least Sam Tanksley would get her off the worst charges, but if their enemies were really determined, she'd go to jail. Marjorie would like that, of course.

The big front door opened, letting in blinding light and the sound of motor horns from MaQuarie Street outside. Jack Hemmingway stepped in and closed off the street again. He began to climb the stairs, two at a time, then stopped short when he saw Col.

"Oh, Col," he said. "I didn't expect I'd find you here."

"I just came back to get a few things," Col said simply. "I'm not leaving my whiskey for my successor." He gave the shadow of his former laugh.

"I'm sorry," Jack said. "There wasn't much I could do. There wasn't anything anyone could do. The evidence was too overwhelming."

"Far too overwhelming," Col said. "Whoever set this up made damned sure that if the devil didn't get me, the deep blue sea would."

"I did warn you," Jack said.

"I know you did," Col said. "I never was very good at taking warnings. My old mother always said I'd come to a bad end. I never listened to her either."

"It need not be such a bad end," Jack suggested. "I don't think they'll press any charges against you . . ."

"That's what Sam said. Let me go to play chess and dangle a fishing line for the rest of my days."

"That could be worse."

"And Sarah," Col said. "What about her? Will she get off without jail? Has Sam said anything?"

"He was working on it."

"I can't imagine her in jail," Col said.

"You should have left her," Jack said quietly. "She was the straw that broke the camel's back. They'd all have left you to live out your term if you hadn't insisted on keeping her around. You must have known that Marjorie was working on it, and Neville . . ."

"What I don't understand," Col said quietly, "is how they got to the house so quickly. Someone must have set me up. But who knew I was going there that night with the Japanese? We only decided ourselves a few minutes earlier, so nobody else could have . . ." he broke off, staring at Jack until the latter looked away. "It was you, wasn't it?" he asked. "You told them. You set me up."

"For your own good, Col," Jack said. "You had to be stopped. You were making a serious mistake with these Japanese. It would never have worked. It would have been wrong for Australia."

"And you talked to *me* about playing God!" Col said, still shaking his head in disbelief.

"You told me I knew nothing about real politics," Jack said smoothly. "As a matter of fact, I've learned a lot from you. I've learned to bend with the wind. The wind wasn't blowing from your quarter any longer."

"You were working for McKinnon?" Col demanded. "That quiet little bastard with his phony public school accent was paying you?"

"Not paying me," Jack said. "Cooperating with me. The only person who was paying me was your wife. And she was just paying me to get rid of Sarah. We'd planned the police raid and the drug plant long before you decided to visit with your Japs. Your arrival made it too good an opportunity to miss . . ." He took a step toward Col, who involuntarily stepped back. "I'm sorry Col, I really liked you, I think you were a good chap, but someone else would have done it if I hadn't. You were on the way out anyway."

Col pushed past him. "I'm going for a walk," he said.

Fifty

LATER THAT AFTERNOON SARAH STOOD OUTSIDE her house, a policeman at her side. It had never looked more desirable than now—the lawns all manicured just so and the gardens a riot of flowers.

"Can you give me a little while?" she asked the policeman. "I'd like to walk around my gardens once more . . ."

The policeman looked suspicious. "You won't try to do a bunk on me, or throw yourself into the harbor, or anything like that?"

Sarah smiled. "I promise," she said. "I'd only like to be alone for a while. You can even keep me in sight if you want to."

The policeman nodded. "That's all right, miss. I'll just sit on this seat here and you do your walk around. No hurry."

"Thank you," Sarah said with a smile. She turned and walked down the raked sandy paths, pausing to stroke flowers on the way as if they were children's faces. She didn't even know where she was going to sleep that night, but she pushed such thoughts from her mind. She was saying good-bye to a dream. *Once I had a place I could call mine,* she thought. *Now I have nothing again—and nowhere to go . . .*

She walked on, down to the shore and stood on the rocks, looking across the harbor. She remembered the Christmas party when she had stood on this spot in the darkness, listening to the laughter. In memory she picked up a pebble and tossed it out across the water, watching it skim and bounce until it sank, sending spreading rings toward the shore.

"At least it's one stage better than breaking rocks with arrows on your clothes," a voice said behind her. She turned and Col stood there—a paler, thinner Col, somehow, dressed simply in an open-necked shirt and plain gray slacks.

"How are you?" she asked.

"Surviving. How about you?"

"Surviving, I hope."

They stood there, looking at each other with understanding and longing.

"They've taken this house," she said at last. "I suppose there's not much I can do about it?"

"Don't ask me," he said. "I've just handed in my resignation."

"I'm sorry."

"So am I," he said. "I hate to be beaten by bastards like that."

She turned away from him, staring out across the harbor. "What do you think you'll do?" she asked.

"I don't know. Become a swagman," he answered, then grinned as she looked sharply at him. "Not a bad life—drinking tea from a billy, sleeping out under the stars, bathe once a year . . ." He faltered and his face became serious again. "Marjorie's already packing up," he said. "She's shipping everything to California as quick as she can. She says she can't face anybody here and California is the only place she knows where it doesn't matter if you've had a past . . ."

Sarah looked away from him, across the water where the last ripples from her thrown pebble were dying. "Oh," she said. "America."

There was a pause. "Only thing to do, really," Col said brightly. "They don't care over there if you're a duchess or a crook . . . and lots of money to be made. Marjorie's buying a farm, I understand."

"Oh," Sarah said again. "You always said you wouldn't mind being a farmer." She tried to say it evenly, but her voice cracked on the last word.

"You can see me riding behind the cattle into the sunset, can you," he asked, "in my cowboy hat with my six-gun at my side?" He chuckled. "No, it wouldn't be a bad life, only I'm not going."

"You're not?" She dared to look at him for the first time.

He shook his head carelessly. "What would I want with America? Everyone talks too fast over there . . . and I don't even like chewing gum." He took a step toward her. "You know me—I'm an Aussie, love. A dinky-die Aussie. I don't let a little thing like being thrown out of Parliament get me down—and I don't care two hoots about what people think—" he paused again.

"But what about Marjorie?" Sarah asked cautiously.

He shrugged his shoulders carelessly. "I told her I wasn't coming with her. She threw one of her tantrums and told me she'd cut me off without a penny—funny, I think she was more fond of me than I ever suspected—either that or she wanted someone to protect her from Billy the Kid!" He looked up at Sarah's face and grinned. "You didn't really think I'd walk out on you, did you? You fancy being a swagman's sheila?"

"I've no better offers right now," Sarah said, gazing at him with love in her eyes. "In fact, I've nowhere to sleep tonight so maybe we'd better hit the road right away."

He laughed. "I daresay I've got a friend or two left who

wouldn't mind putting us up for a couple of nights!'' He put his arm protectively around her.

''And what then?'' Sarah asked, resting her head against his shoulder. ''I suppose I've still got that land out at Ivanhoe.''

''Heaven forbid,'' Col said, laughing. ''I'm not that desperate. I did manage to put a little bit aside here and there, you know—even though you tried to get my kickbacks voted down!''

Sarah looked at him with wonder and began to laugh, too. ''You're an old rogue, you know that?''

''Of course I do. So do you—that's what you like about me.'' He gazed out past her, down the harbor. ''I'm not sure Marjorie will divorce me. She doesn't believe in divorce. We'll have to wait and see if she meets a nice rich American rancher who changes her ideas on the subject. Will you mind?''

''What, living in sin?'' she asked and laughed again. ''But I suppose we ought to get away from Sydney. I don't think we'd be too welcome here—Colonel Neville would see to that.''

''That bastard,'' Col growled.

''You should buy a newspaper and give him a dose of his own medicine,'' Sarah said.

Col shook his head. ''He'll get what's coming to him soon enough, without my help, love,'' he said. ''That slump I've been predicting—it will come soon enough. Then everyone will blame England for letting them down and champions of the old country, like our friend Neville, will be out on their ears.''

''I don't know if I can wait that long,'' Sarah said. ''I've a great desire to push him off the Gap right now.''

He turned her toward him. ''Violent little thing, aren't you? I can see I've got my work cut out for me keeping you in check. Tell you what, though. I thought about going up to Queensland, nice country up there and not many people. You can buy land for pennies, in fact, I think they pay you to live there. I don't want to retire, mind you. I'm too young to sit on the porch. What do you think of breeding racehorses? I've always fancied myself winning the Melbourne Cup . . .''

''My racehorse!'' Sarah exclaimed delightedly. ''My colt from Lytton Argus. The police don't know about him. We'll win the Melbourne Cup and show them all!''

''That's right,'' Col said. ''Lytton Argus! You could always marry him instead. Much better prospect than sticking with me. He'll keep you in diamonds and caviar and probably make you a rich young widow before too long. I should go for it if I wer you."

Sarah's arm came around his neck. "I don't want to be a ric young widow, thank you," she said. "I daresay you're not th best choice, but I've never been known for making the righ choices in my life up till now. So if I'm stuck with you for th rest of my life, I've only myself to blame."

"Like I said once before, you need your bloody head examined," Col said, and he kissed her, full and hard on the mout while the constable on the hill looked on.

About the Author

JANET QUIN-HARKIN was born in Bath, England, and educated in England, Austria, and Germany. Her first ambition was to be a lion tamer, but since nobody gave her a lion to practice on, she had to look elsewhere. Always very attracted to the stage, she studied acting and when she graduated from college, went into drama production with the B.B.C. in London.

She has been writing all her life. Her mother claims she wrote her first poem at age four. She had a short story accepted by the time she was sixteen and wrote several plays for the B.B.C. while working there.

On a visit to Australia in search of sunshine, she met her husband, fellow Englishman John Quin-Harkin. Immediately after marriage they moved to California and have lived there for twenty-three years, apart from a short stay in Texas. They have four children who have been great inspiration for the forty-six children's books she has written, which range from award-winning picture books to young adult novels. Her young adult books are known worldwide and have sold more than five million copies.

MADAM SARAH is her first venture back into adult writing since her early TV and radio plays. She enjoyed the depth of research it required, spending a great deal of time with relatives and friends in Australia and using archives, old magazines, and time-tables to check on the historical accuracy.